Experience

MOUNTAINHEAD

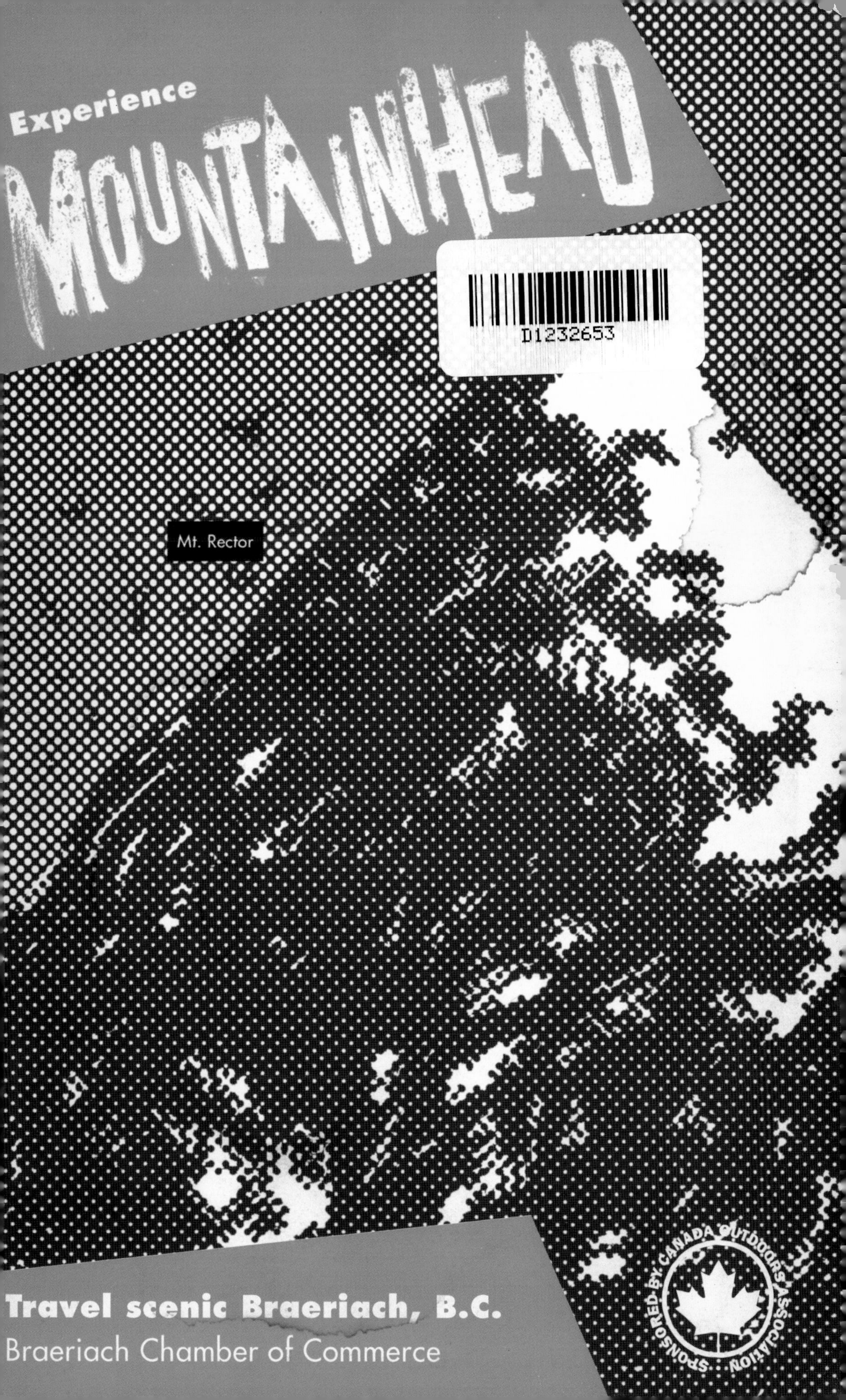
Mt. Rector

Travel scenic Braeriach, B.C.

Braeriach Chamber of Commerce

SPONSORED BY CANADA OUTDOORS ASSOCIATION

ISBN: 978-1-68405-633-0

23 22 21 20 1 2 3 4

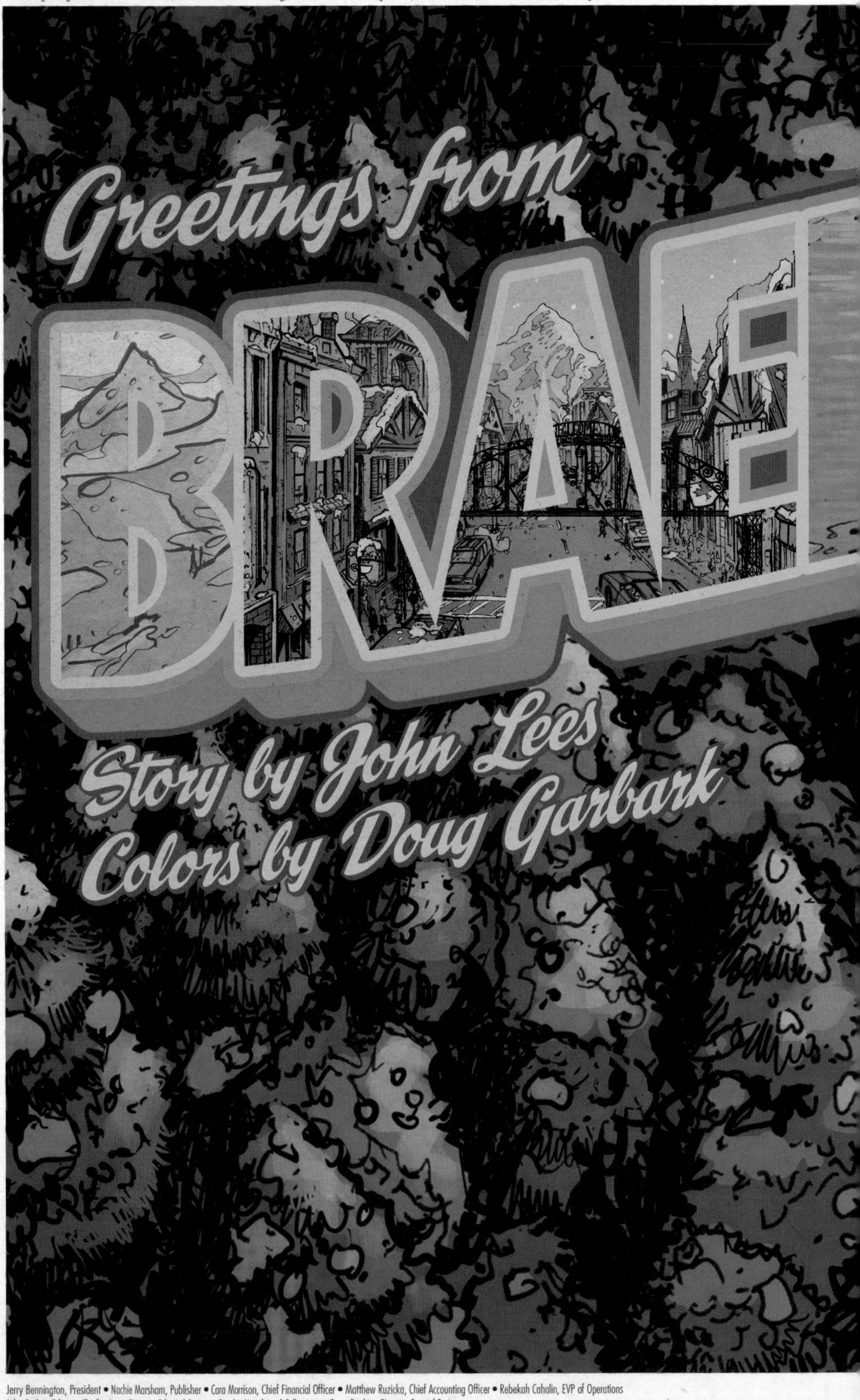
Greetings from
Story by John Lees
Colors by Doug Garbark

Art by Ryan Lee
Letters by Shawn Lee

COVER ARTIST: **RYAN LEE**

SERIES EDITOR: **BOBBY CURNOW**

COLLECTION EDITORS: **ALONZO SIMON** & **ZAC BOONE**

COLLECTION DESIGNER: **SHAWN LEE**

For international rights, contact licensing@idwpublishing.com

Facebook: facebook.com/idwpublishing • Twitter: @idwpublishing • YouTube: youtube.com/idwpublishing • Tumblr: tumblr.idwpublishing.com • Instagram: instagram.com/idwpublishing

Blake Kobashigawa, VP of Sales • Lorelei Bunjes, VP of Technology & Information Services • Anna Morrow, Sr Marketing Director • Tara McCrillis, Director of Design & Production
Mike Ford, Director of Operations • Shauna Monteforte, Manufacturing Operations Director • Ted Adams and Robbie Robbins, IDW Founders

BRAERIACH
BRAERIACH CHAMBER OF COMMERCE

ART BY RYAN LEE

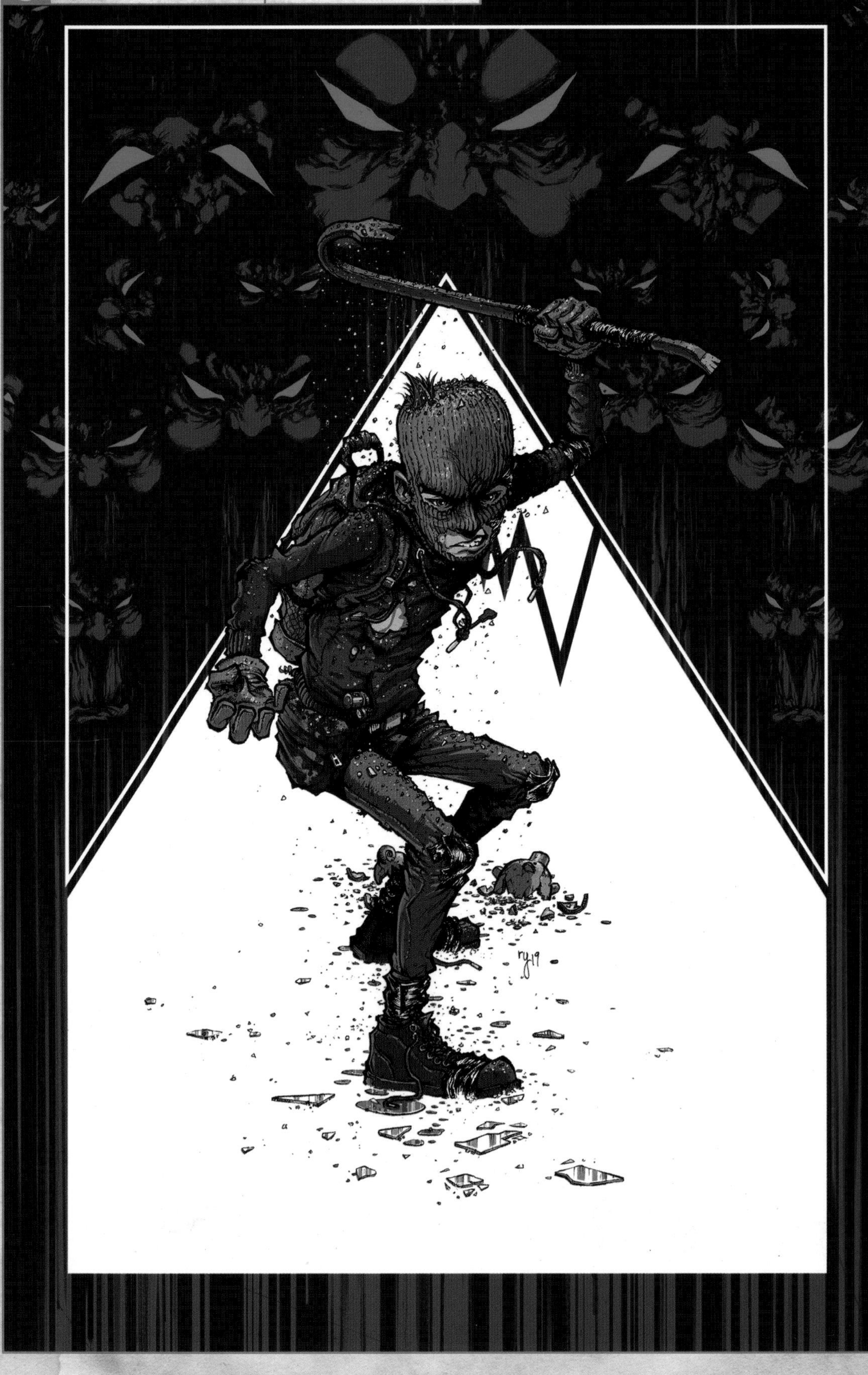

ry 19

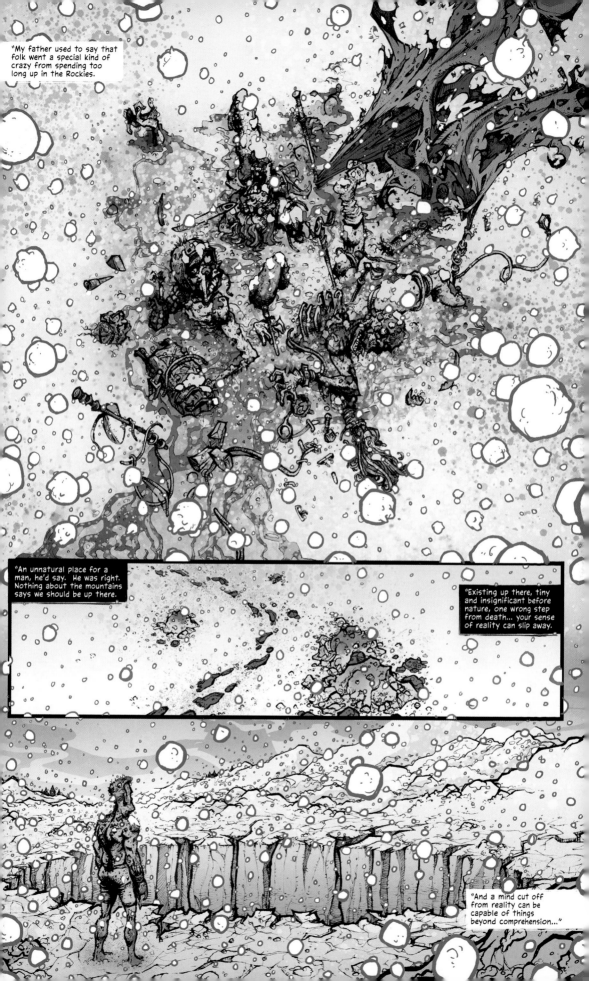

"My father used to say that folk went a special kind of crazy from spending too long up in the Rockies.

"An unnatural place for a man, he'd say. He was right. Nothing about the mountains says we should be up there.

"Existing up there, tiny and insignificant before nature, one wrong step from death... your sense of reality can slip away.

"And a mind cut off from reality can be capable of things beyond comprehension..."

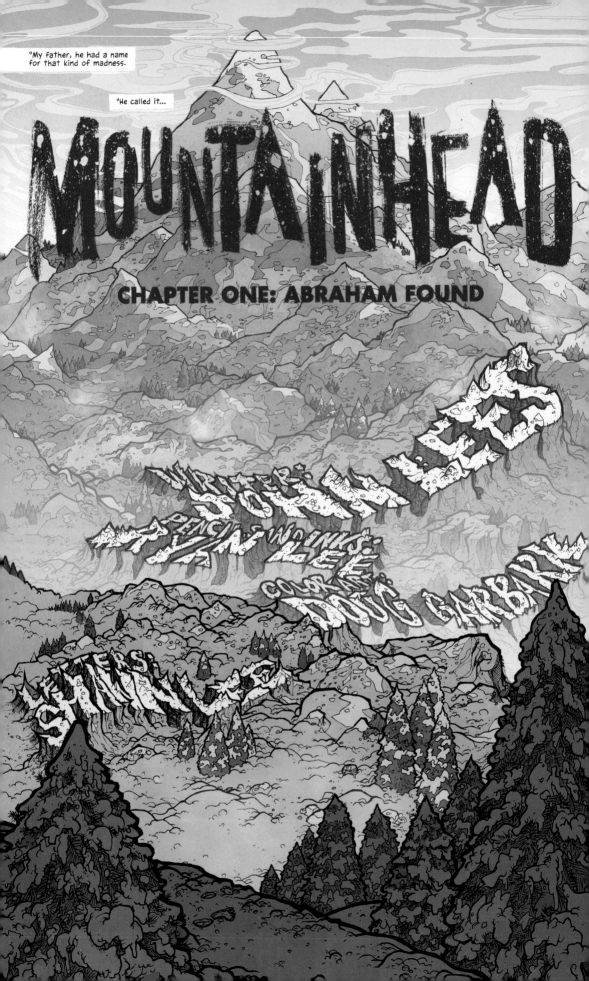

"My father, he had a name for that kind of madness.

"He called it...

MOUNTAINHEAD

CHAPTER ONE: ABRAHAM FOUND

WRITER JOHN LEES

PENCILS W/ INKS

COLOR BY DOUG GARBARK

LETTERS

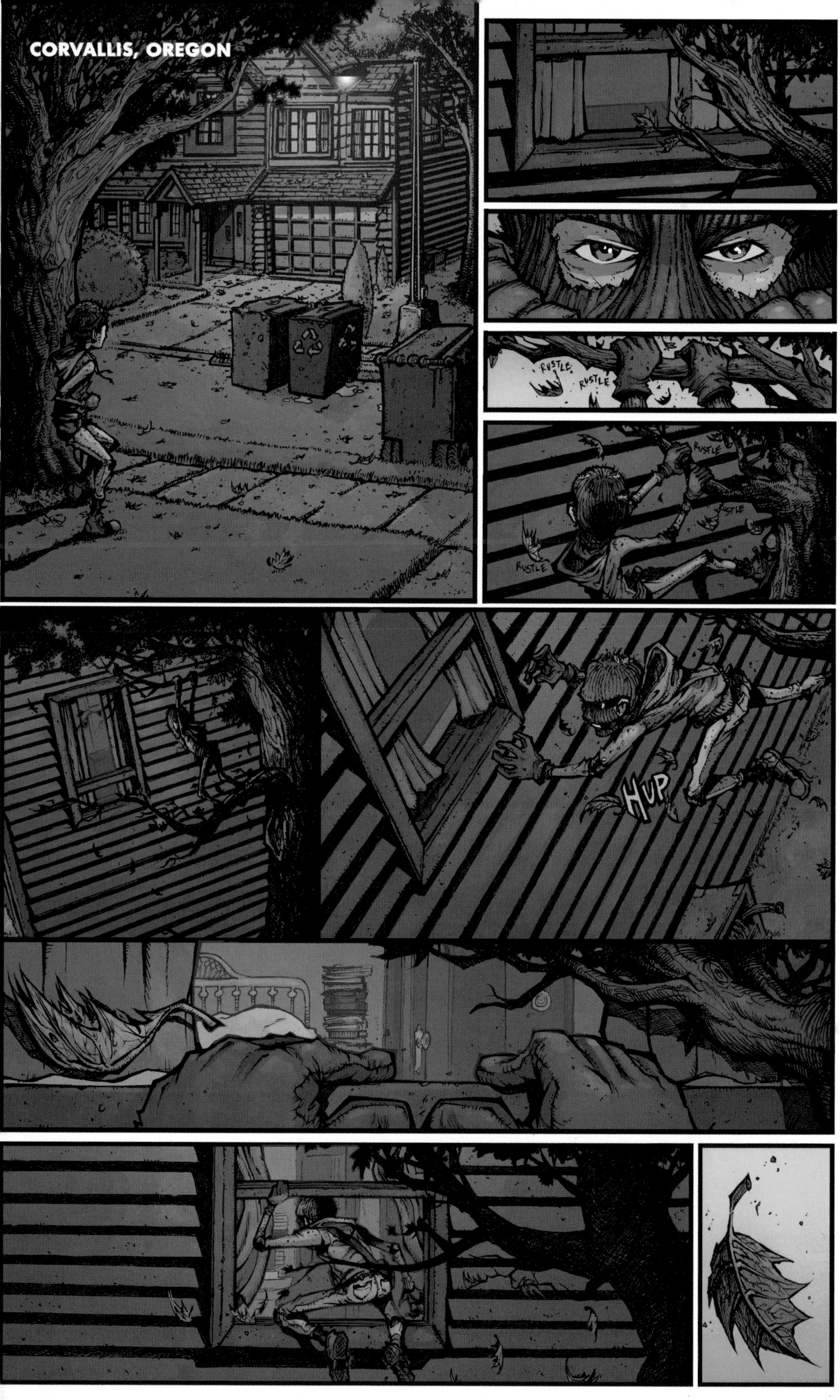

CORVALLIS, OREGON
RUSTLE
RUSTLE
RUSTLE
RUSTLE
RUSTLE
HUP

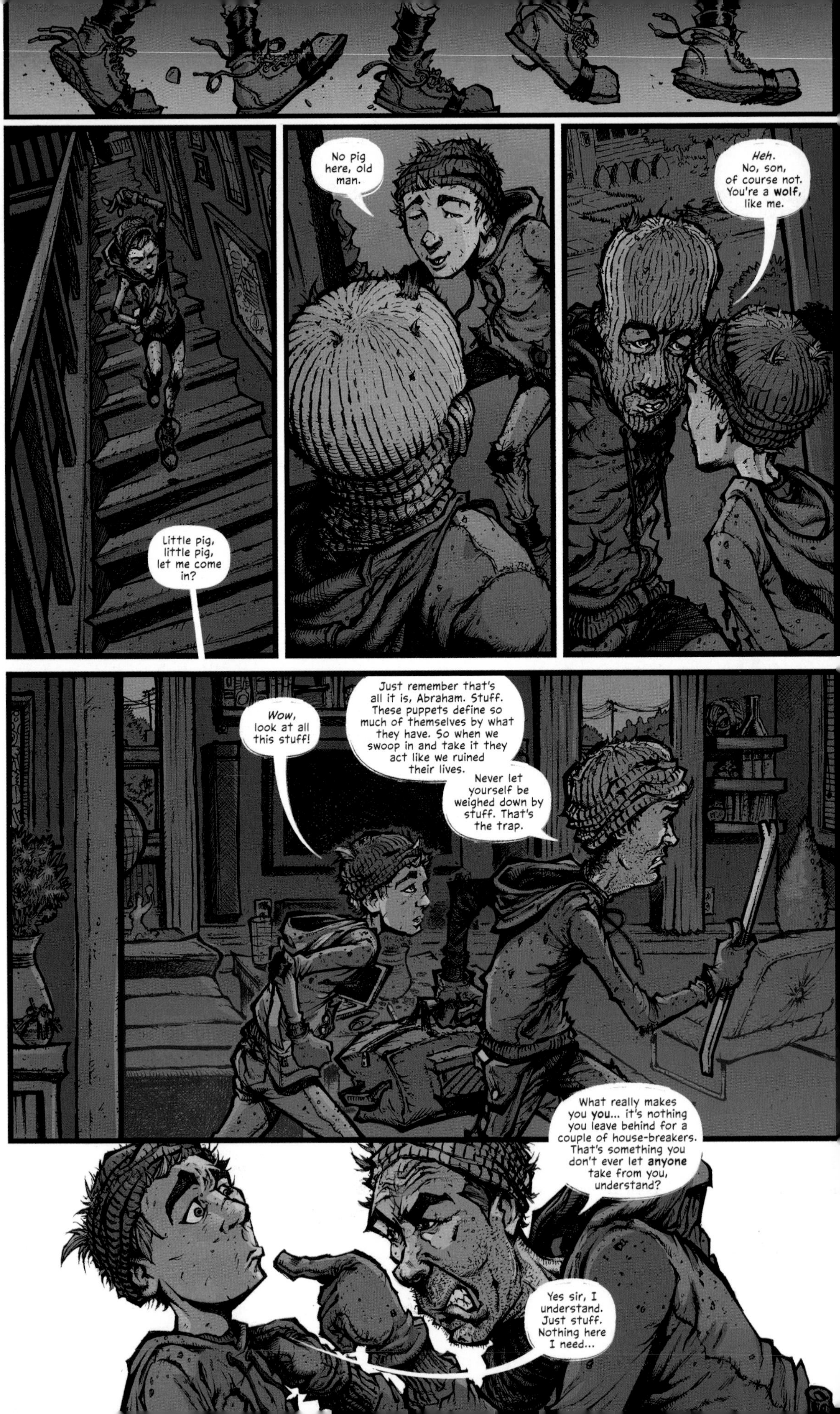
Little pig, little pig, let me come in?
No pig here, old man.
Heh. No, son, of course not. You're a **wolf**, like me.
Wow, look at all this stuff!
Just remember that's all it is, Abraham. Stuff. These puppets define so much of themselves by what they have. So when we swoop in and take it they act like we ruined their lives.
Never let yourself be weighed down by stuff. That's the trap.
What really makes you **you**... it's nothing you leave behind for a couple of house-breakers. That's something you don't ever let **anyone** take from you, understand?
Yes sir, I understand. Just stuff. Nothing here I need...

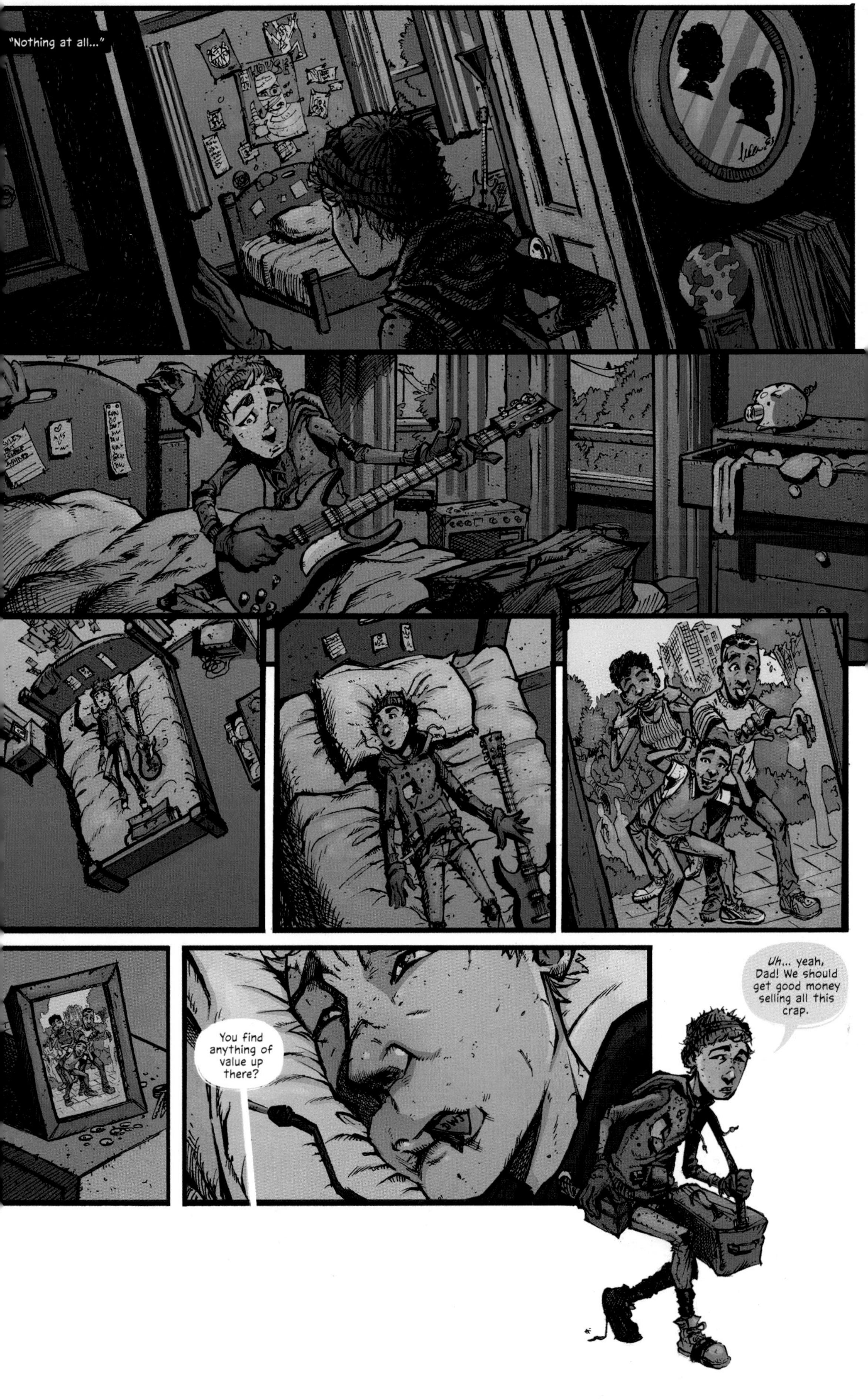

"Nothing at all..."
You find anything of value up there?
Uh... yeah, Dad! We should get good money selling all this crap.

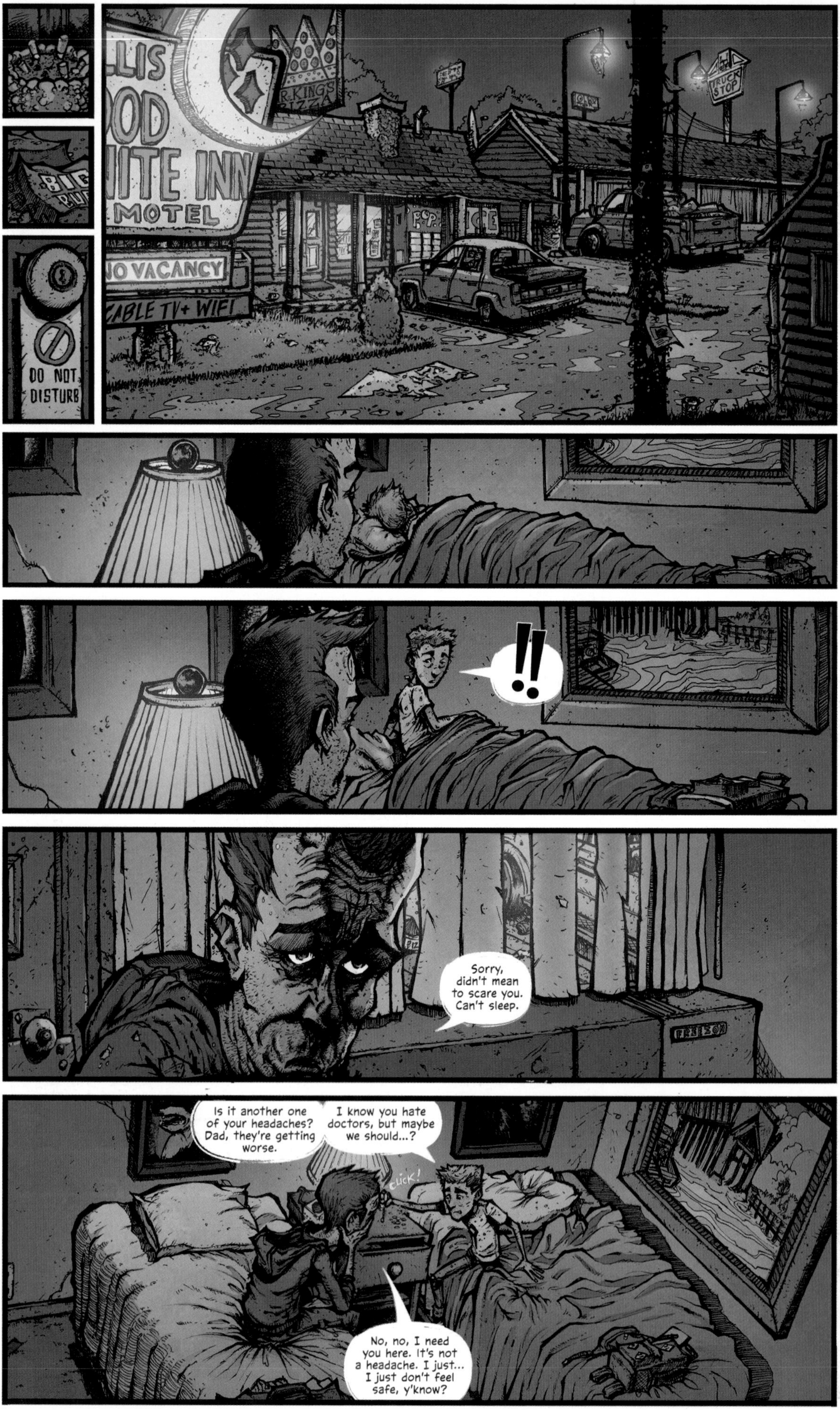

BIG
DO NOT DISTURB
MOTEL
NO VACANCY
CABLE TV + WIFI
TRUCK STOP
!!
Sorry, didn't mean to scare you. Can't sleep.
Is it another one of your headaches? Dad, they're getting worse.
I know you hate doctors, but maybe we should...?
CLICK!
No, no, I need you here. It's not a headache. I just... I just don't feel safe, y'know?

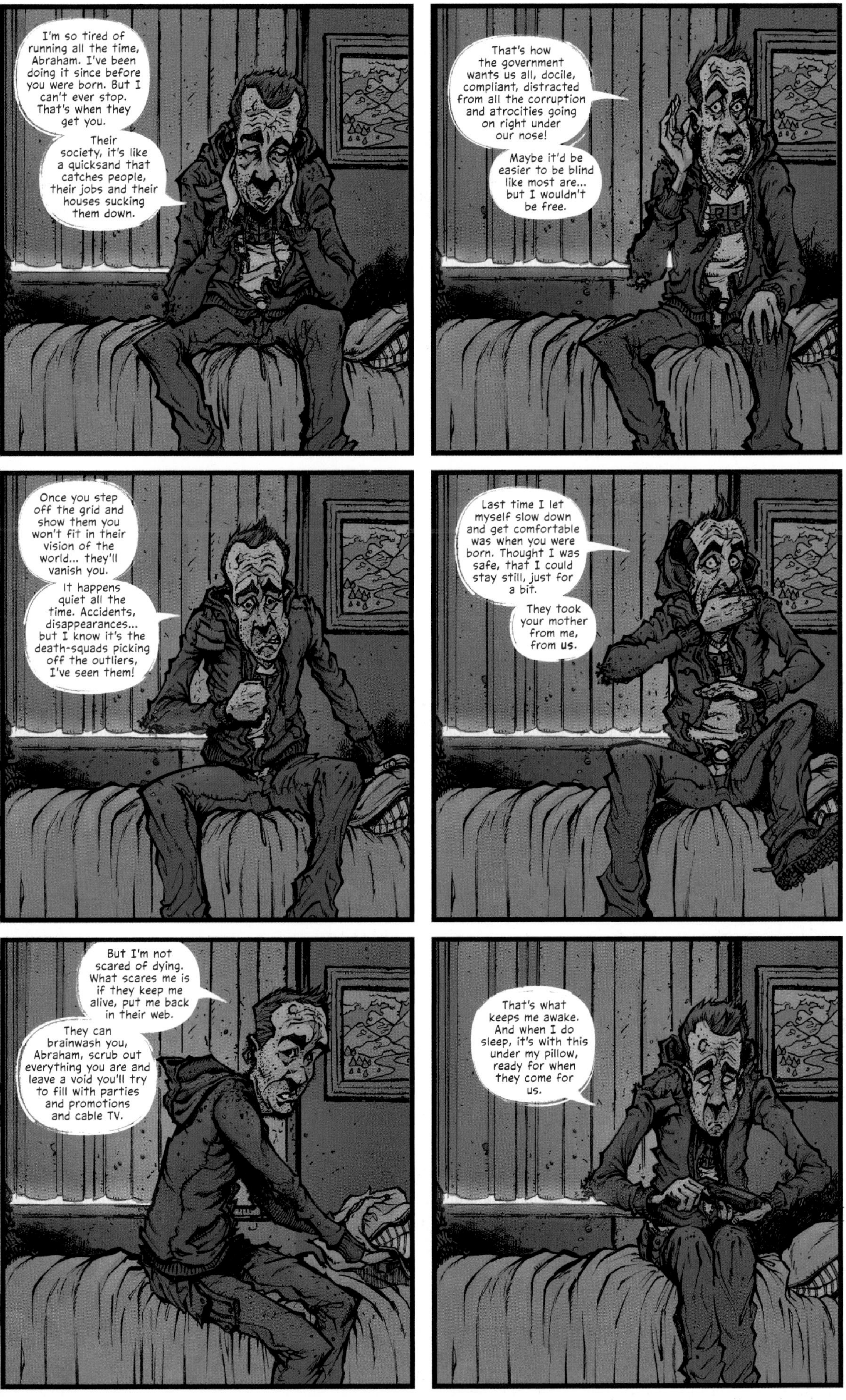
I'm so tired of running all the time, Abraham. I've been doing it since before you were born. But I can't ever stop. That's when they get you.
Their society, it's like a quicksand that catches people, their jobs and their houses sucking them down.
That's how the government wants us all, docile, compliant, distracted from all the corruption and atrocities going on right under our nose!
Maybe it'd be easier to be blind like most are... but I wouldn't be free.
Once you step off the grid and show them you won't fit in their vision of the world... they'll vanish you.
It happens quiet all the time. Accidents, disappearances... but I know it's the death-squads picking off the outliers, I've seen them!
Last time I let myself slow down and get comfortable was when you were born. Thought I was safe, that I could stay still, just for a bit.
They took your mother from me, from **us**.
But I'm not scared of dying. What scares me is if they keep me alive, put me back in their web.
They can brainwash you, Abraham, scrub out everything you are and leave a void you'll try to fill with parties and promotions and cable TV.
That's what keeps me awake. And when I do sleep, it's with this under my pillow, ready for when they come for us.

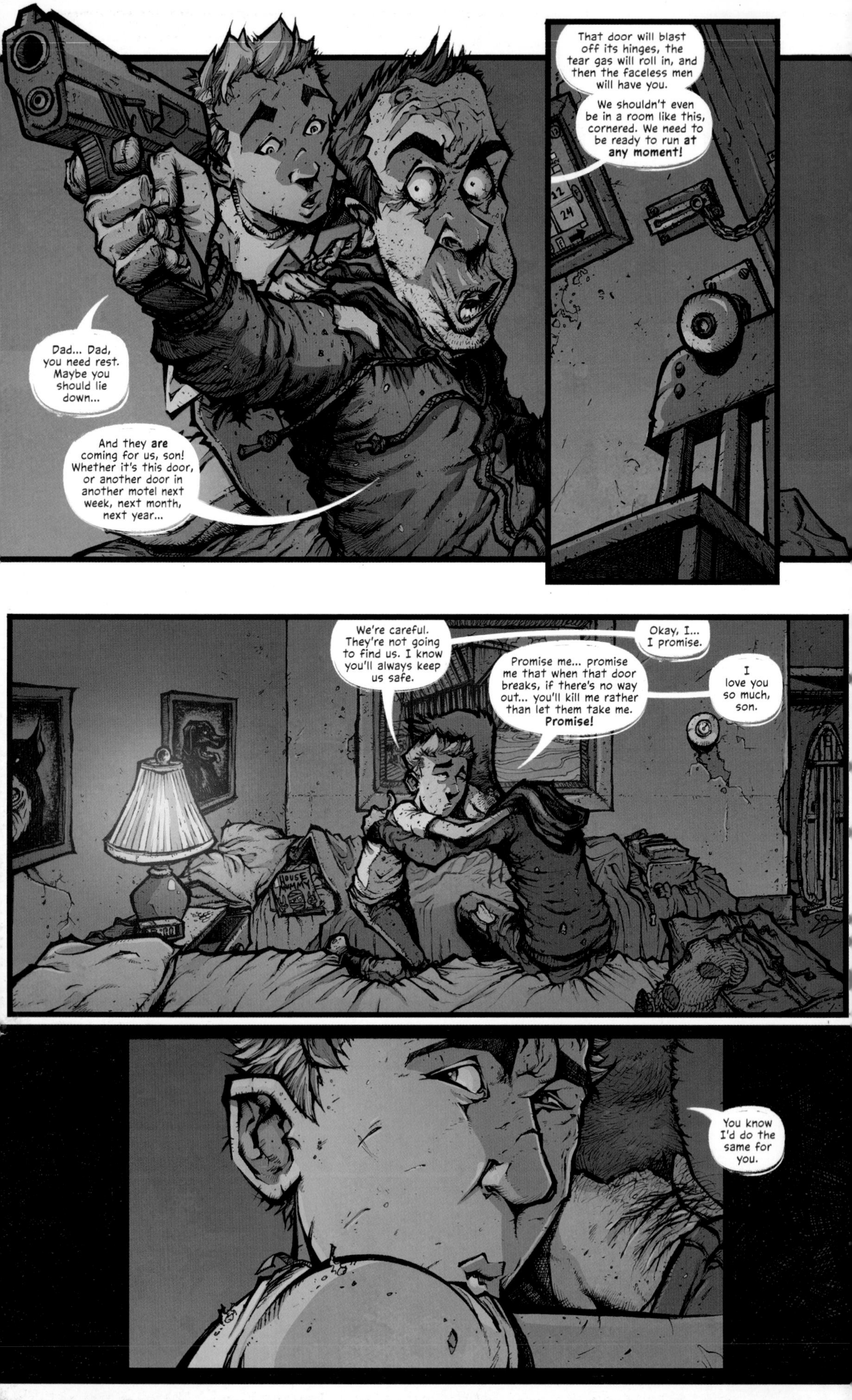
Dad... Dad, you need rest. Maybe you should lie down...
And they are coming for us, son! Whether it's this door, or another door in another motel next week, next month, next year...
That door will blast off its hinges, the tear gas will roll in, and then the faceless men will have you.
We shouldn't even be in a room like this, cornered. We need to be ready to run at any moment!
12
24
We're careful. They're not going to find us. I know you'll always keep us safe.
Promise me... promise me that when that door breaks, if there's no way out... you'll kill me rather than let them take me. Promise!
Okay, I... I promise.
I love you so much, son.
HOUSE MUMMY
You know I'd do the same for you.

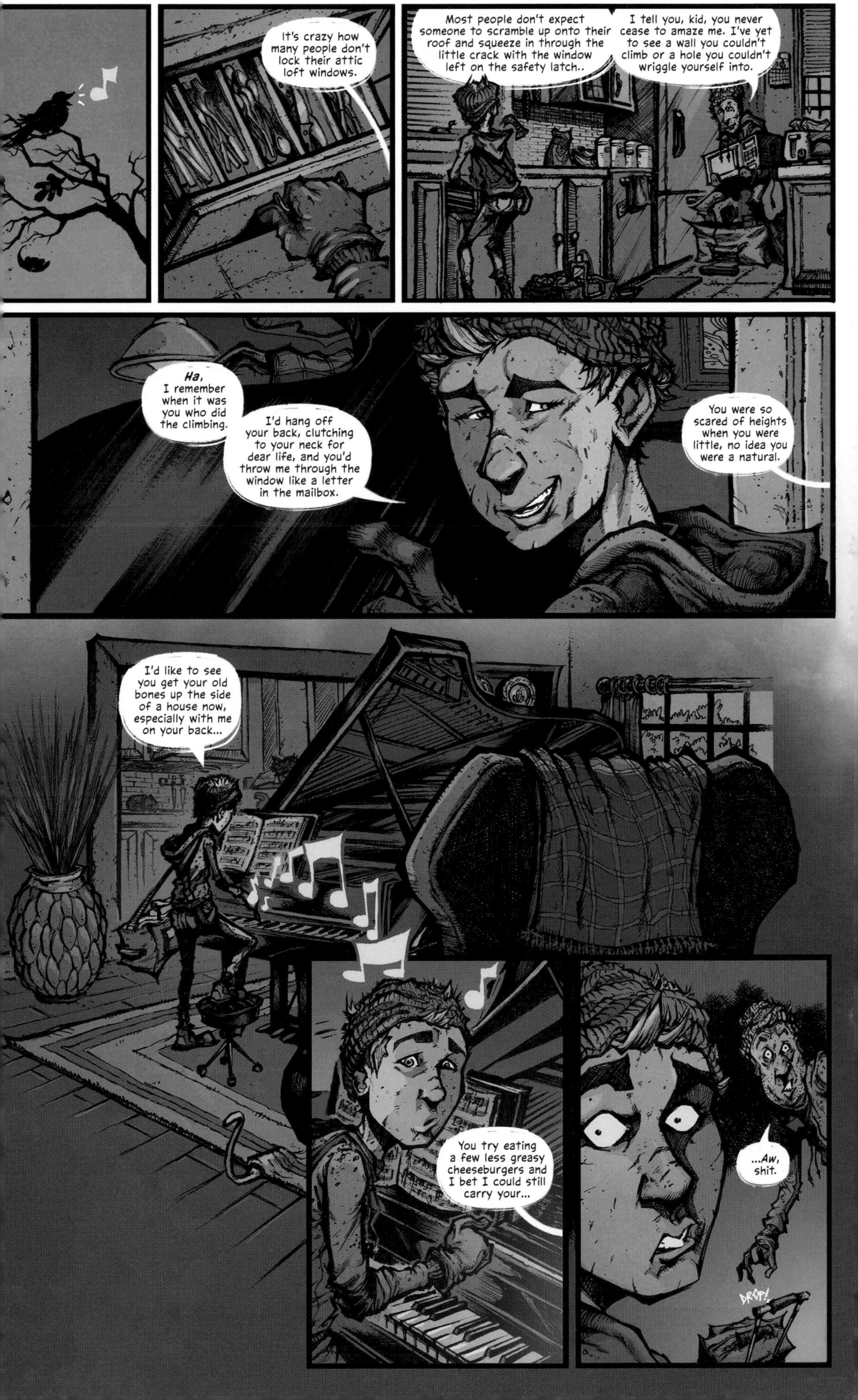
It's crazy how many people don't lock their attic loft windows.
Most people don't expect someone to scramble up onto their roof and squeeze in through the little crack with the window left on the safety latch..
I tell you, kid, you never cease to amaze me. I've yet to see a wall you couldn't climb or a hole you couldn't wriggle yourself into.
Ha, I remember when it was you who did the climbing.
I'd hang off your back, clutching to your neck for dear life, and you'd throw me through the window like a letter in the mailbox.
You were so scared of heights when you were little, no idea you were a natural.
I'd like to see you get your old bones up the side of a house now, especially with me on your back...
You try eating a few less greasy cheeseburgers and I bet I could still carry your...
...Aw, shit.
DROP!

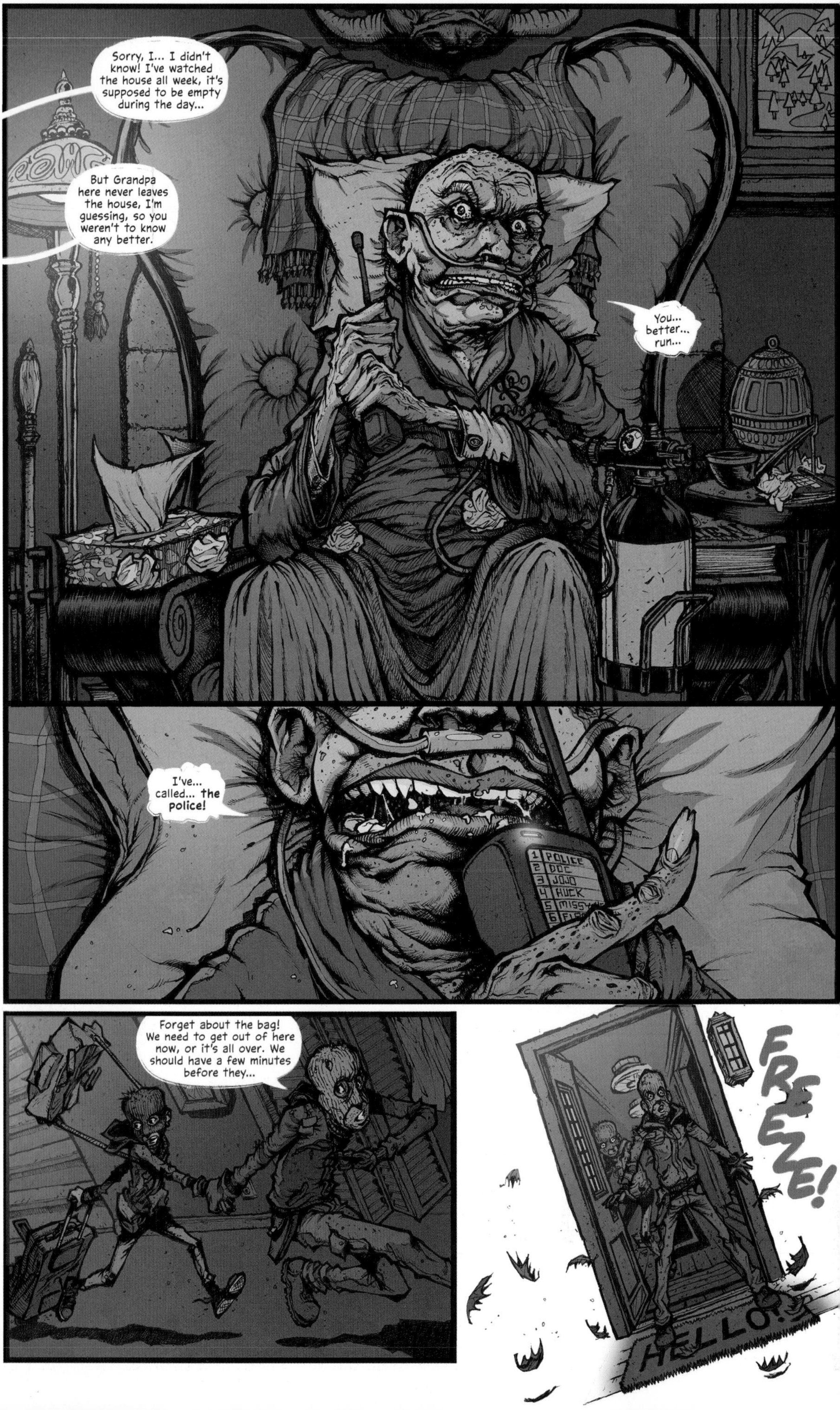
Sorry, I... I didn't know! I've watched the house all week, it's supposed to be empty during the day...
But Grandpa here never leaves the house, I'm guessing, so you weren't to know any better.
You... better... run...
I've... called... the police!
1 POLICE
2 DOC
3 JOJO
4 HUCK
Forget about the bag! We need to get out of here now, or it's all over. We should have a few minutes before they...
FREEZE!
HELLO!

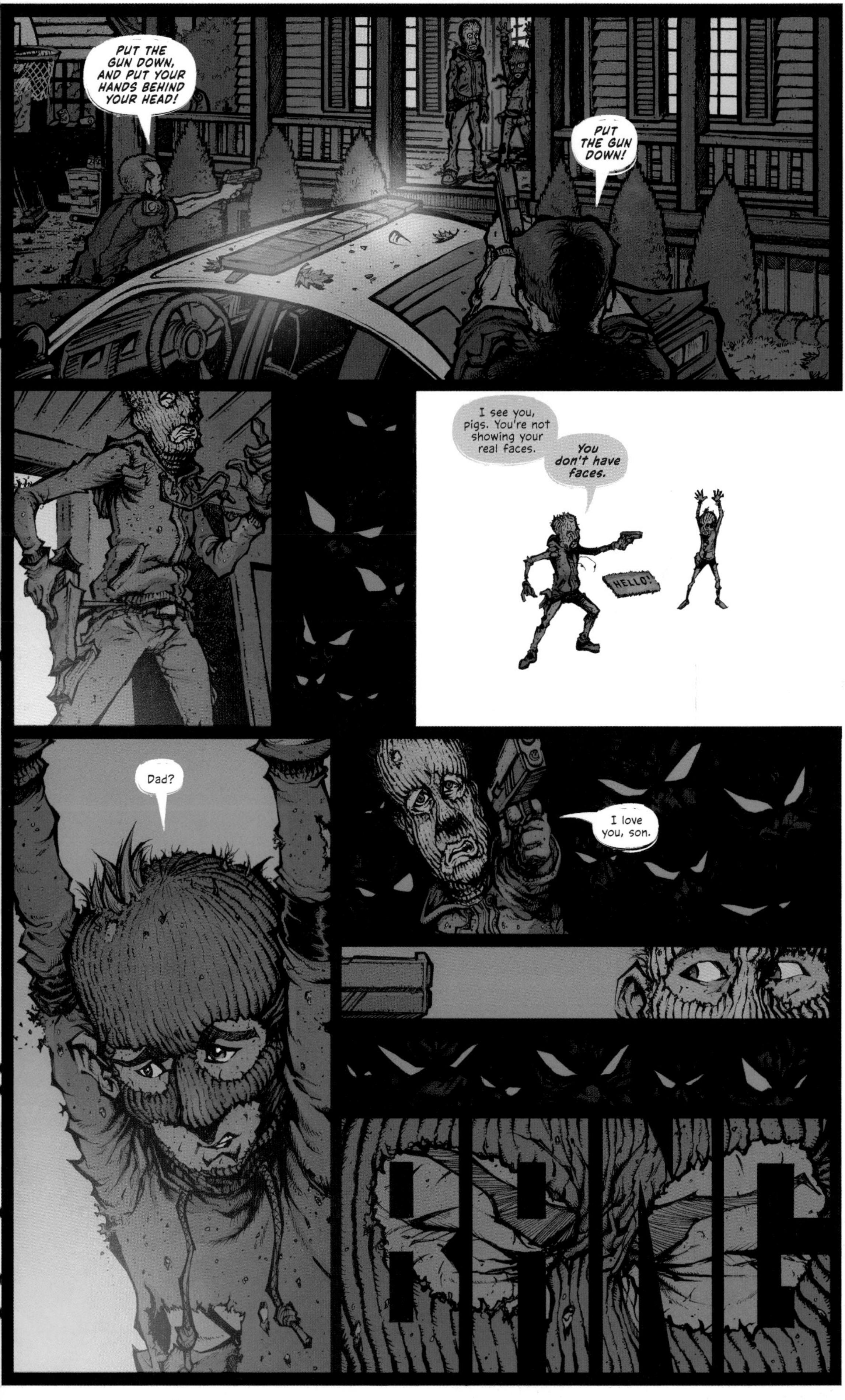
PUT THE GUN DOWN, AND PUT YOUR HANDS BEHIND YOUR HEAD!
PUT THE GUN DOWN!
I see you, pigs. You're not showing your real faces.
You don't have faces.
HELLO!
Dad?
I love you, son.

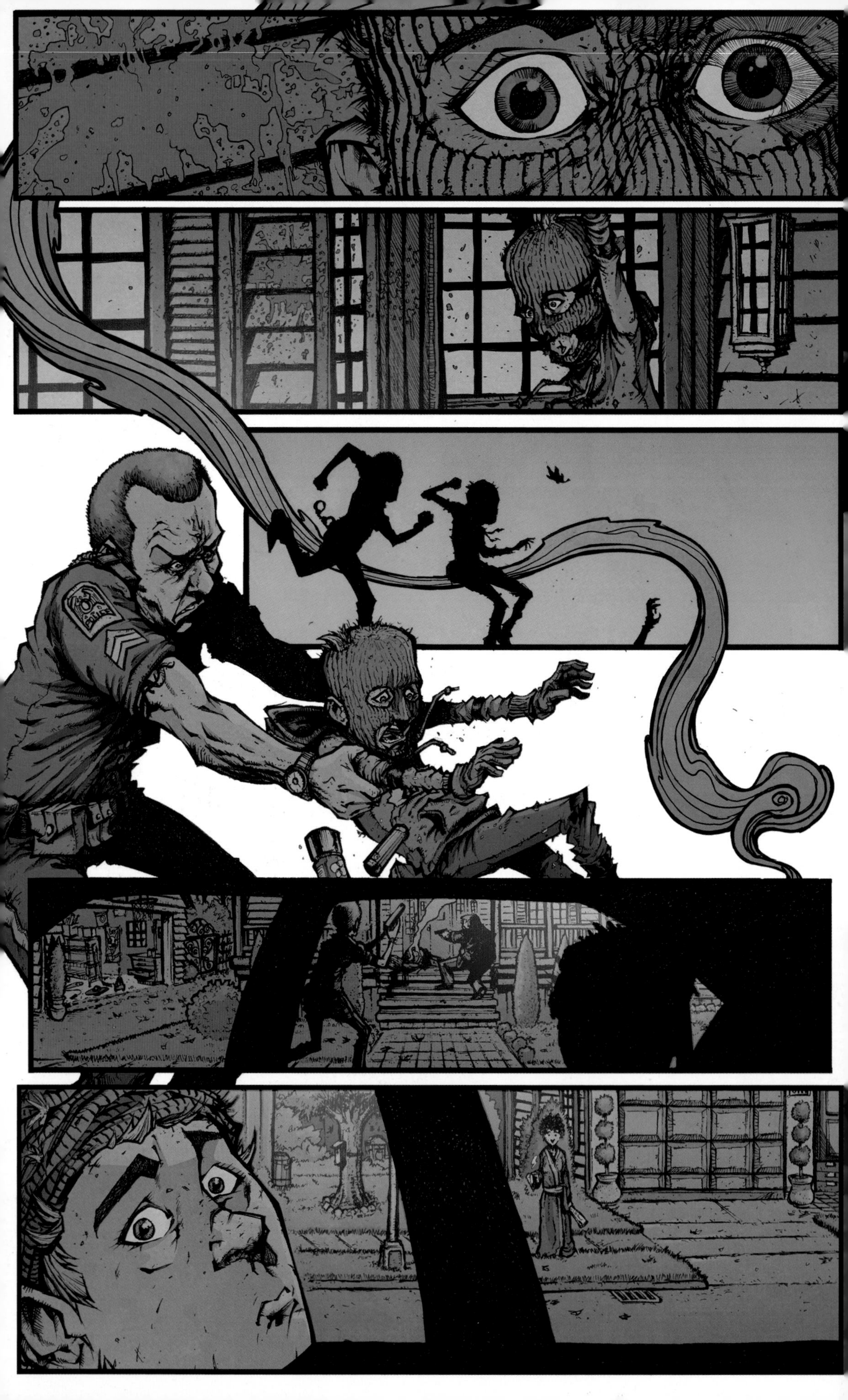

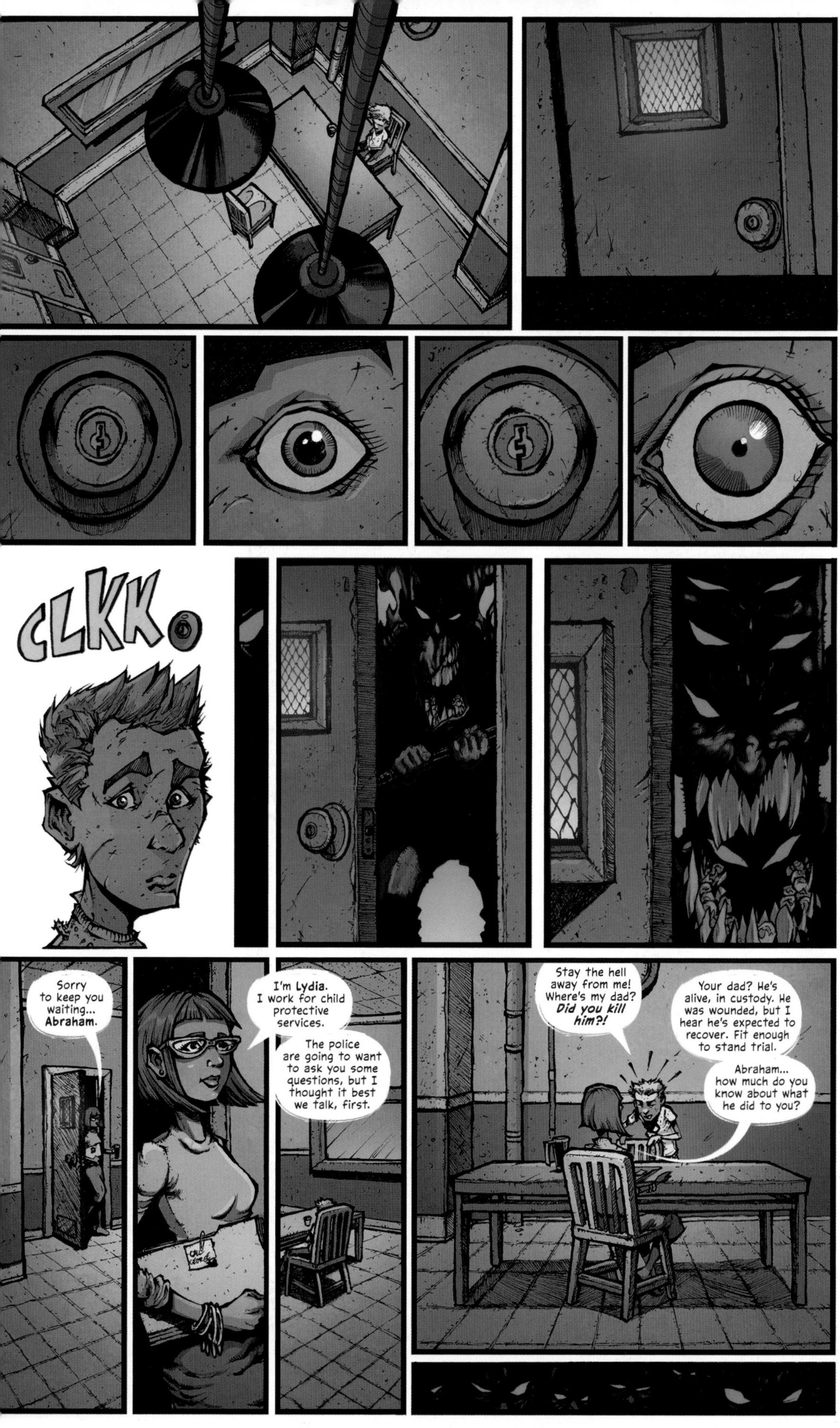
CLKK
Sorry to keep you waiting... **Abraham.**
I'm **Lydia.** I work for child protective services.
The police are going to want to ask you some questions, but I thought it best we talk, first.
Stay the hell away from me! Where's my dad? ***Did you kill him?!***
Your dad? He's alive, in custody. He was wounded, but I hear he's expected to recover. Fit enough to stand trial.
Abraham... how much do you know about what he did to you?

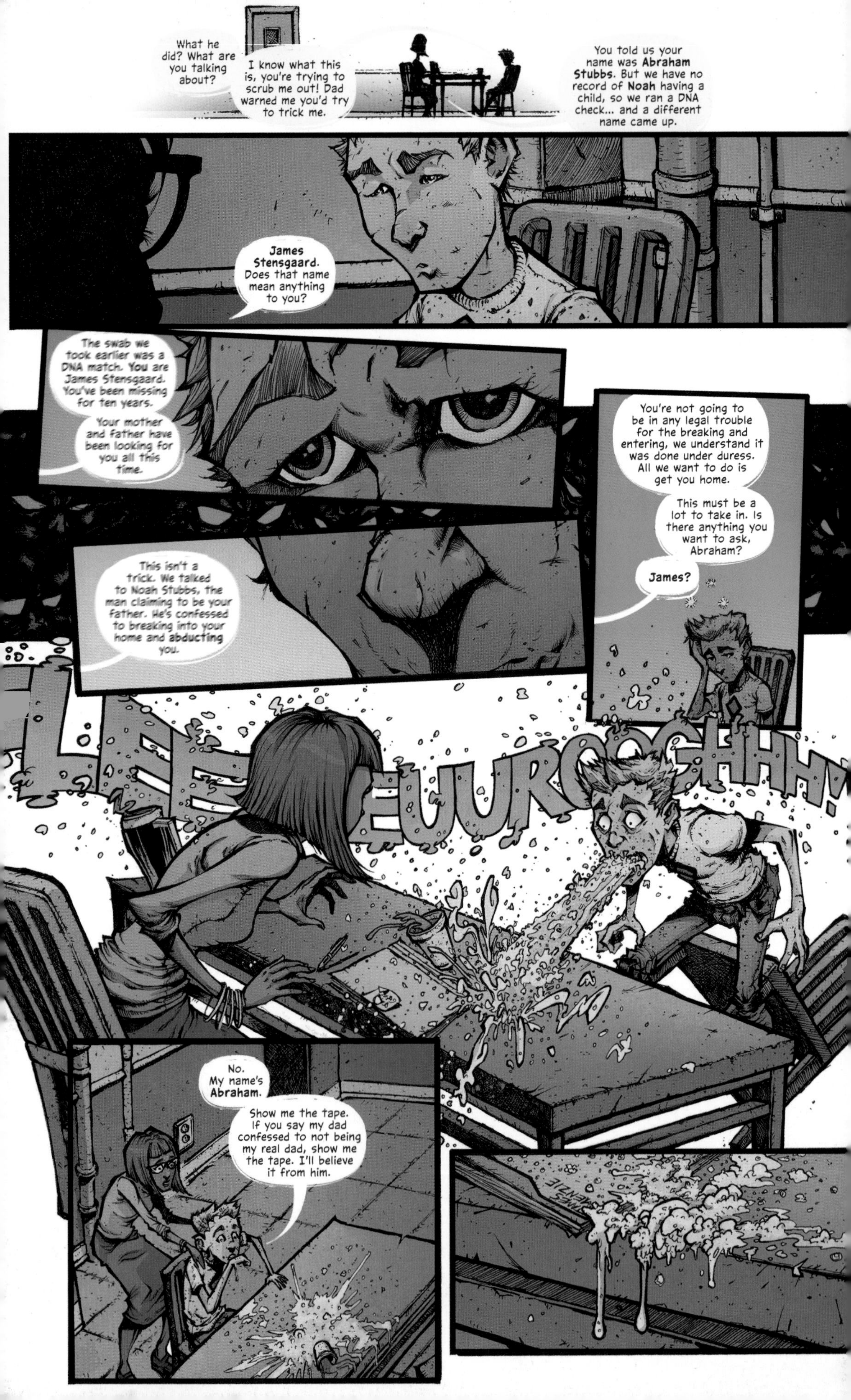

What he did? What are you talking about?
I know what this is, you're trying to scrub me out! Dad warned me you'd try to trick me.
You told us your name was **Abraham Stubbs**. But we have no record of **Noah** having a child, so we ran a DNA check... and a different name came up.
James Stensgaard. Does that name mean anything to you?
The swab we took earlier was a DNA match. **You** are James Stensgaard. You've been missing for ten years.
Your mother and father have been looking for you all this time.
This isn't a trick. We talked to Noah Stubbs, the man claiming to be your father. He's confessed to breaking into your home and **abducting** you.
You're not going to be in any legal trouble for the breaking and entering, we understand it was done under duress. All we want to do is get you home.
This must be a lot to take in. Is there anything you want to ask, Abraham?
James?
EEEUUUROOGHHH!
No. My name's **Abraham**.
Show me the tape. If you say my dad confessed to not being my real dad, show me the tape. I'll believe it from him.

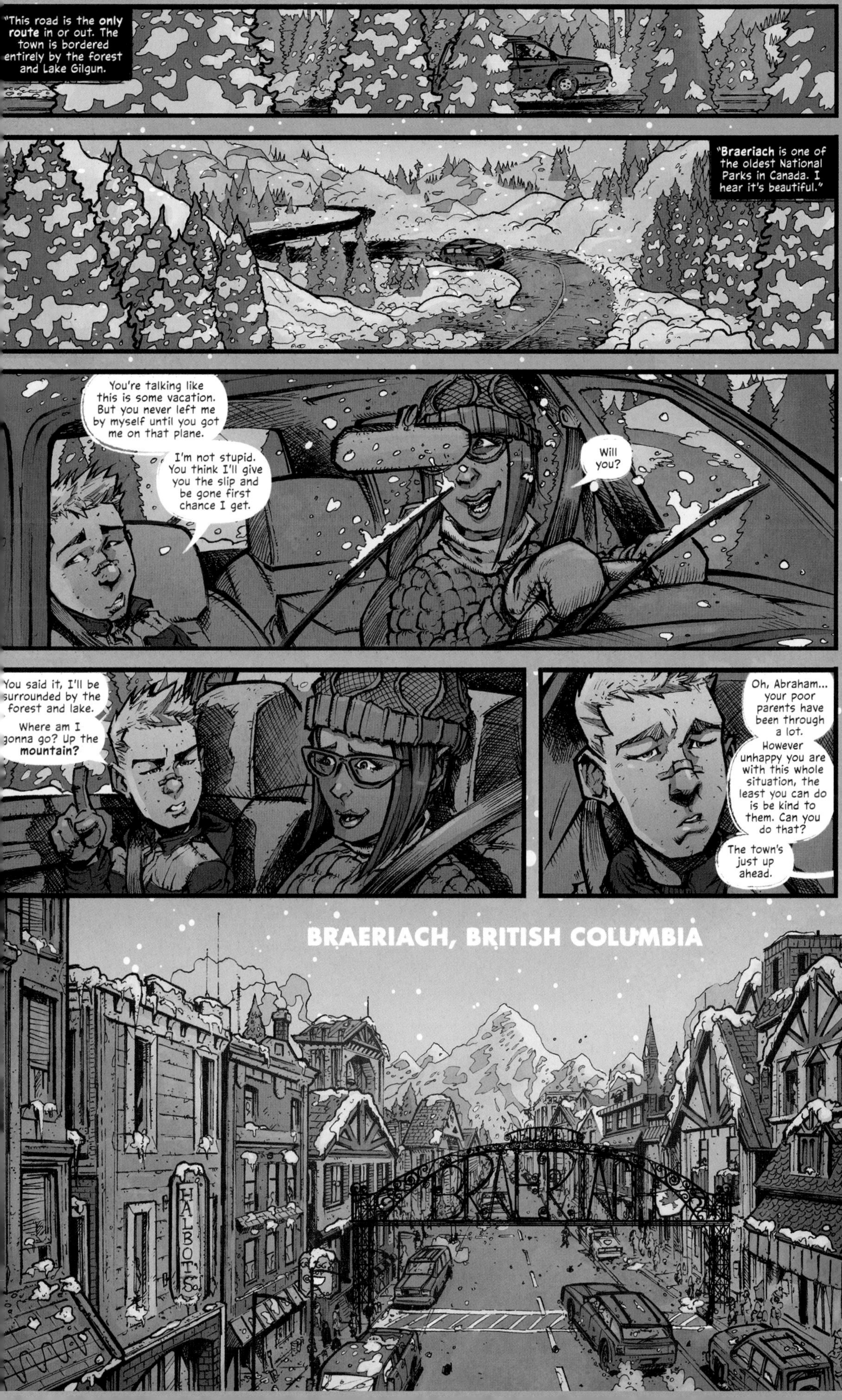
"This road is the **only route** in or out. The town is bordered entirely by the forest and Lake Gilgun.
"**Braeriach** is one of the oldest National Parks in Canada. I hear it's beautiful."
You're talking like this is some vacation. But you never left me by myself until you got me on that plane.
I'm not stupid. You think I'll give you the slip and be gone first chance I get.
Will you?
You said it, I'll be surrounded by the forest and lake.
Where am I gonna go? Up the **mountain?**
Oh, Abraham... your poor parents have been through a lot.
However unhappy you are with this whole situation, the least you can do is be kind to them. Can you do that?
The town's just up ahead.
BRAERIACH, BRITISH COLUMBIA
HALBOTS

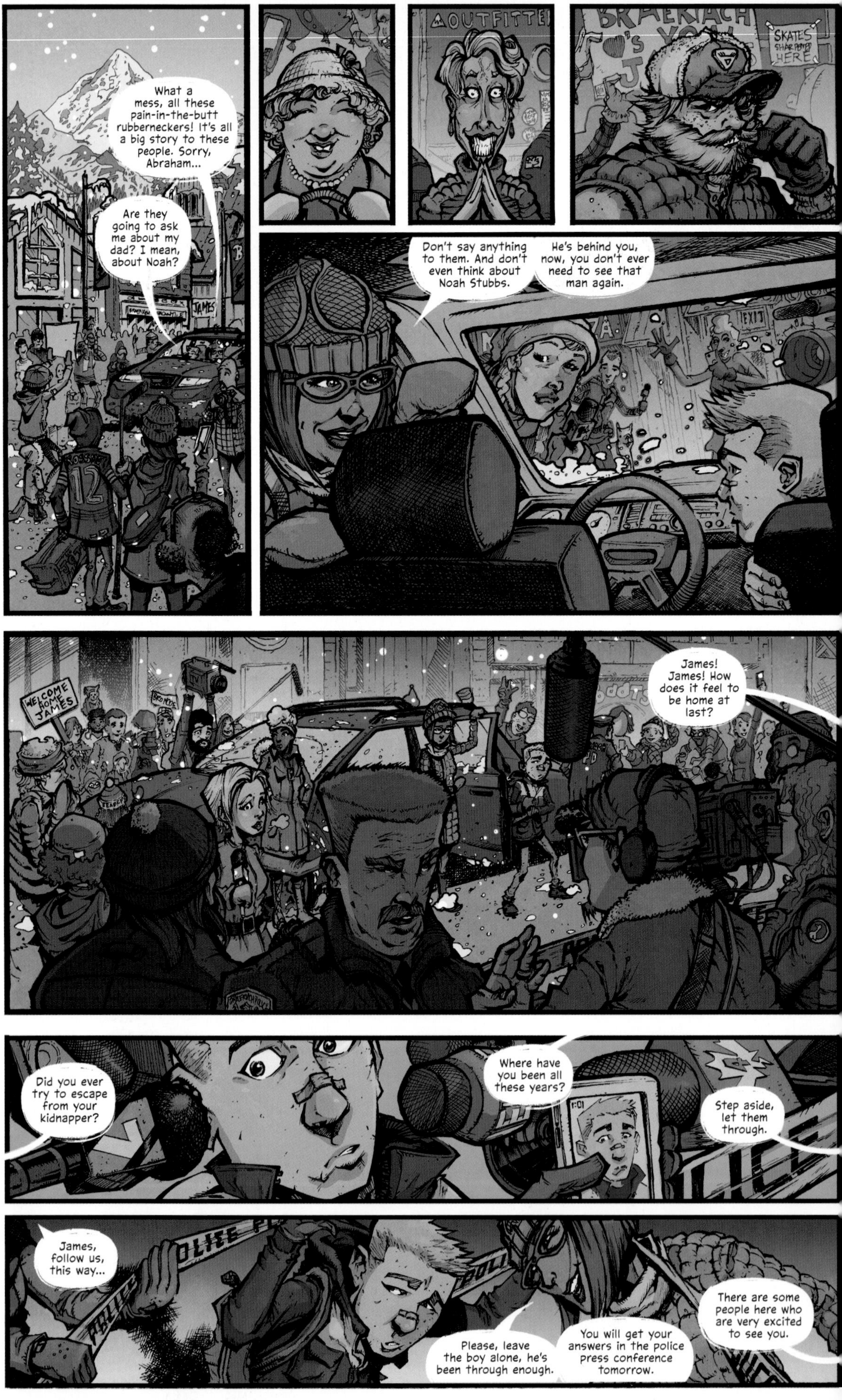
What a mess, all these pain-in-the-butt rubberneckers! It's all a big story to these people. Sorry, Abraham...
Are they going to ask me about my dad? I mean, about Noah?
OUTFITTE
SKATES SHARPENED HERE
Don't say anything to them. And don't even think about Noah Stubbs.
He's behind you, now, you don't ever need to see that man again.
WELCOME HOME JAMES
James! James! How does it feel to be home at last?
Did you ever try to escape from your kidnapper?
Where have you been all these years?
Step aside, let them through.
James, follow us, this way...
There are some people here who are very excited to see you.
Please, leave the boy alone, he's been through enough.
You will get your answers in the police press conference tomorrow.

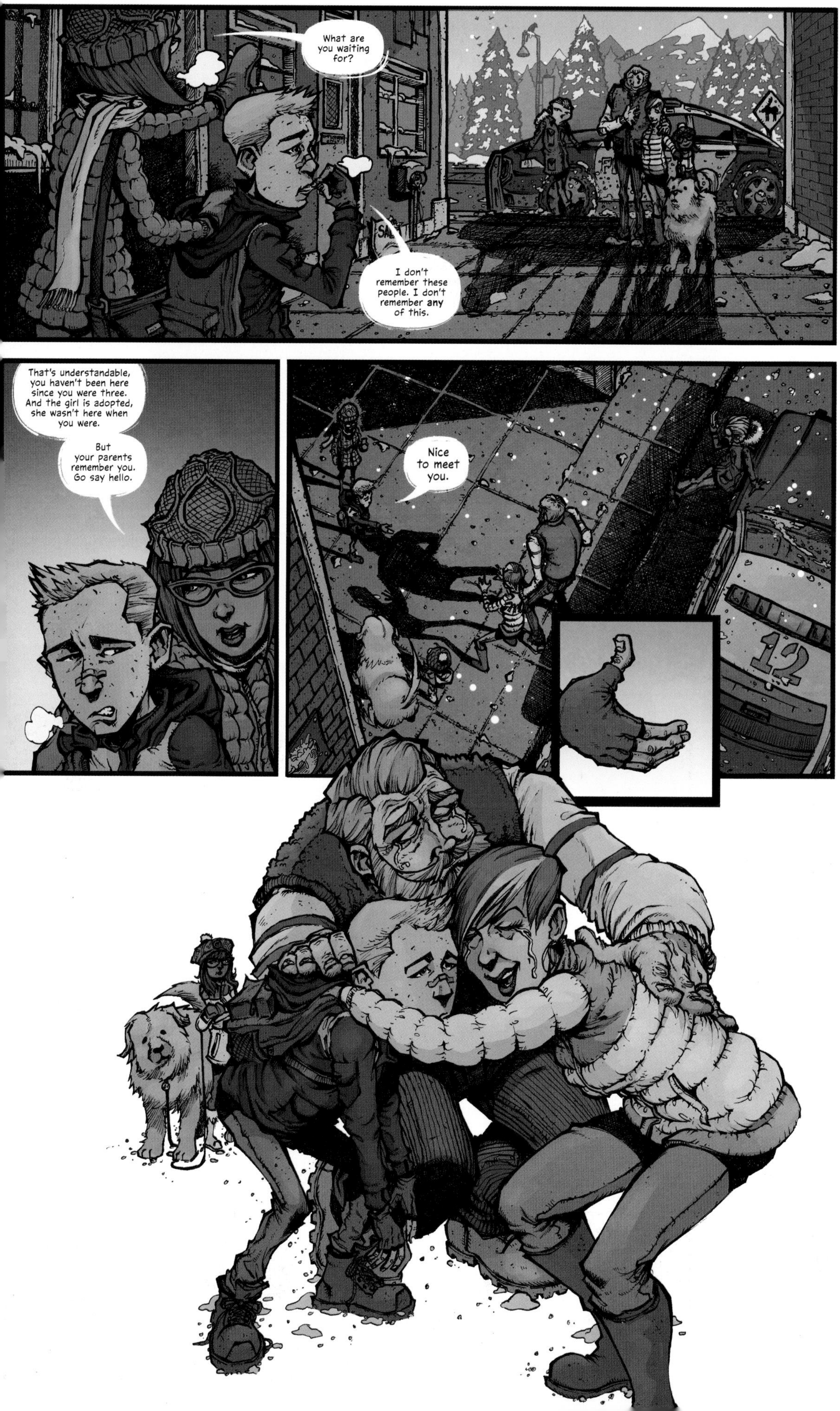

What are you waiting for?
I don't remember these people. I don't remember any of this.
That's understandable, you haven't been here since you were three. And the girl is adopted, she wasn't here when you were.
But your parents remember you. Go say hello.
Nice to meet you.
12

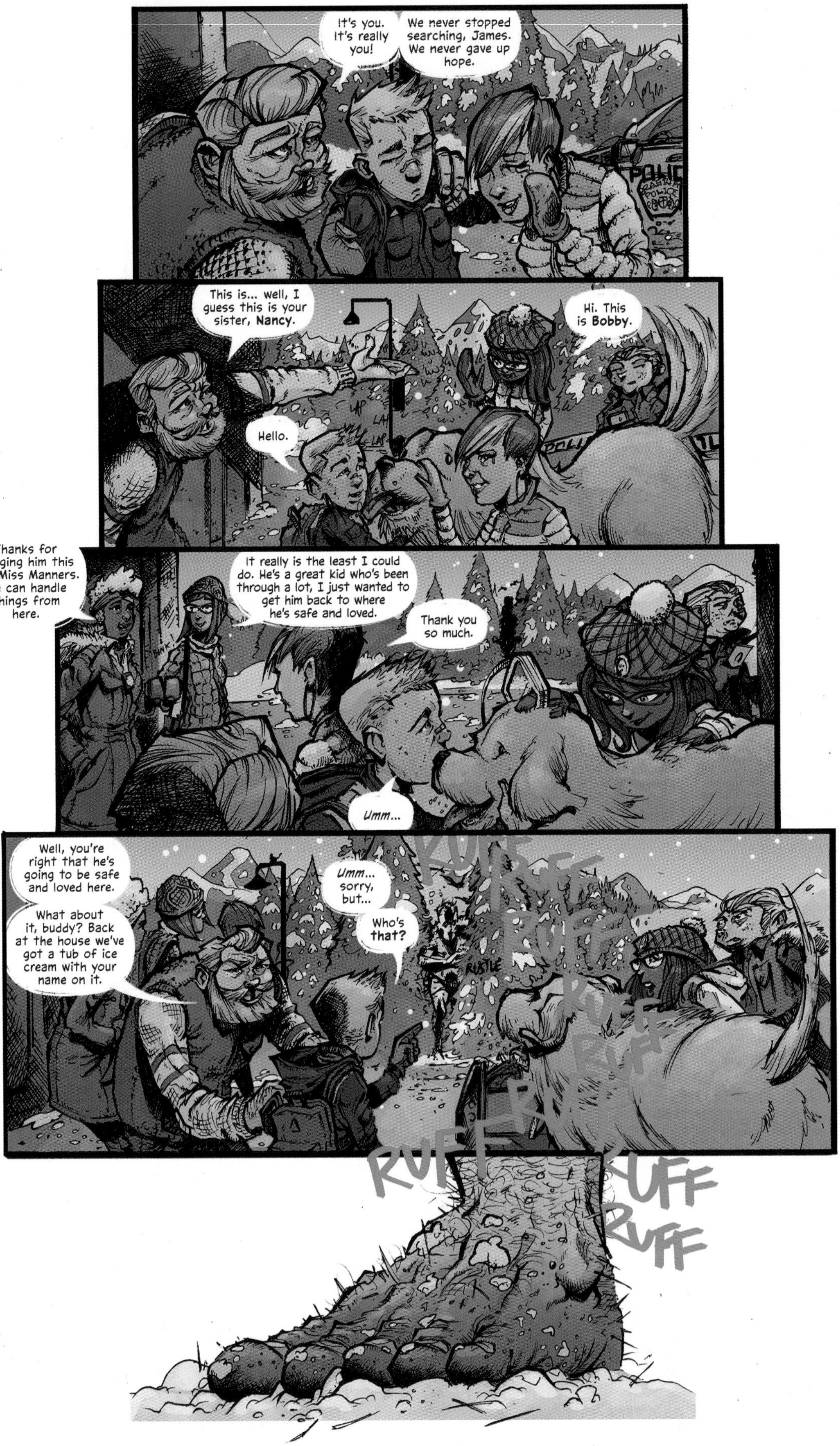
It's you. It's really you!
We never stopped searching, James. We never gave up hope.
POLICE
This is... well, I guess this is your sister, Nancy.
Hi. This is Bobby.
Hello.
Thanks for bringing him this far, Miss Manners. We can handle things from here.
It really is the least I could do. He's a great kid who's been through a lot, I just wanted to get him back to where he's safe and loved.
Thank you so much.
Umm...
Well, you're right that he's going to be safe and loved here.
What about it, buddy? Back at the house we've got a tub of ice cream with your name on it.
Umm... sorry, but...
Who's that?
RUSTLE
RUFF RUFF RUFF RUFF RUFF RUFF RUFF RUFF RUFF

SHAKE
SHAKE
RUSTLE
Please...
...Help me.
Call dispatch, get an ambulance down here!
WHUD
That's Theo Halbot, Ryan's dad!
Stay back, Bobby!
RUFF RUFF RUFF RUFF
RUFF RUFF RUFF RUFF RUFF

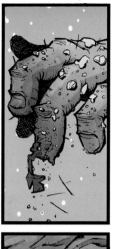

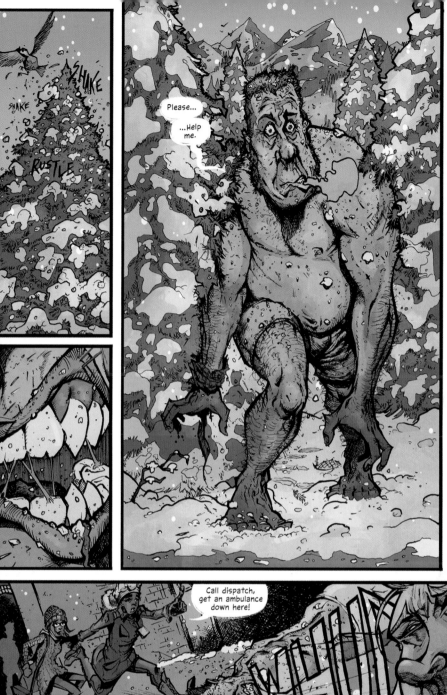

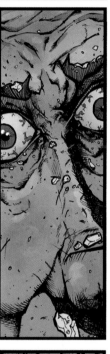

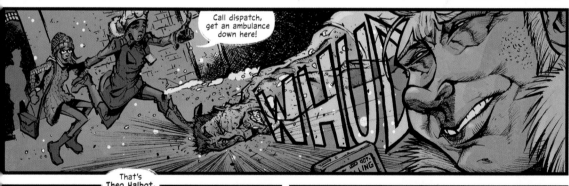

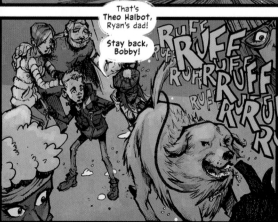

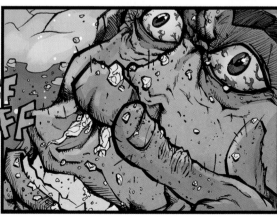

"What a crazy day."

SHK SHK SHK SHK

They've got Theo Halbot in the hospital. He went climbing up **Mount Rector** with a group but the others are still missing.

You've been awful quiet, James. I know you must have a lot on your mind, a lot of questions you want to ask.

I can't imagine what that monster put you through. When you're ready, maybe we can talk about it.

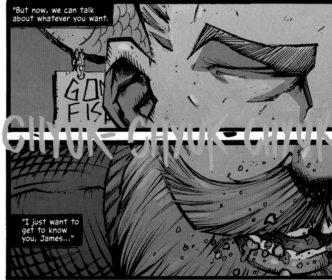

"But now, we can talk about whatever you want.

GO FISH

CHUK CHUK CHUK

"I just want to get to know you, James..."

Don't call me James. I've been Abraham for ten years.

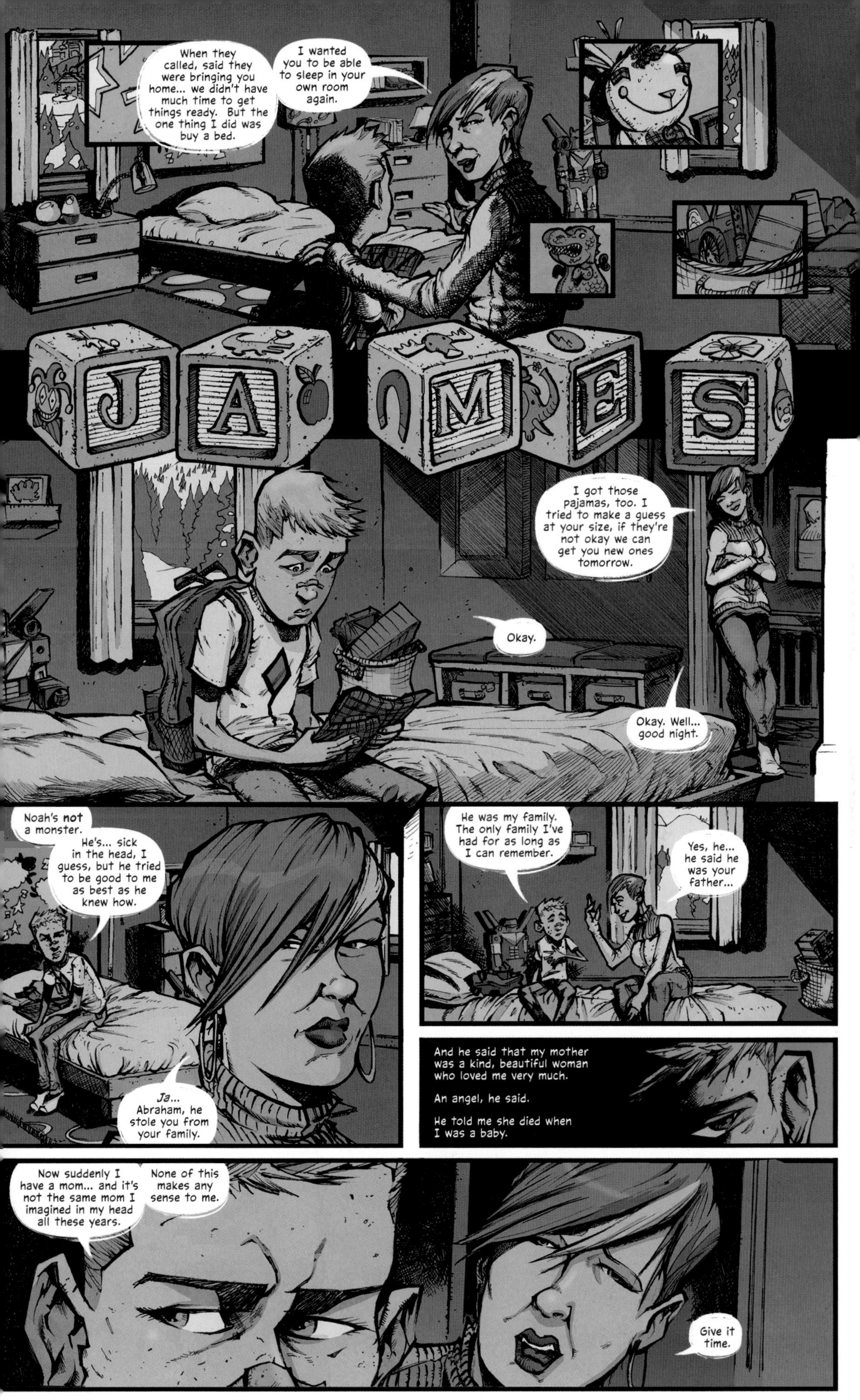
When they called, said they were bringing you home... we didn't have much time to get things ready. But the one thing I did was buy a bed.
I wanted you to be able to sleep in your own room again.
JAMES
I got those pajamas, too. I tried to make a guess at your size, if they're not okay we can get you new ones tomorrow.
Okay.
Okay. Well... good night.
Noah's **not** a monster.
He's... sick in the head, I guess, but he tried to be good to me as best as he knew how.
Ja... Abraham, he stole you from your family.
He was my family. The only family I've had for as long as I can remember.
Yes, he... he said he was your father...
And he said that my mother was a kind, beautiful woman who loved me very much.
An angel, he said.
He told me she died when I was a baby.
Now suddenly I have a mom... and it's not the same mom I imagined in my head all these years.
None of this makes any sense to me.
Give it time.

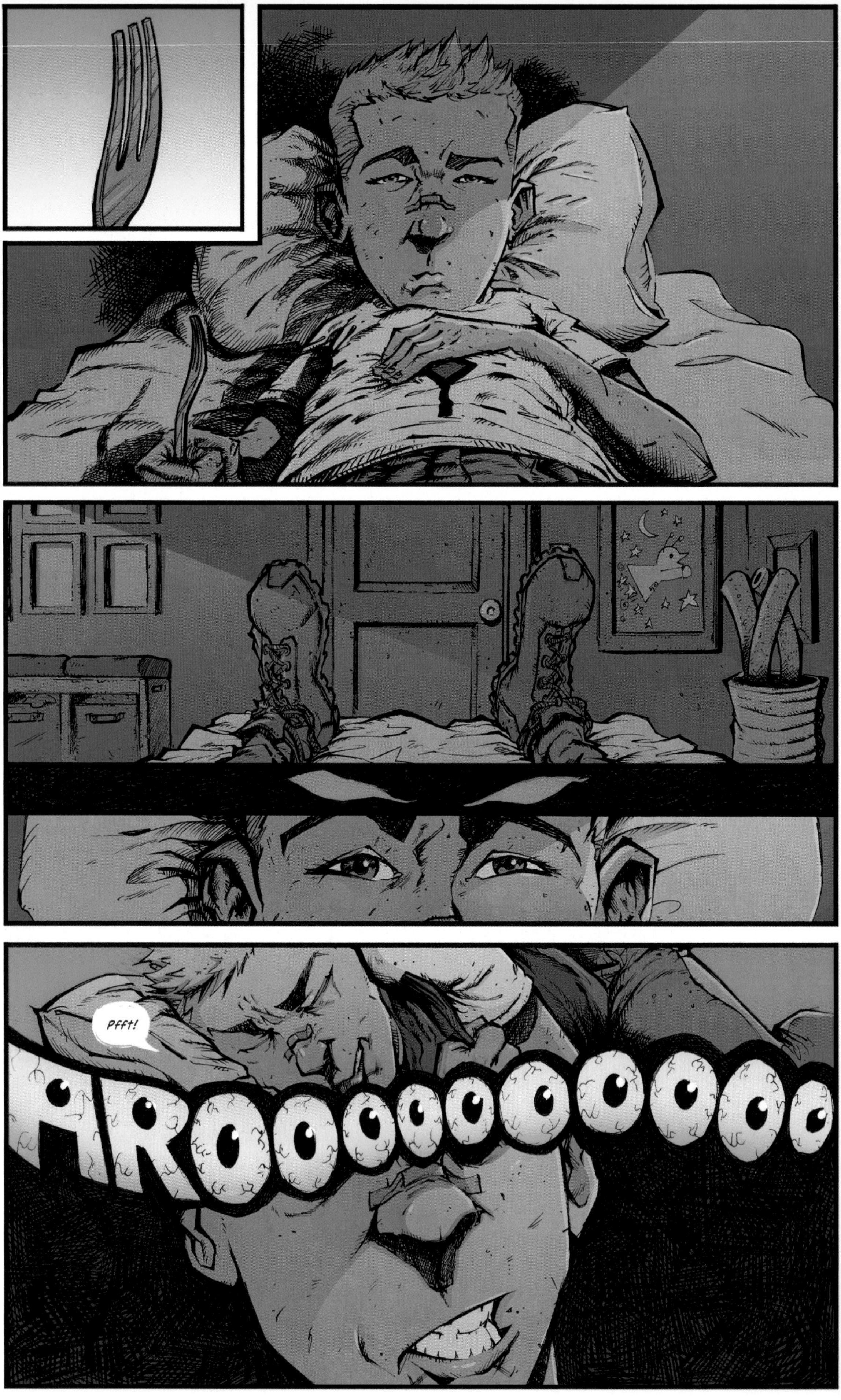
Pfft!
AROOOOOOOOOOOO

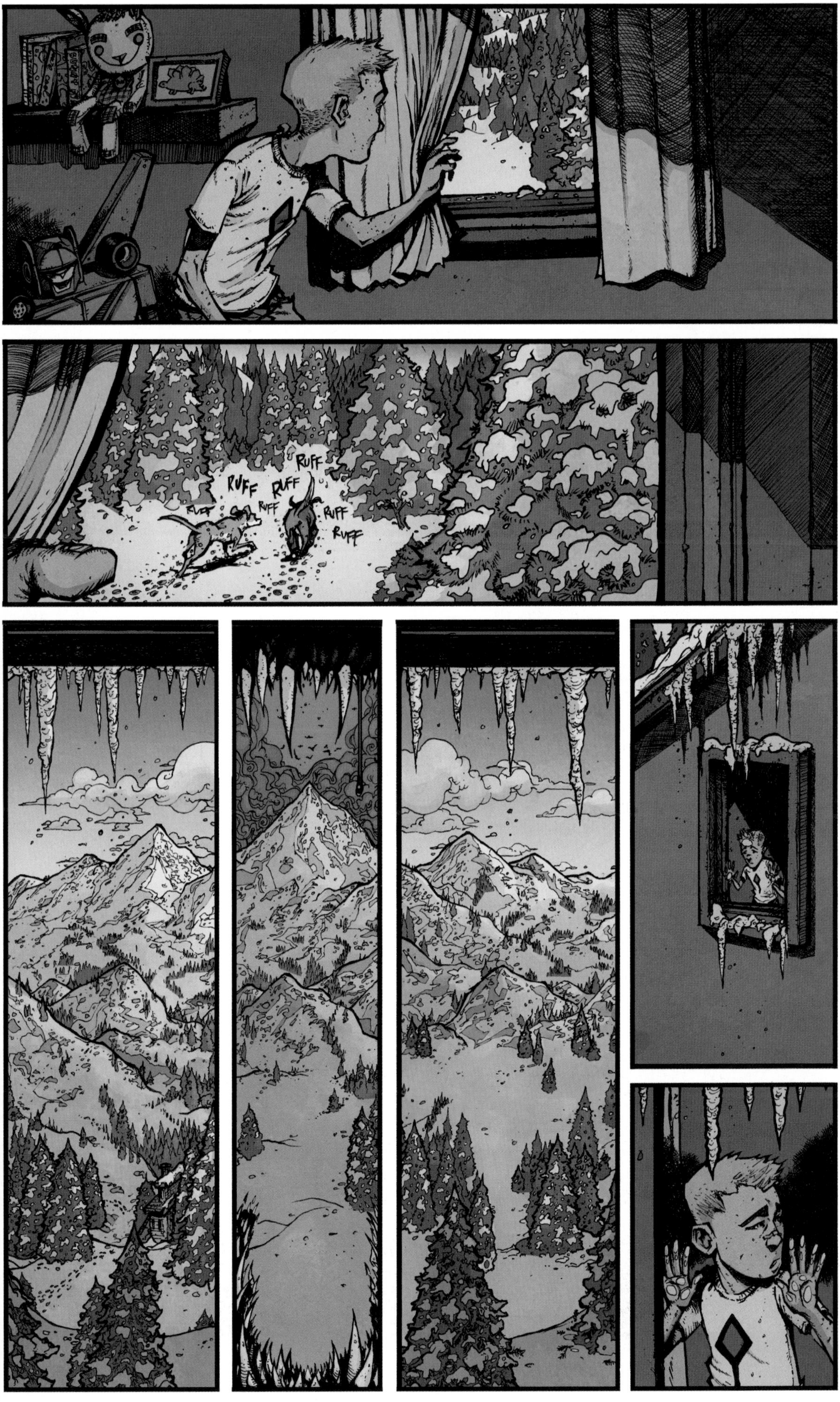
RUFF
RUFF
RUFF
RUFF
RUFF
RUFF
RUFF

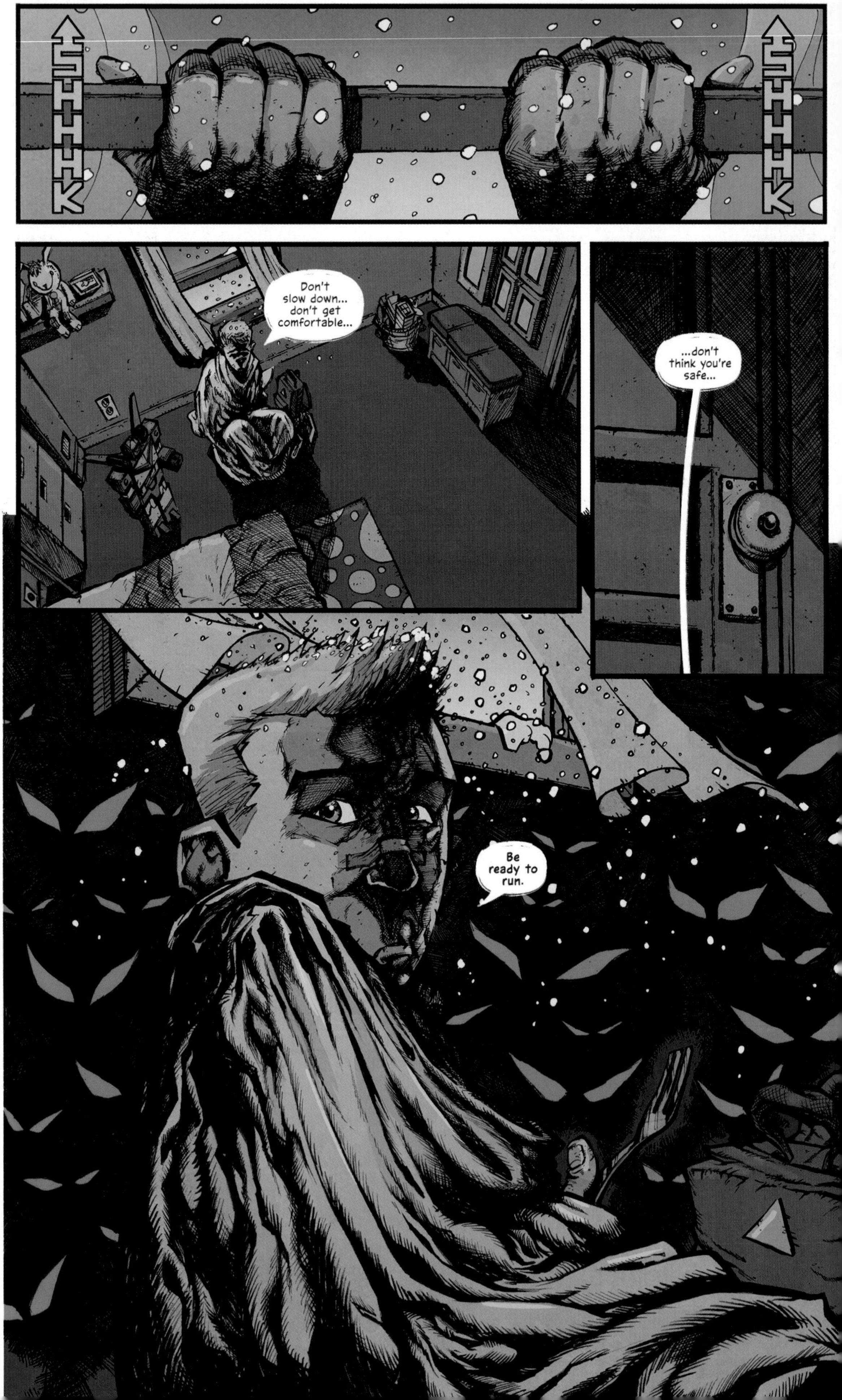
SHHHK
SHHHK
Don't slow down... don't get comfortable...
...don't think you're safe...
Be ready to run.

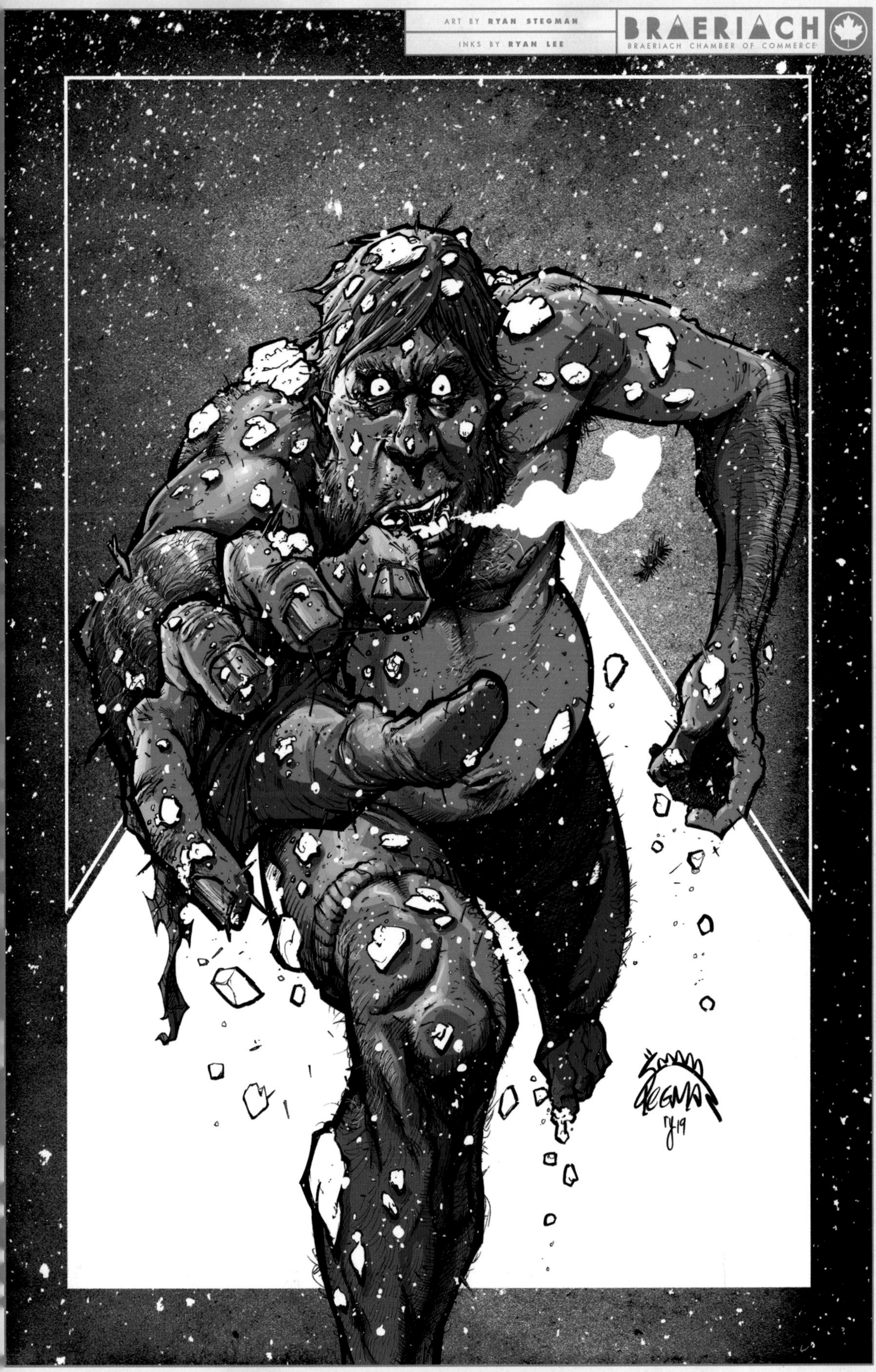
ART BY RYAN STEGMAN
INKS BY RYAN LEE
BRAERIACH
BRAERIACH CHAMBER OF COMMERCE

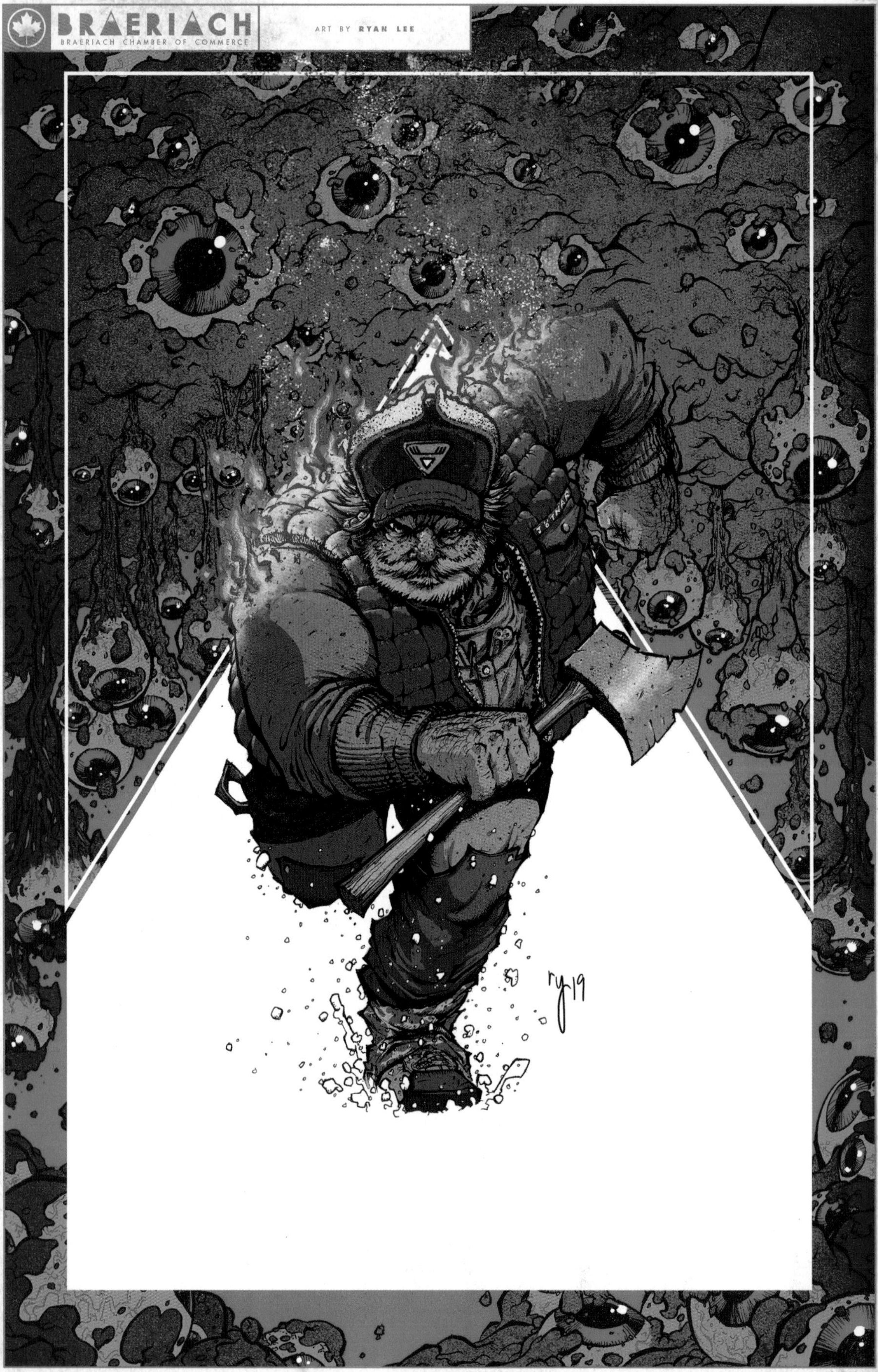
BRAERIACH
BRAERIACH CHAMBER OF COMMERCE
ART BY RYAN LEE

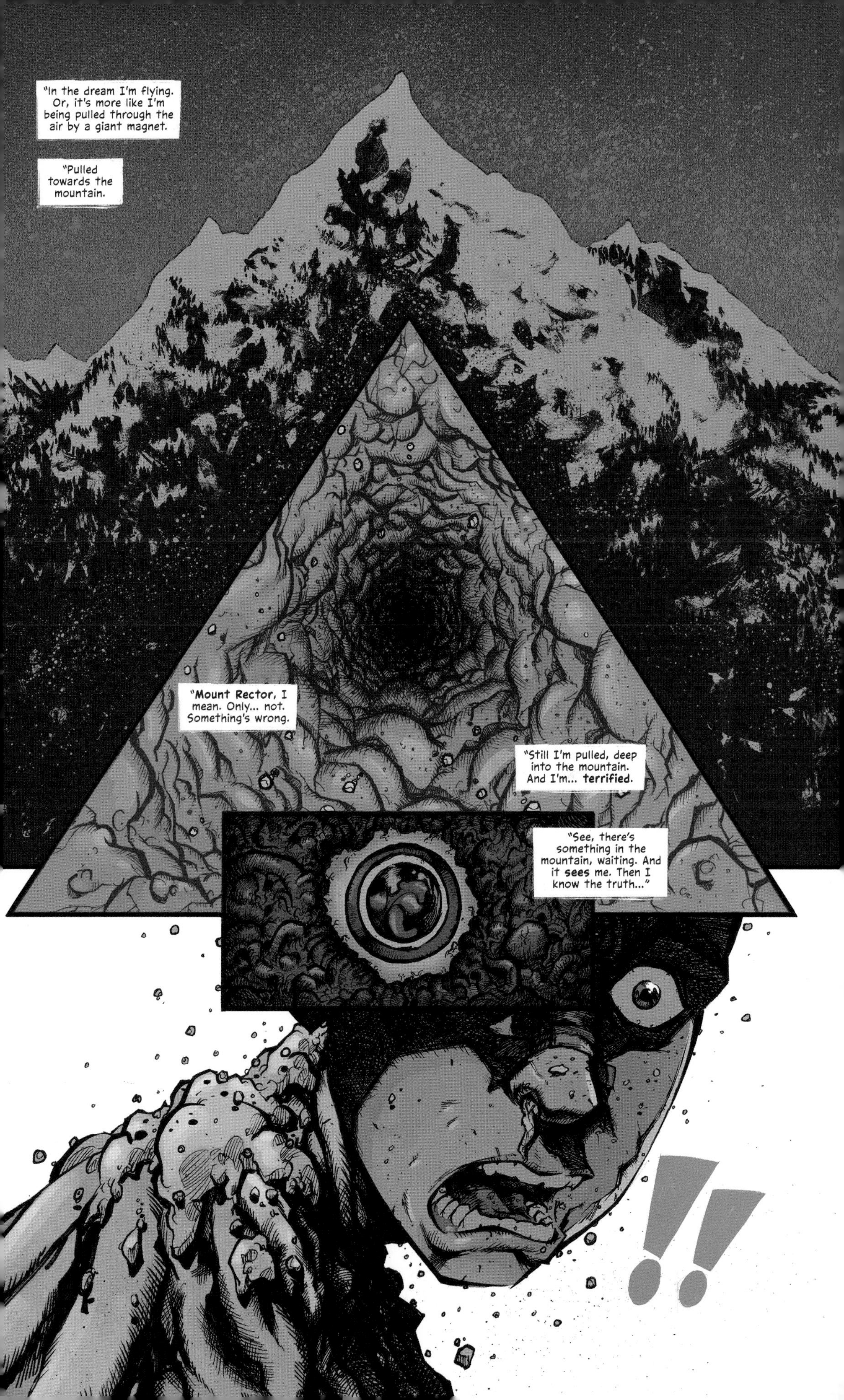
"In the dream I'm flying. Or, it's more like I'm being pulled through the air by a giant magnet.
"Pulled towards the mountain.
"Mount Rector, I mean. Only... not. Something's wrong.
"Still I'm pulled, deep into the mountain. And I'm... terrified.
"See, there's something in the mountain, waiting. And it sees me. Then I know the truth..."
!!

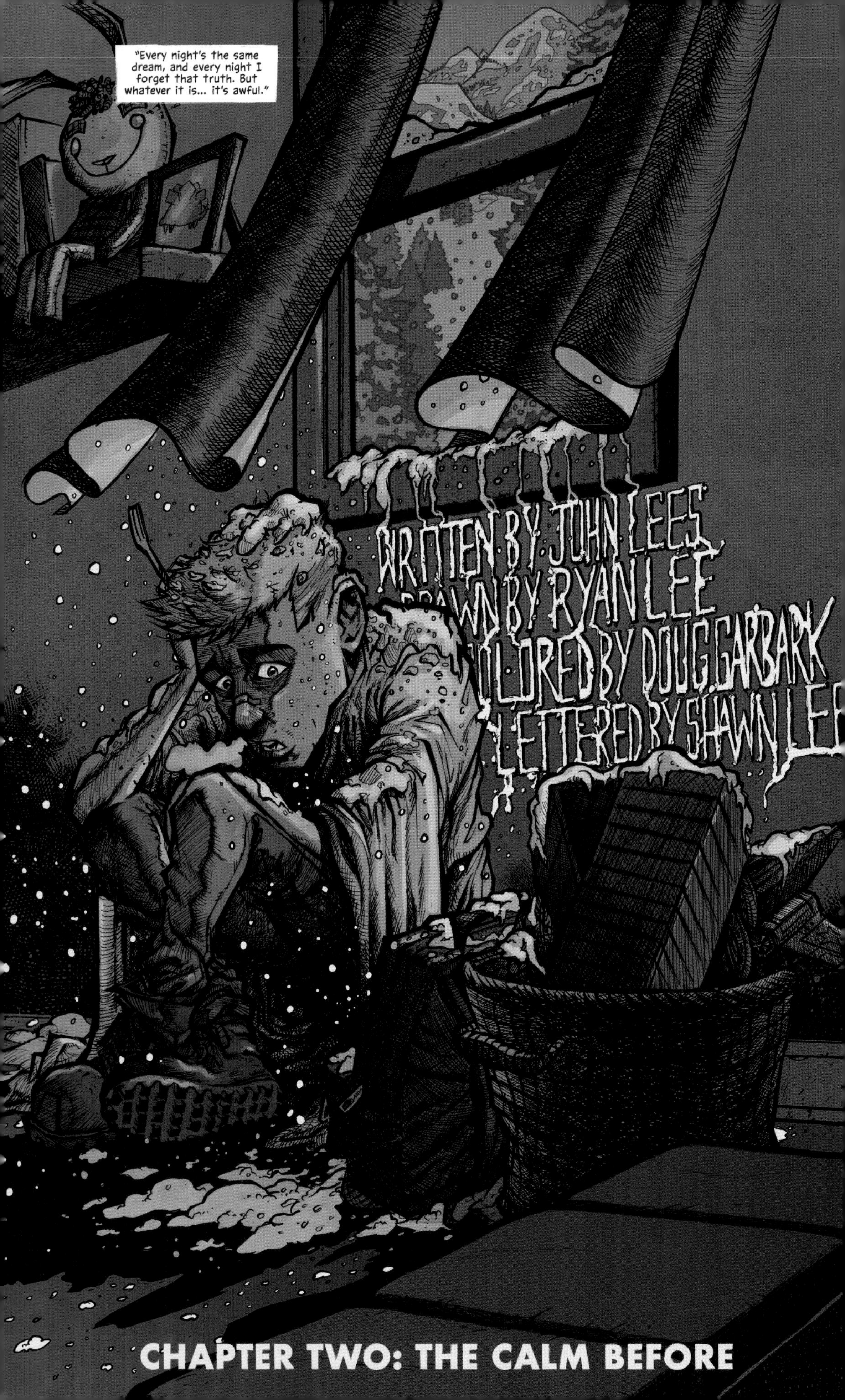
"Every night's the same dream, and every night I forget that truth. But whatever it is... it's awful."
WRITTEN BY JOHN LEES,
BY RYAN LEE
LORED BY DOUG GARBARK
LETTERED BY SHAWN LEE
CHAPTER TWO: THE CALM BEFORE

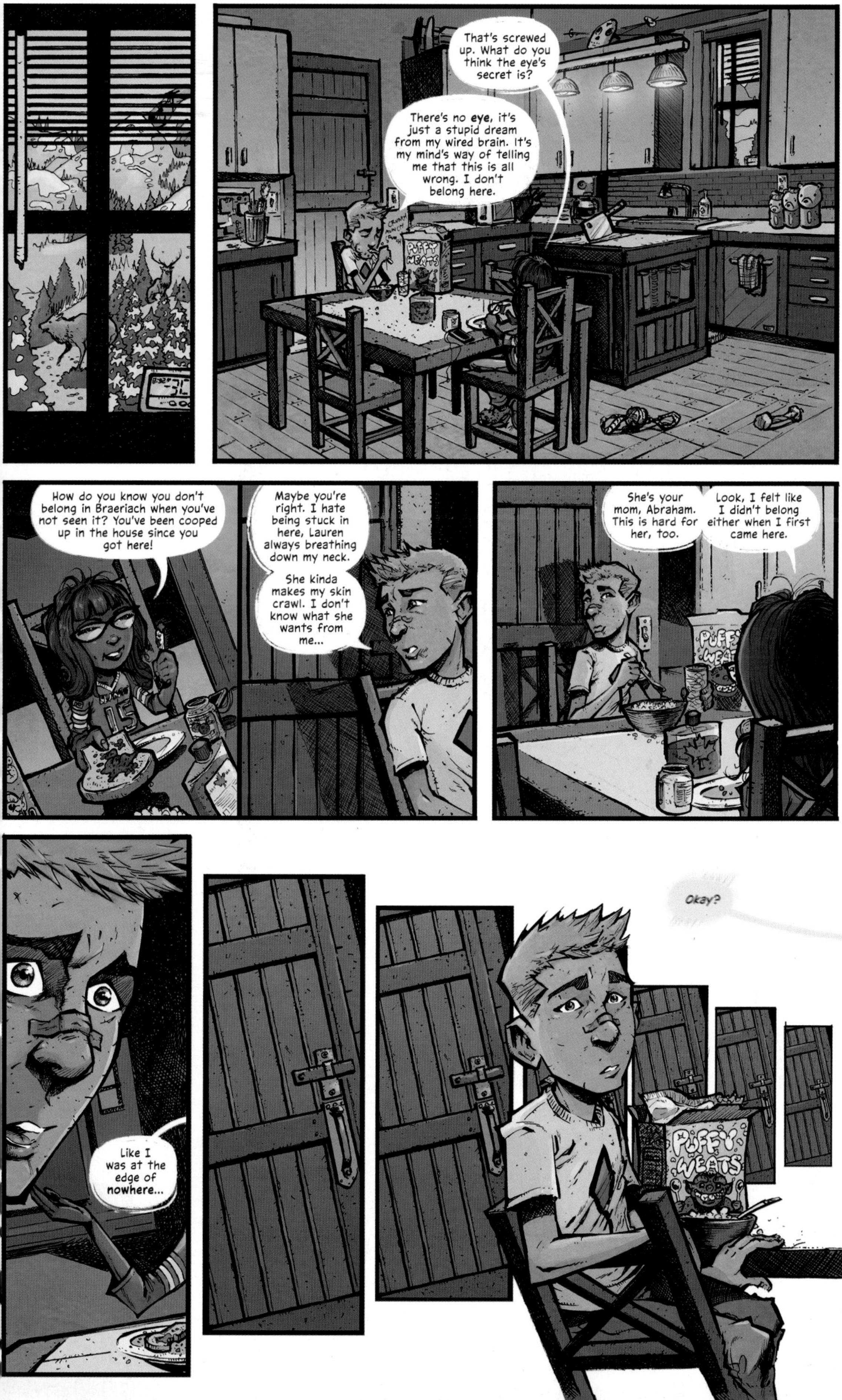
That's screwed up. What do you think the eye's secret is?
There's no eye, it's just a stupid dream from my wired brain. It's my mind's way of telling me that this is all wrong. I don't belong here.
How do you know you don't belong in Braeriach when you've not seen it? You've been cooped up in the house since you got here!
Maybe you're right. I hate being stuck in here, Lauren always breathing down my neck.
She kinda makes my skin crawl. I don't know what she wants from me...
She's your mom, Abraham. This is hard for her, too.
Look, I felt like I didn't belong either when I first came here.
Like I was at the edge of nowhere...
Okay?

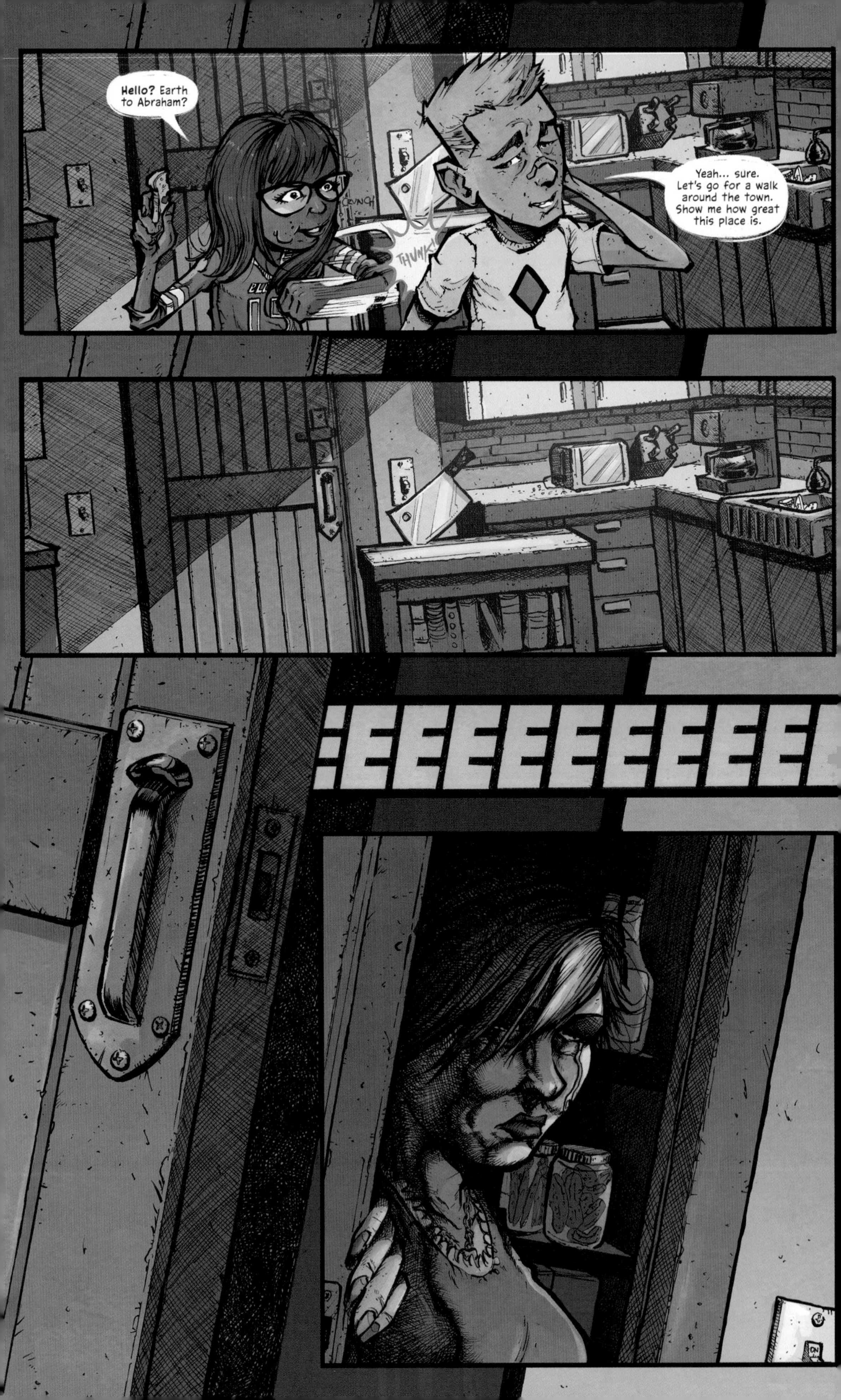
Hello? Earth to Abraham?
CRUNCH
THUNK!
Yeah... sure. Let's go for a walk around the town. Show me how great this place is.
EEEEEEEEEEE
ON

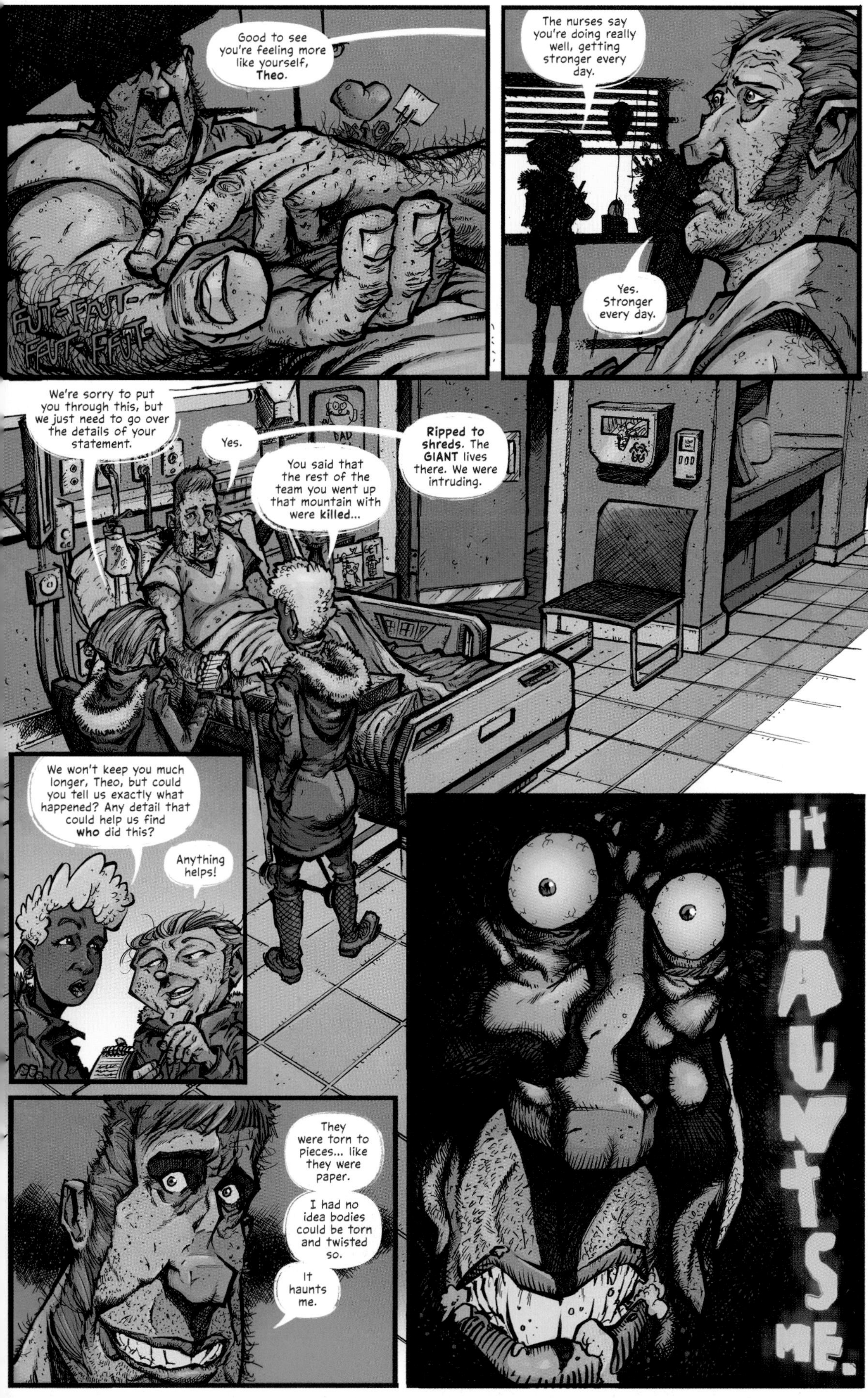
Good to see you're feeling more like yourself, **Theo.**
FUT-FAUT-FAUT-FFUT-
The nurses say you're doing really well, getting stronger every day.
Yes. Stronger every day.
We're sorry to put you through this, but we just need to go over the details of your statement.
Yes.
You said that the rest of the team you went up that mountain with were **killed**...
Ripped to shreds. The **GIANT** lives there. We were intruding.
We won't keep you much longer, Theo, but could you tell us exactly what happened? Any detail that could help us find **who** did this?
Anything helps!
They were torn to pieces... like they were paper.
I had no idea bodies could be torn and twisted so.
It haunts me.
IT HAUNTS ME.

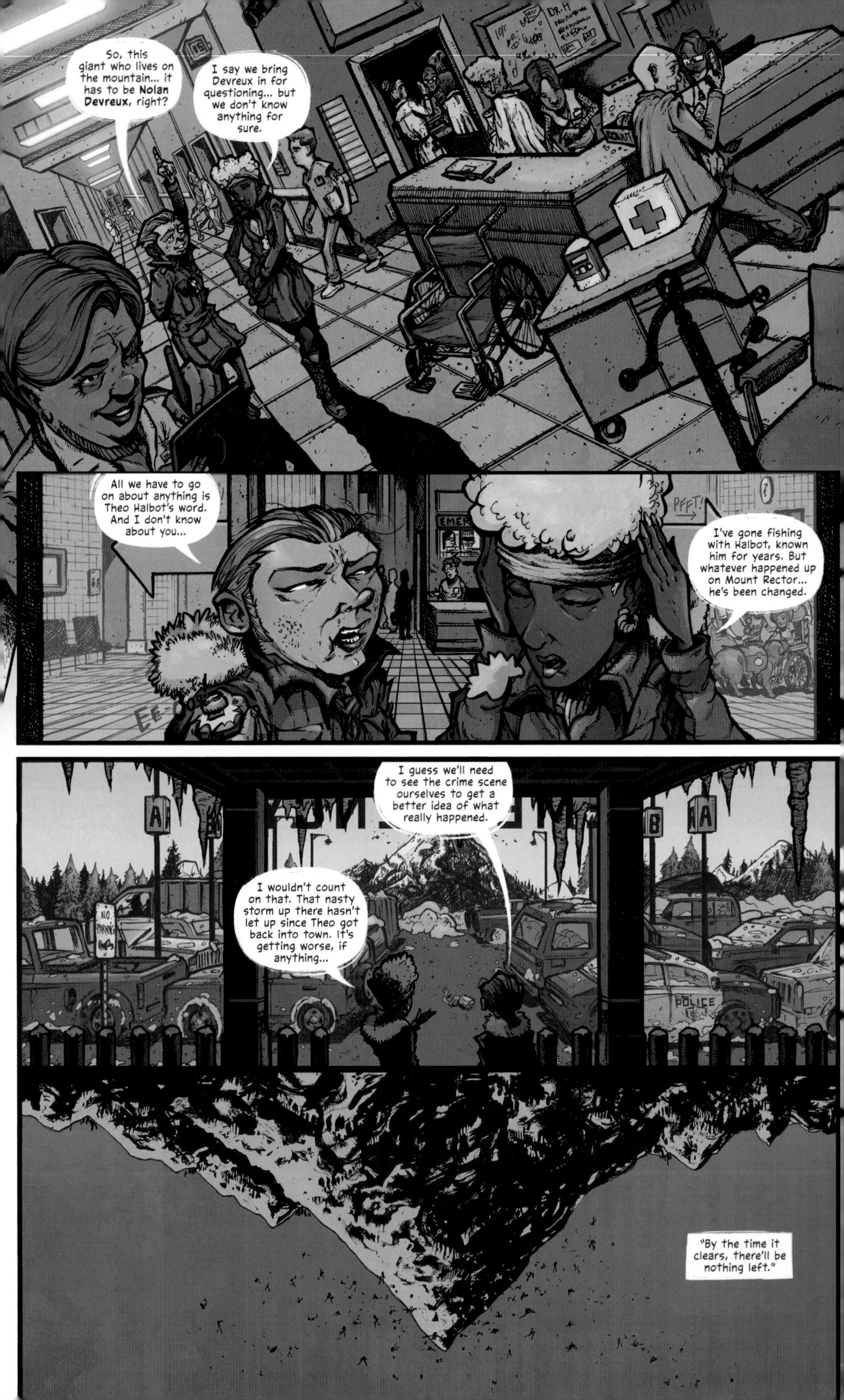

So, this giant who lives on the mountain... it has to be **Nolan Devreux**, right?
I say we bring Devreux in for questioning... but we don't know anything for sure.
All we have to go on about anything is Theo Halbot's word. And I don't know about you...
PFFT!
I've gone fishing with Halbot, known him for years. But whatever happened up on Mount Rector... he's been changed.
I guess we'll need to see the crime scene ourselves to get a better idea of what really happened.
I wouldn't count on that. That nasty storm up there hasn't let up since Theo got back into town. It's getting worse, if anything...
NO PARKING
POLICE
"By the time it clears, there'll be nothing left."

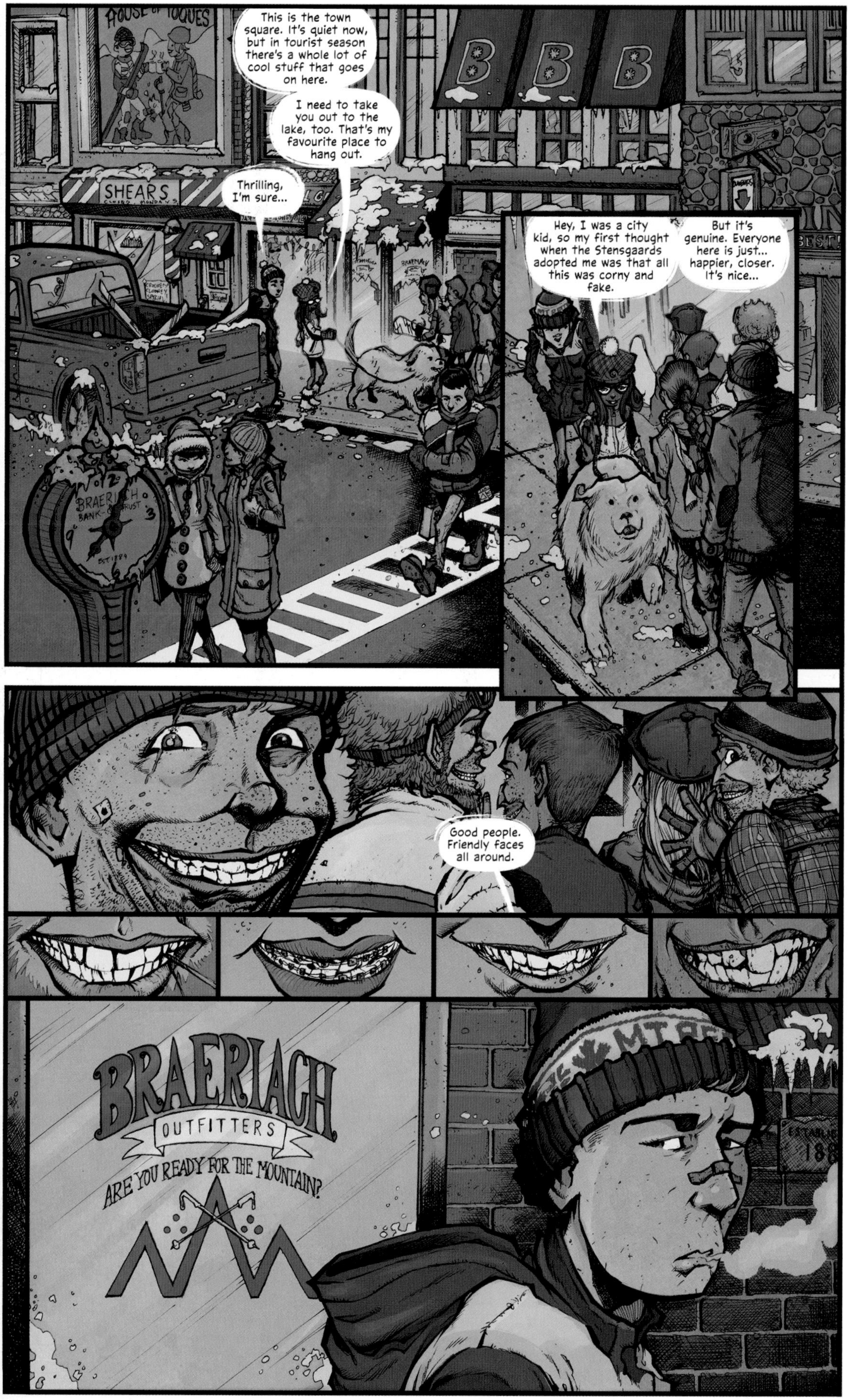

HOUSE OF TOQUES
This is the town square. It's quiet now, but in tourist season there's a whole lot of cool stuff that goes on here.
I need to take you out to the lake, too. That's my favourite place to hang out.
SHEARS
Thrilling, I'm sure...
BRAERIACH BANK & TRUST
Hey, I was a city kid, so my first thought when the Stensgaards adopted me was that all this was corny and fake.
But it's genuine. Everyone here is just... happier, closer. It's nice...
Good people. Friendly faces all around.
BRAERIACH
OUTFITTERS
ARE YOU READY FOR THE MOUNTAIN?

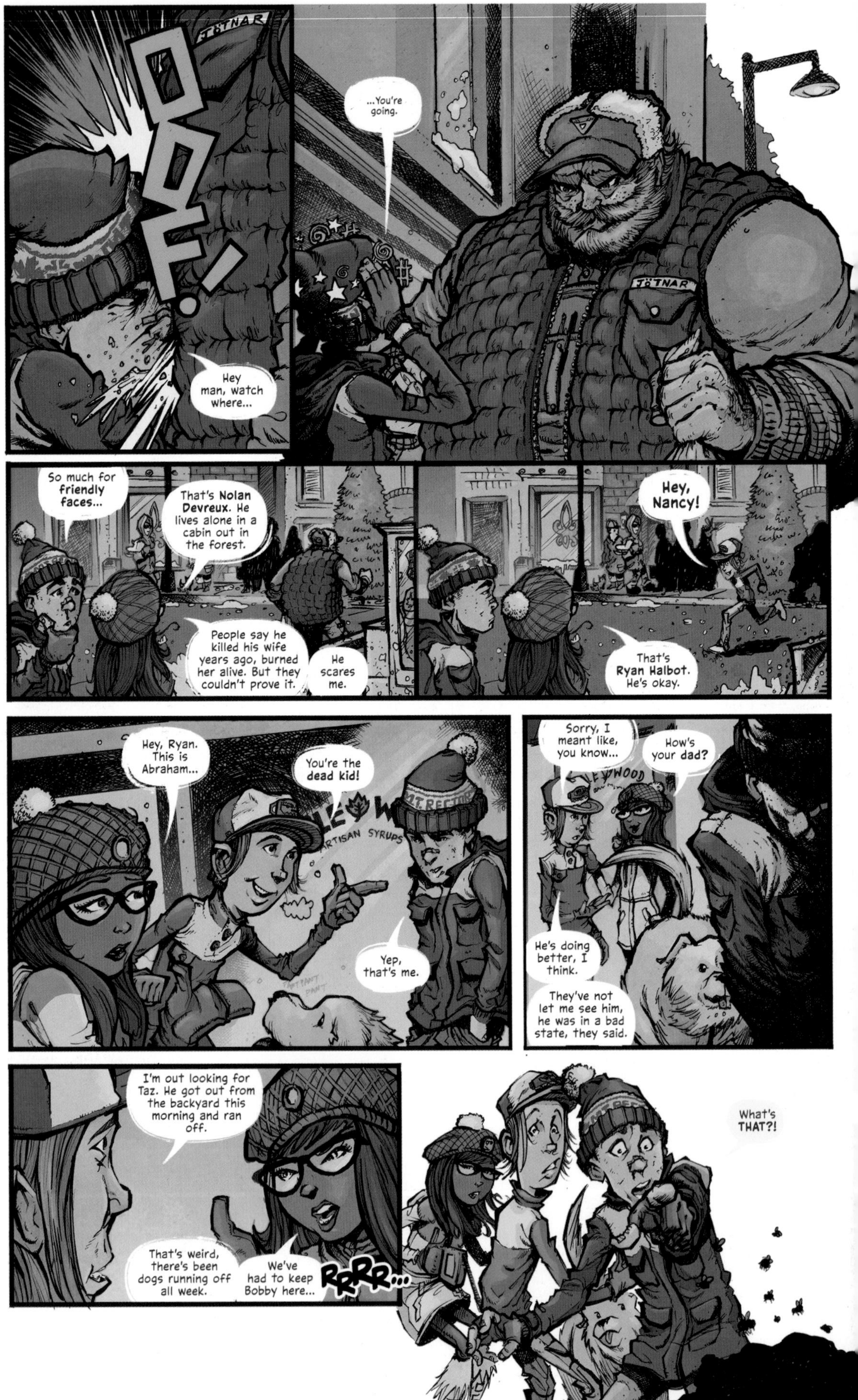
JÖTNAR
OOF!
Hey man, watch where...
...You're going.
JÖTNAR
So much for friendly faces...
That's Nolan Devreux. He lives alone in a cabin out in the forest.
People say he killed his wife years ago, burned her alive. But they couldn't prove it.
He scares me.
Hey, Nancy!
That's Ryan Halbot. He's okay.
Hey, Ryan. This is Abraham...
You're the dead kid!
ARTISAN SYRUPS
Yep, that's me.
PANT PANT PANT
Sorry, I meant like, you know...
How's your dad?
He's doing better, I think.
They've not let me see him, he was in a bad state, they said.
I'm out looking for Taz. He got out from the backyard this morning and ran off.
That's weird, there's been dogs running off all week.
We've had to keep Bobby here...
RRRR...
What's THAT?!

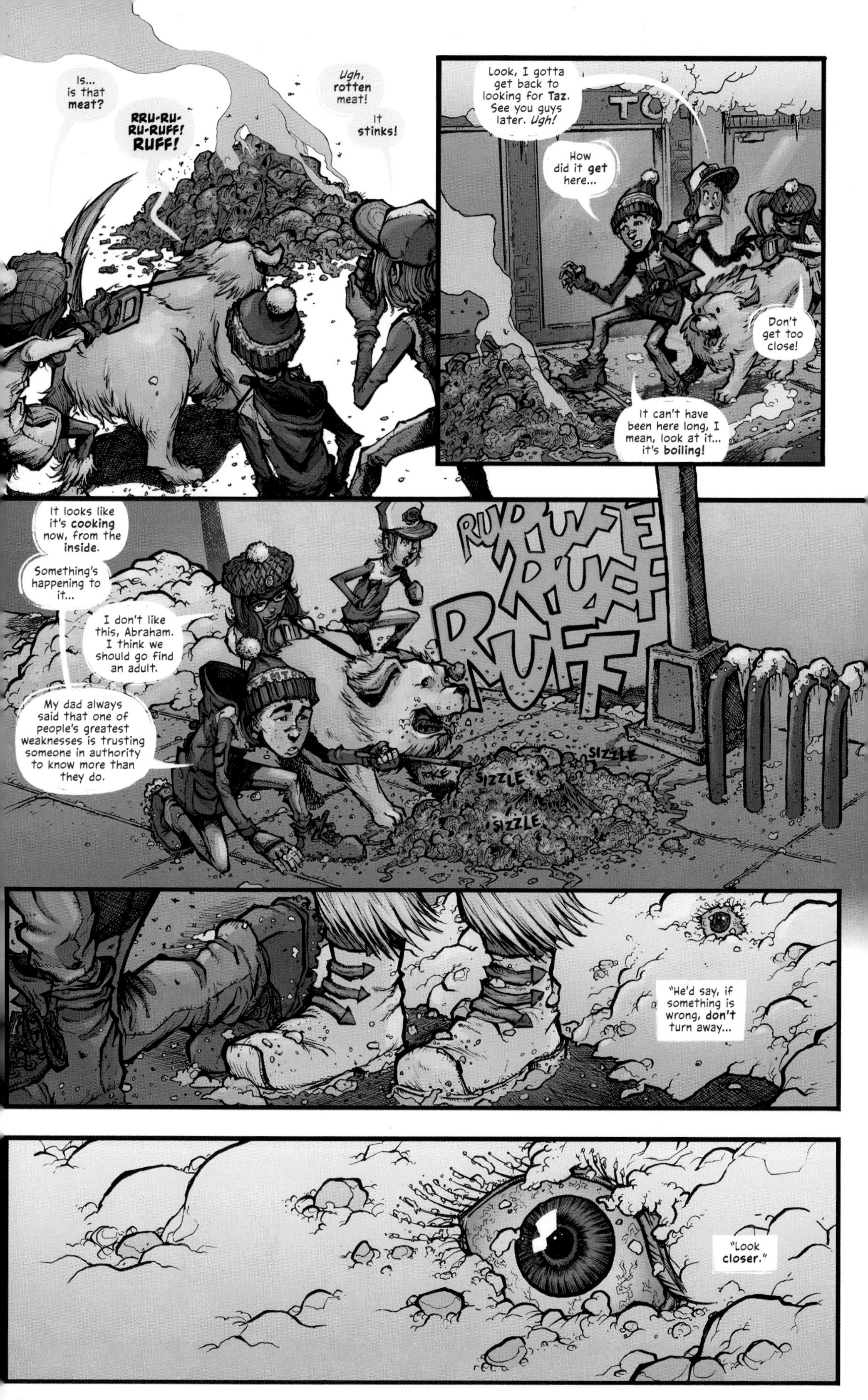

Is... is that **meat?**
RRU-RU-RU-RUFF! RUFF!
Ugh, **rotten** meat!
It **stinks!**
Look, I gotta get back to looking for **Taz.** See you guys later. *Ugh!*
How did it **get** here...
Don't get too close!
It can't have been here long, I mean, look at it... it's **boiling!**
It looks like it's **cooking** now, from the **inside.**
Something's happening to it...
I don't like this, Abraham. I think we should go find an adult.
My dad always said that one of people's greatest weaknesses is trusting someone in authority to know more than they do.
RUFF
RUFF
RUFF
SIZZLE
SIZZLE
SIZZLE
"He'd say, if something is wrong, **don't** turn away...
"Look **closer.**"

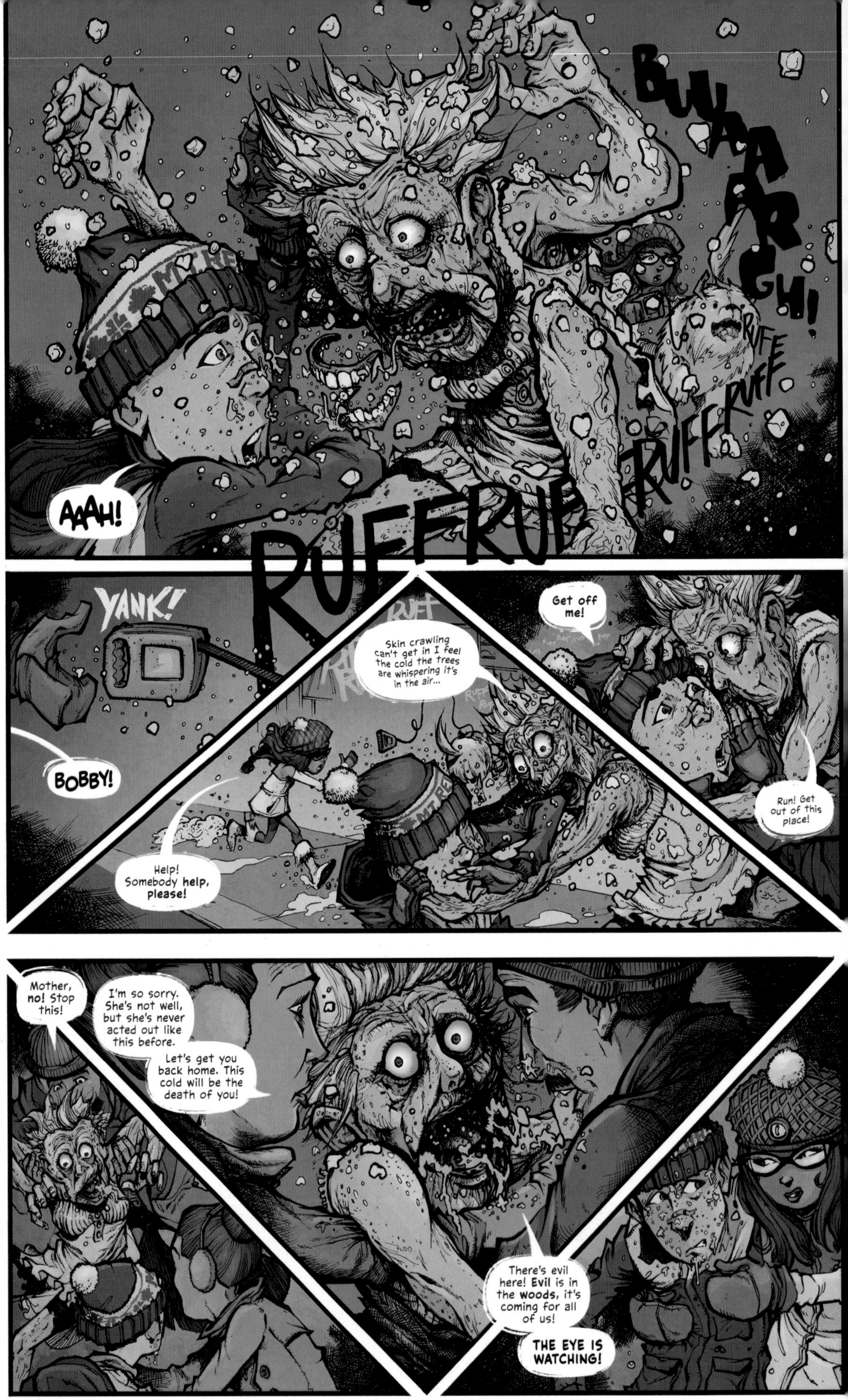
BUUAARGH!
RUFF
RUFF
RUFF!
AAAH!
RUFFRUF
YANK!
BOBBY!
Skin crawling can't get in I feel the cold the trees are whispering it's in the air...
Help! Somebody help, please!
Get off me!
Run! Get out of this place!
Mother, no! Stop this!
I'm so sorry. She's not well, but she's never acted out like this before.
Let's get you back home. This cold will be the death of you!
There's evil here! Evil is in the woods, it's coming for all of us!
THE EYE IS WATCHING!

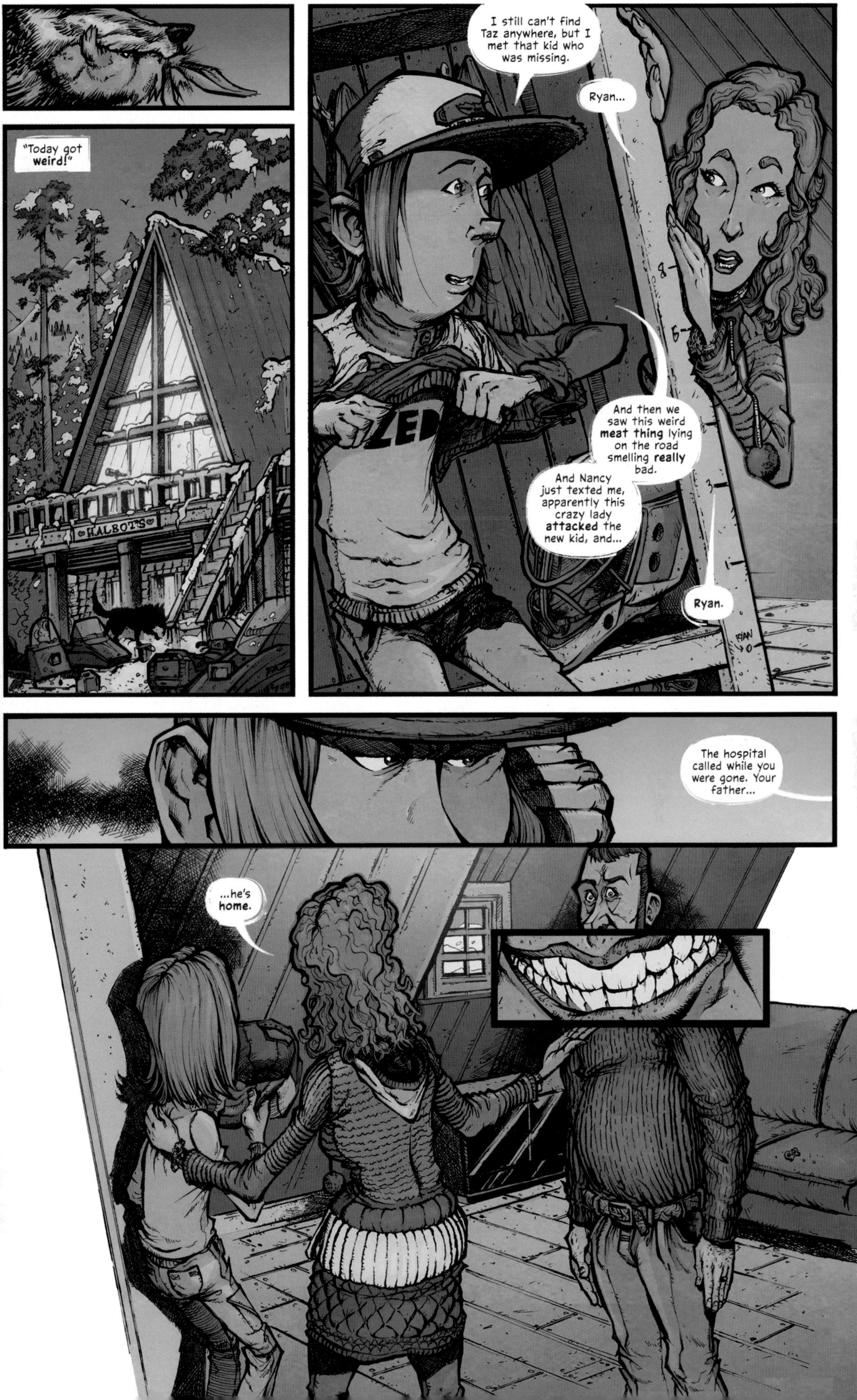
"Today got weird!"
HALBOTS
I still can't find Taz anywhere, but I met that kid who was missing.
Ryan...
And then we saw this weird **meat thing** lying on the road smelling **really** bad.
And Nancy just texted me, apparently this crazy lady **attacked** the new kid, and...
Ryan.
RYAN
The hospital called while you were gone. Your father...
...he's **home.**

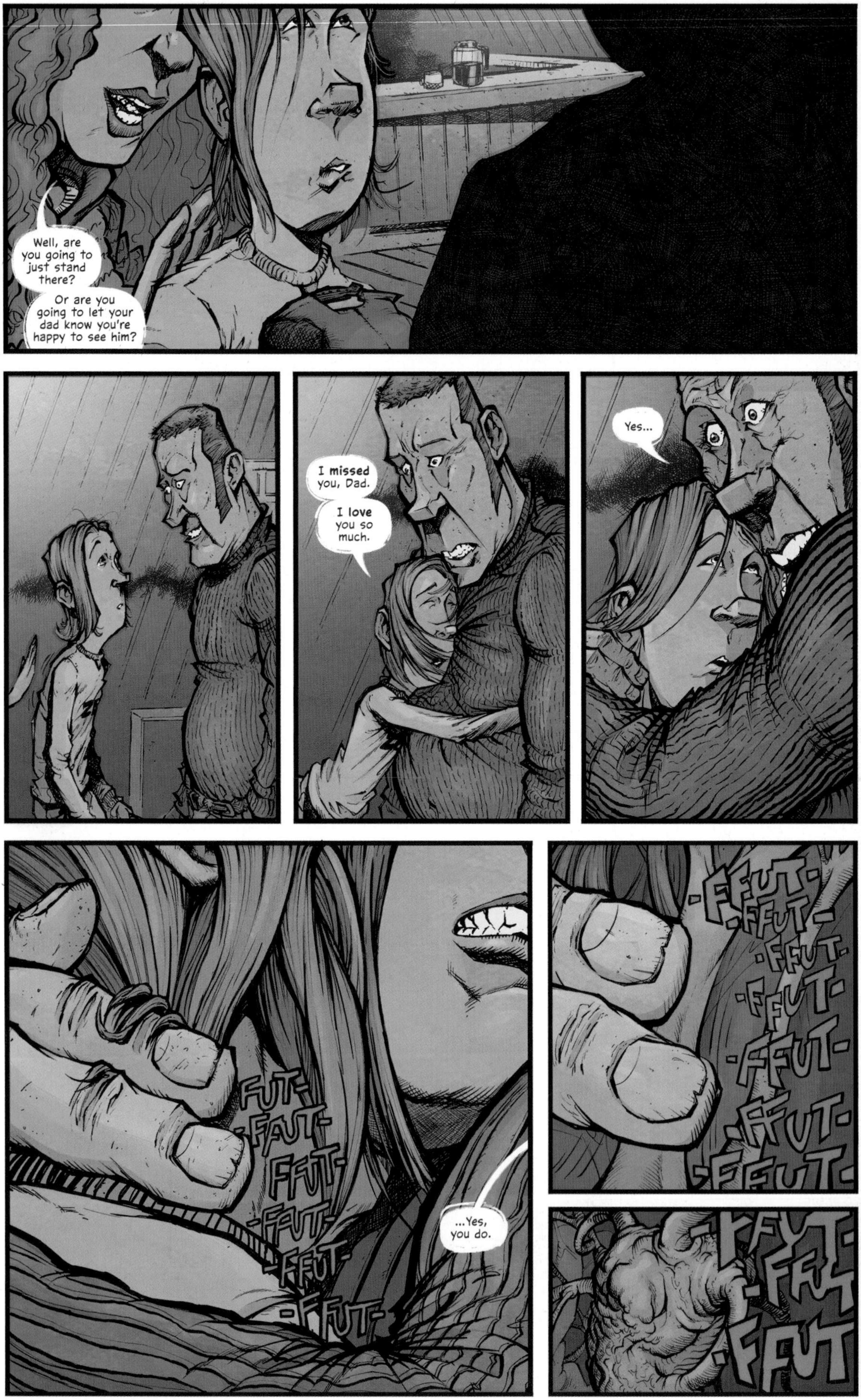

Well, are you going to just stand there?
Or are you going to let your dad know you're happy to see him?
I missed you, Dad.
I love you so much.
Yes...
FUT- -FFUT- FFUT- -FFUT- -FFUT -FFUT-
...Yes, you do.
-FFUT- -FFUT- -FFUT- -FFUT- -FFUT- -FFUT- -FFUT-
-FFUT- -FFUT -FFUT

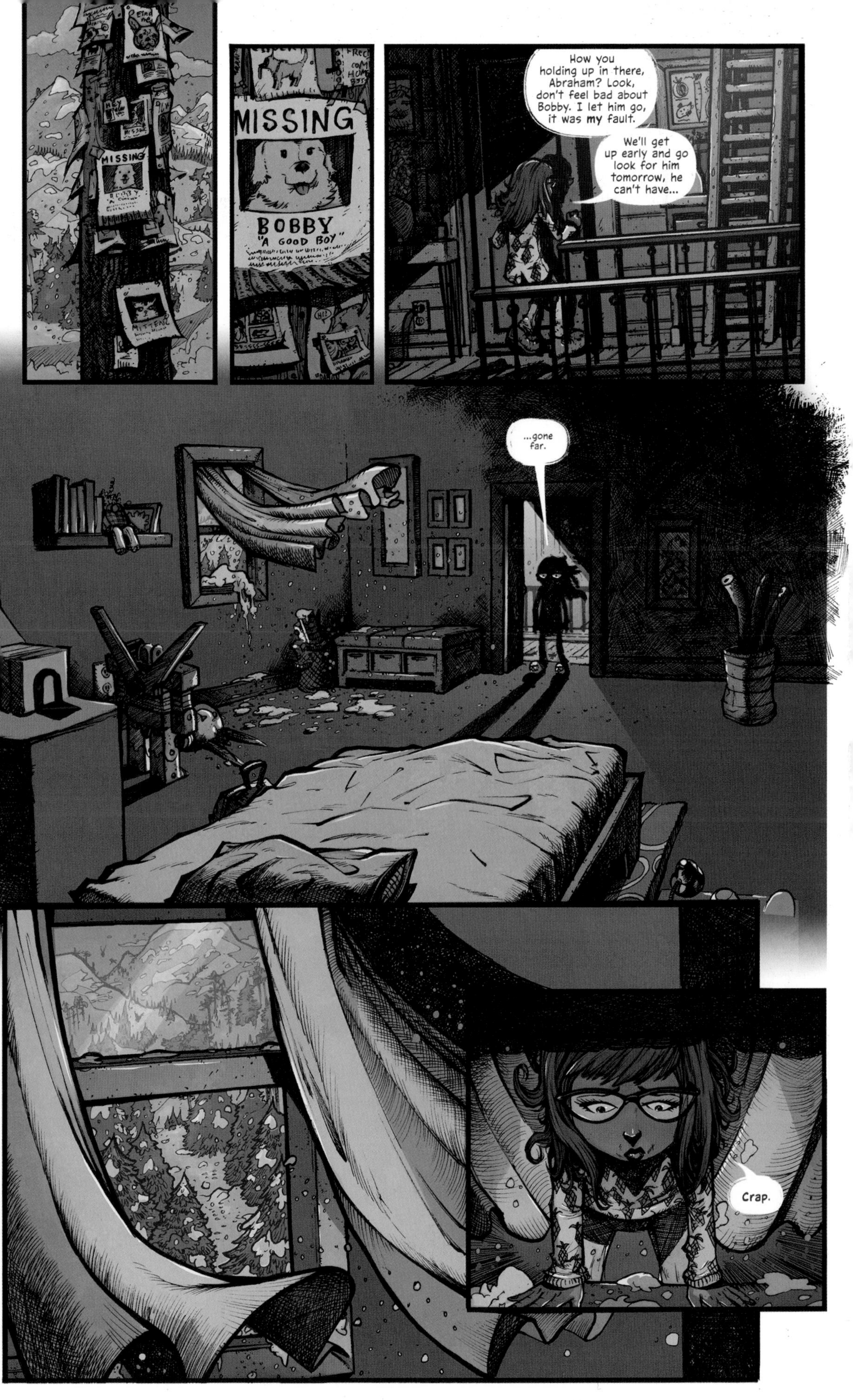
MISSING
MISSING
BOBBY
"A GOOD BOY"
How you holding up in there, Abraham? Look, don't feel bad about Bobby. I let him go, it was my fault.
We'll get up early and go look for him tomorrow, he can't have...
...gone far.
Crap.

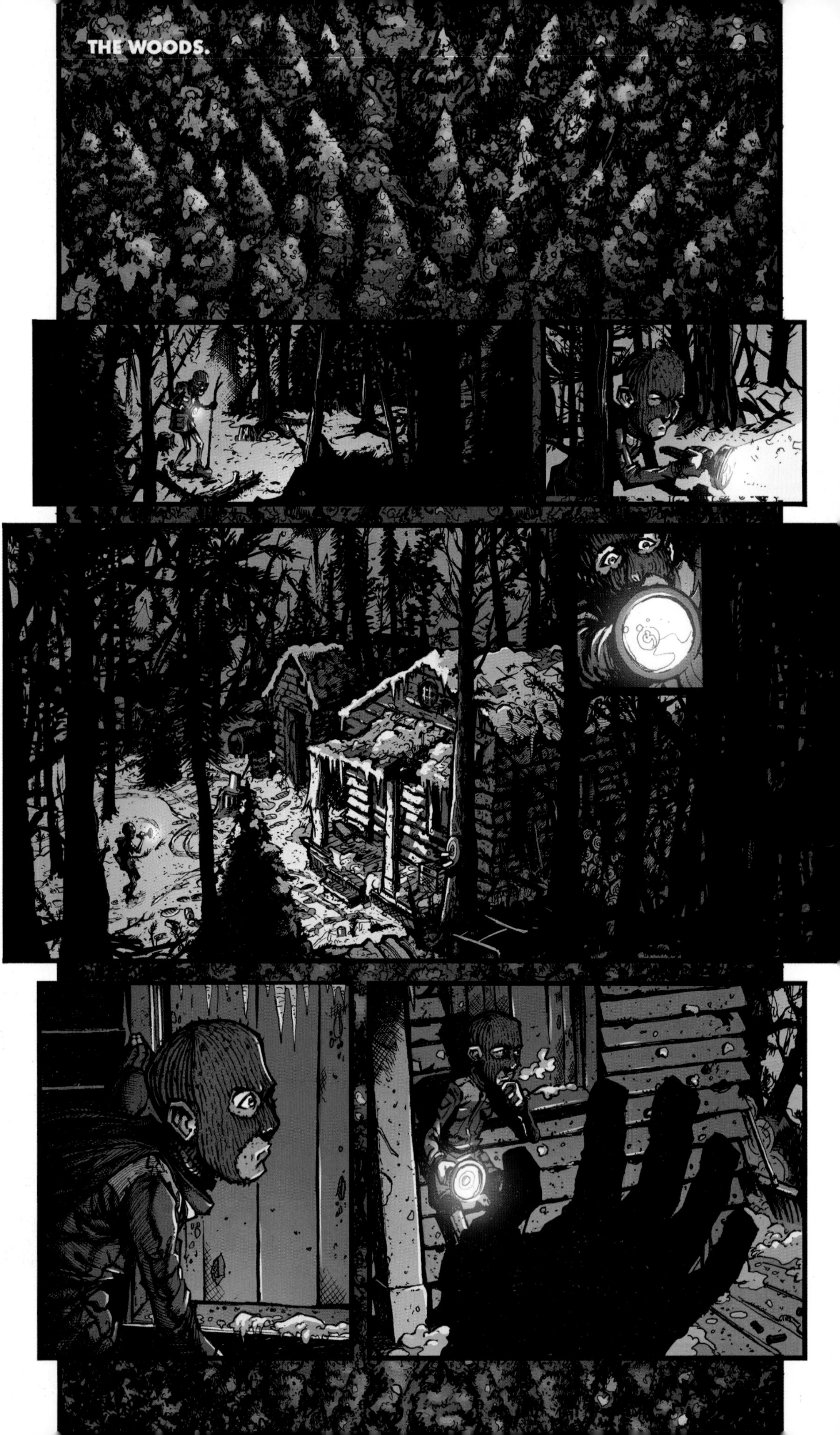
THE WOODS.

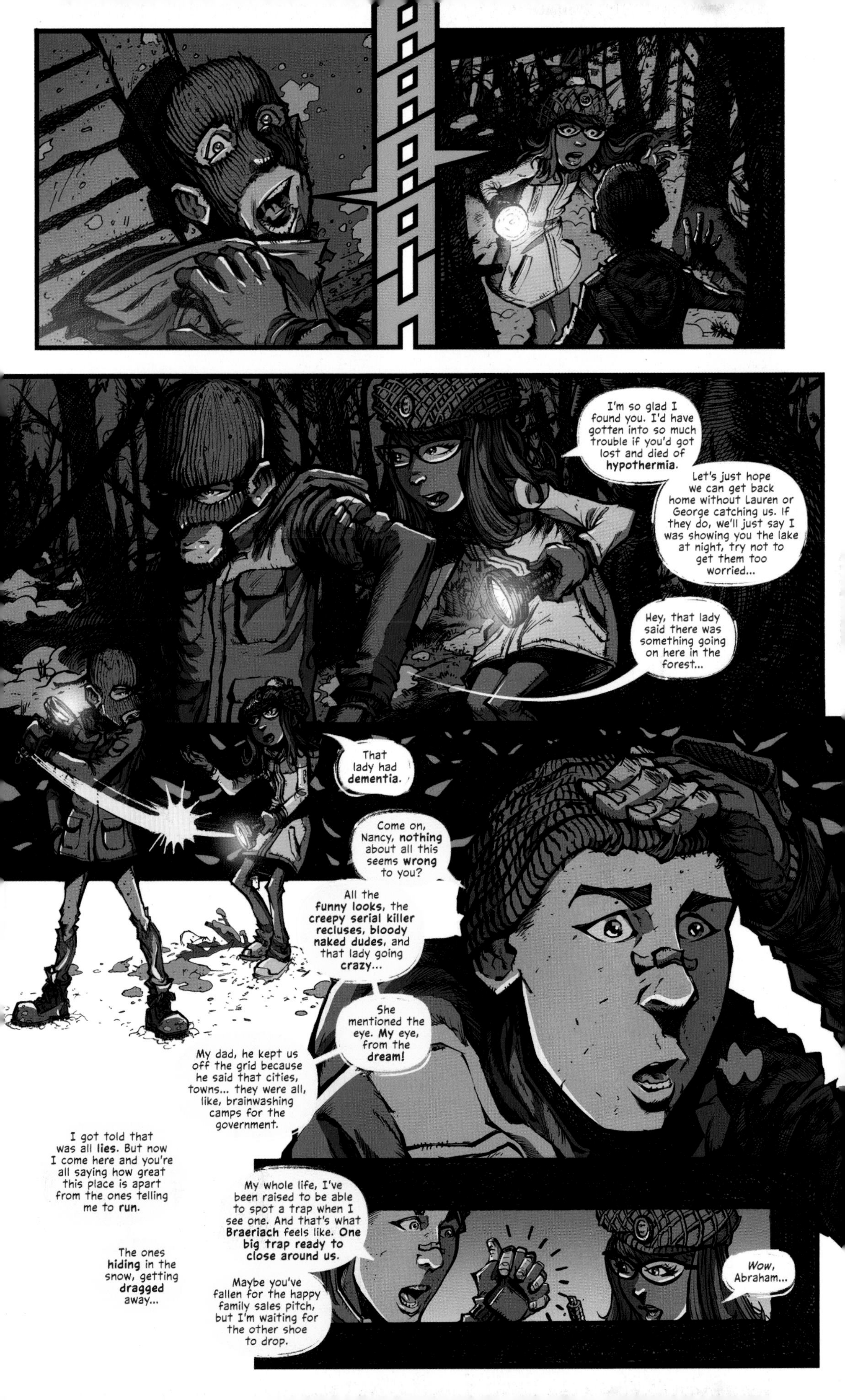
AAAAAAH
I'm so glad I found you. I'd have gotten into so much trouble if you'd got lost and died of **hypothermia**.
Let's just hope we can get back home without Lauren or George catching us. If they do, we'll just say I was showing you the lake at night, try not to get them too worried...
Hey, that lady said there was something going on here in the forest...
That lady had **dementia**.
Come on, Nancy, **nothing** about all this seems **wrong** to you?
All the **funny looks**, the **creepy serial killer recluses, bloody naked dudes**, and that lady going **crazy**...
She mentioned the eye. **My** eye, from the **dream!**
My dad, he kept us off the grid because he said that cities, towns... they were all, like, brainwashing camps for the government.
I got told that was all **lies**. But now I come here and you're all saying how great this place is apart from the ones telling me to **run**.
The ones **hiding** in the snow, getting **dragged** away...
My whole life, I've been raised to be able to spot a trap when I see one. And that's what **Braeriach** feels like. **One big trap ready to close around us.**
Maybe you've fallen for the happy family sales pitch, but I'm waiting for the other shoe to drop.
Wow, Abraham...

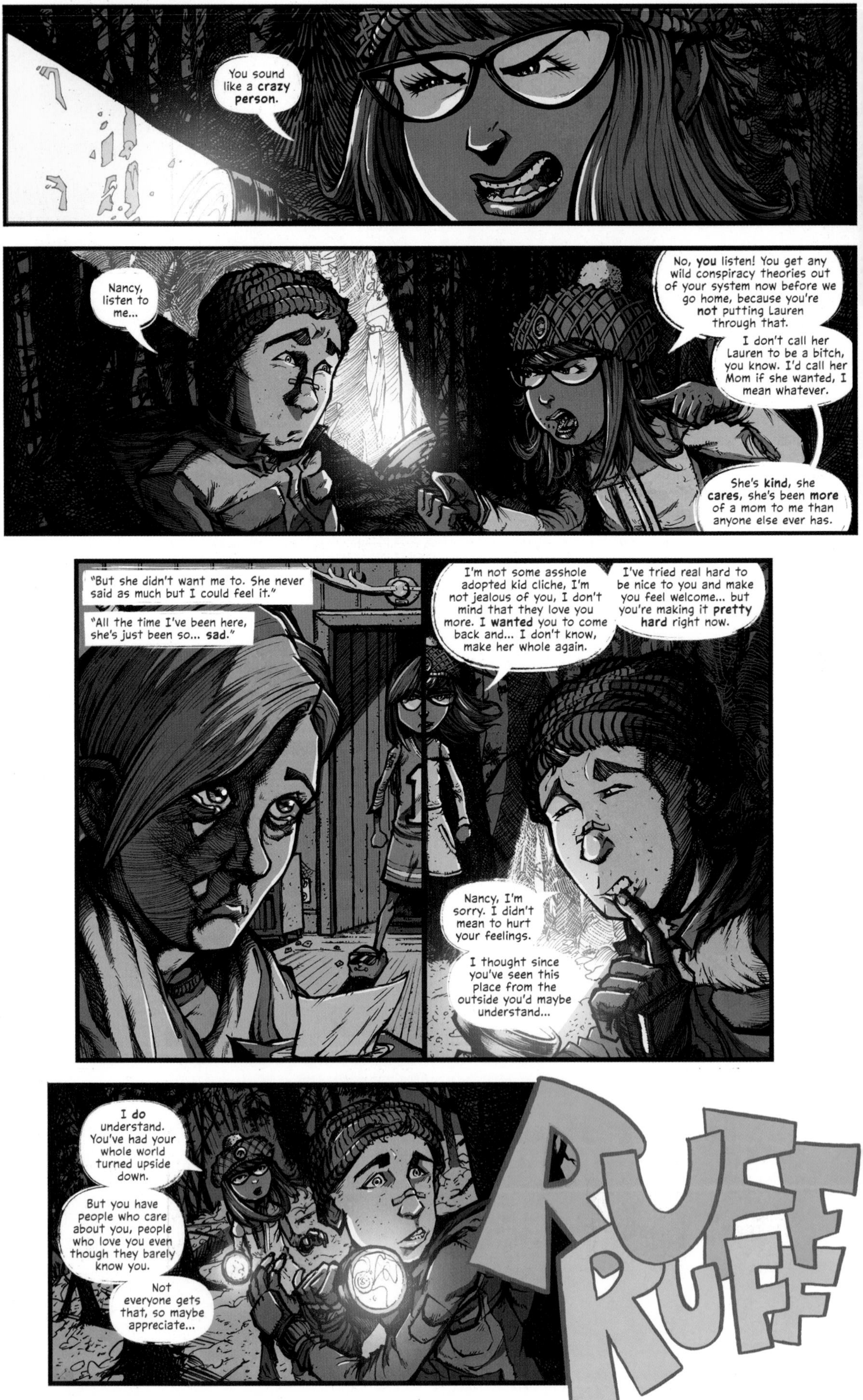

You sound like a crazy person.
Nancy, listen to me...
No, you listen! You get any wild conspiracy theories out of your system now before we go home, because you're not putting Lauren through that.
I don't call her Lauren to be a bitch, you know. I'd call her Mom if she wanted, I mean whatever.
She's kind, she cares, she's been more of a mom to me than anyone else ever has.
"But she didn't want me to. She never said as much but I could feel it."
"All the time I've been here, she's just been so... sad."
I'm not some asshole adopted kid cliche, I'm not jealous of you, I don't mind that they love you more. I wanted you to come back and... I don't know, make her whole again.
I've tried real hard to be nice to you and make you feel welcome... but you're making it pretty hard right now.
Nancy, I'm sorry. I didn't mean to hurt your feelings.
I thought since you've seen this place from the outside you'd maybe understand...
I do understand. You've had your whole world turned upside down.
But you have people who care about you, people who love you even though they barely know you.
Not everyone gets that, so maybe appreciate...
RUFF
RUFF

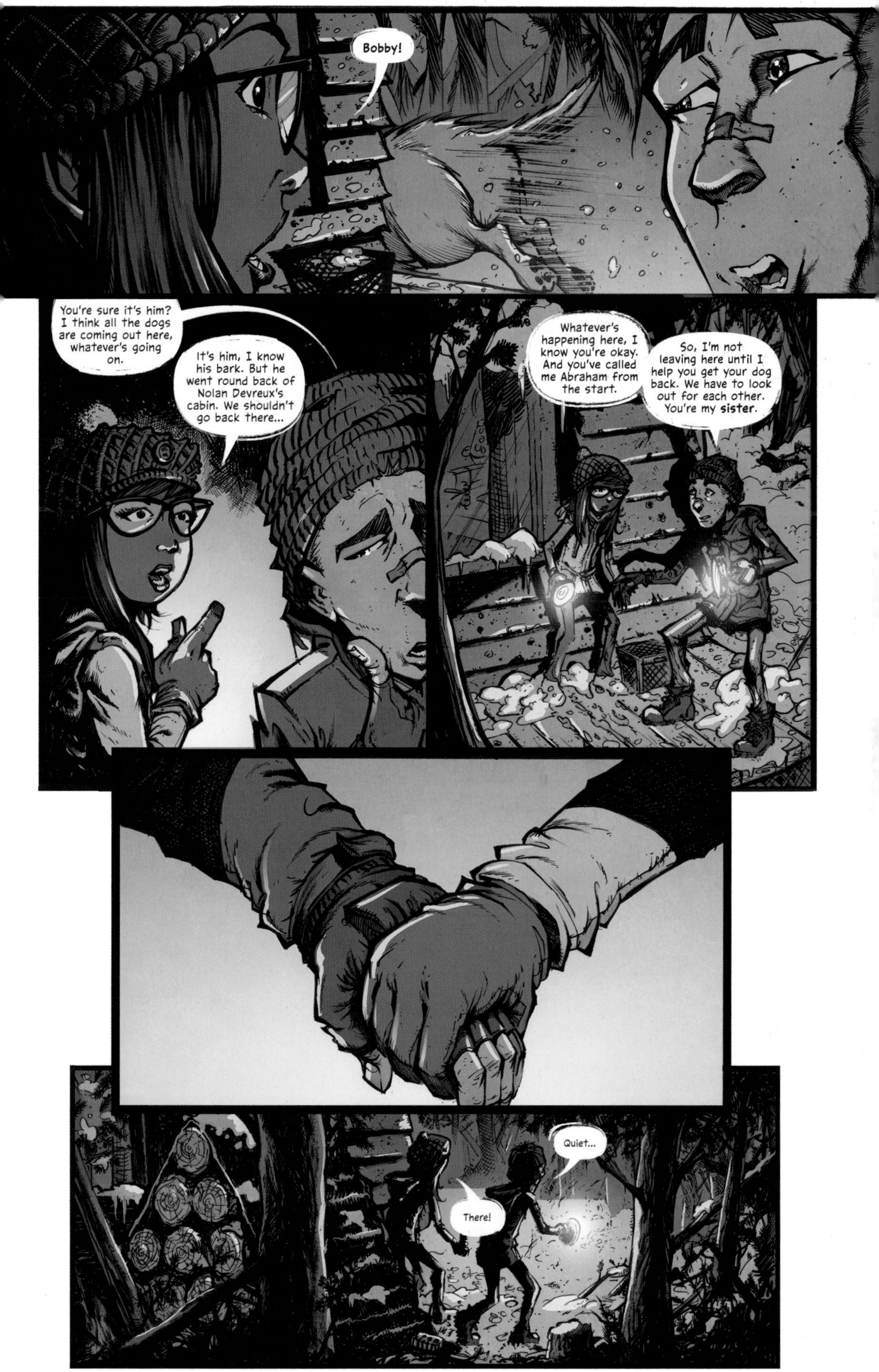
Bobby!
You're sure it's him? I think all the dogs are coming out here, whatever's going on.
It's him, I know his bark. But he went round back of Nolan Devreux's cabin. We shouldn't go back there...
Whatever's happening here, I know you're okay. And you've called me Abraham from the start.
So, I'm not leaving here until I help you get your dog back. We have to look out for each other. You're my **sister**.
Quiet...
There!

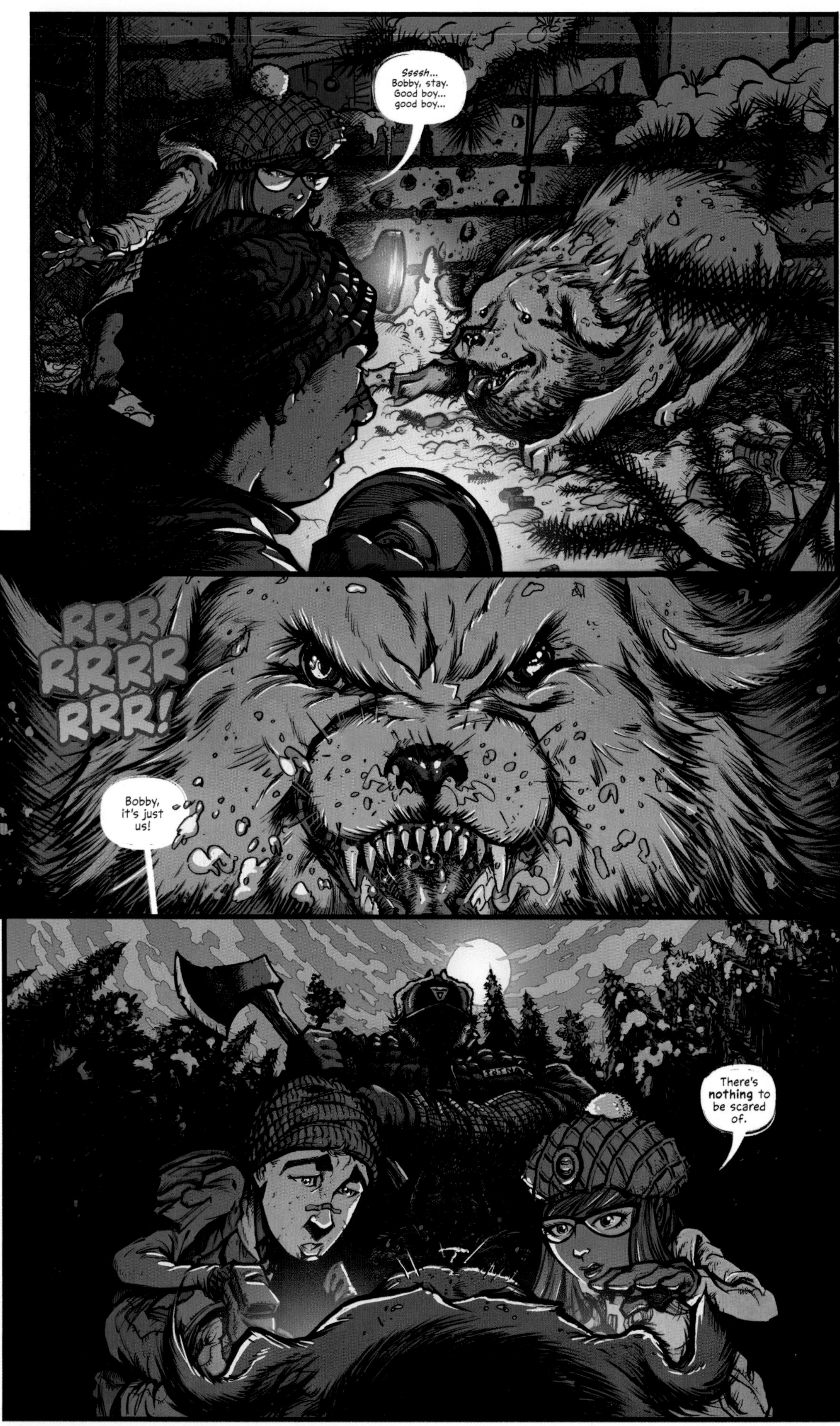
Ssssh... Bobby, stay. Good boy... good boy...
RRR RRRR RRR!
Bobby, it's just us!
There's **nothing** to be scared of.

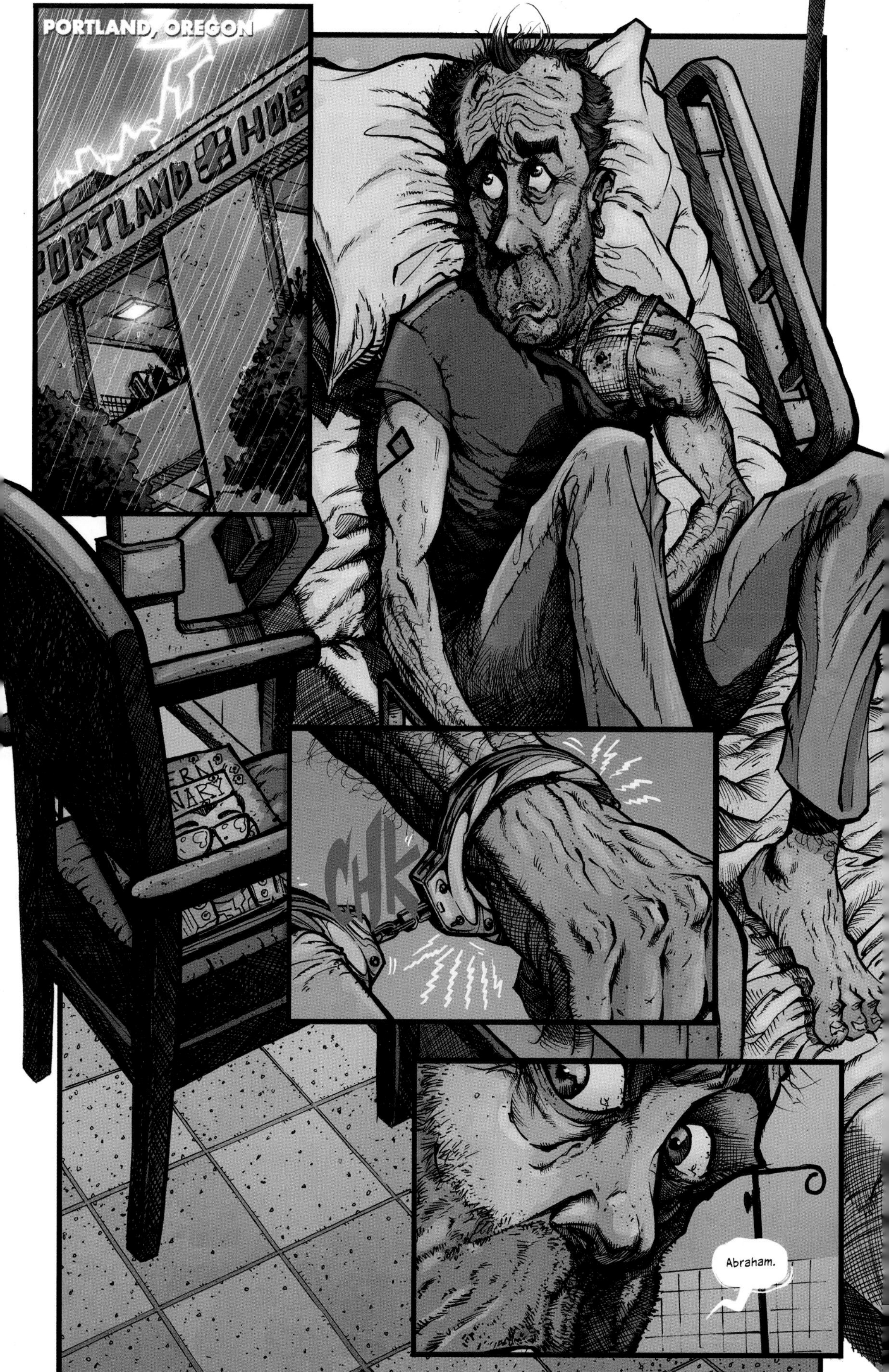
PORTLAND, OREGON
PORTLAND HOS
CHK
Abraham.

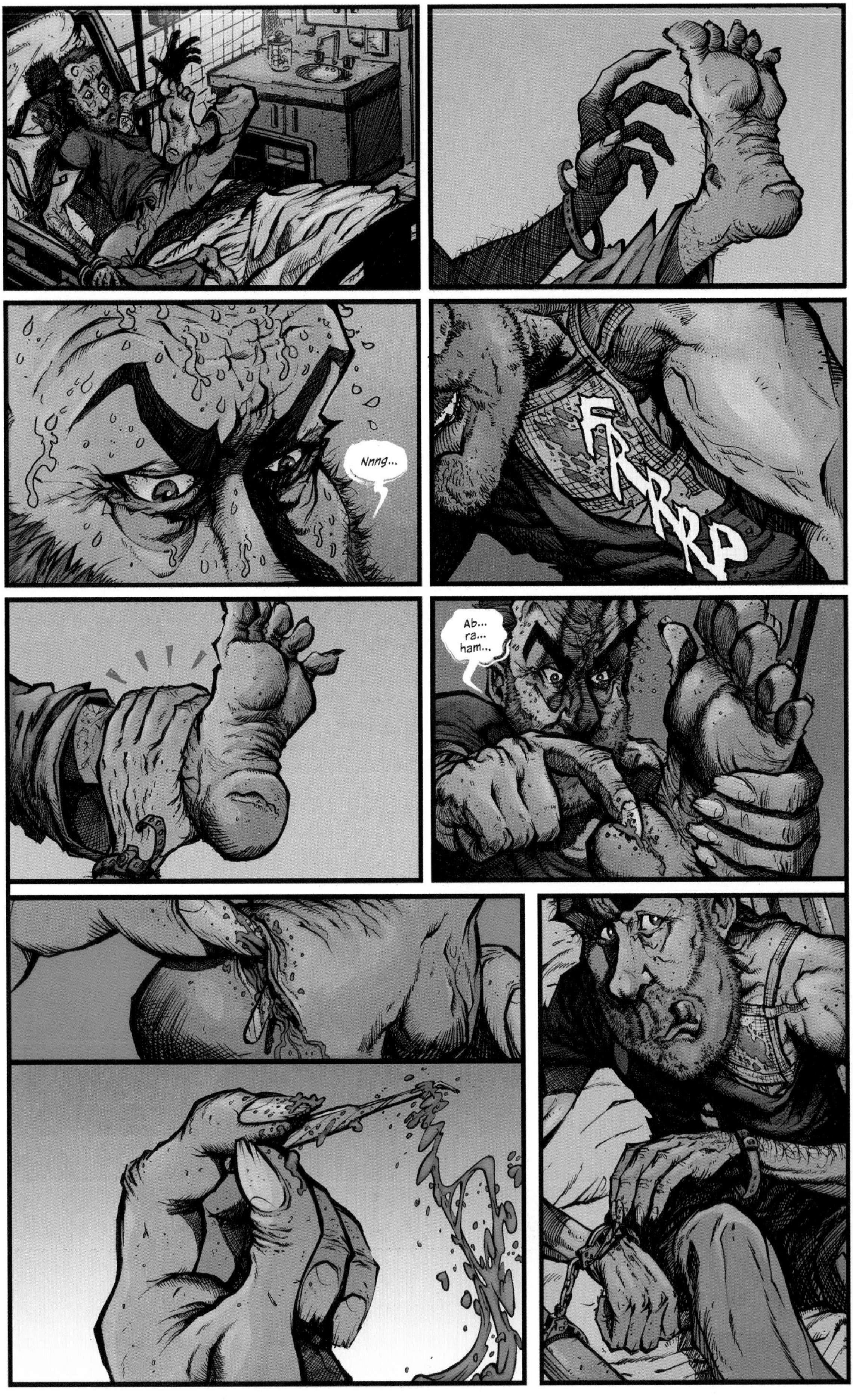
Nnng...
FRRRRP
Ab... ra... ham...

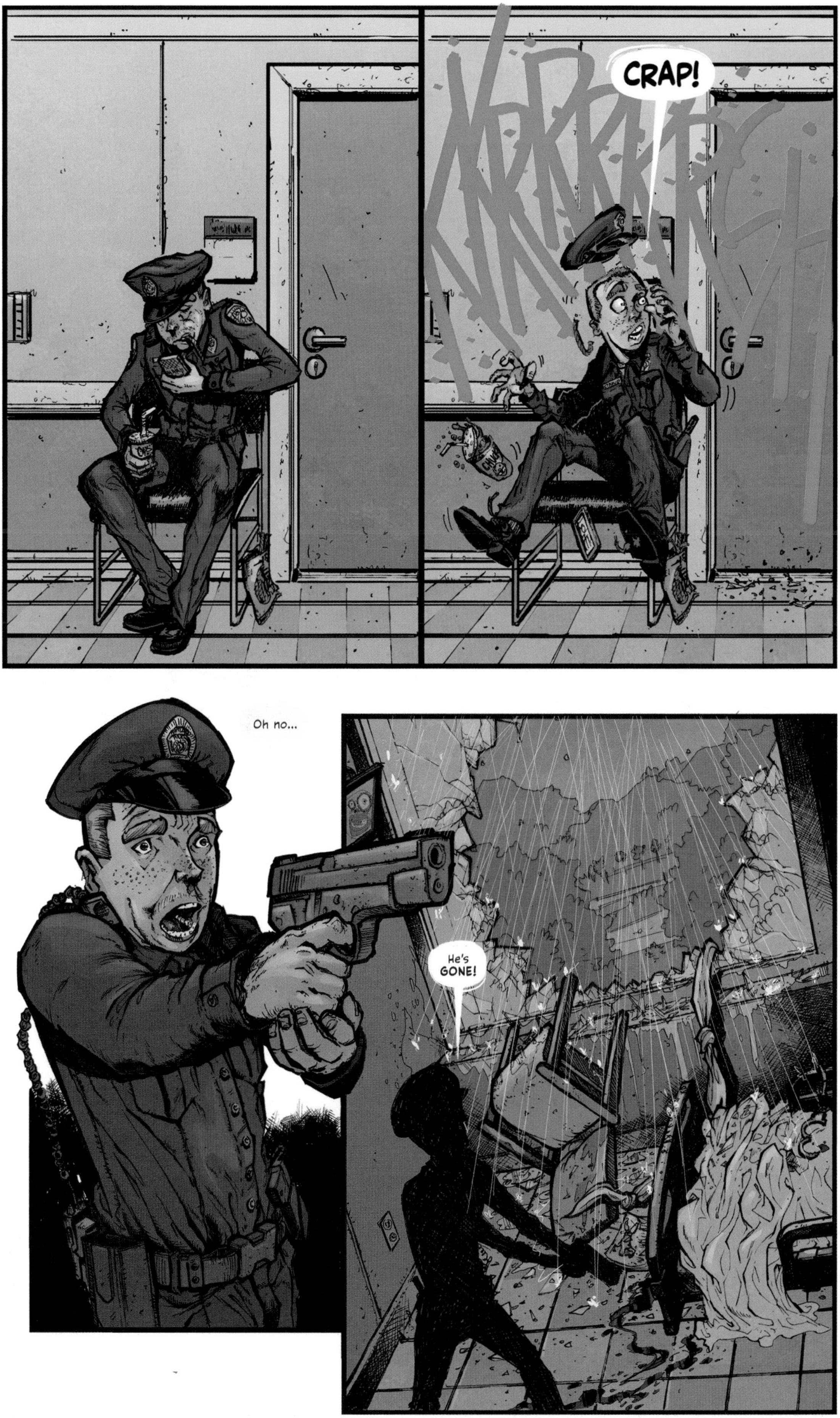
CRAP!
Oh no...
He's GONE!

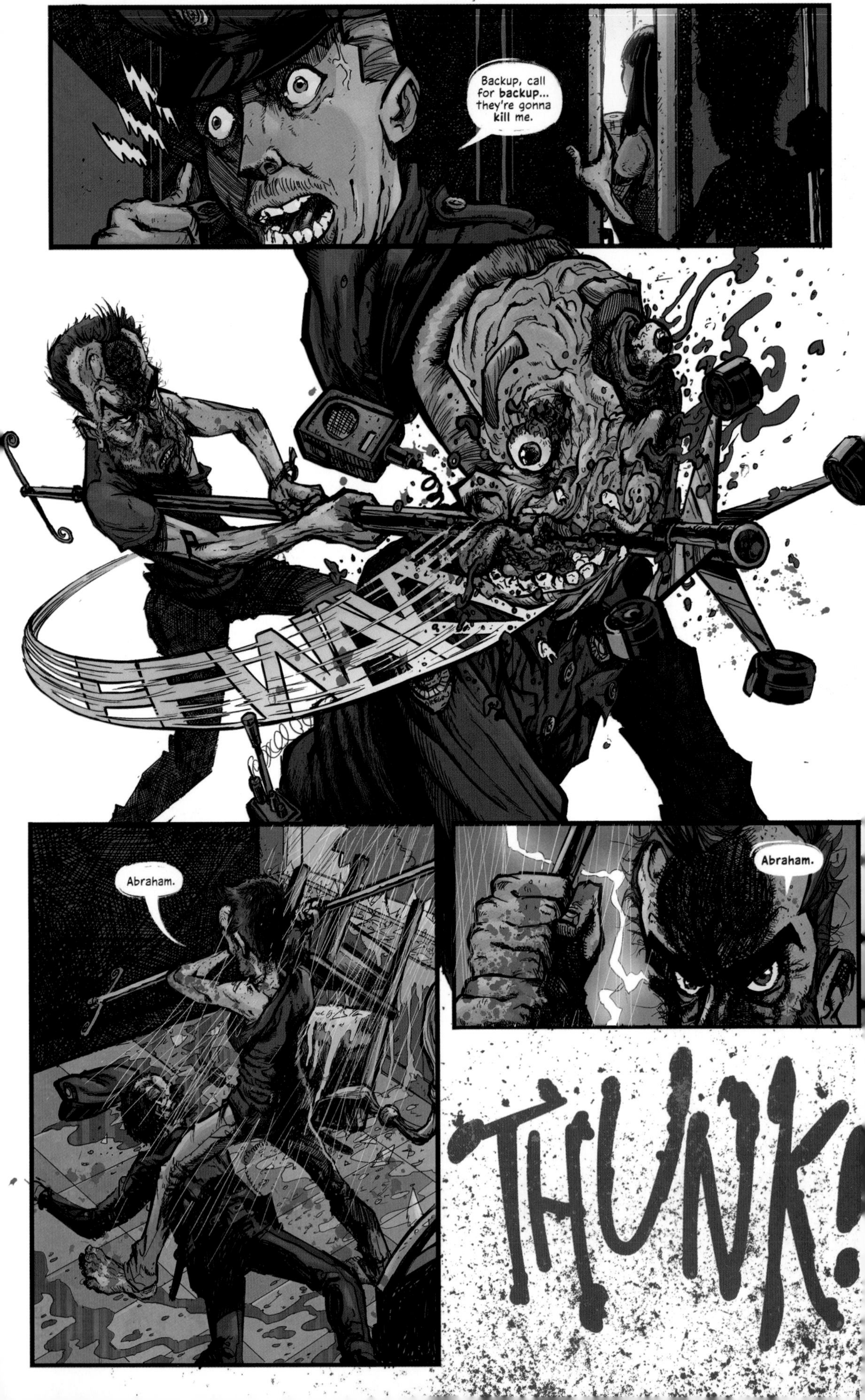
Backup, call for backup... they're gonna kill me.
Abraham.
Abraham.
THUNK!

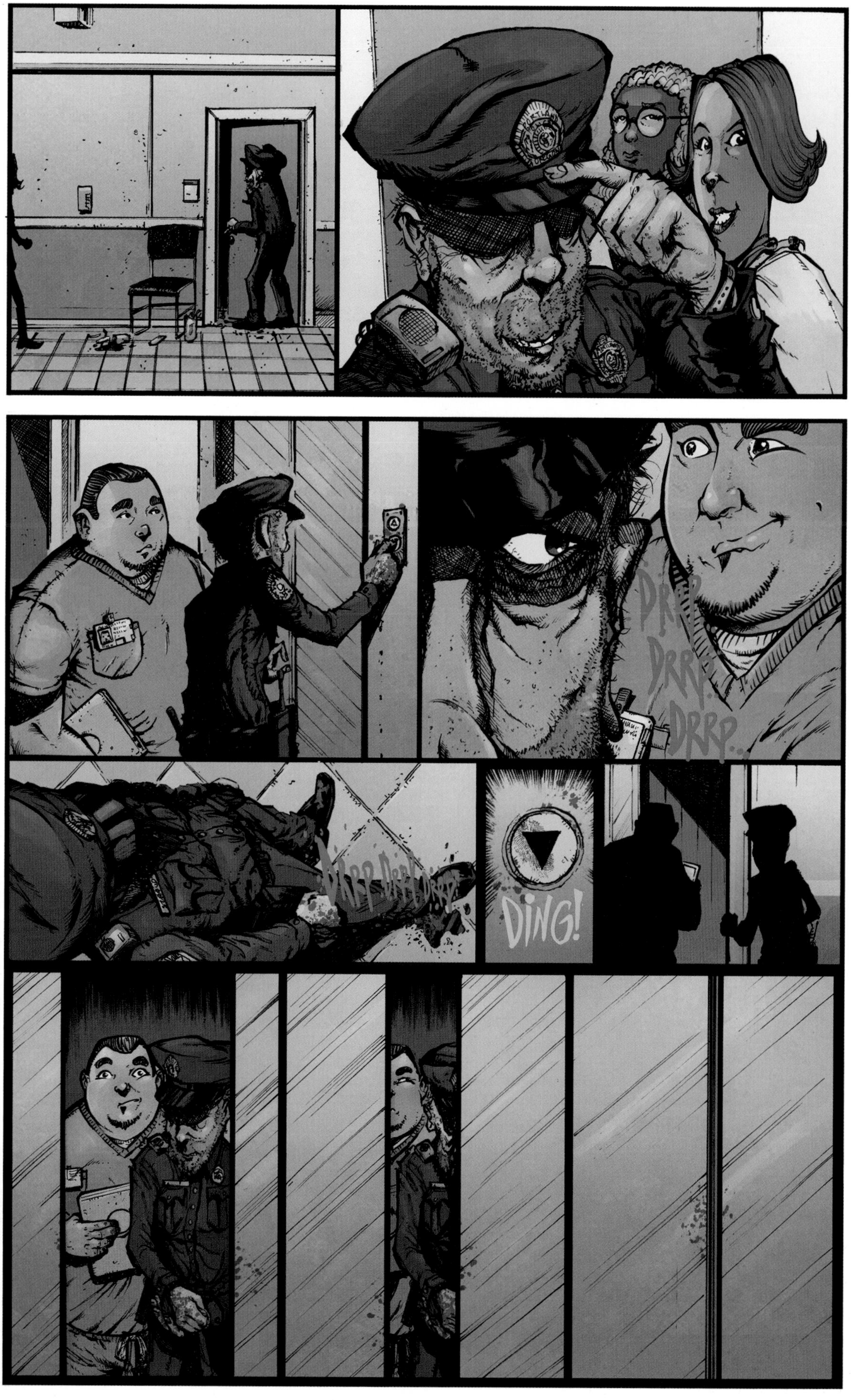
DRRP.
DRRP.
DRRP..
DRRP. DRRP. DRRP.
DING!

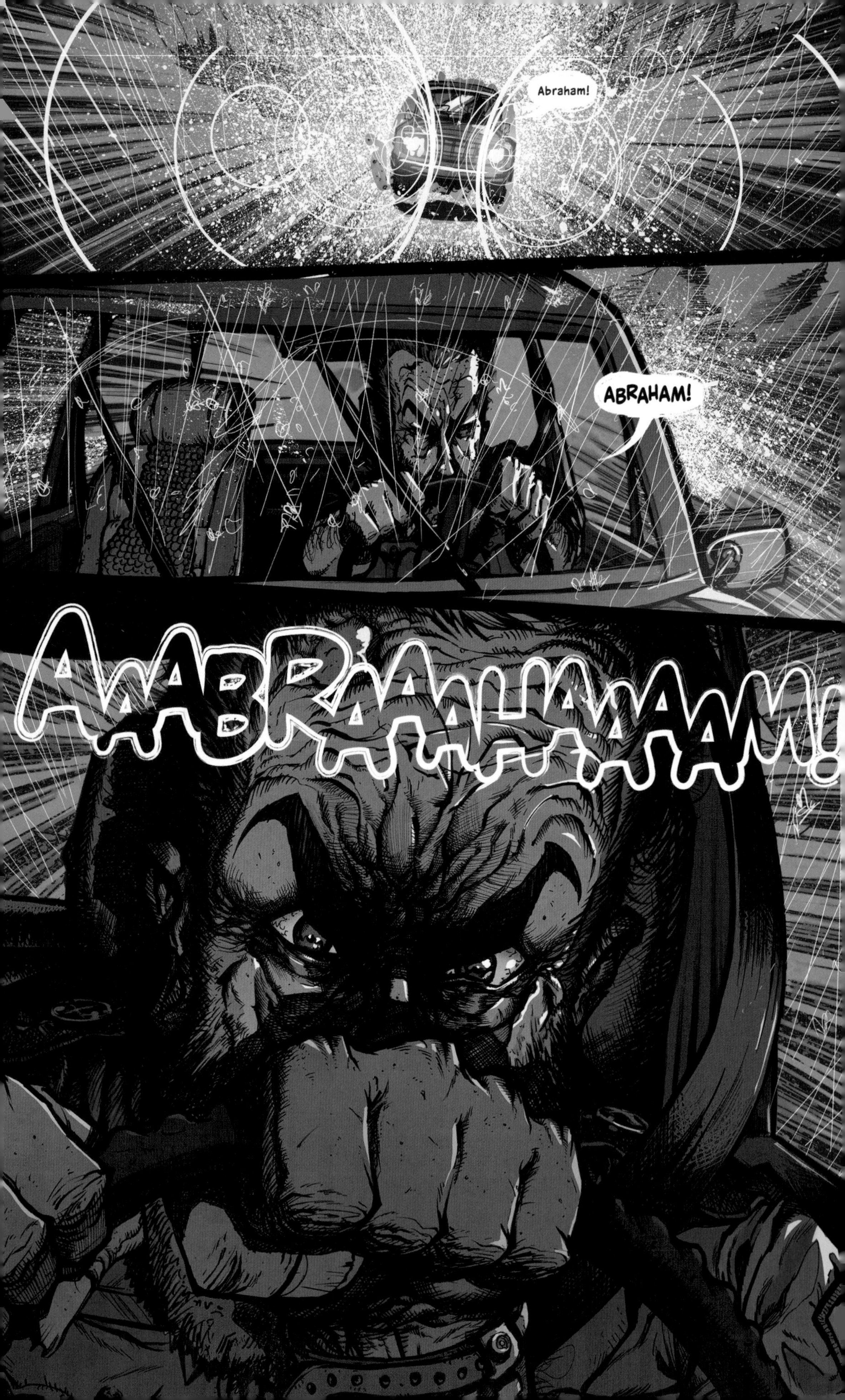
Abraham!
ABRAHAM!
AABRAAHAAAM!

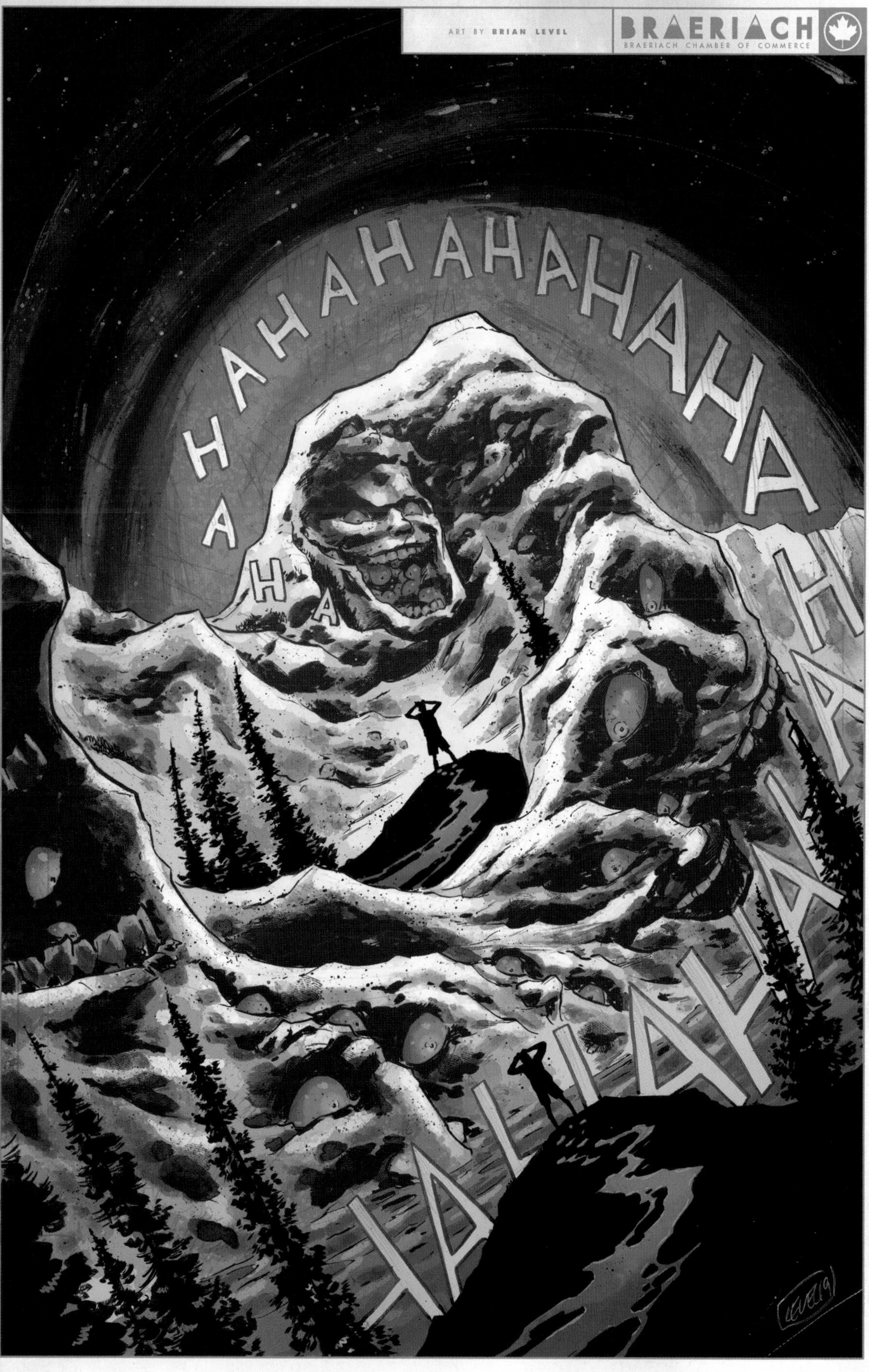
HAHAHAHAHAHAHAHA
HAHA

BRAERIACH
BRAERIACH CHAMBER OF COMMERCE

ART BY RYAN LEE

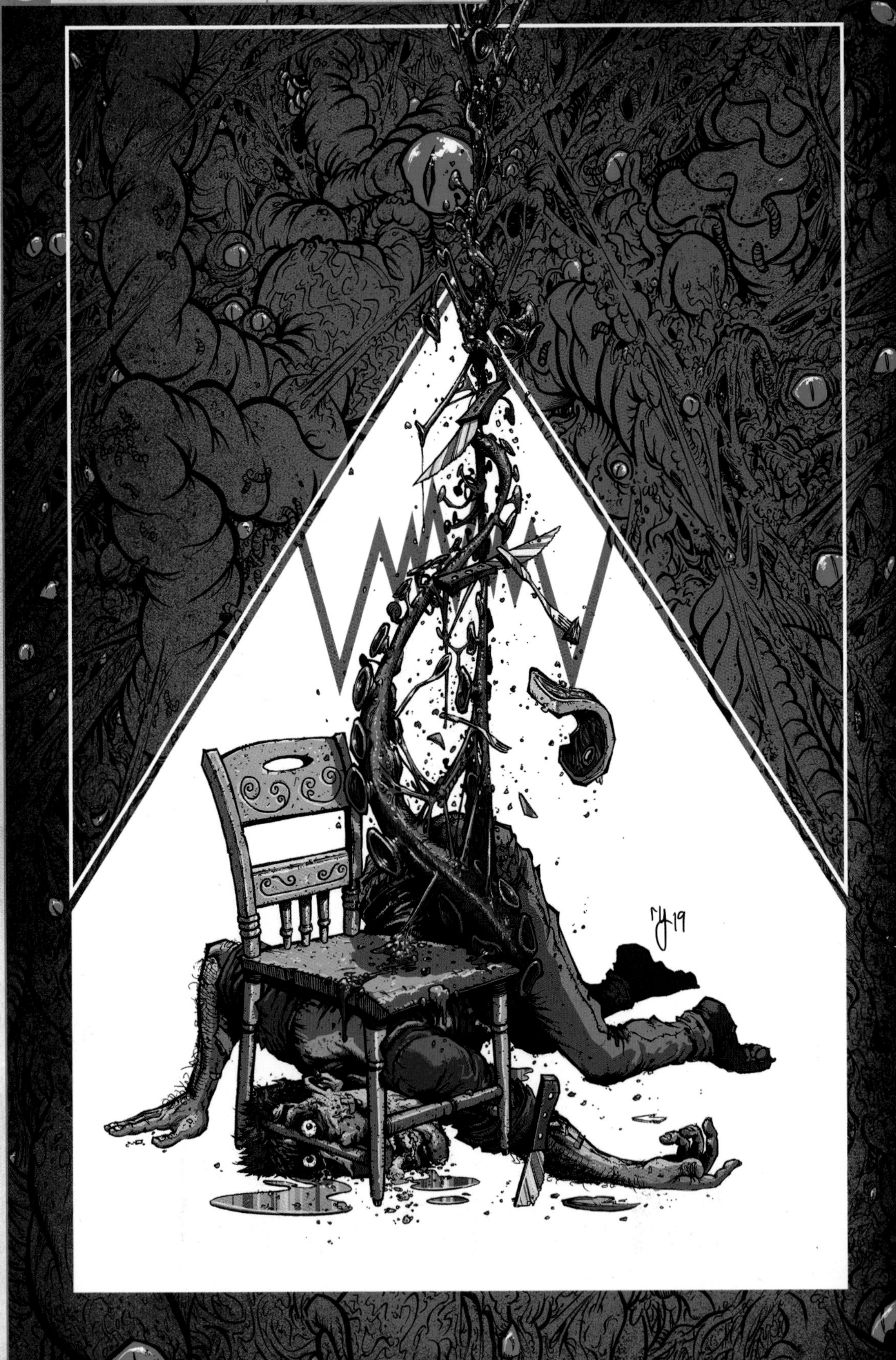

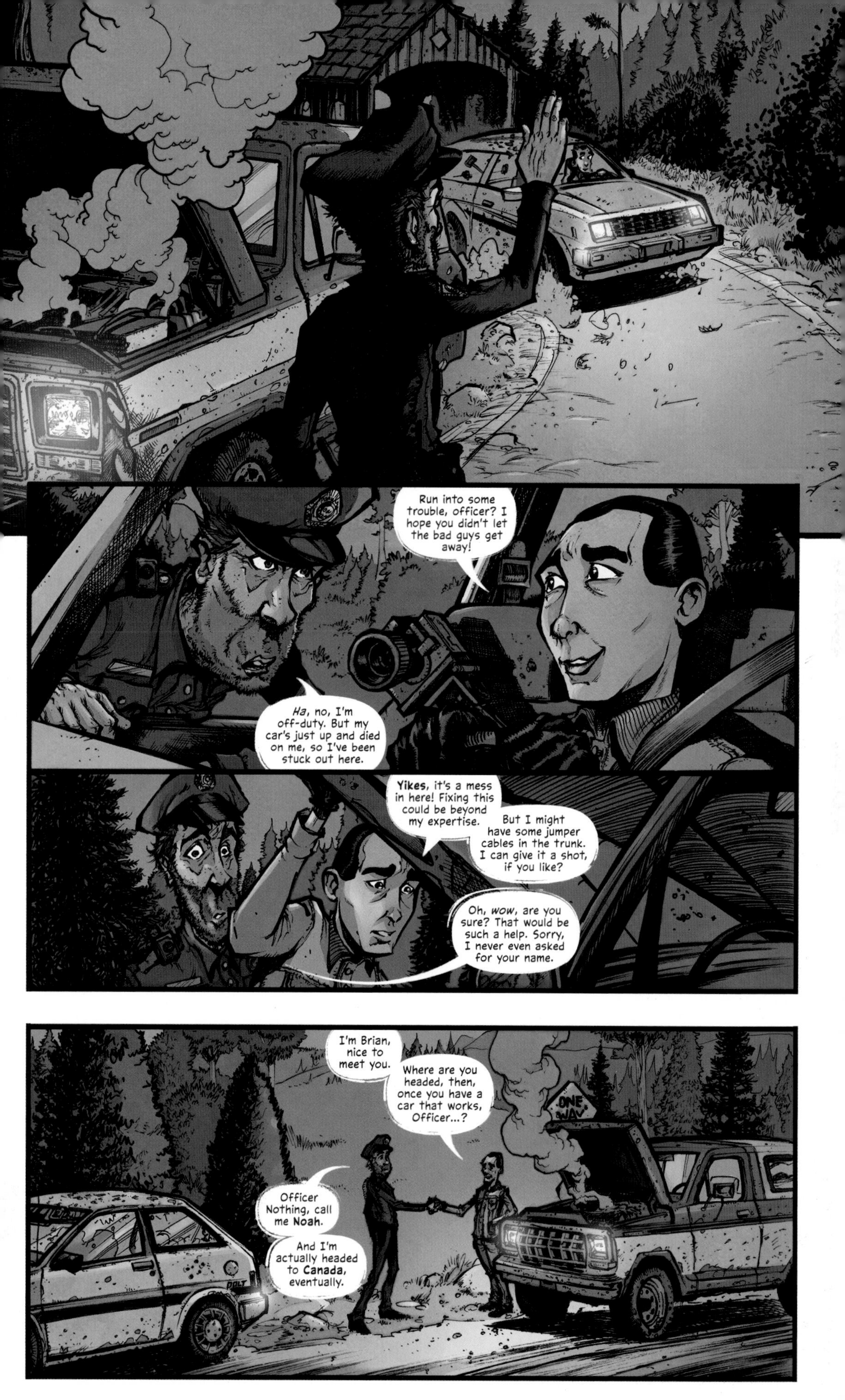

Run into some trouble, officer? I hope you didn't let the bad guys get away!
Ha, no, I'm off-duty. But my car's just up and died on me, so I've been stuck out here.
Yikes, it's a mess in here! Fixing this could be beyond my expertise.
But I might have some jumper cables in the trunk. I can give it a shot, if you like?
Oh, *wow*, are you sure? That would be such a help. Sorry, I never even asked for your name.
I'm Brian, nice to meet you.
Where are you headed, then, once you have a car that works, Officer...?
Officer Nothing, call me **Noah**.
And I'm actually headed to **Canada**, eventually.
ONE WAY

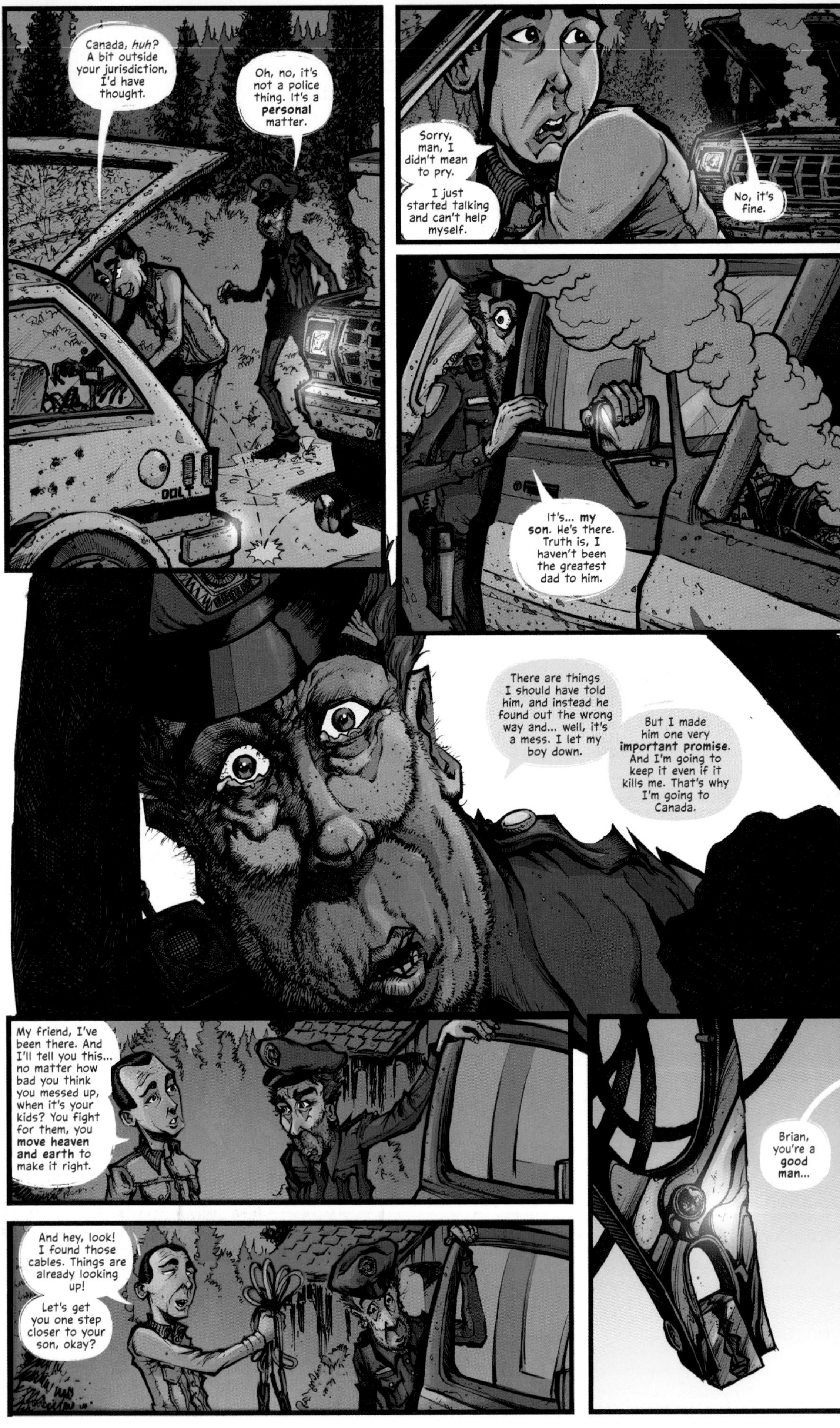
Canada, *huh*? A bit outside your jurisdiction, I'd have thought.
Oh, no, it's not a police thing. It's a **personal** matter.
Sorry, man, I didn't mean to pry.
I just started talking and can't help myself.
No, it's fine.
It's... **my son**. He's there. Truth is, I haven't been the greatest dad to him.
There are things I should have told him, and instead he found out the wrong way and... well, it's a mess. I let my boy down.
But I made him one very **important promise**. And I'm going to keep it even if it kills me. That's why I'm going to Canada.
My friend, I've been there. And I'll tell you this... no matter how bad you think you messed up, when it's your kids? You fight for them, you **move heaven and earth** to make it right.
Brian, you're a **good man**...
And hey, look! I found those cables. Things are already looking up!
Let's get you one step closer to your son, okay?

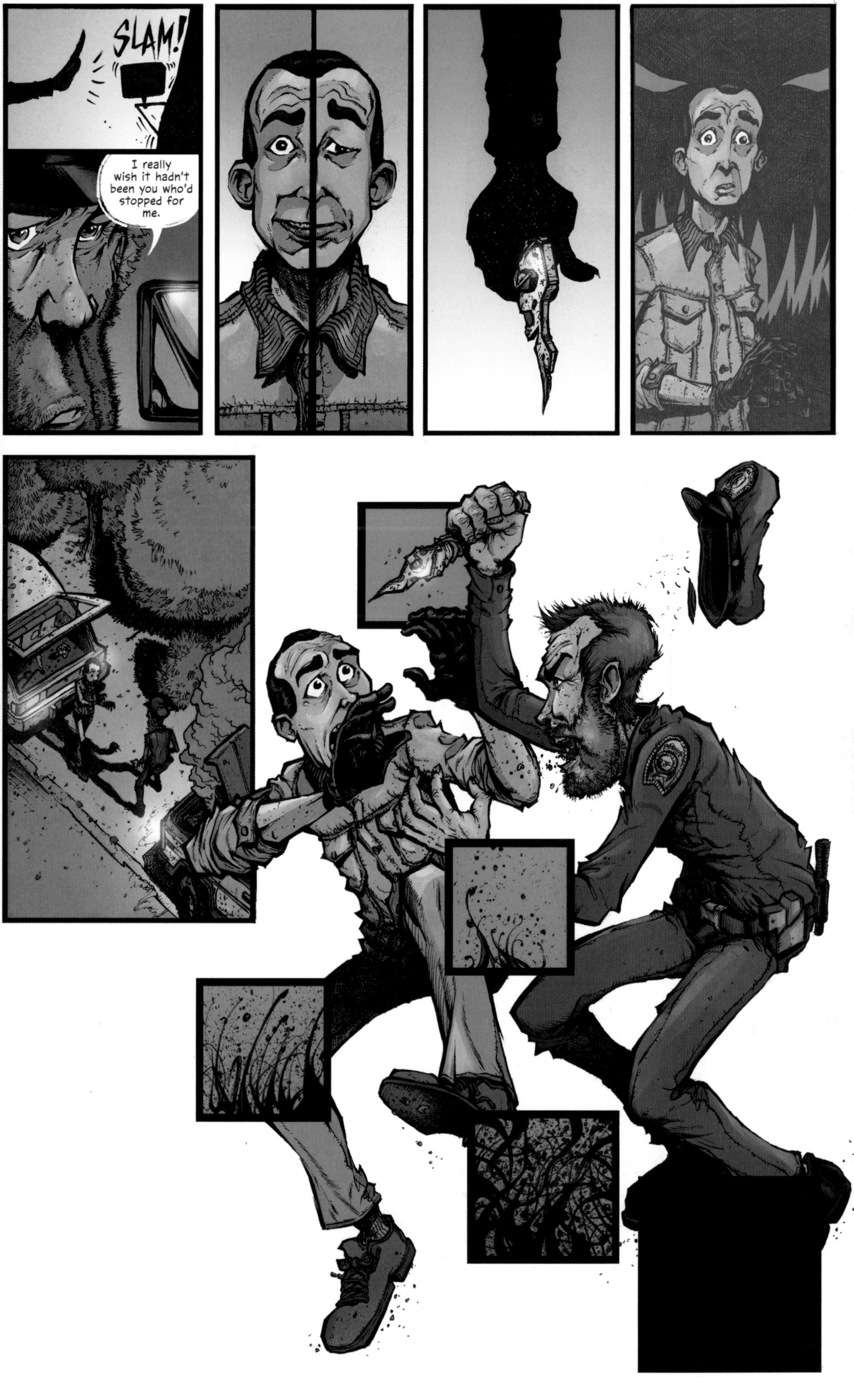
SLAM!
I really wish it hadn't been you who'd stopped for me.

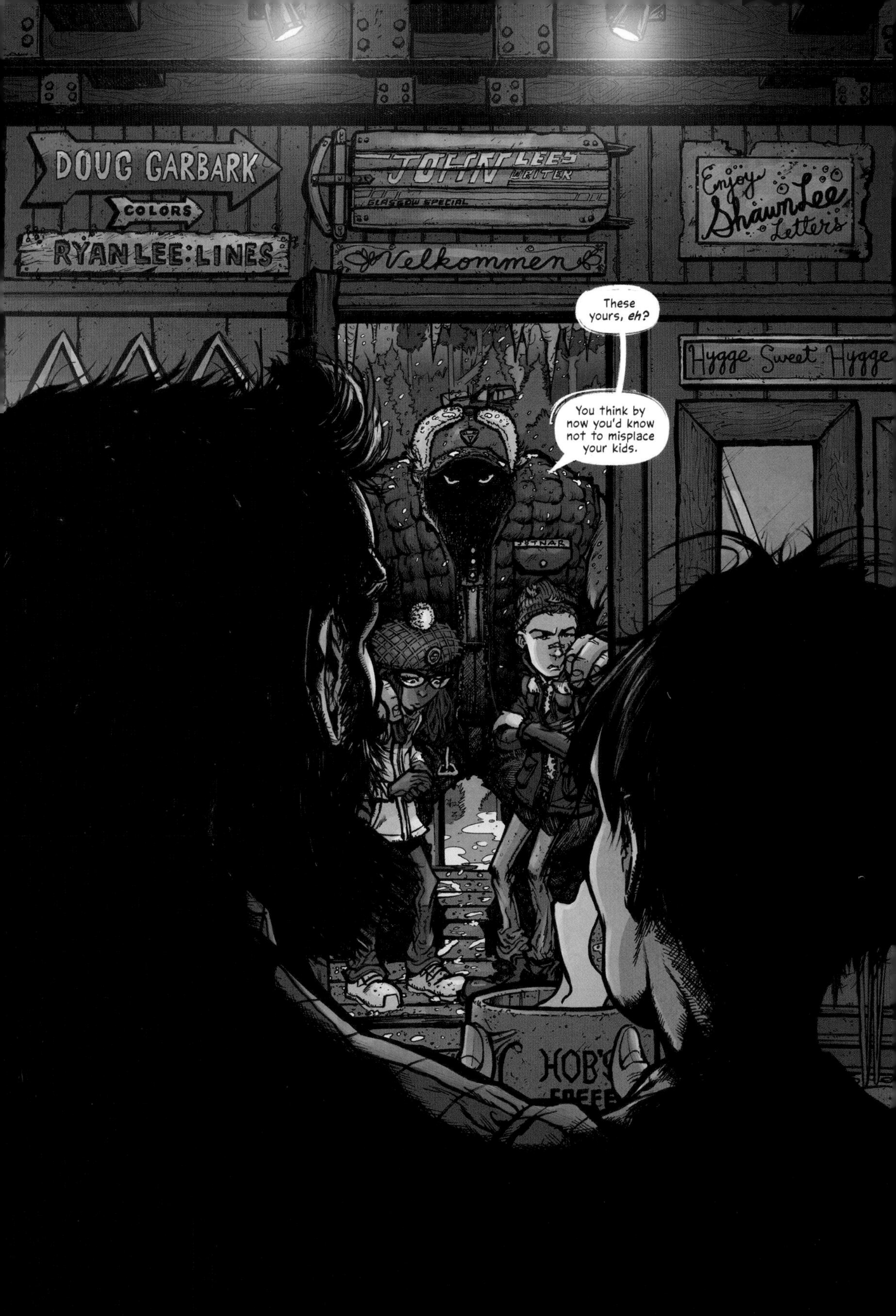
DOUG GARBARK
COLORS
RYAN LEE: LINES
JOHN LEES
WRITER
GLASGOW SPECIAL
Velkommen
Enjoy Shawn Lee Letters
These yours, *eh?*
You think by now you'd know not to misplace your kids.
Hygge Sweet Hygge
HOB'S

CHAPTER THREE: THE OTHER SHOE

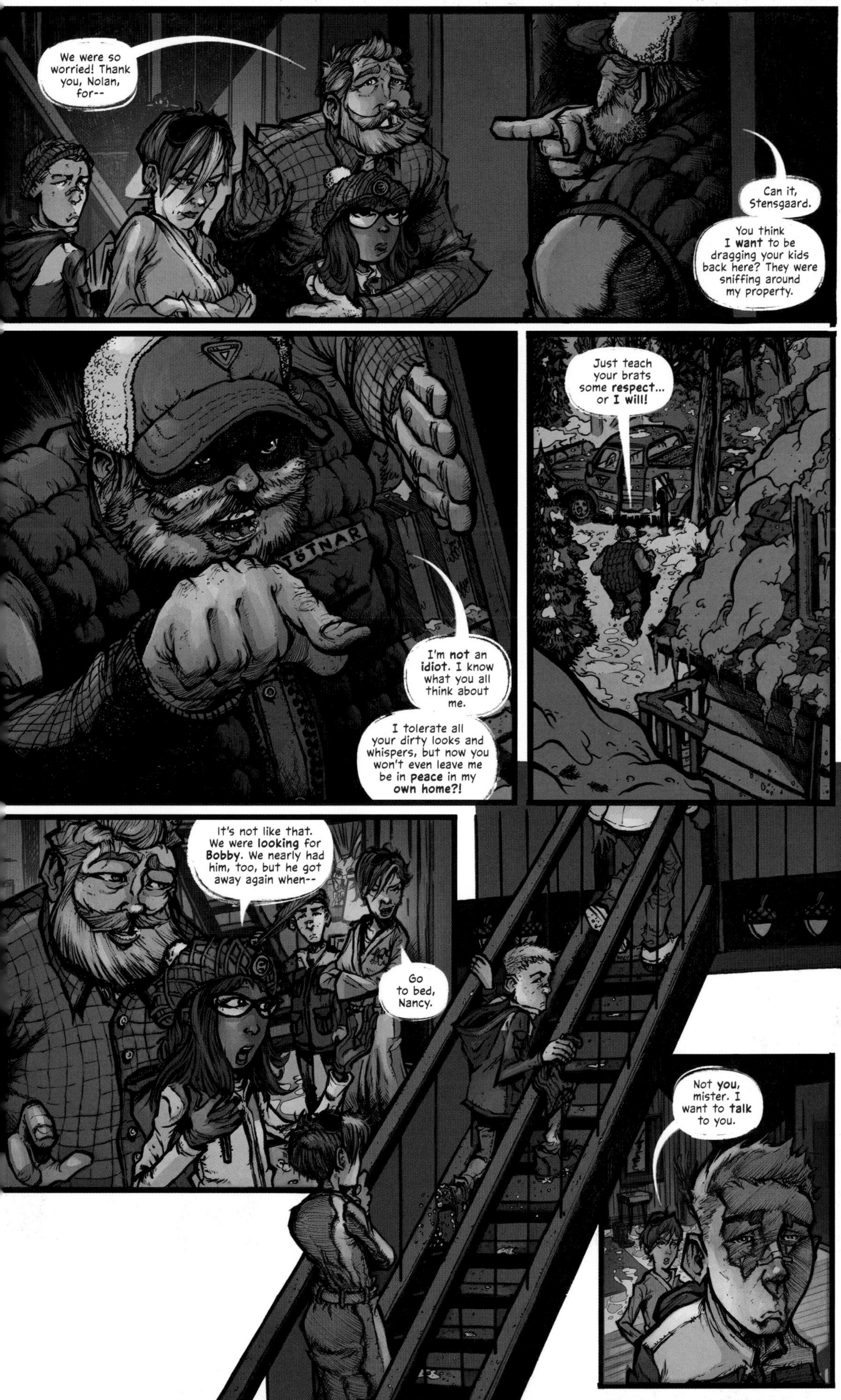

We were so worried! Thank you, Nolan, for--
Can it, Stensgaard.
You think I **want** to be dragging your kids back here? They were sniffing around my property.
TÖTNAR
I'm **not** an **idiot**. I know what you all think about me.
I tolerate all your dirty looks and whispers, but now you won't even leave me be in **peace** in my **own home?!**
Just teach your brats some **respect**... or **I will!**
It's not like that. We were **looking** for **Bobby**. We nearly had him, too, but he got away again when--
Go to bed, Nancy.
Not **you**, mister. I want to **talk** to you.

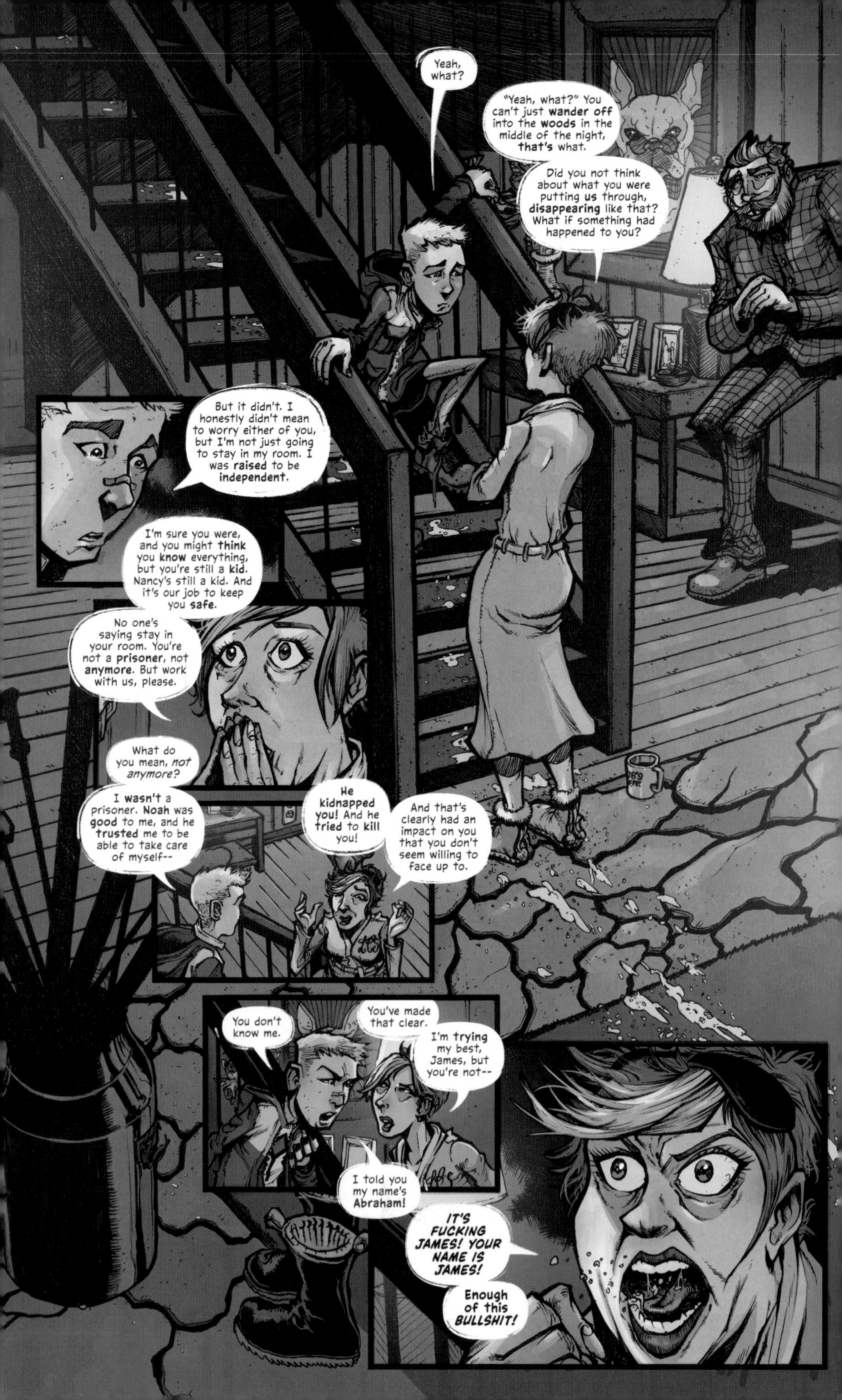

Yeah, what?
"Yeah, what?" You can't just wander off into the woods in the middle of the night, that's what.
Did you not think about what you were putting us through, disappearing like that? What if something had happened to you?
But it didn't. I honestly didn't mean to worry either of you, but I'm not just going to stay in my room. I was raised to be independent.
I'm sure you were, and you might think you know everything, but you're still a kid. Nancy's still a kid. And it's our job to keep you safe.
No one's saying stay in your room. You're not a prisoner, not anymore. But work with us, please.
What do you mean, not anymore?
I wasn't a prisoner. Noah was good to me, and he trusted me to be able to take care of myself--
He kidnapped you! And he tried to kill you!
And that's clearly had an impact on you that you don't seem willing to face up to.
You don't know me.
You've made that clear.
I'm trying my best, James, but you're not--
I told you my name's Abraham!
IT'S FUCKING JAMES! YOUR NAME IS JAMES!
Enough of this BULLSHIT!

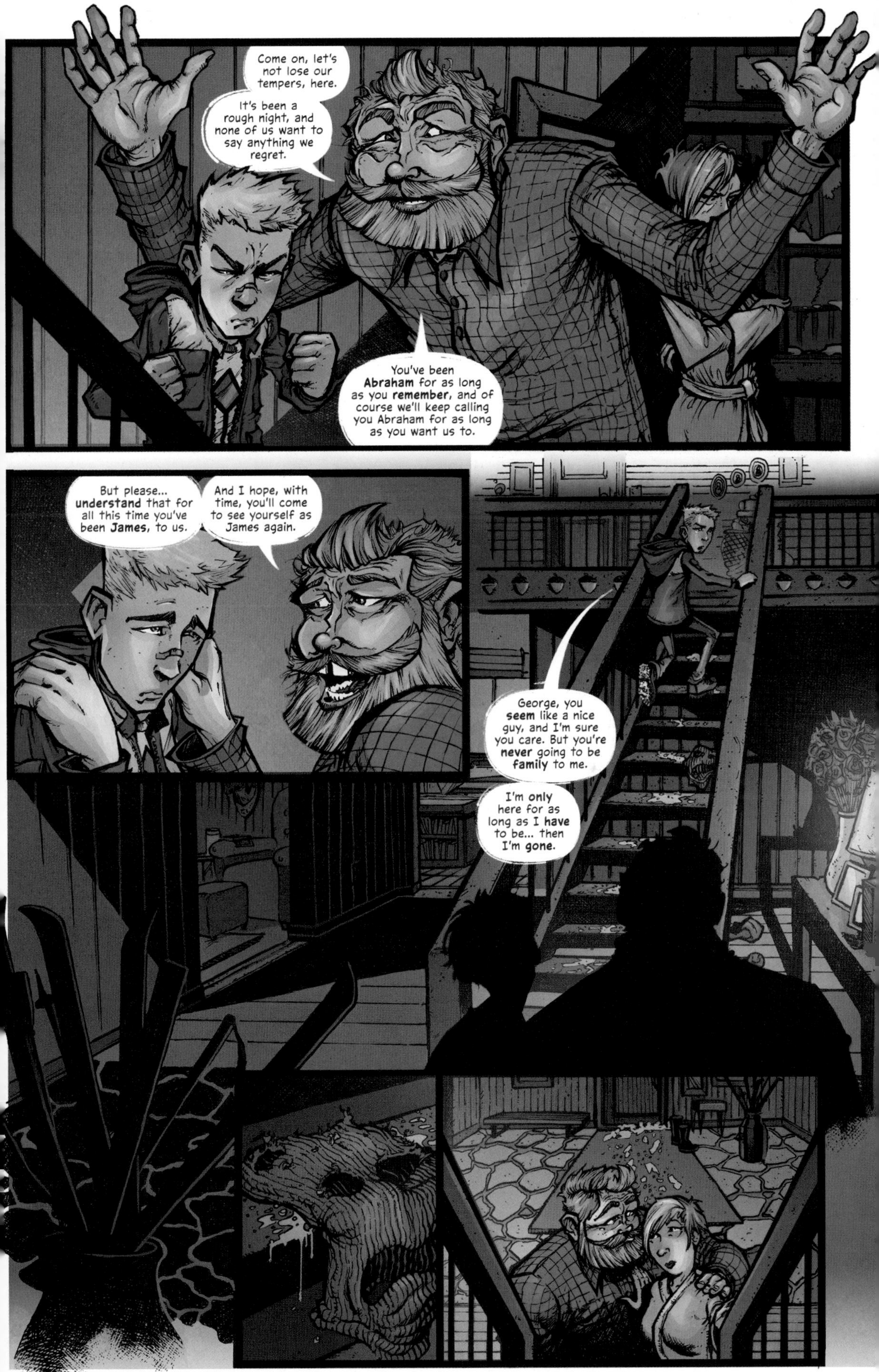
Come on, let's not lose our tempers, here.
It's been a rough night, and none of us want to say anything we regret.
You've been **Abraham** for as long as you **remember**, and of course we'll keep calling you Abraham for as long as you want us to.
But please... **understand** that for all this time you've been **James**, to us.
And I hope, with time, you'll come to see yourself as James again.
George, you **seem** like a nice guy, and I'm sure you care. But you're **never** going to be **family** to me.
I'm **only** here for as long as I **have** to be... then I'm **gone**.

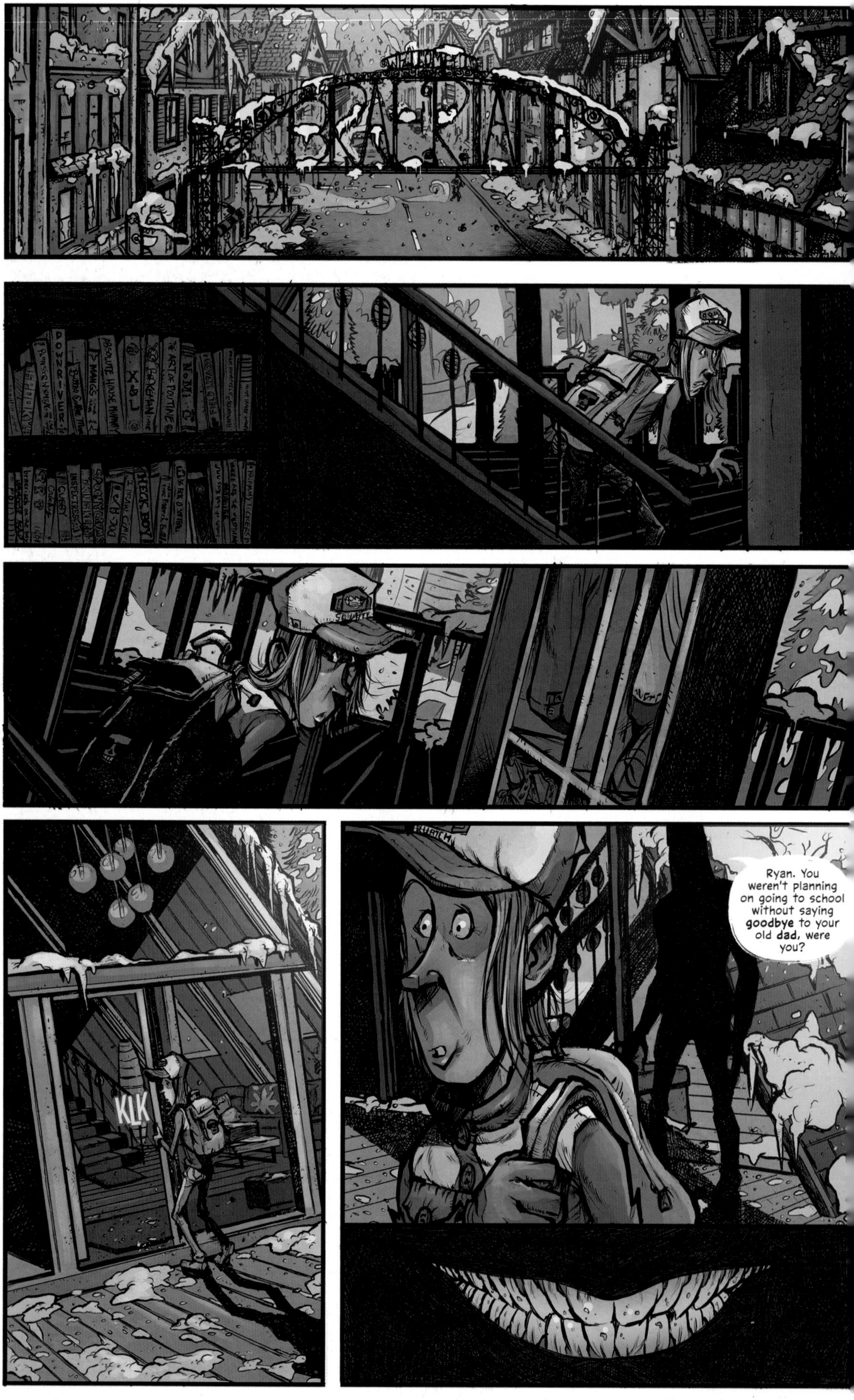
KLK
Ryan. You weren't planning on going to school without saying **goodbye** to your old **dad**, were you?

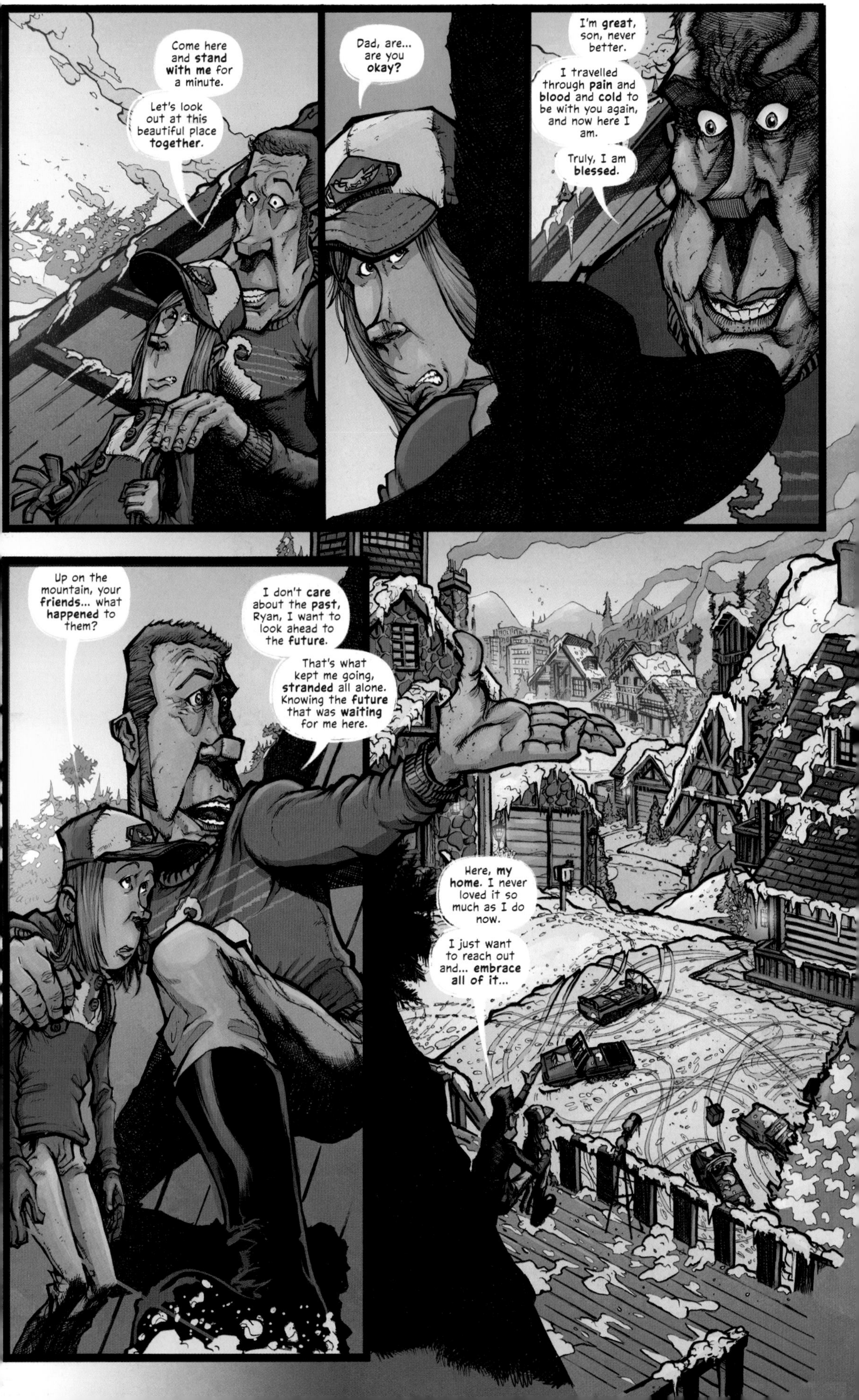

Come here and **stand with me** for a minute.
Let's look out at this beautiful place **together**.
Dad, are... are you **okay?**
I'm **great**, son, never better.
I travelled through **pain** and **blood** and **cold** to be with you again, and now here I am.
Truly, I am **blessed**.
Up on the mountain, your **friends**... what **happened** to them?
I don't **care** about the **past**, Ryan, I want to look ahead to the **future**.
That's what kept me going, **stranded** all alone. Knowing the **future** that was **waiting** for me here.
Here, **my home**. I never loved it so much as I do now.
I just want to reach out and... **embrace all of it**...

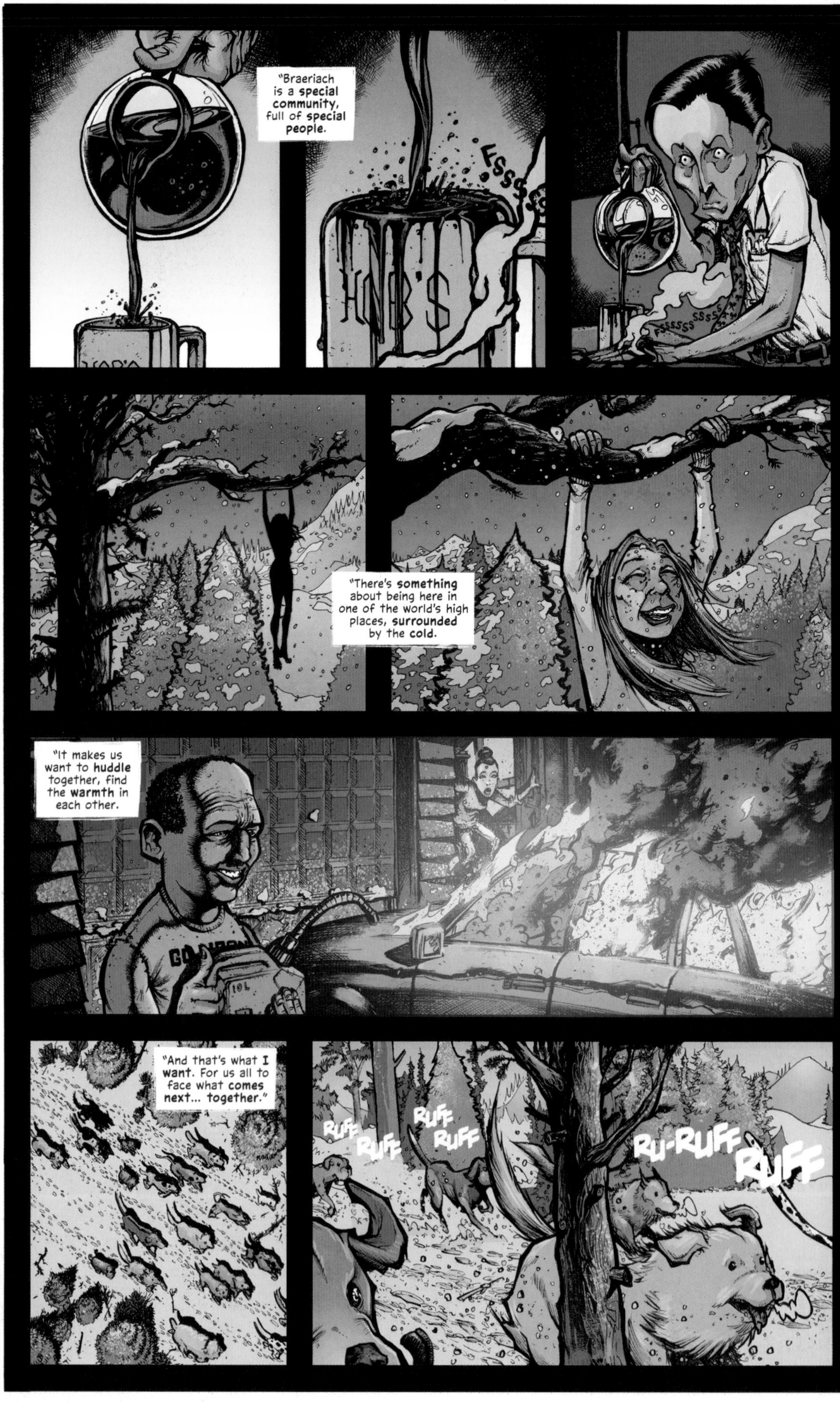
"Braeriach is a special community, full of special people.
FSSSS
HOB'S
FSSSSSSS SSSSS
"There's something about being here in one of the world's high places, surrounded by the cold.
"It makes us want to huddle together, find the warmth in each other.
"And that's what I want. For us all to face what comes next... together."
RUFF
RUFF
RUFF
RUFF
RU-RUFF
RUFF

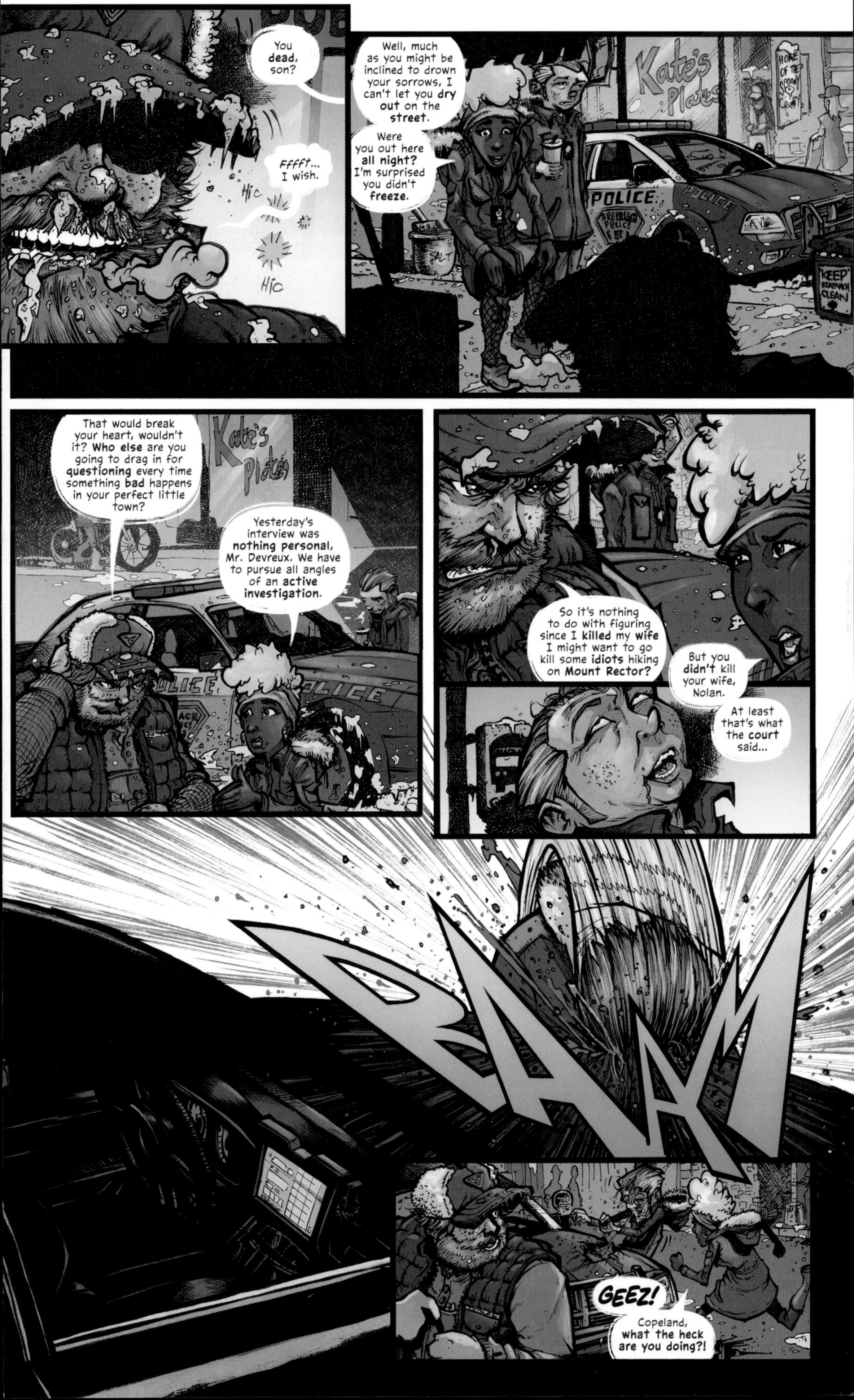

You dead, son?
Fffft... I wish.
Hic
Hic
Well, much as you might be inclined to drown your sorrows, I can't let you dry out on the street.
Were you out here all night? I'm surprised you didn't freeze.
Kate's Plates
POLICE
KEEP
CLEAN
That would break your heart, wouldn't it? Who else are you going to drag in for questioning every time something bad happens in your perfect little town?
Yesterday's interview was nothing personal, Mr. Devreux. We have to pursue all angles of an active investigation.
So it's nothing to do with figuring since I killed my wife I might want to go kill some idiots hiking on Mount Rector?
But you didn't kill your wife, Nolan.
At least that's what the court said...
BAM
GEEZ!
Copeland, what the heck are you doing?!

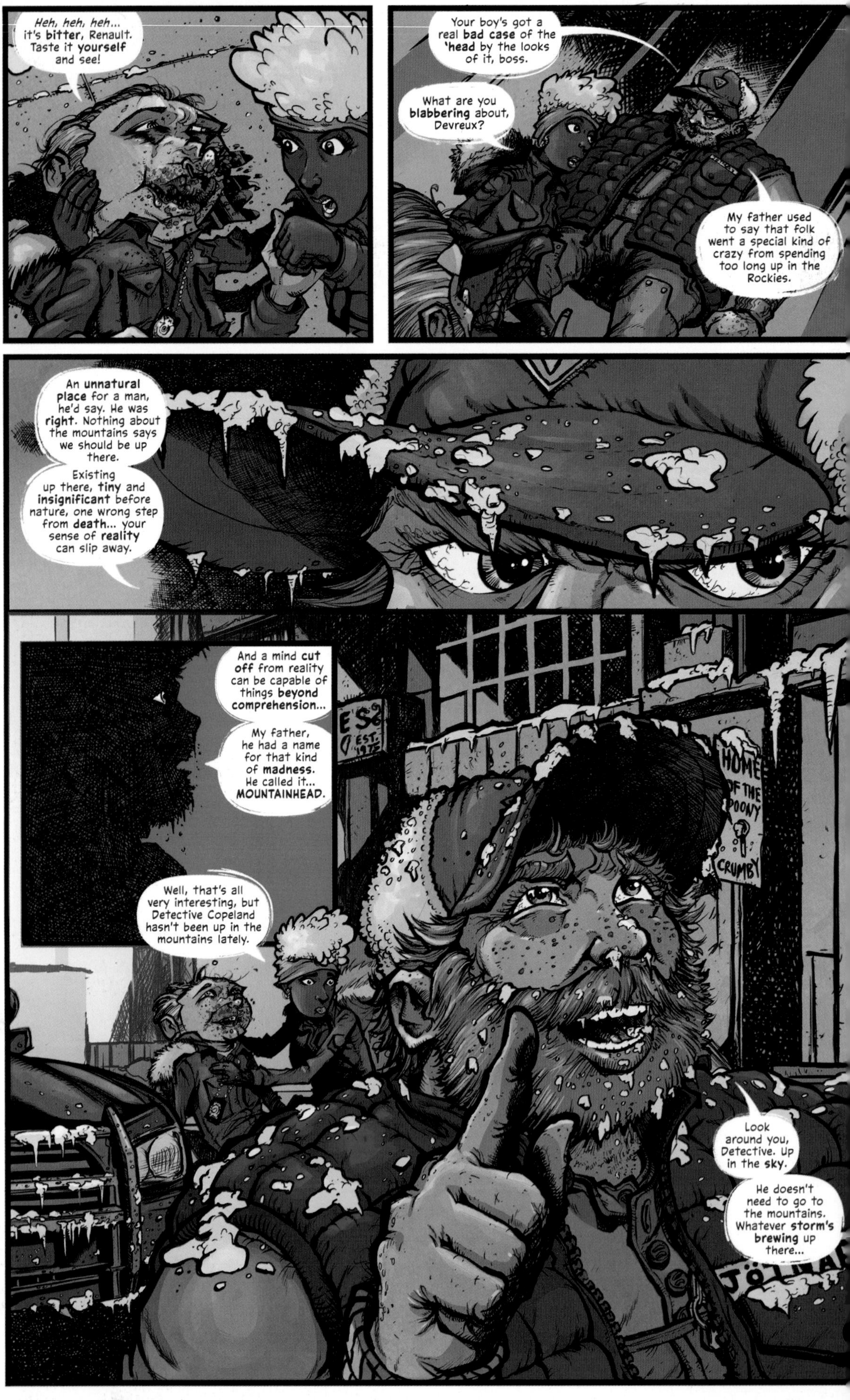
Heh, heh, heh... it's bitter, Renault. Taste it yourself and see!
Your boy's got a real bad case of the 'head by the looks of it, boss.
What are you blabbering about, Devreux?
My father used to say that folk went a special kind of crazy from spending too long up in the Rockies.
An unnatural place for a man, he'd say. He was right. Nothing about the mountains says we should be up there.
Existing up there, tiny and insignificant before nature, one wrong step from death... your sense of reality can slip away.
And a mind cut off from reality can be capable of things beyond comprehension...
My father, he had a name for that kind of madness. He called it... MOUNTAINHEAD.
Well, that's all very interesting, but Detective Copeland hasn't been up in the mountains lately.
Look around you, Detective. Up in the sky.
He doesn't need to go to the mountains. Whatever storm's brewing up there...

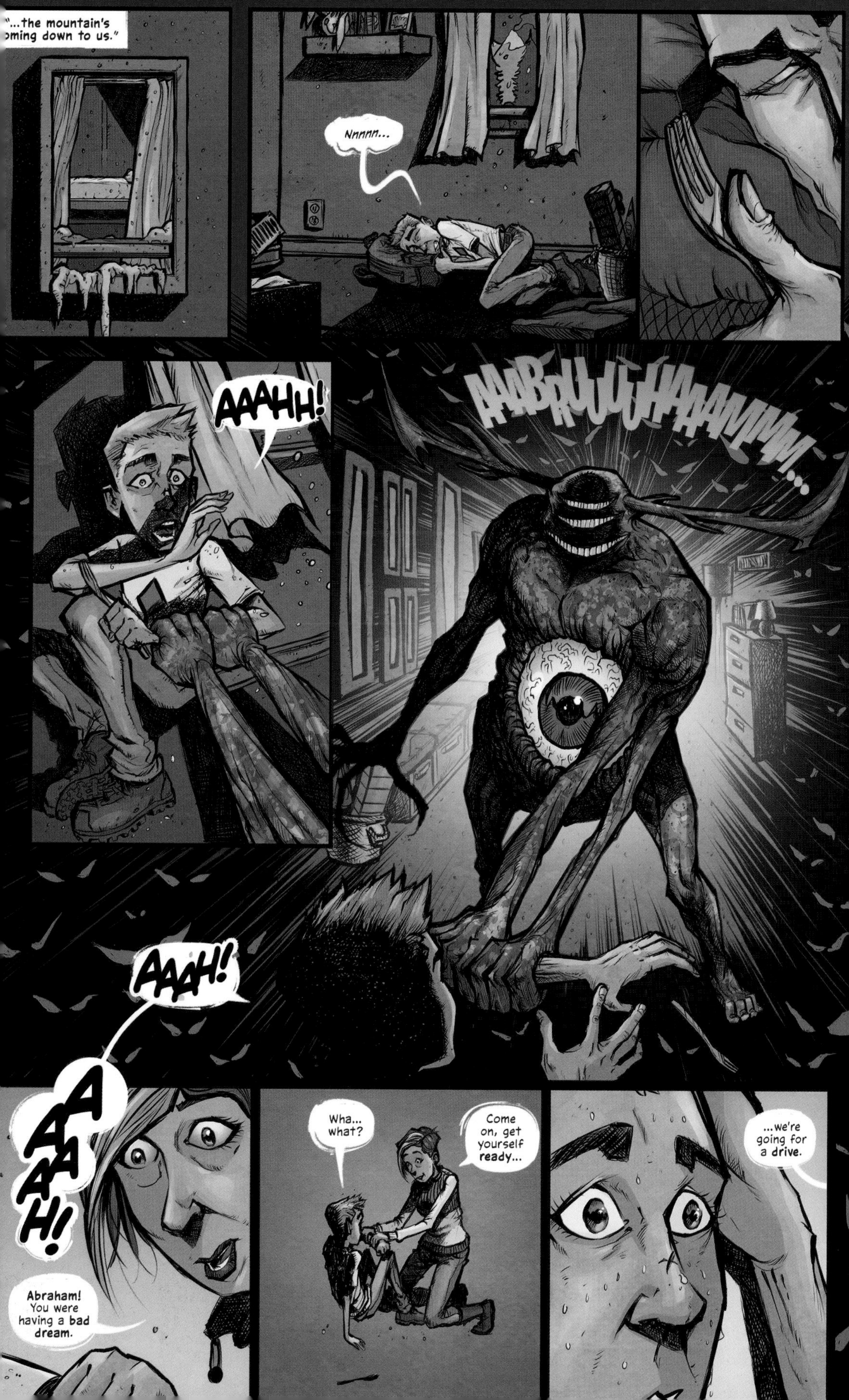
"...the mountain's
oming down to us."
Nnnnn...
AAAHH!
AAABRUUUUHHAAANMMM...
AAAH!
AAAAH!
Abraham! You were having a bad dream.
Wha... what?
Come on, get yourself ready...
...we're going for a drive.

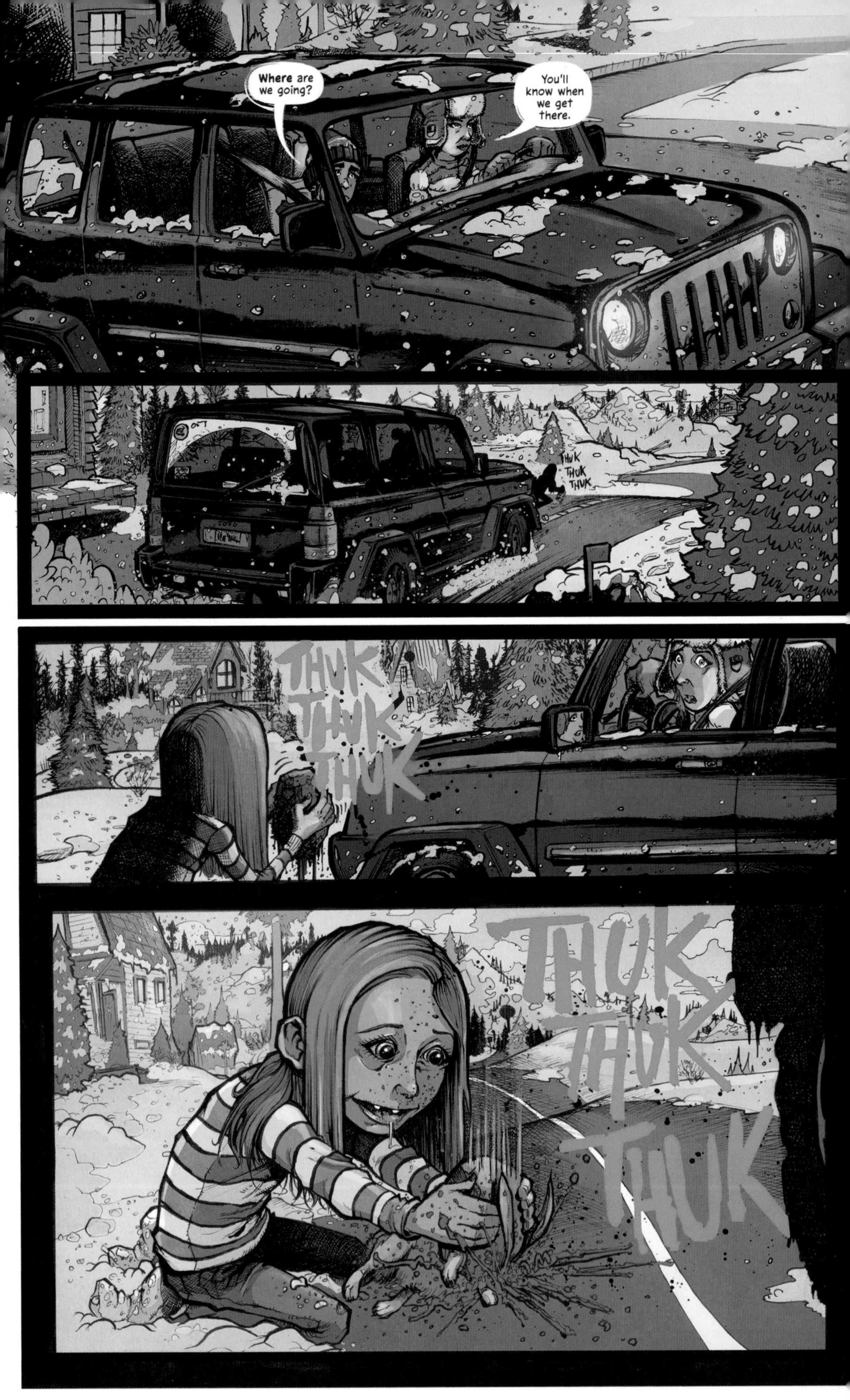

Where are we going?
You'll know when we get there.
THUK THUK THUK
THUK THUK THUK
THUK THUK THUK

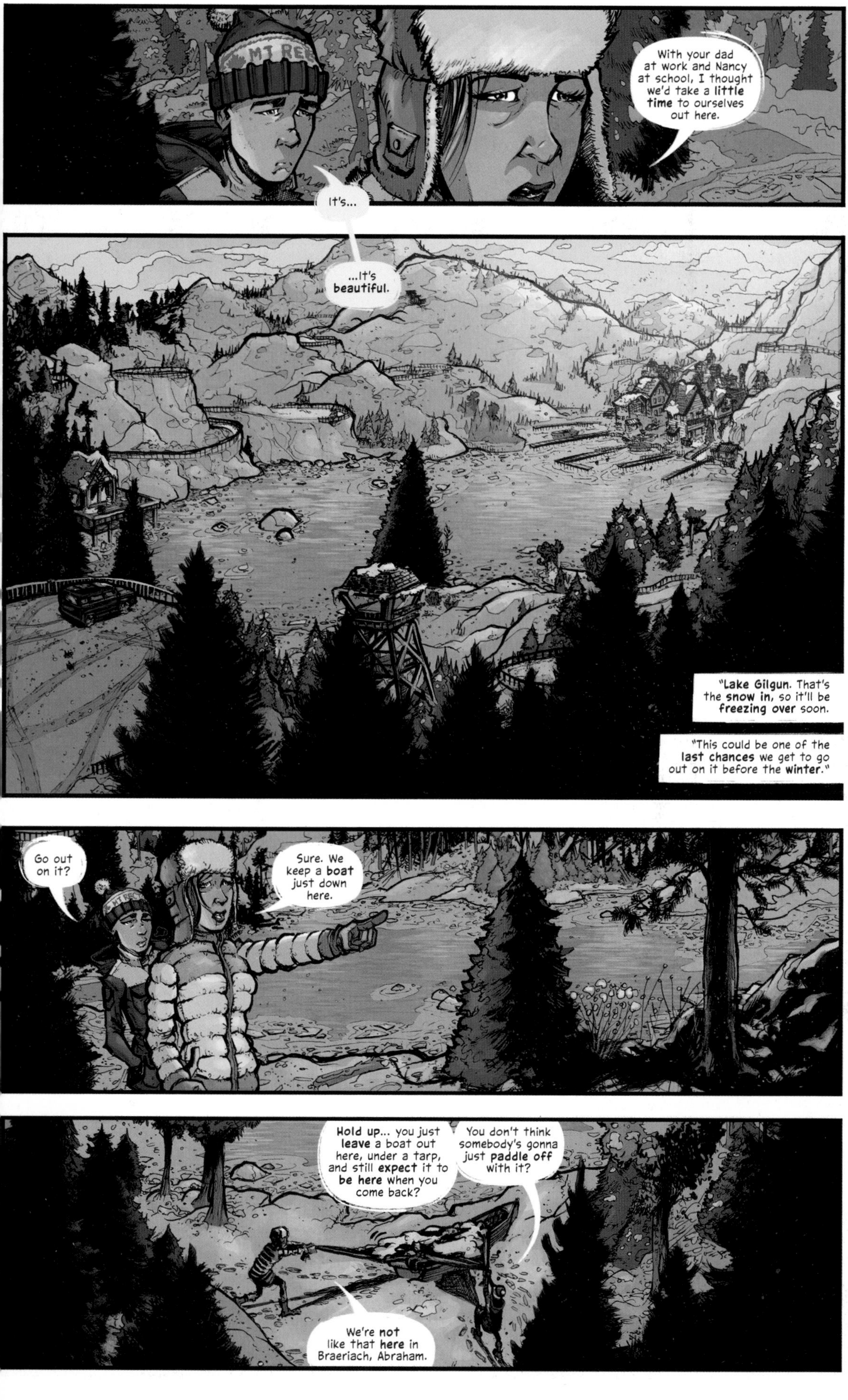

With your dad at work and Nancy at school, I thought we'd take a little time to ourselves out here.
It's...
...It's beautiful.
"Lake Gilgun. That's the snow in, so it'll be freezing over soon.
"This could be one of the last chances we get to go out on it before the winter."
Go out on it?
Sure. We keep a boat just down here.
Hold up... you just leave a boat out here, under a tarp, and still expect it to be here when you come back?
You don't think somebody's gonna just paddle off with it?
We're not like that here in Braeriach, Abraham.

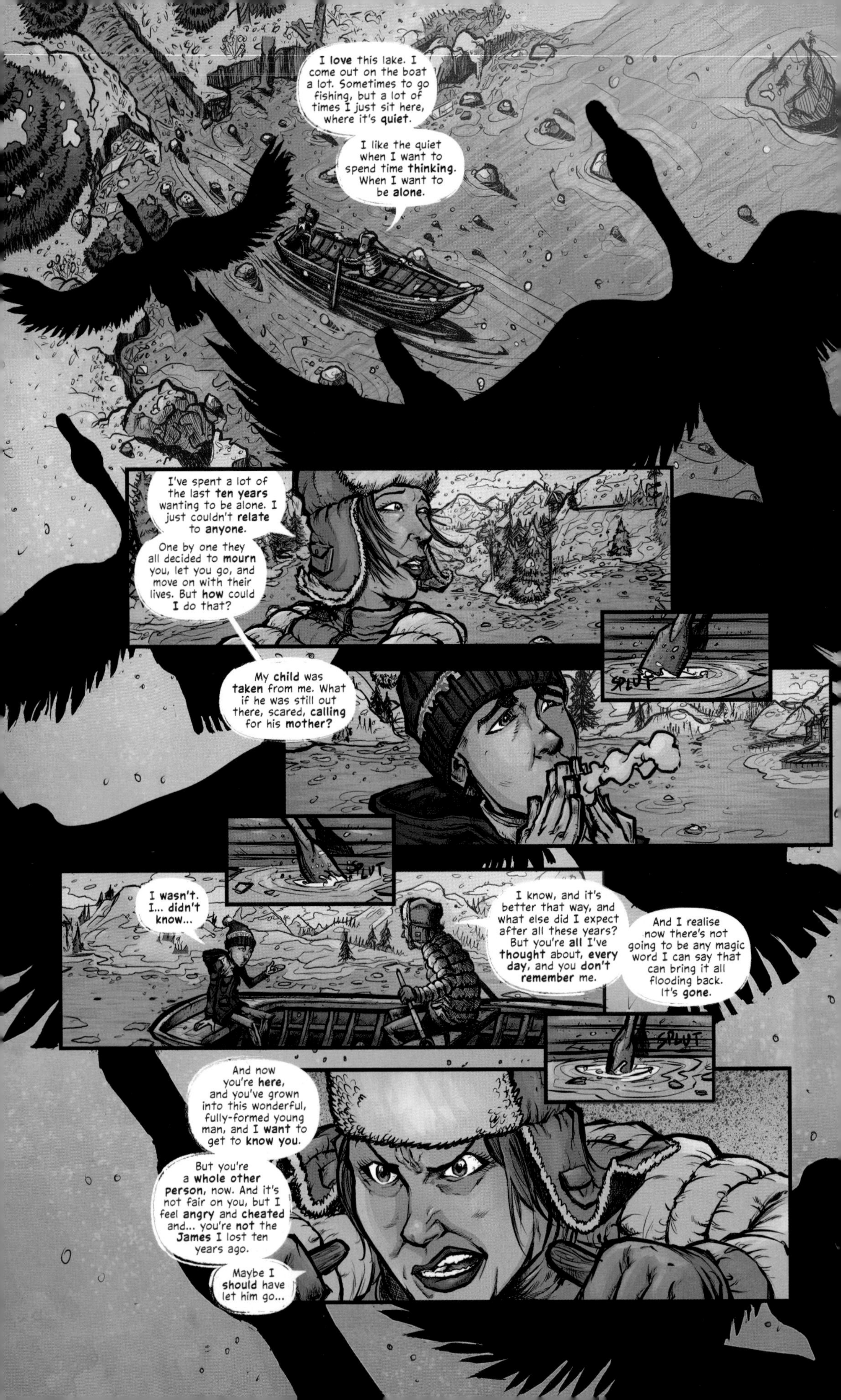
I love this lake. I come out on the boat a lot. Sometimes to go fishing, but a lot of times I just sit here, where it's quiet.
I like the quiet when I want to spend time thinking. When I want to be alone.
I've spent a lot of the last ten years wanting to be alone. I just couldn't relate to anyone.
One by one they all decided to mourn you, let you go, and move on with their lives. But how could I do that?
SPLUT
My child was taken from me. What if he was still out there, scared, calling for his mother?
SPLUT
I wasn't. I... didn't know...
I know, and it's better that way, and what else did I expect after all these years? But you're all I've thought about, every day, and you don't remember me.
And I realise now there's not going to be any magic word I can say that can bring it all flooding back. It's gone.
SPLUT
And now you're here, and you've grown into this wonderful, fully-formed young man, and I want to get to know you.
But you're a whole other person, now. And it's not fair on you, but I feel angry and cheated and... you're not the James I lost ten years ago.
Maybe I should have let him go...

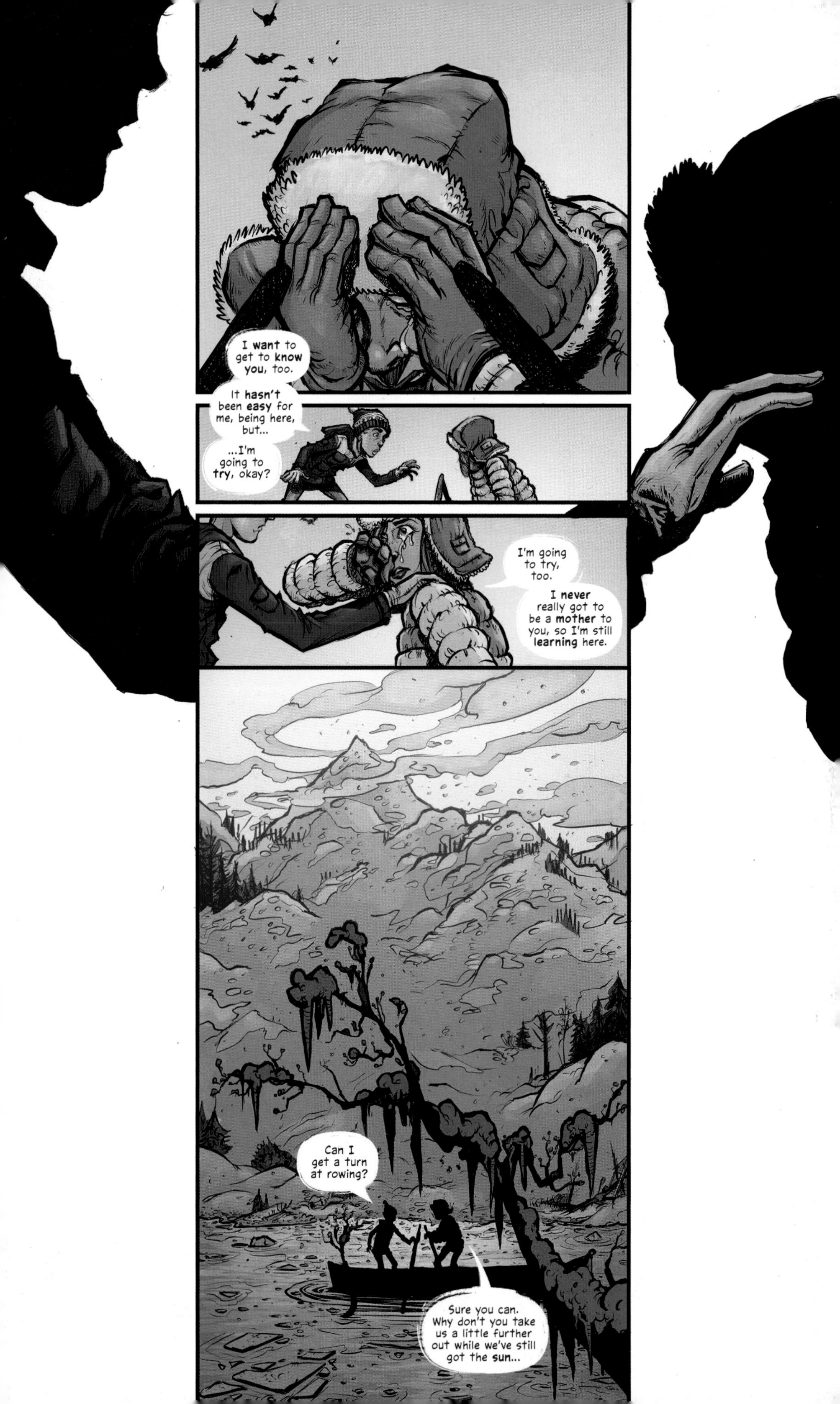
I want to get to know you, too.
It hasn't been easy for me, being here, but...
...I'm going to try, okay?
I'm going to try, too.
I never really got to be a mother to you, so I'm still learning here.
Can I get a turn at rowing?
Sure you can. Why don't you take us a little further out while we've still got the sun...

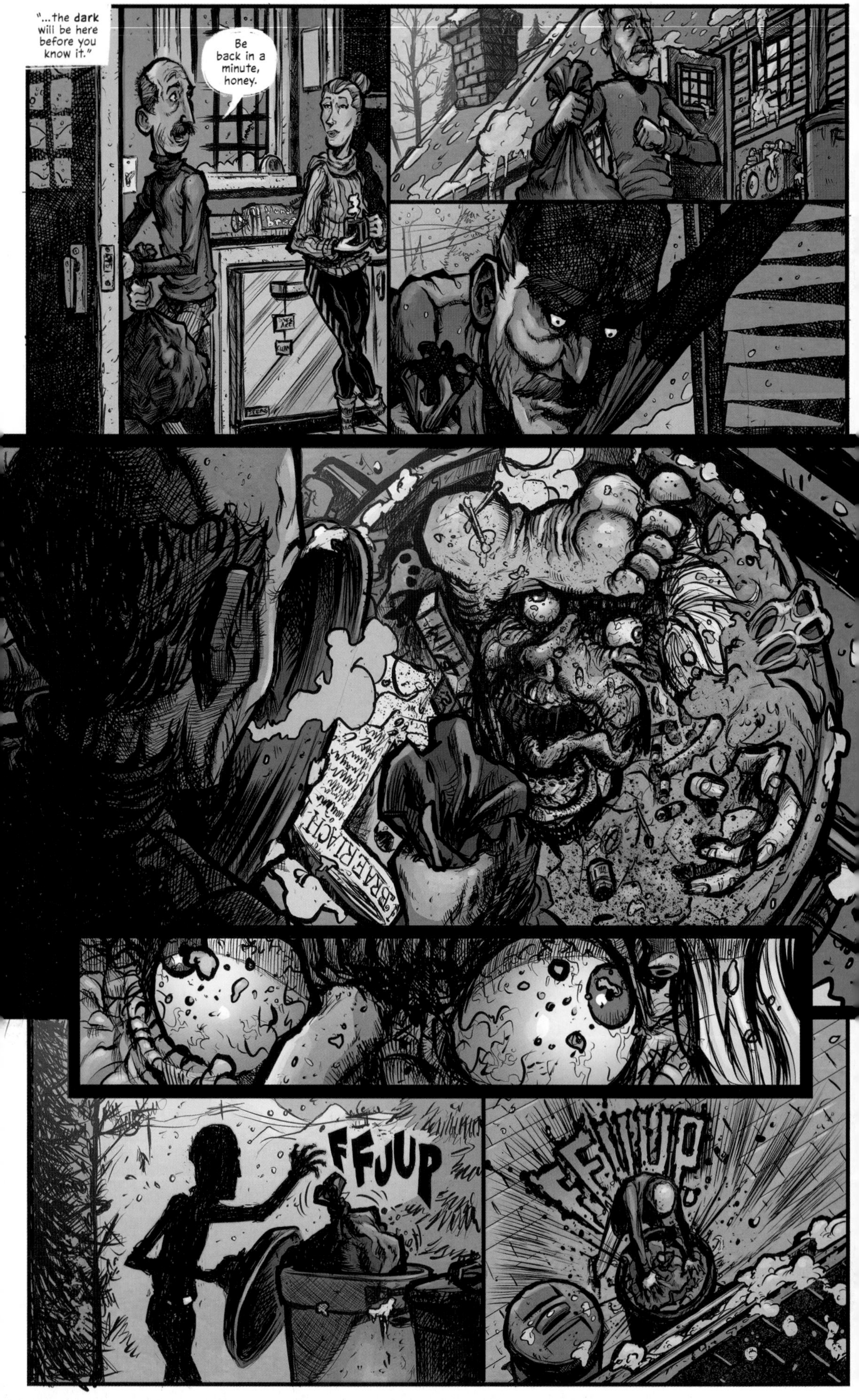
"...the dark will be here before you know it."
Be back in a minute, honey.
FFJUP

"At last... I'm beginning to feel **myself** again."

I have **returned** to you, my family. Daddy's **here**.

You have **given** all your **love** to me... and I want to **share** with you what has given my **heart** joy.

THE MOUNTAIN. The mountain is **beauty**. The mountain is **truth**.

Theo, please... you're **hurting** me. And you're **scaring** Ryan...

It has **slept** in the dark for so **long**, my darling, but it is **awake** now, and it is **coming**.

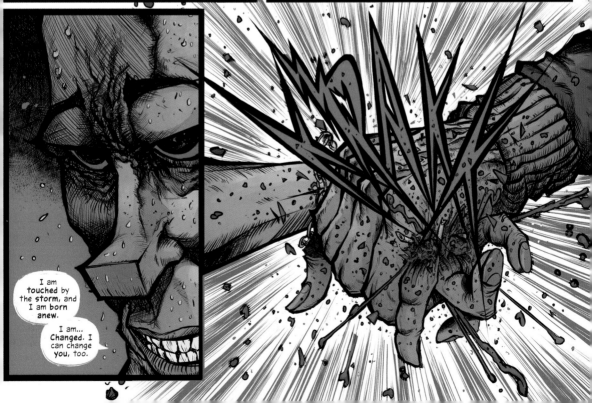

I am **touched** by the **storm**, and I am **born** anew.

I am... Changed. I can change you, too.

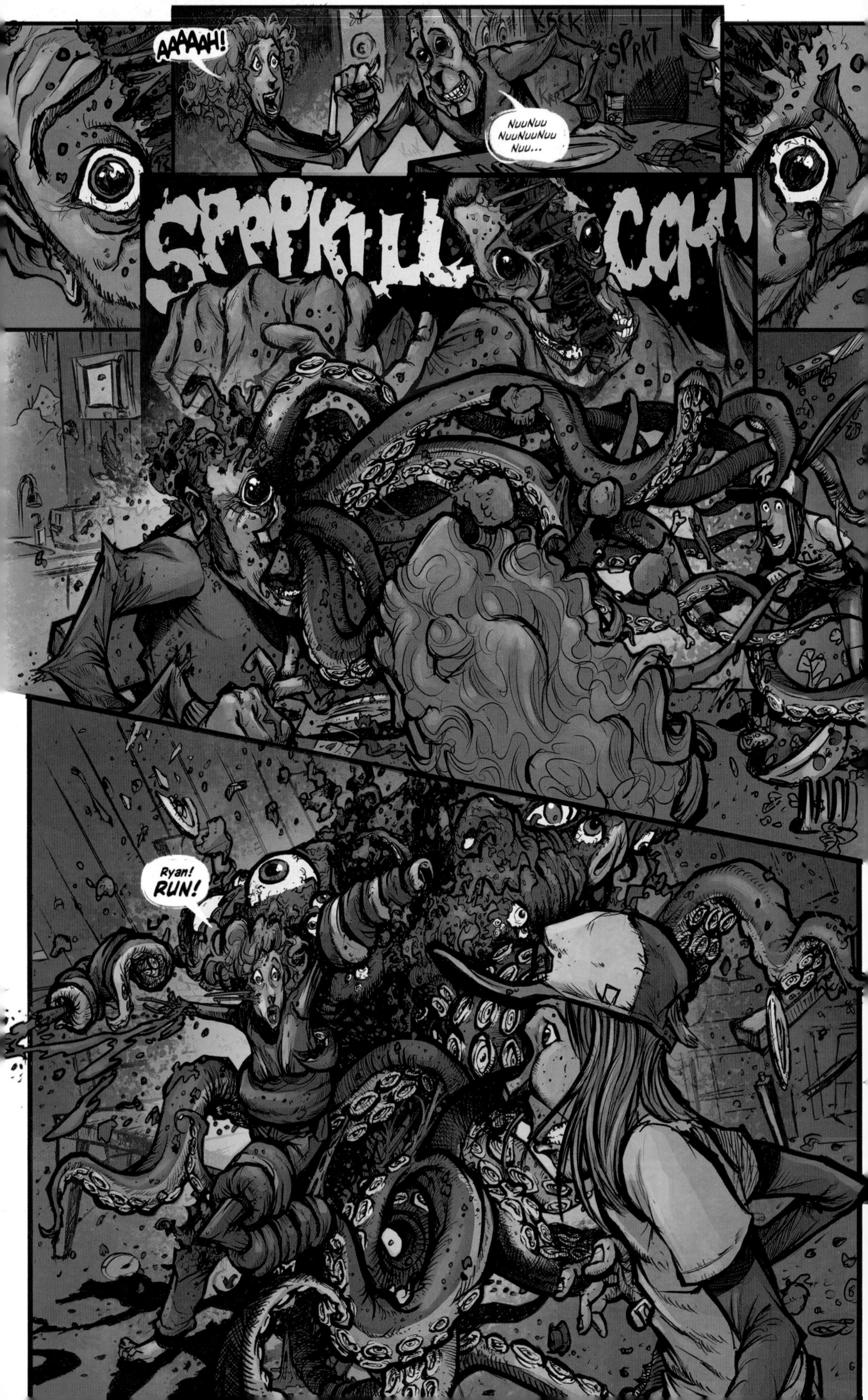
AAAAH!
SPRKT
NuuNuu NuuNuuNuu Nuu...
Ryan! RUN!

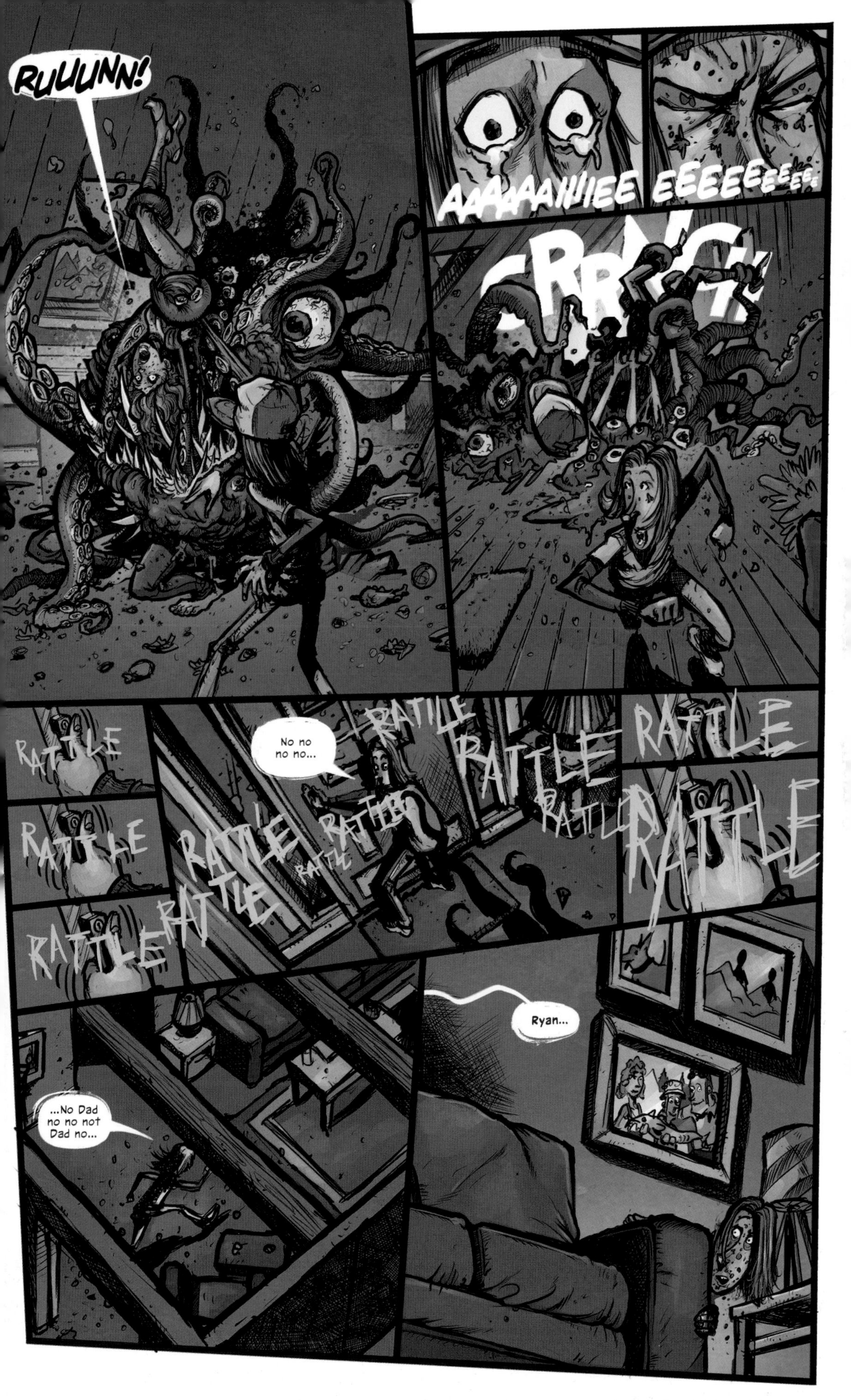
RUUUNN!
AAAAAIIIIIEE EEEEEEEEE
CRRNCH!
RATTLE
RATTLE
RATTLE RATTLE
No no
no no...
RATTLE
RATTLE
RATTLE
RATTLE
RATTLE
RATTLE
...No Dad
no no not
Dad no...
Ryan...

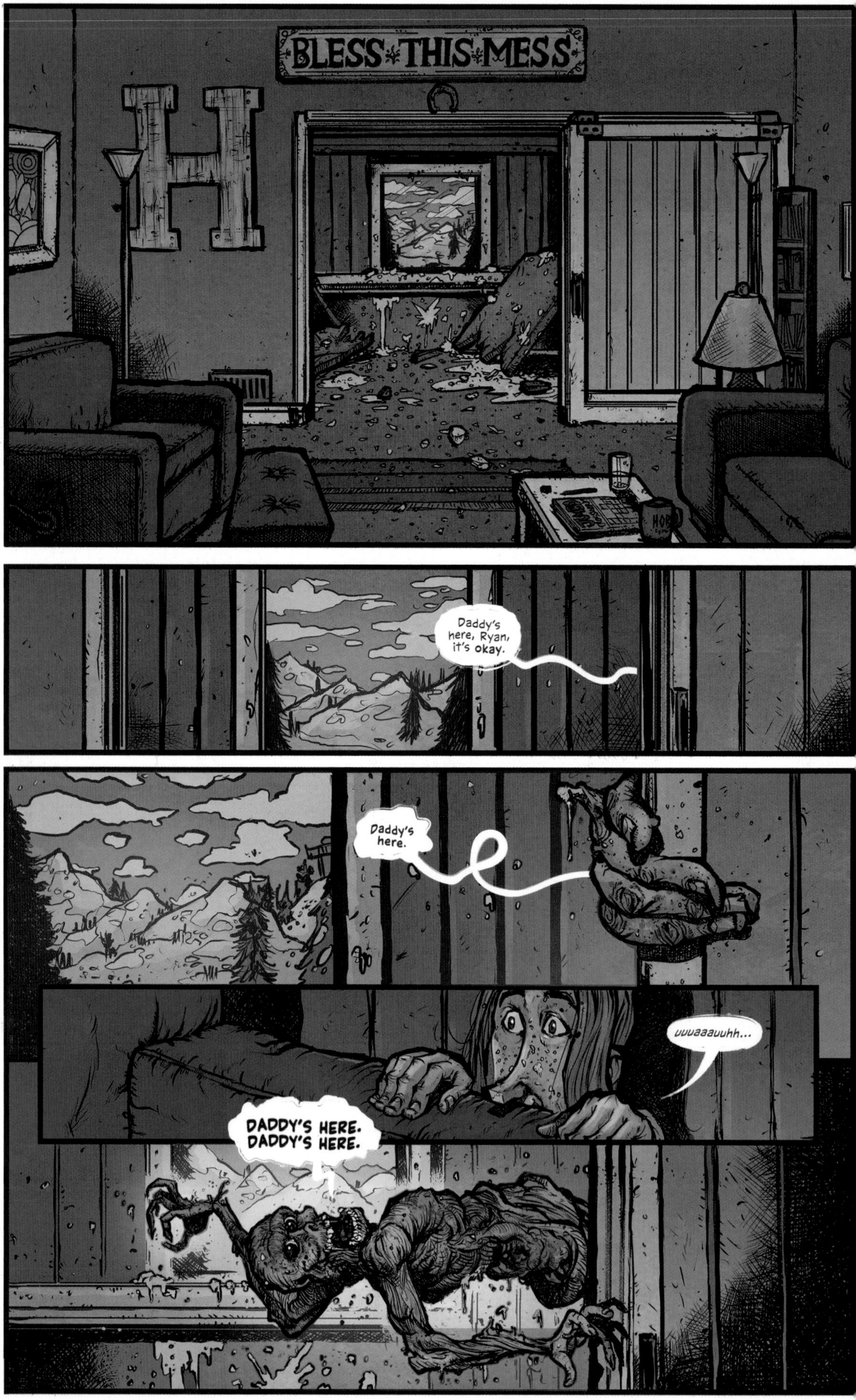
BLESS THIS MESS
Daddy's here, Ryan, it's okay.
Daddy's here.
uuuaaauuhh...
DADDY'S HERE. DADDY'S HERE.

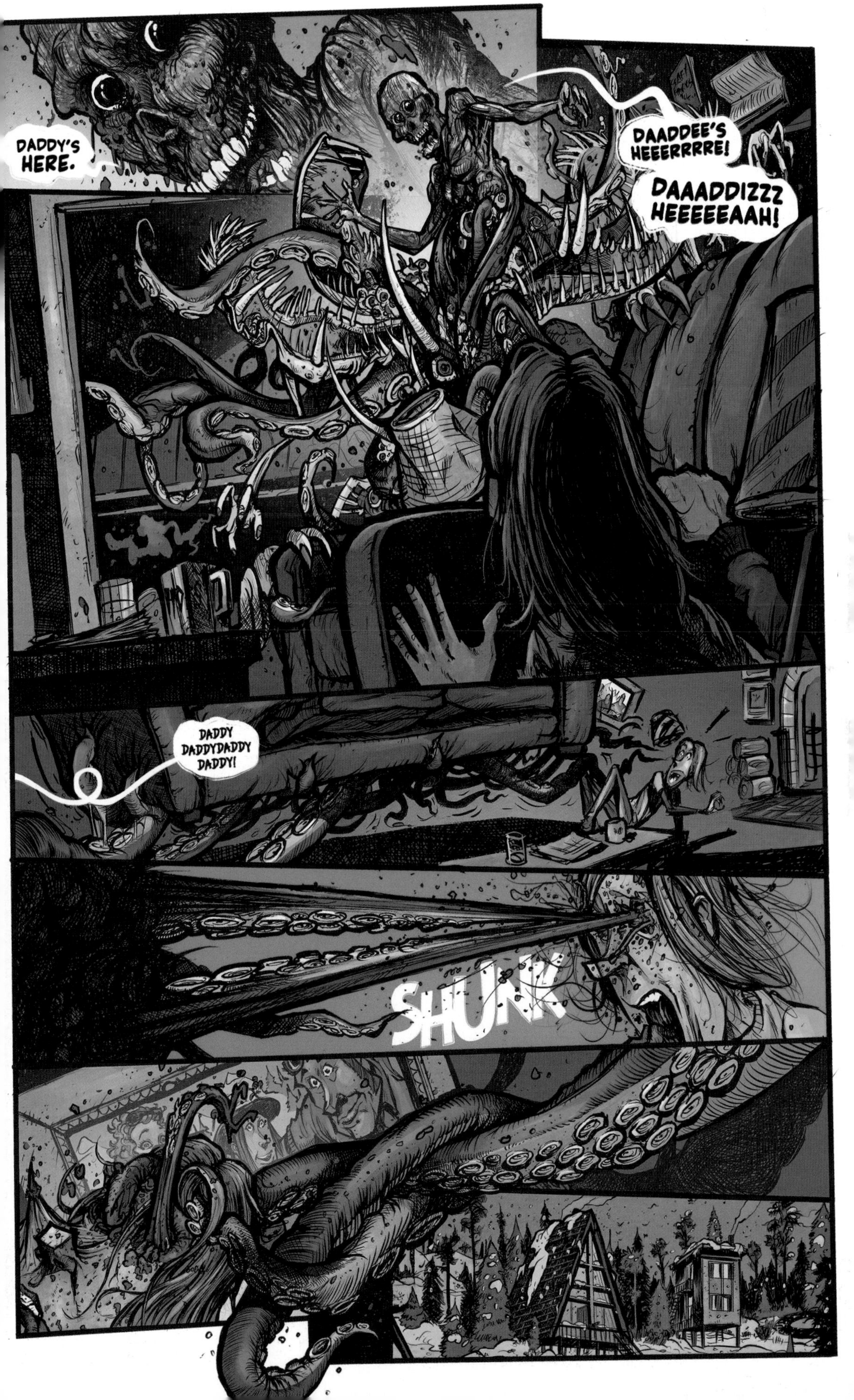
DADDY'S HERE.
DAADDEE'S HEEERRRRE!
DAAADDIZZZ HEEEEEAAH!
DADDY DADDYDADDY DADDY!
SHUNK

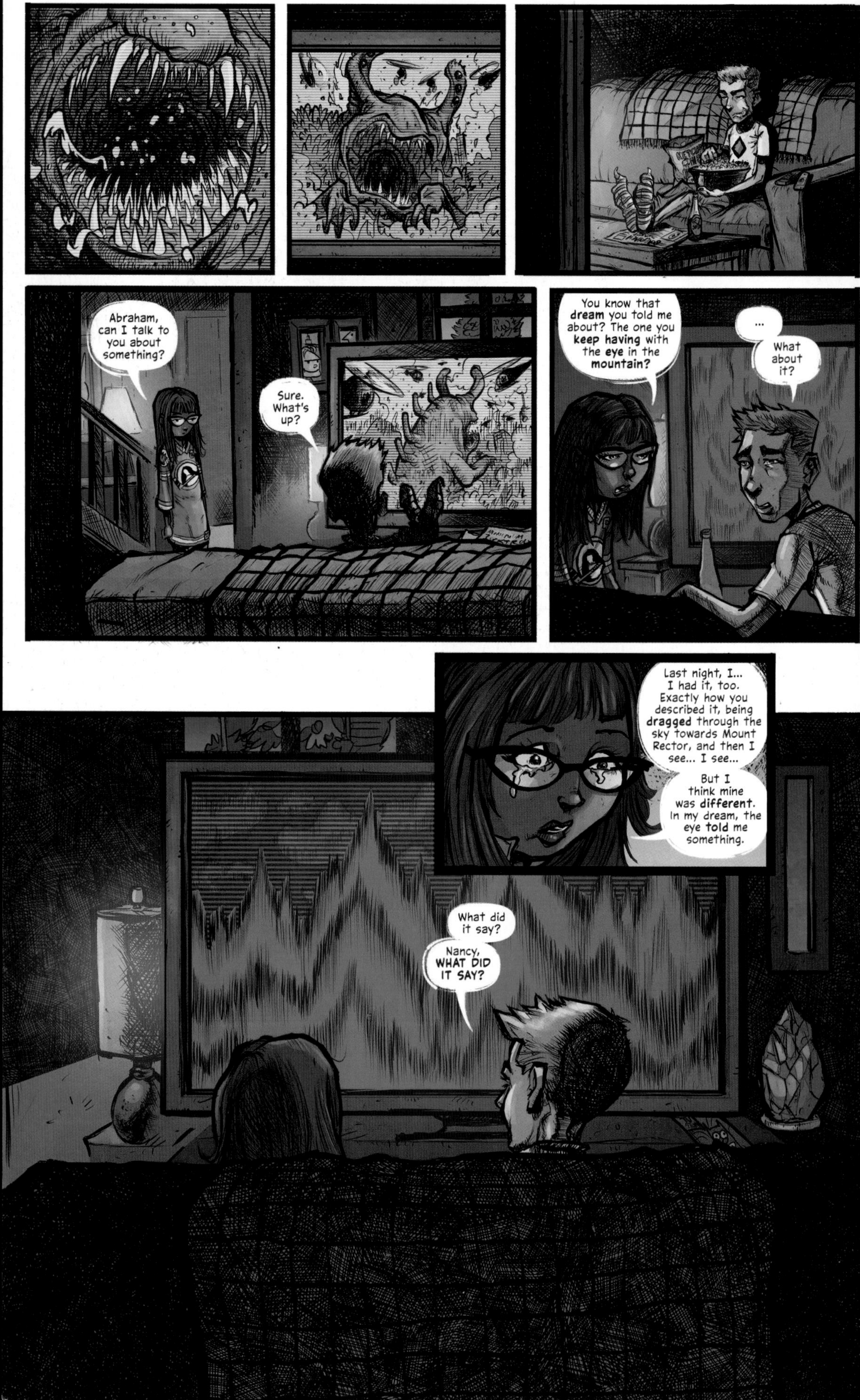
Abraham, can I talk to you about something?
Sure. What's up?
You know that dream you told me about? The one you keep having with the eye in the mountain?
...
What about it?
Last night, I... I had it, too. Exactly how you described it, being dragged through the sky towards Mount Rector, and then I see... I see...
But I think mine was different. In my dream, the eye told me something.
What did it say?
Nancy, WHAT DID IT SAY?

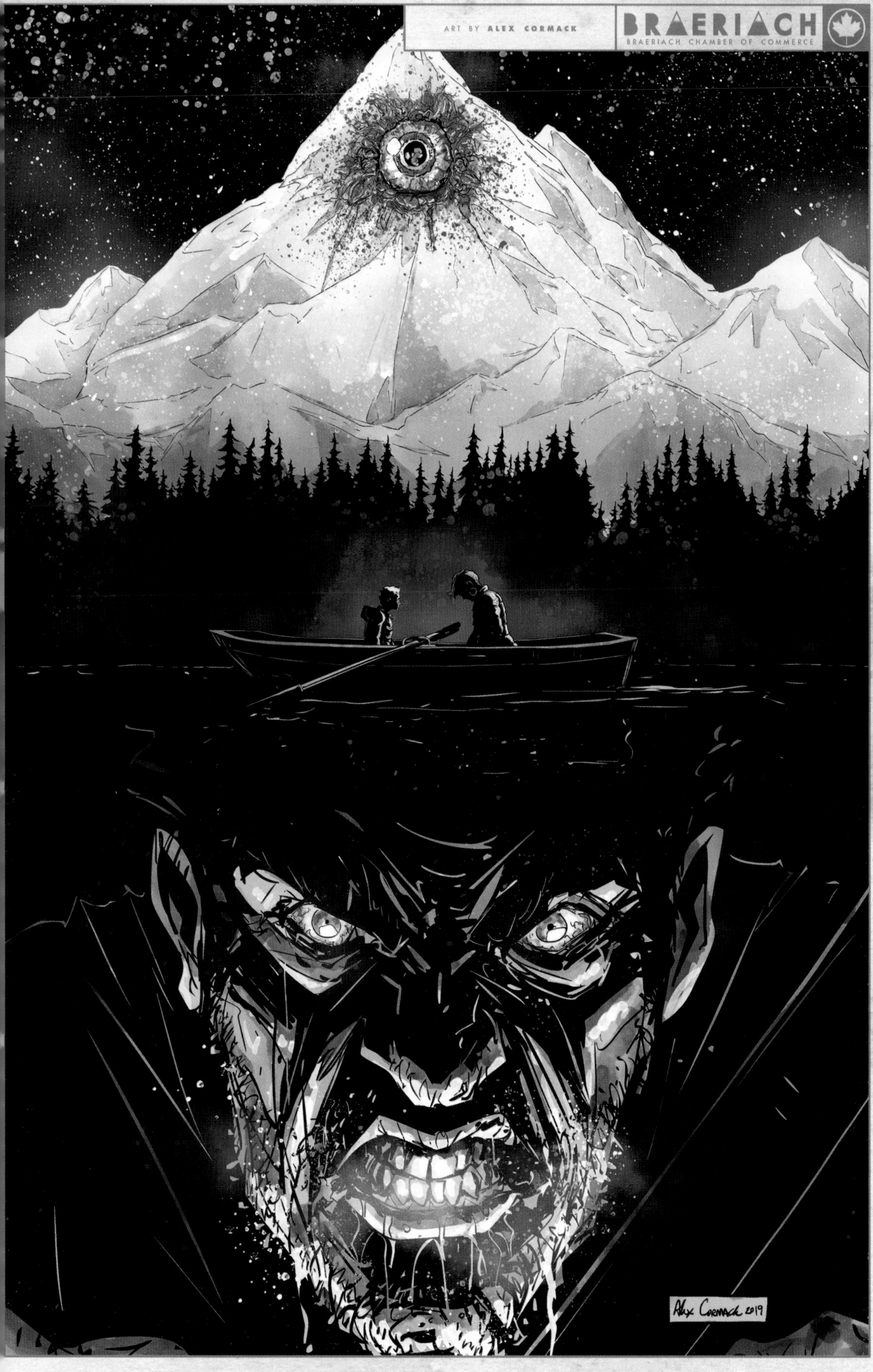

ART BY ALEX CORMACK
BRAERIACH
BRAERIACH CHAMBER OF COMMERCE
Alex Cormack 2019

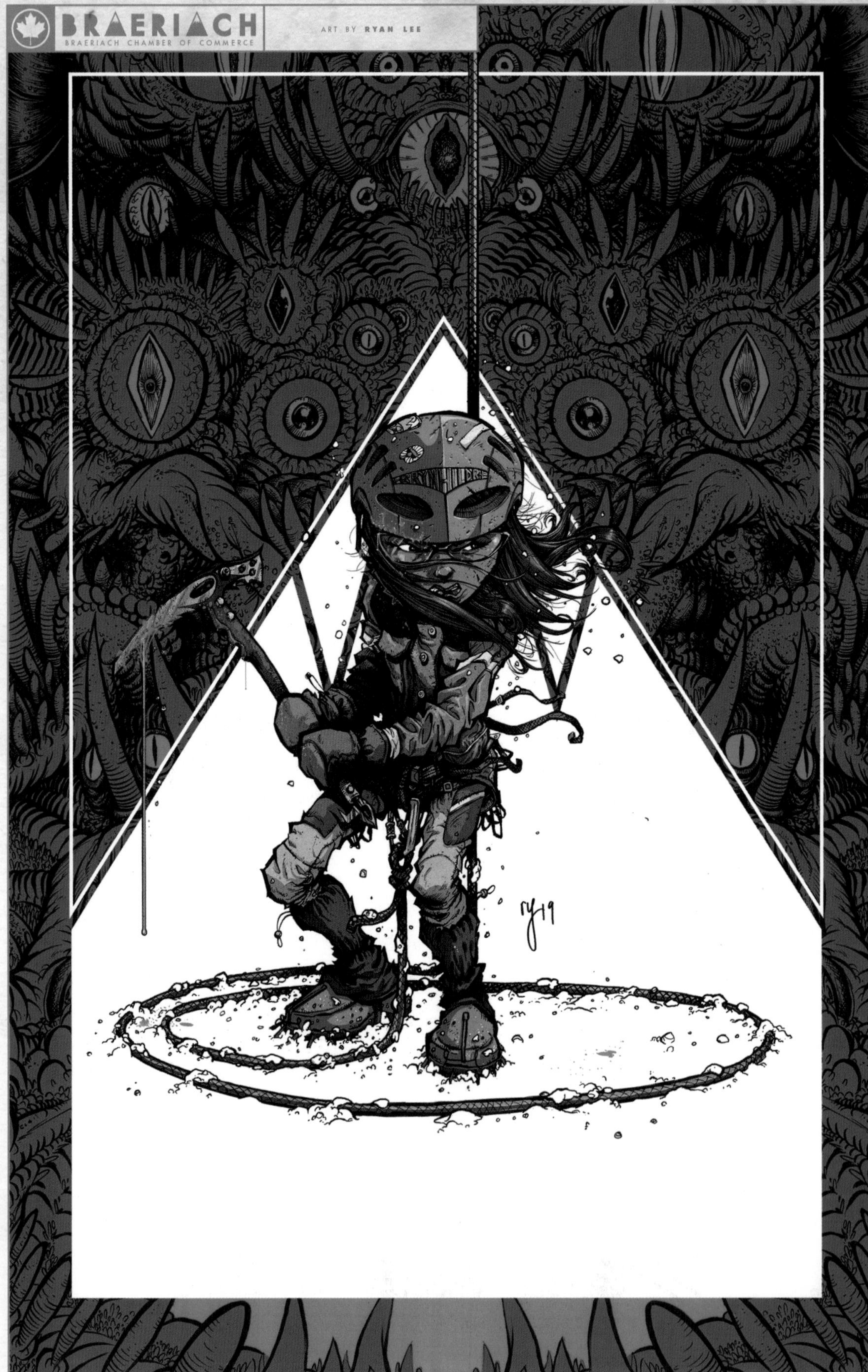
BRAERIACH
BRAERIACH CHAMBER OF COMMERCE
ART BY RYAN LEE
ry 19

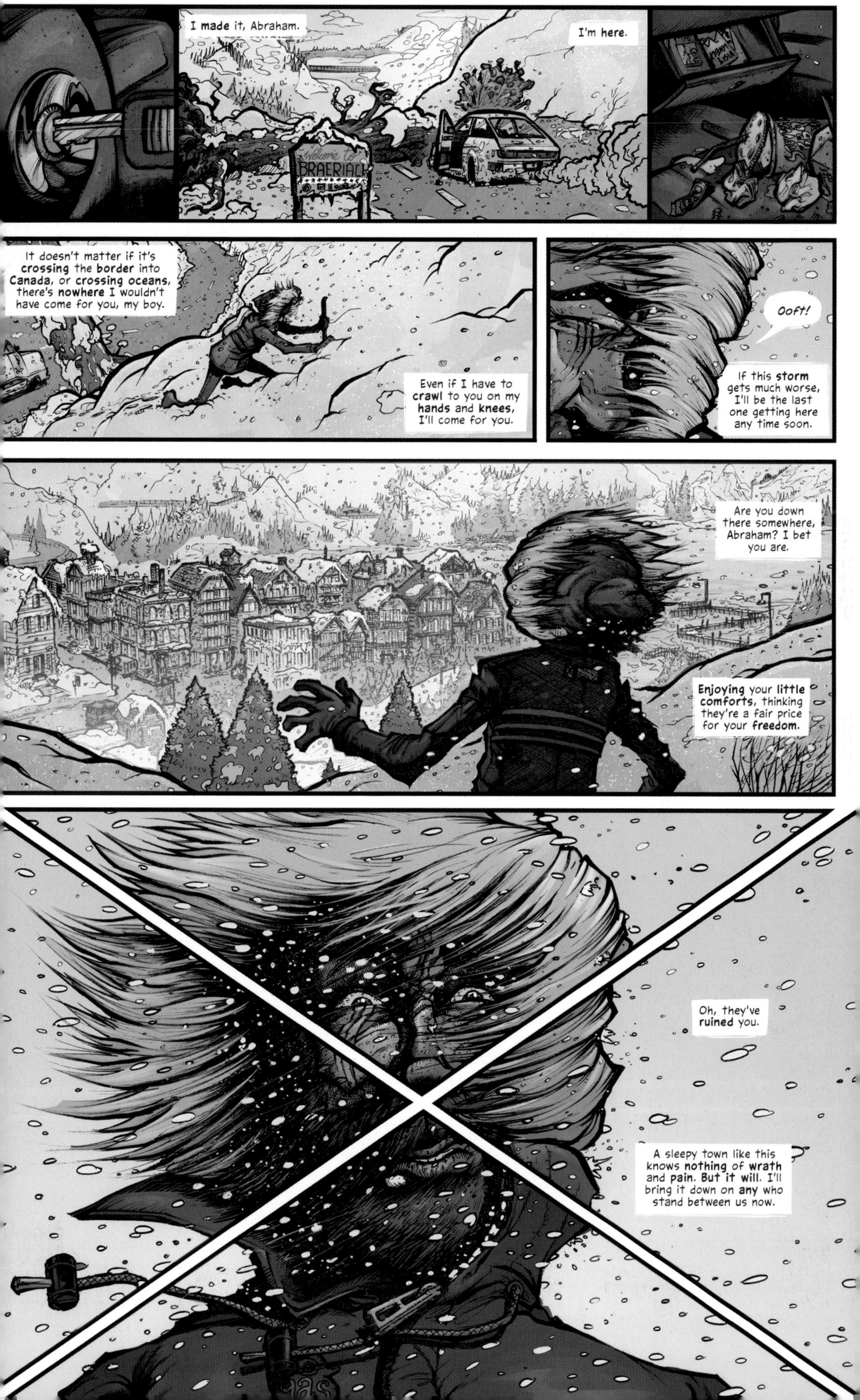
I made it, Abraham.
I'm here.
Welcome to BRAERIACH
It doesn't matter if it's crossing the border into Canada, or crossing oceans, there's nowhere I wouldn't have come for you, my boy.
Even if I have to crawl to you on my hands and knees, I'll come for you.
Ooft!
If this storm gets much worse, I'll be the last one getting here any time soon.
Are you down there somewhere, Abraham? I bet you are.
Enjoying your little comforts, thinking they're a fair price for your freedom.
Oh, they've ruined you.
A sleepy town like this knows nothing of wrath and pain. But it will. I'll bring it down on any who stand between us now.

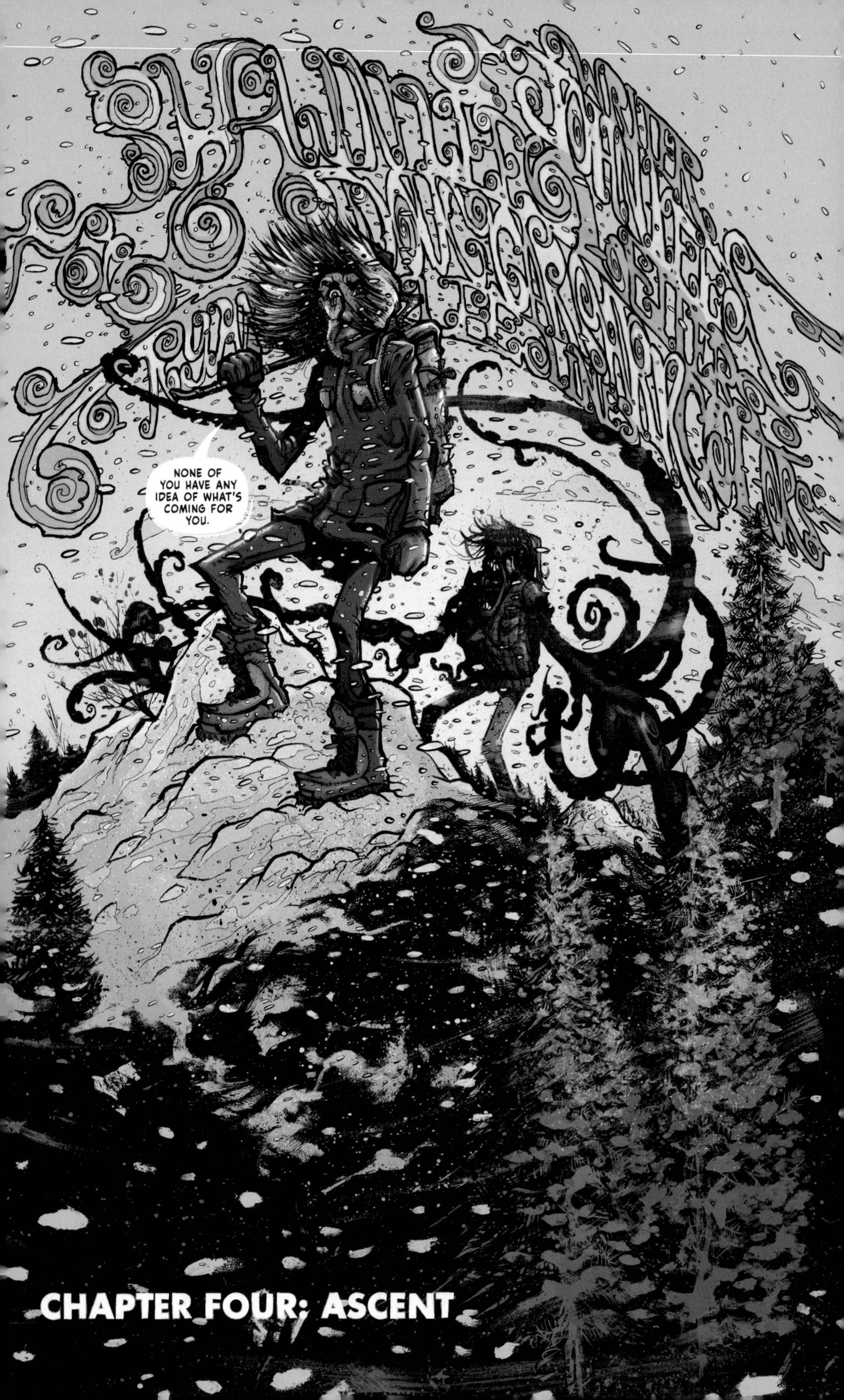
NONE OF YOU HAVE ANY IDEA OF WHAT'S COMING FOR YOU.
CHAPTER FOUR: ASCENT

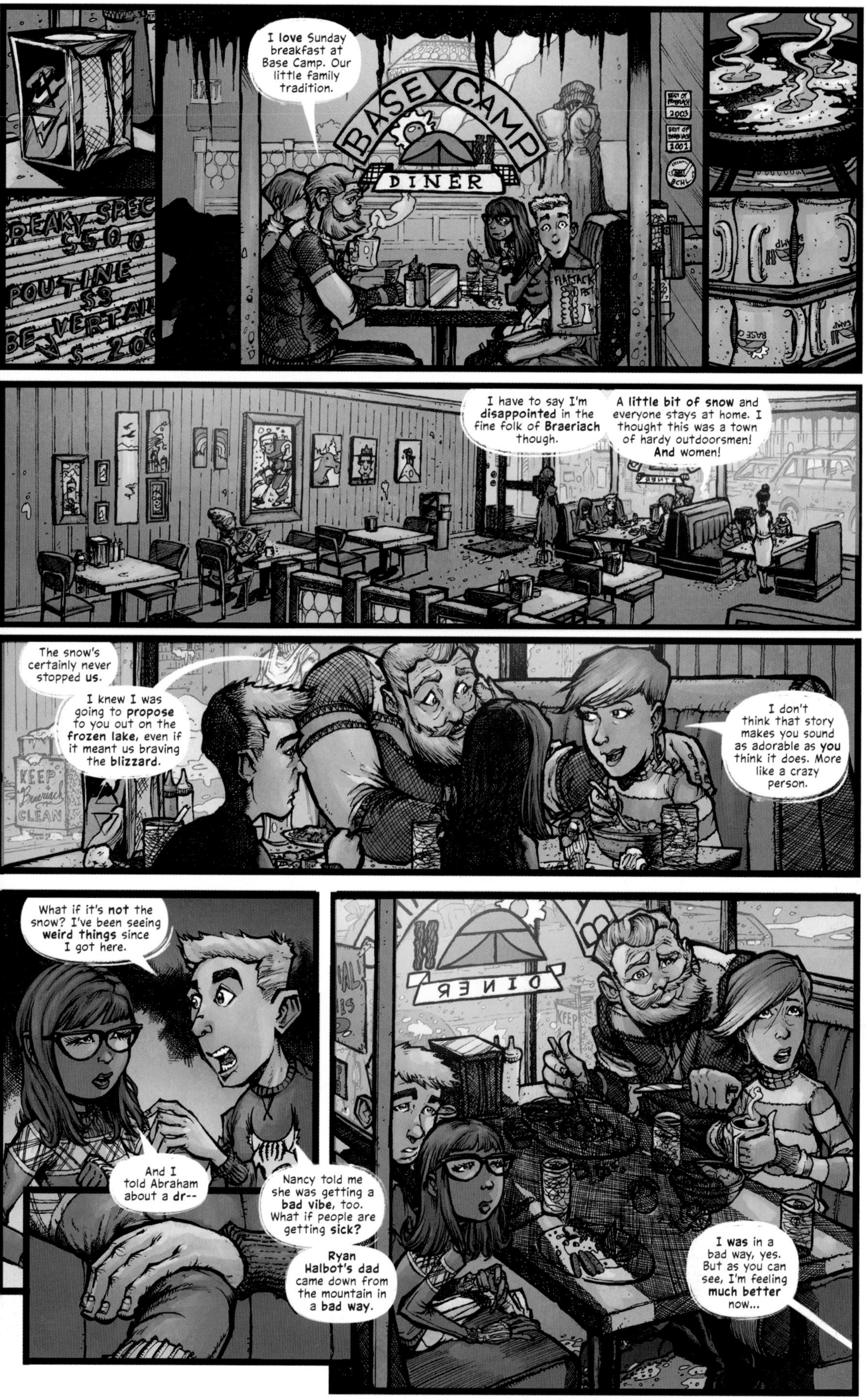

SPEAKY SPEC $500
POUTINE $3
BE VERTAIL $200
I love Sunday breakfast at Base Camp. Our little family tradition.
BASE CAMP
DINER
BEST OF BRAERIACH 2003
BEST OF BRAERIACH 2002
FLAPJACK FEST
I have to say I'm disappointed in the fine folk of Braeriach though.
A little bit of snow and everyone stays at home. I thought this was a town of hardy outdoorsmen! And women!
The snow's certainly never stopped us.
I knew I was going to propose to you out on the frozen lake, even if it meant us braving the blizzard.
KEEP Braeriach CLEAN
I don't think that story makes you sound as adorable as you think it does. More like a crazy person.
What if it's not the snow? I've been seeing weird things since I got here.
And I told Abraham about a dr--
Nancy told me she was getting a bad vibe, too. What if people are getting sick?
Ryan Halbot's dad came down from the mountain in a bad way.
DINER
KEEP
I was in a bad way, yes. But as you can see, I'm feeling much better now...

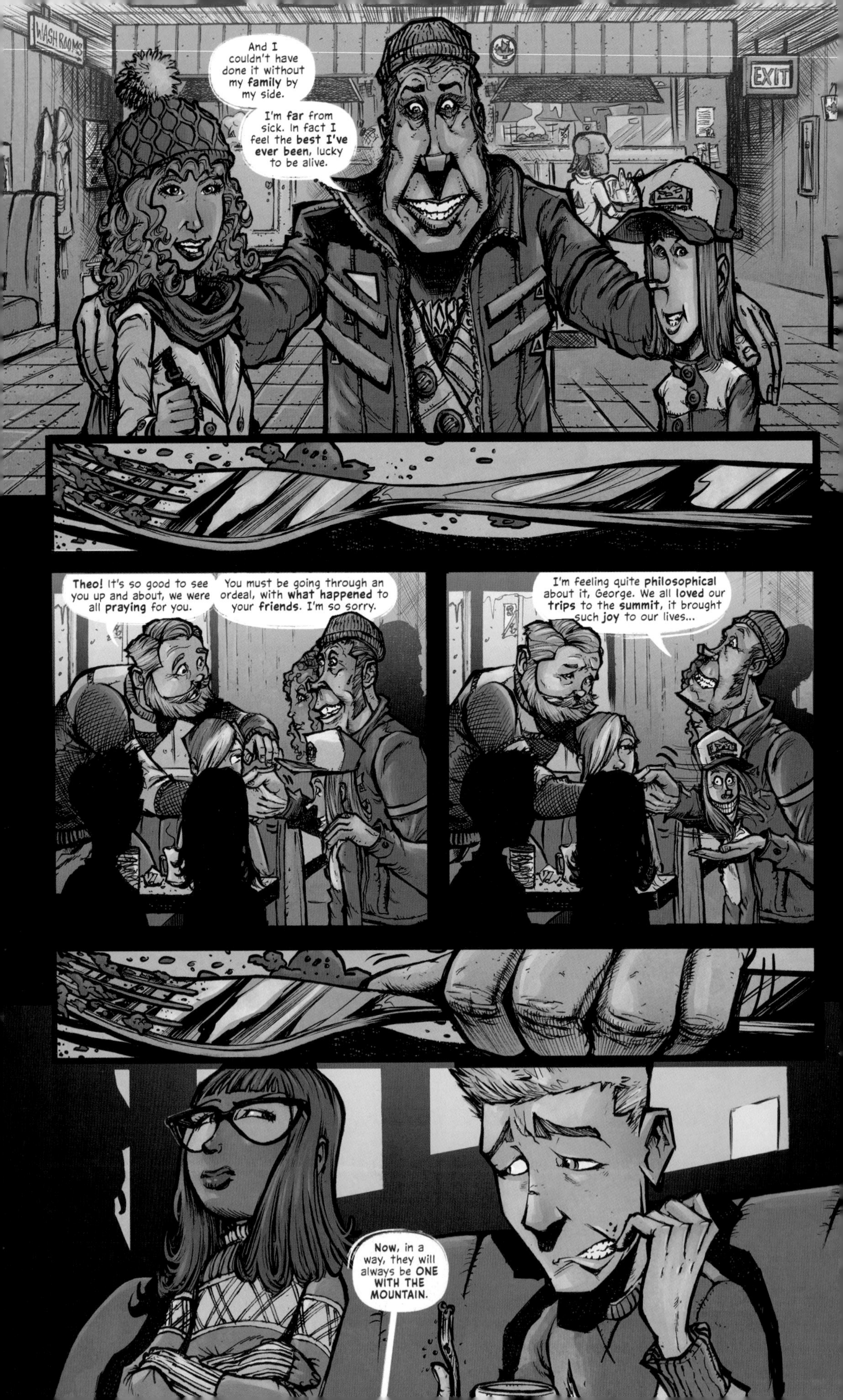
WASH ROOMS
EXIT
And I couldn't have done it without my **family** by my side.
I'm **far** from sick. In fact I feel the **best I've ever been**, lucky to be alive.
Theo! It's so good to see you up and about, we were all **praying** for you.
You must be going through an ordeal, with **what happened** to your **friends**. I'm so sorry.
I'm feeling quite **philosophical** about it, George. We all **loved** our **trips** to the **summit**, it brought such **joy** to our lives...
Now, in a way, they will always be **ONE WITH THE MOUNTAIN.**

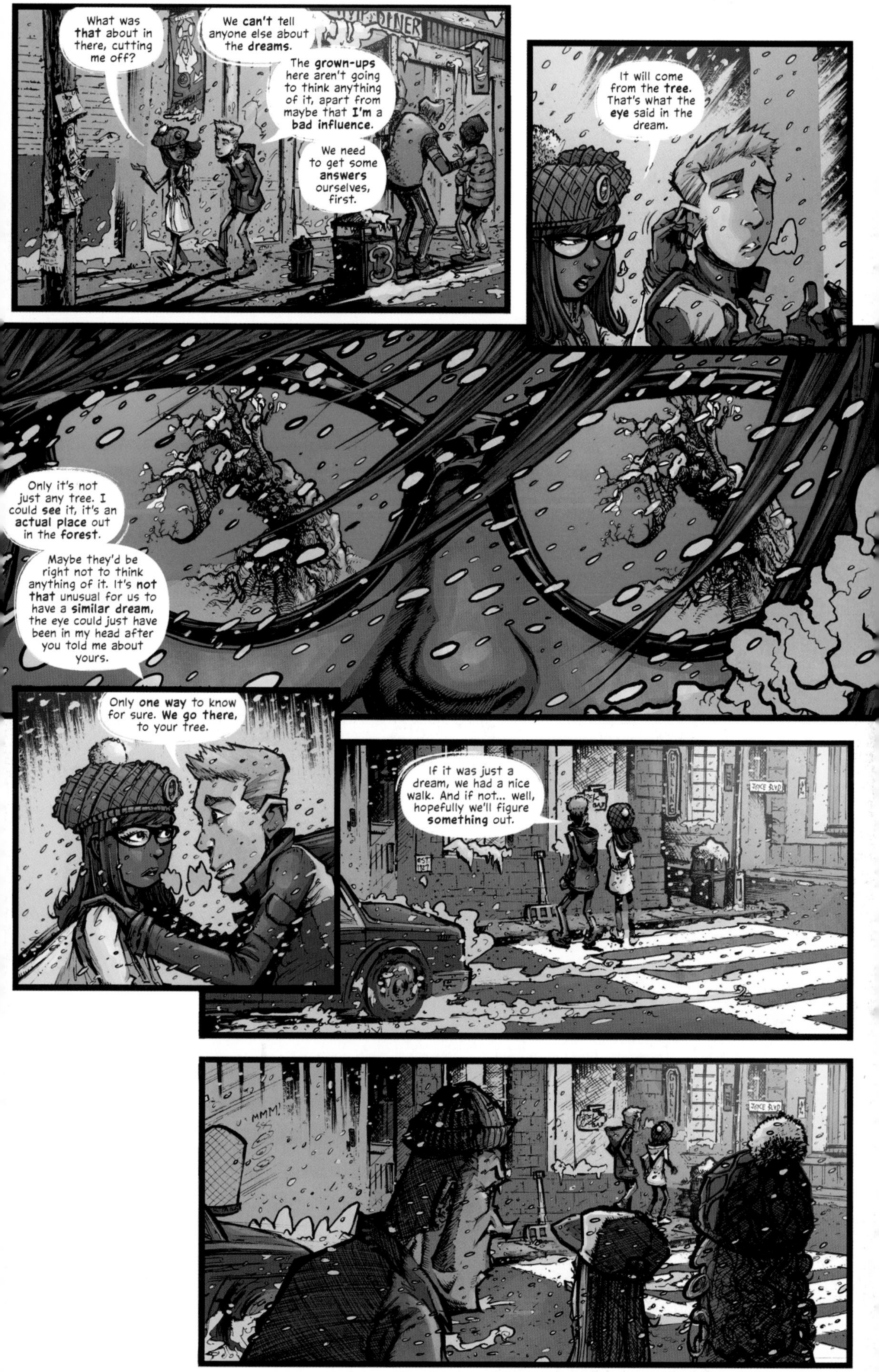
DINER
What was that about in there, cutting me off?
We can't tell anyone else about the dreams.
The grown-ups here aren't going to think anything of it, apart from maybe that I'm a bad influence.
We need to get some answers ourselves, first.
It will come from the tree. That's what the eye said in the dream.
Only it's not just any tree. I could see it, it's an actual place out in the forest.
Maybe they'd be right not to think anything of it. It's not that unusual for us to have a similar dream, the eye could just have been in my head after you told me about yours.
Only one way to know for sure. We go there, to your tree.
If it was just a dream, we had a nice walk. And if not... well, hopefully we'll figure something out.
JOYCE BLVD
MMM!
JOYCE BLVD

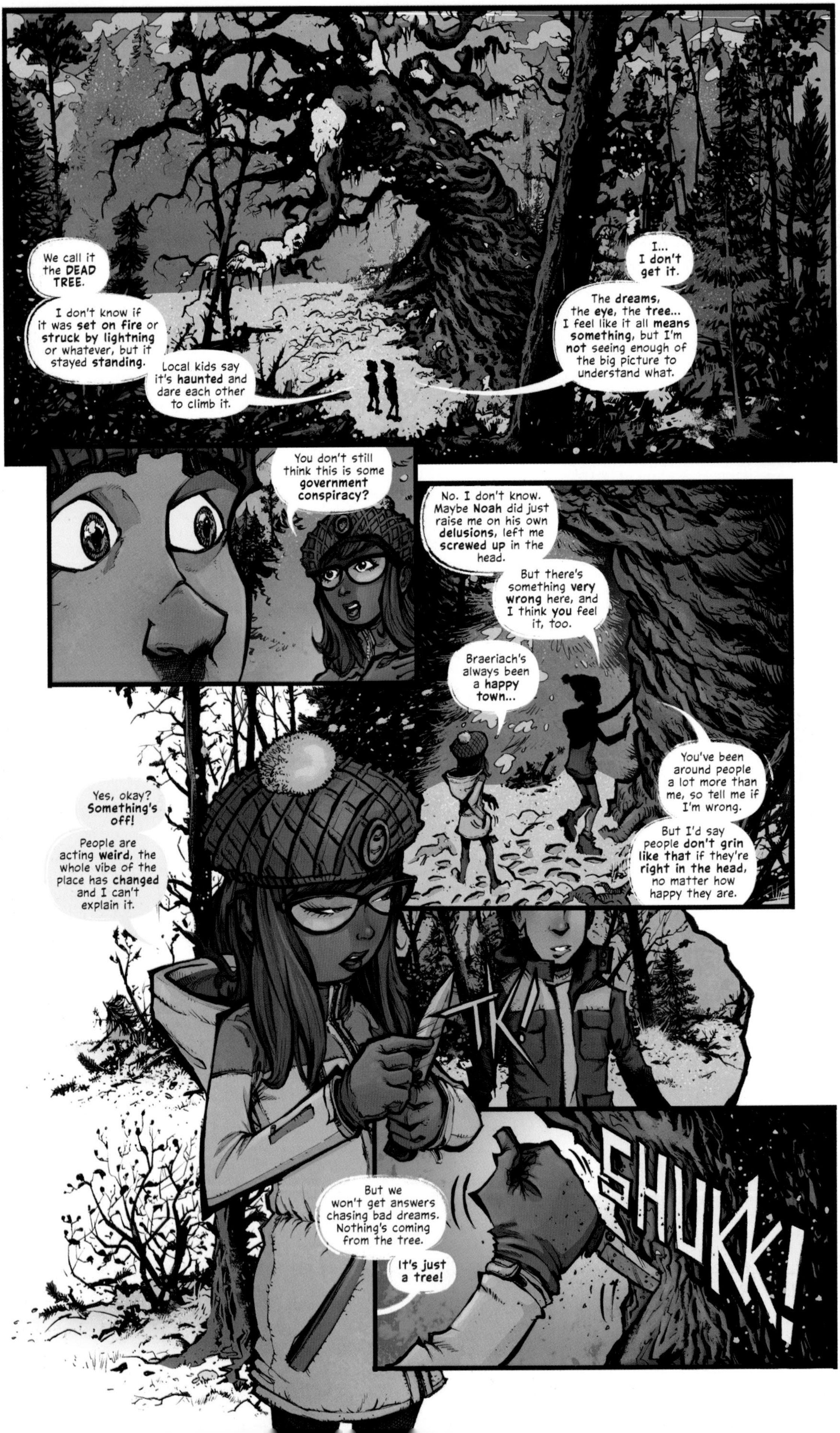

We call it the DEAD TREE.
I don't know if it was set on fire or struck by lightning or whatever, but it stayed standing.
Local kids say it's haunted and dare each other to climb it.
I... I don't get it.
The dreams, the eye, the tree... I feel like it all means something, but I'm not seeing enough of the big picture to understand what.
You don't still think this is some government conspiracy?
No. I don't know. Maybe Noah did just raise me on his own delusions, left me screwed up in the head.
But there's something very wrong here, and I think you feel it, too.
Braeriach's always been a happy town...
You've been around people a lot more than me, so tell me if I'm wrong.
But I'd say people don't grin like that if they're right in the head, no matter how happy they are.
Yes, okay? Something's off!
People are acting weird, the whole vibe of the place has changed and I can't explain it.
TK!
But we won't get answers chasing bad dreams. Nothing's coming from the tree.
It's just a tree!
SHUKK!

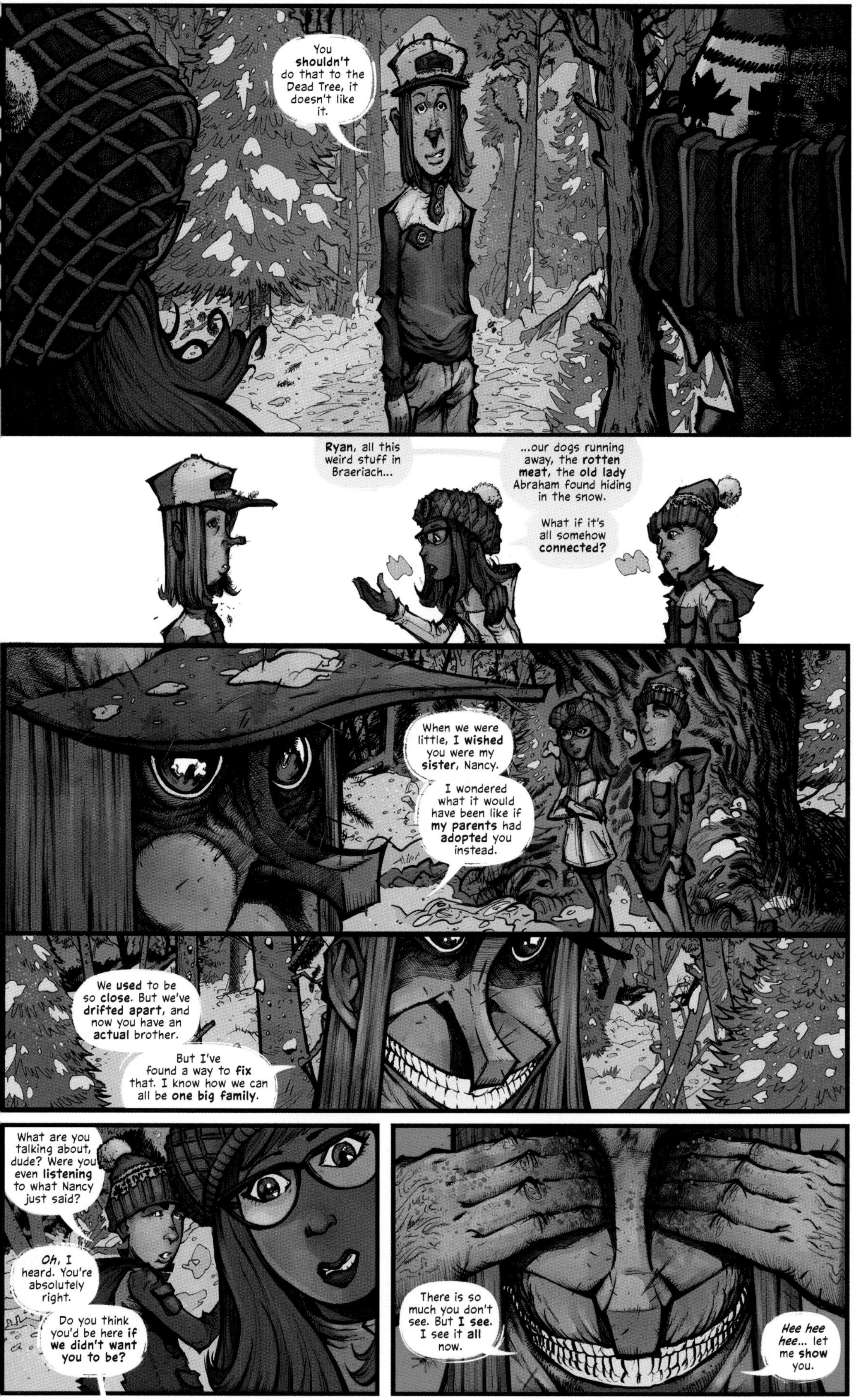
You **shouldn't** do that to the Dead Tree, it doesn't like it.
Ryan, all this weird stuff in Braeriach...
...our dogs running away, the **rotten meat**, the **old lady** Abraham found hiding in the snow.
What if it's all somehow **connected?**
When we were little, I **wished** you were my **sister**, Nancy.
I wondered what it would have been like if **my parents** had **adopted** you instead.
We **used** to be so **close**. But we've **drifted apart**, and now you have an **actual** brother.
But I've found a way to **fix** that. I know how we can all be **one big family**.
What are you talking about, dude? Were you even **listening** to what Nancy just said?
Oh, I heard. You're absolutely right.
Do you think you'd be here **if we didn't want you to be?**
There is so much you don't see. But **I see**. I see it **all** now.
Hee hee hee... let me **show** you.

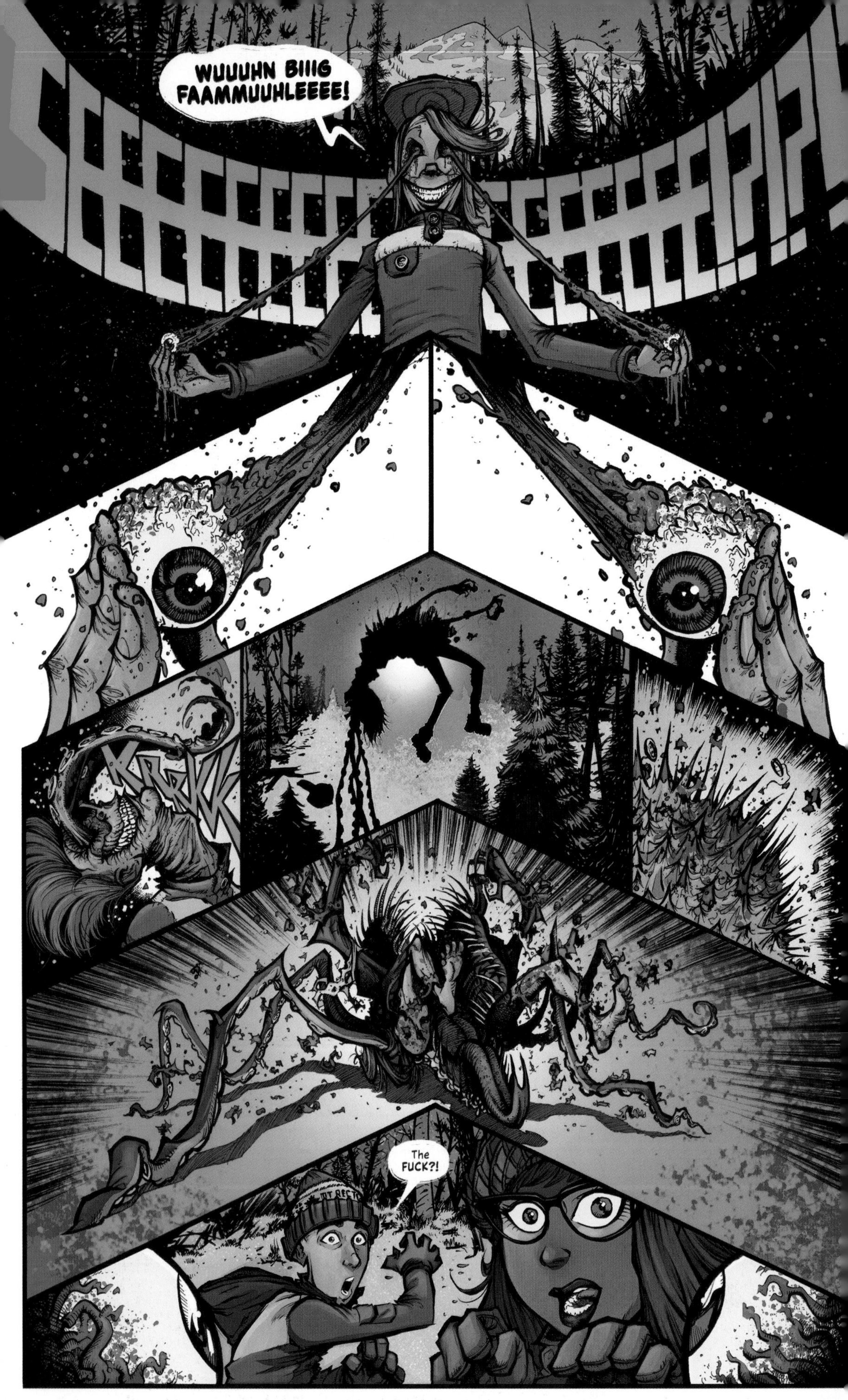
WUUUHN BIIIG FAAMMUUHLEEEE!
The FUCK?!

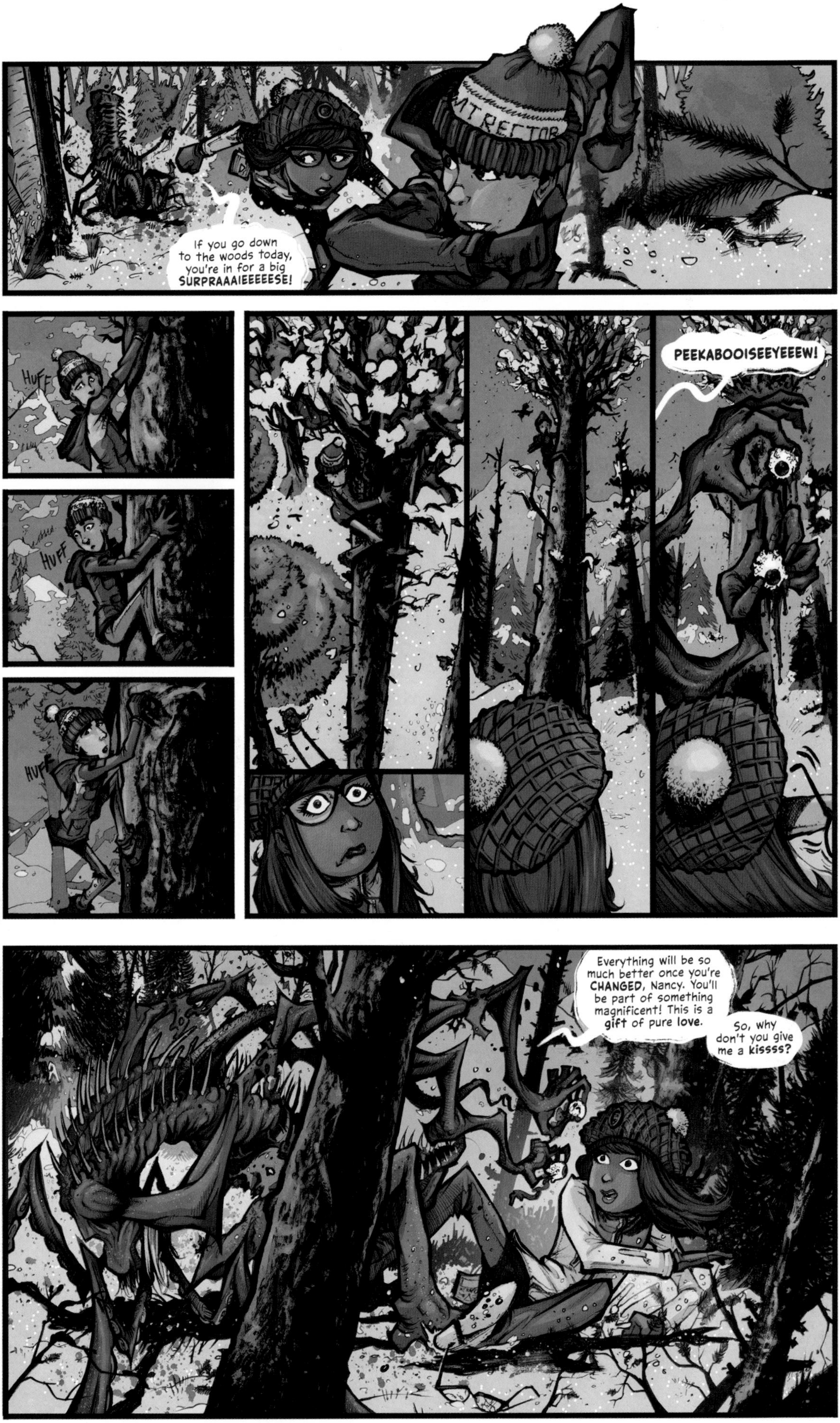
If you go down to the woods today, you're in for a big SURPRAAAIEEEEESE!
HUFF
HUFF
HUFF
PEEKABOOISEEYEEEW!
Everything will be so much better once you're CHANGED, Nancy. You'll be part of something magnificent! This is a gift of pure love.
So, why don't you give me a kissss?

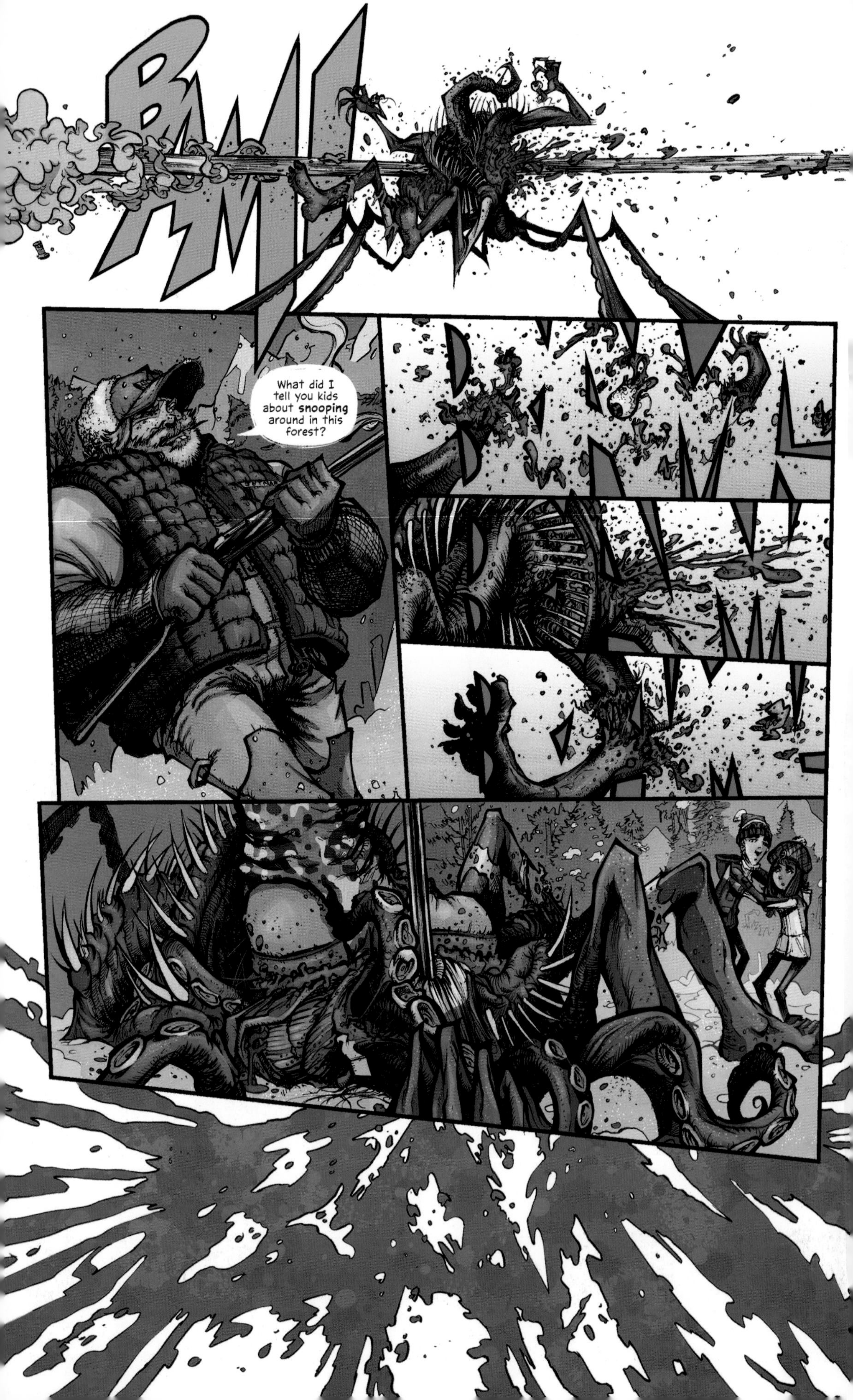
What did I tell you kids about **snooping** around in this forest?

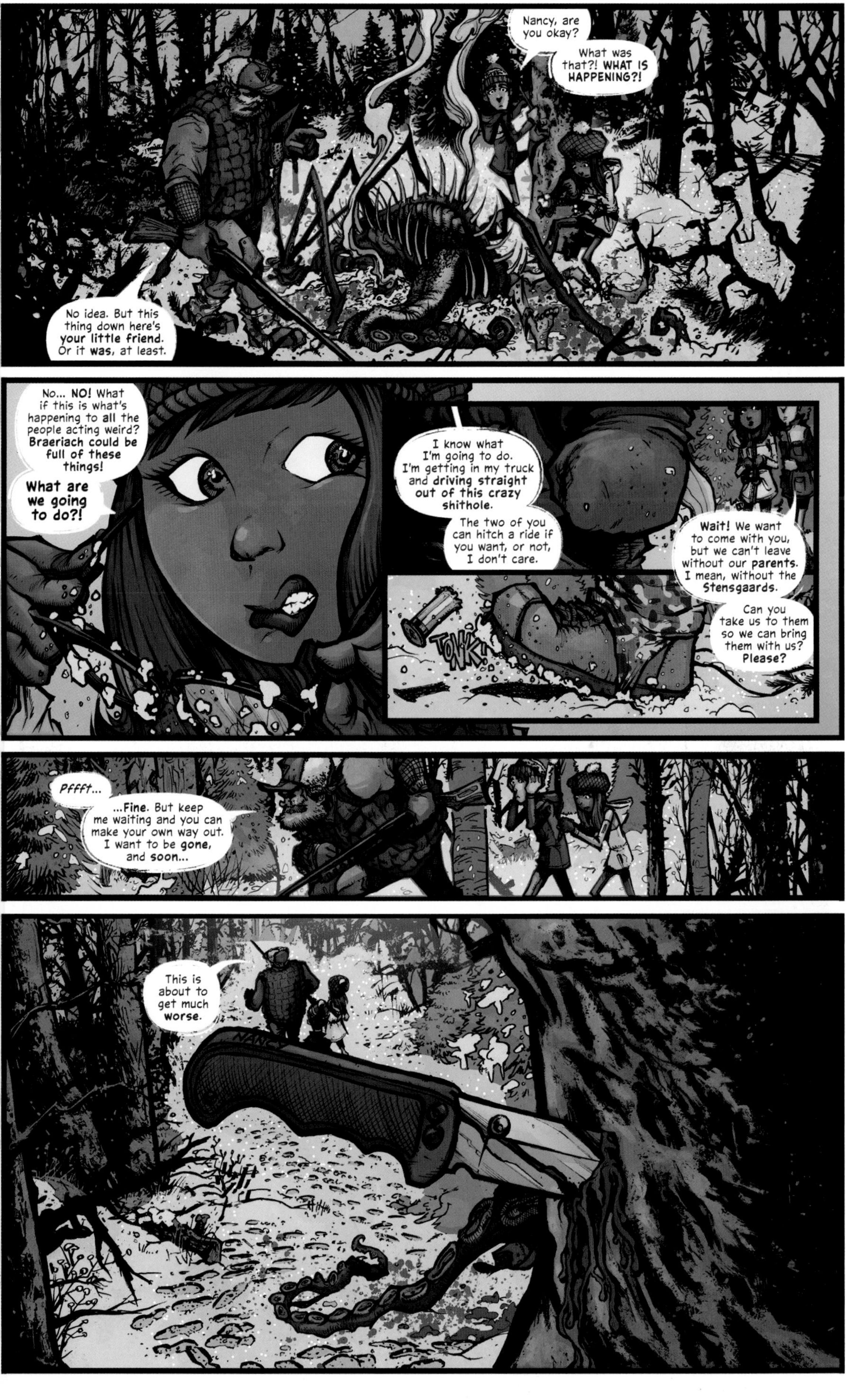
Nancy, are you okay?
What was that?! **WHAT IS HAPPENING?!**
No idea. But this thing down here's **your little friend**. Or it **was**, at least.
No... **NO!** What if this is what's happening to **all** the people acting weird? **Braeriach could be full of these things!**
What are we going to do?!
I know what I'm going to do. I'm getting in my truck and **driving straight out of this crazy shithole.**
The two of you can hitch a ride if you want, or not, I don't care.
Wait! We want to come with you, but we can't leave without our **parents**. I mean, without the **Stensgaards**.
TONK!
Can you take us to them so we can bring them with us? **Please?**
Pffft...
...**Fine**. But keep me waiting and you can make your own way out. I want to be **gone**, and **soon**...
This is about to get much **worse**.
NANCY

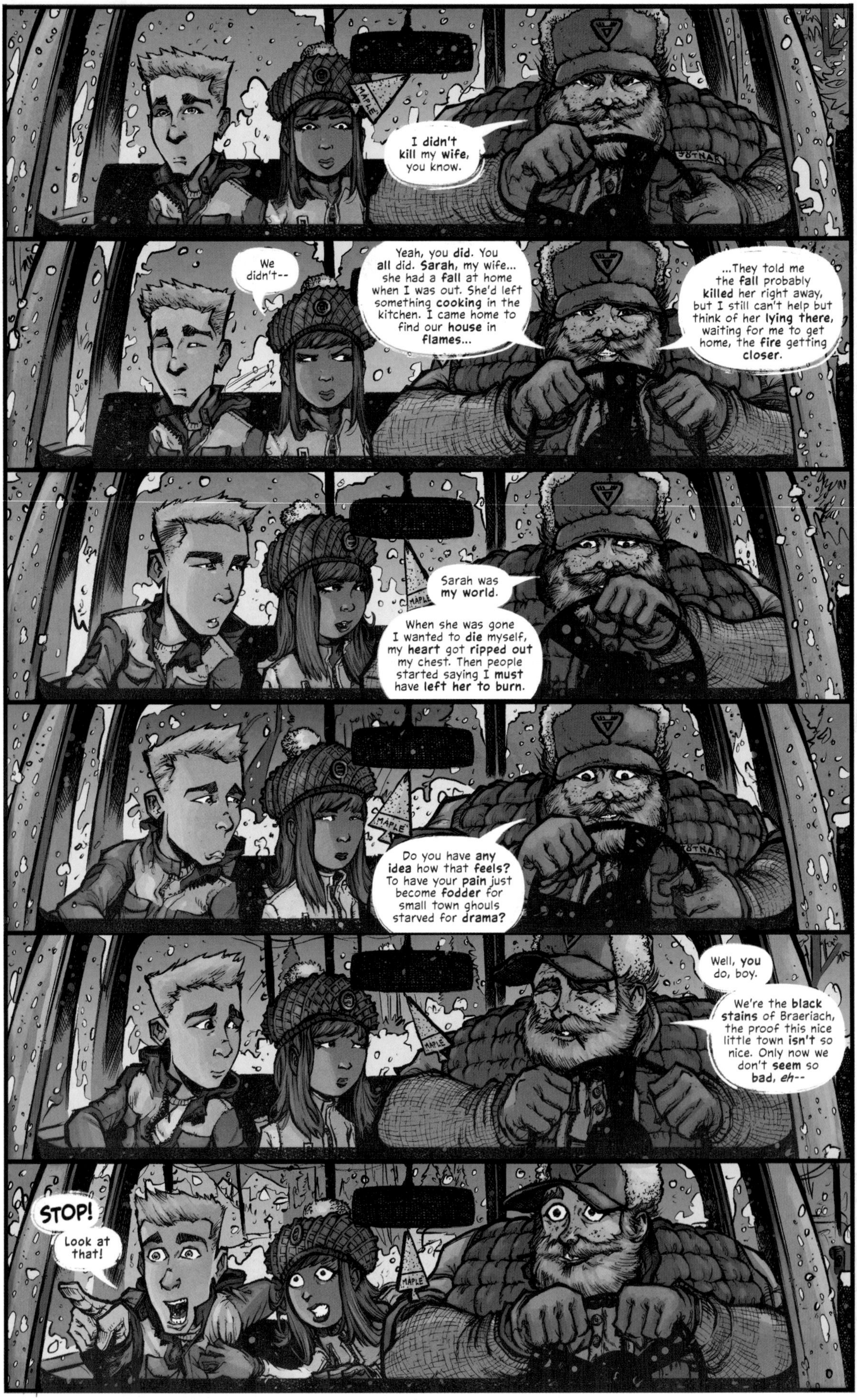

I didn't kill my wife, you know.
We didn't--
Yeah, you did. You all did. Sarah, my wife... she had a fall at home when I was out. She'd left something cooking in the kitchen. I came home to find our house in flames...
...They told me the fall probably killed her right away, but I still can't help but think of her lying there, waiting for me to get home, the fire getting closer.
Sarah was my world.
When she was gone I wanted to die myself, my heart got ripped out my chest. Then people started saying I must have left her to burn.
Do you have any idea how that feels? To have your pain just become fodder for small town ghouls starved for drama?
Well, you do, boy.
We're the black stains of Braeriach, the proof this nice little town isn't so nice. Only now we don't seem so bad, eh--
STOP!
Look at that!

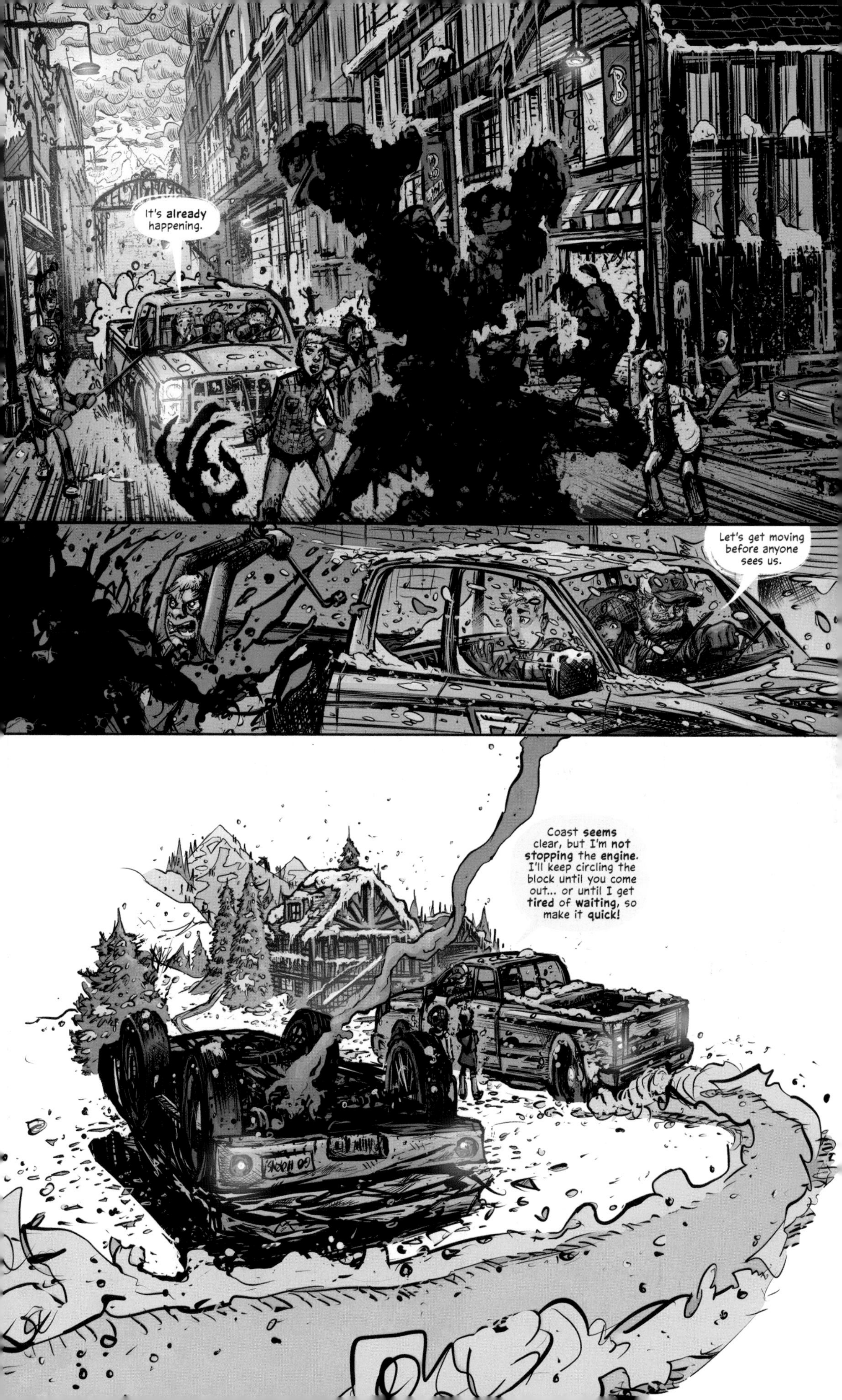
It's already happening.
Let's get moving before anyone sees us.
Coast seems clear, but I'm not stopping the engine. I'll keep circling the block until you come out... or until I get tired of waiting, so make it quick!
GO HORNS

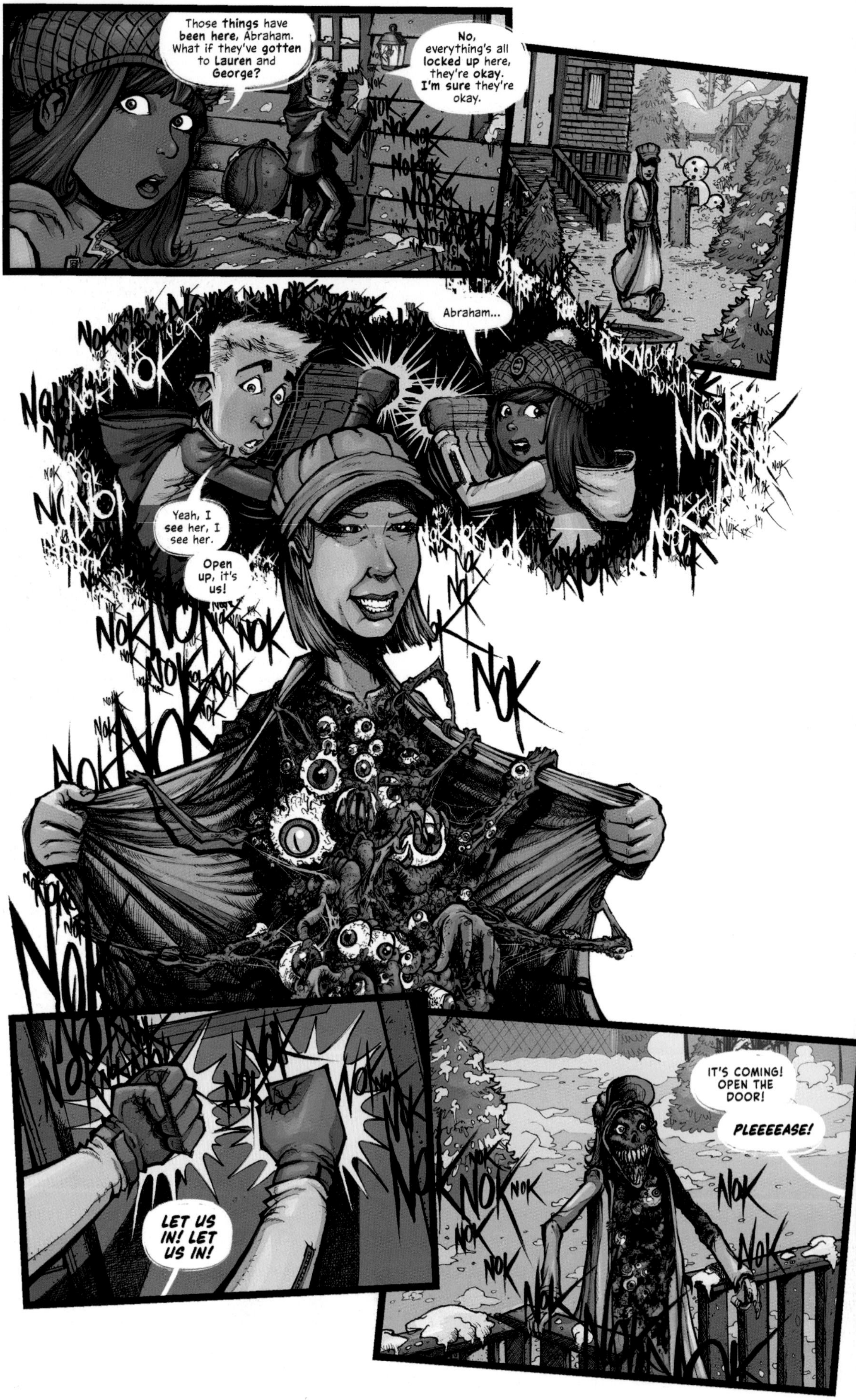

Those **things** have **been here**, Abraham. What if they've **gotten** to **Lauren** and **George?**
No, everything's all **locked up** here, they're **okay. I'm sure** they're okay.
NOK NOK NOK NOK
Abraham...
NOK NOK NOK
Yeah, I see her, I see her.
Open up, it's us!
NOK NOK NOK
NOK
NOK
LET US IN! LET US IN!
NOK NOK
IT'S COMING! OPEN THE DOOR!
PLEEEEASE!
NOK NOK NOK
NOK
NOK

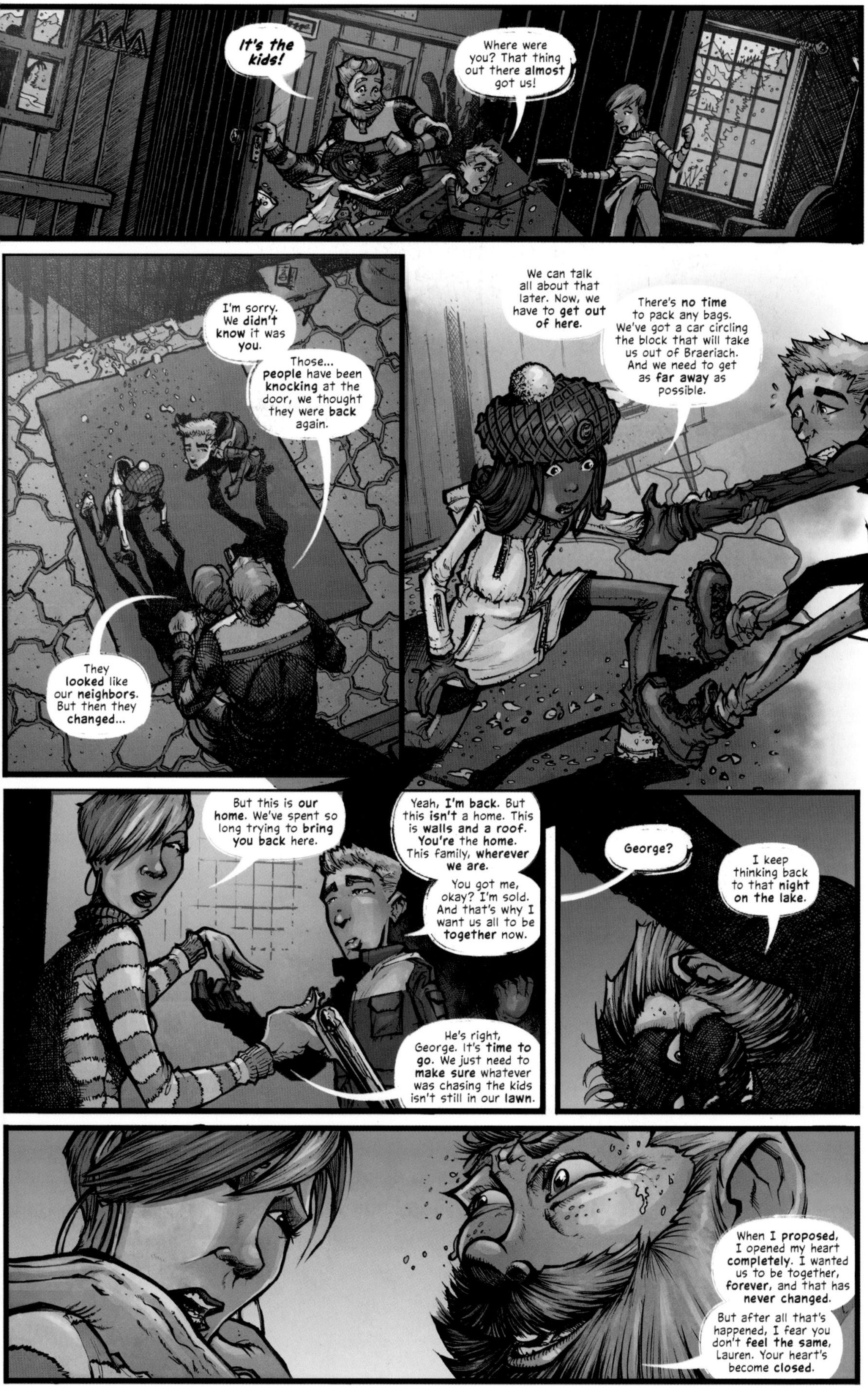
It's the kids!
Where were you? That thing out there almost got us!
I'm sorry. We didn't know it was you.
Those... people have been knocking at the door, we thought they were back again.
They looked like our neighbors. But then they changed...
We can talk all about that later. Now, we have to get out of here.
There's no time to pack any bags. We've got a car circling the block that will take us out of Braeriach. And we need to get as far away as possible.
But this is our home. We've spent so long trying to bring you back here.
Yeah, I'm back. But this isn't a home. This is walls and a roof. You're the home. This family, wherever we are.
You got me, okay? I'm sold. And that's why I want us all to be together now.
He's right, George. It's time to go. We just need to make sure whatever was chasing the kids isn't still in our lawn.
George?
I keep thinking back to that night on the lake.
When I proposed, I opened my heart completely. I wanted us to be together, forever, and that has never changed.
But after all that's happened, I fear you don't feel the same, Lauren. Your heart's become closed.

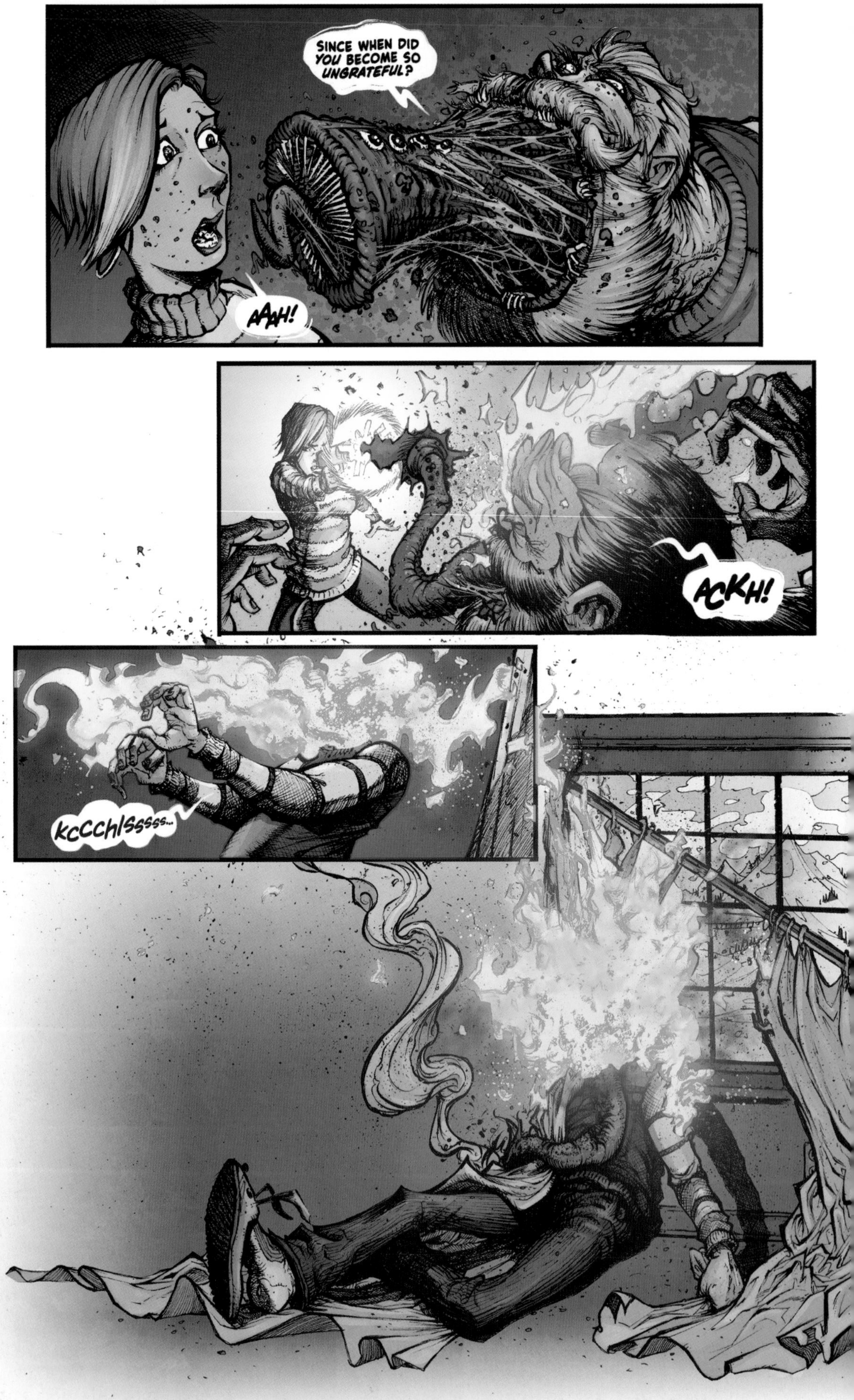
SINCE WHEN DID YOU BECOME SO UNGRATEFUL?
AAAH!
ACKH!
kcCchlsssss...

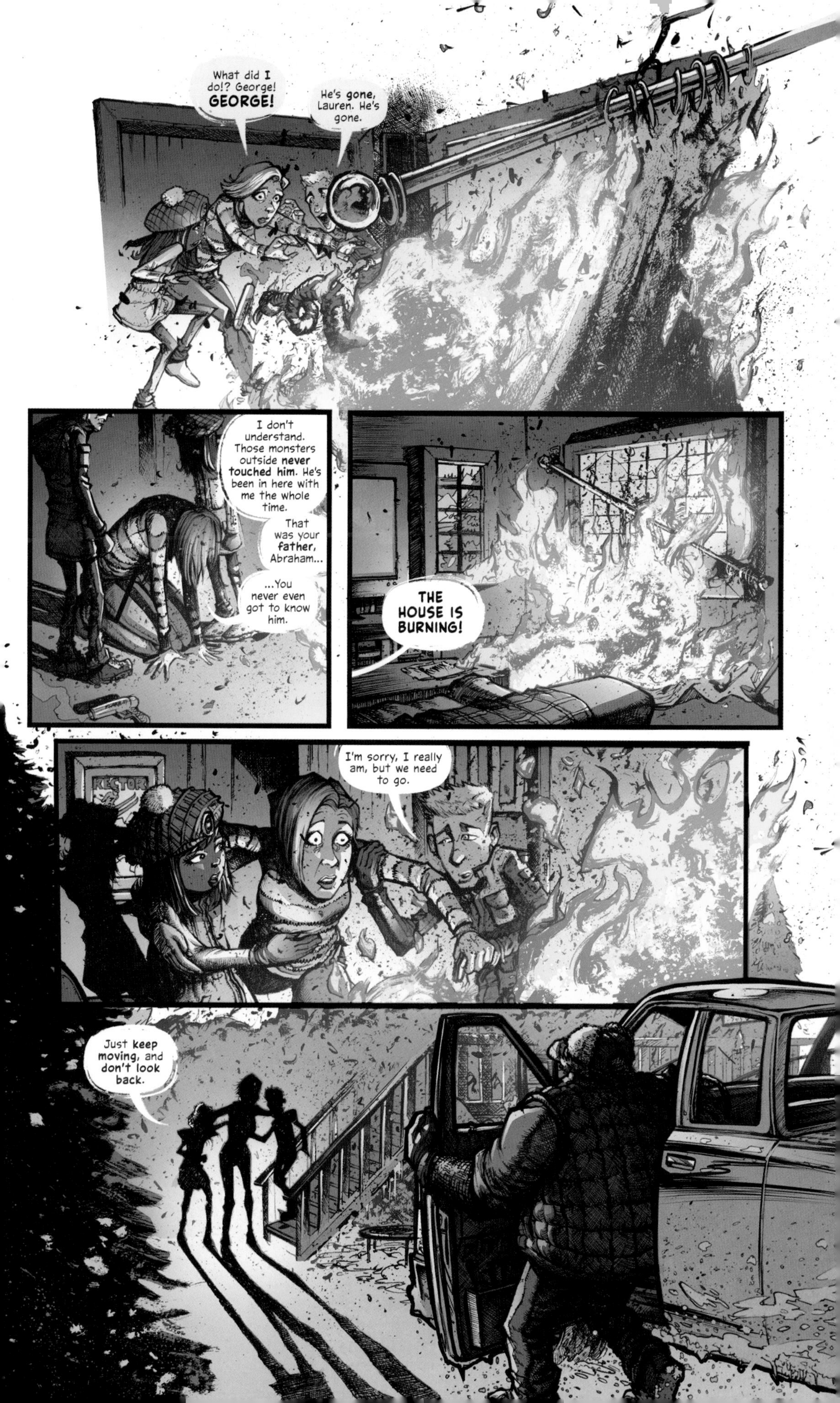

What did I do!? George! GEORGE!
He's gone, Lauren. He's gone.
I don't understand. Those monsters outside never touched him. He's been in here with me the whole time.
That was your father, Abraham...
...You never even got to know him.
THE HOUSE IS BURNING!
I'm sorry, I really am, but we need to go.
Just keep moving, and don't look back.

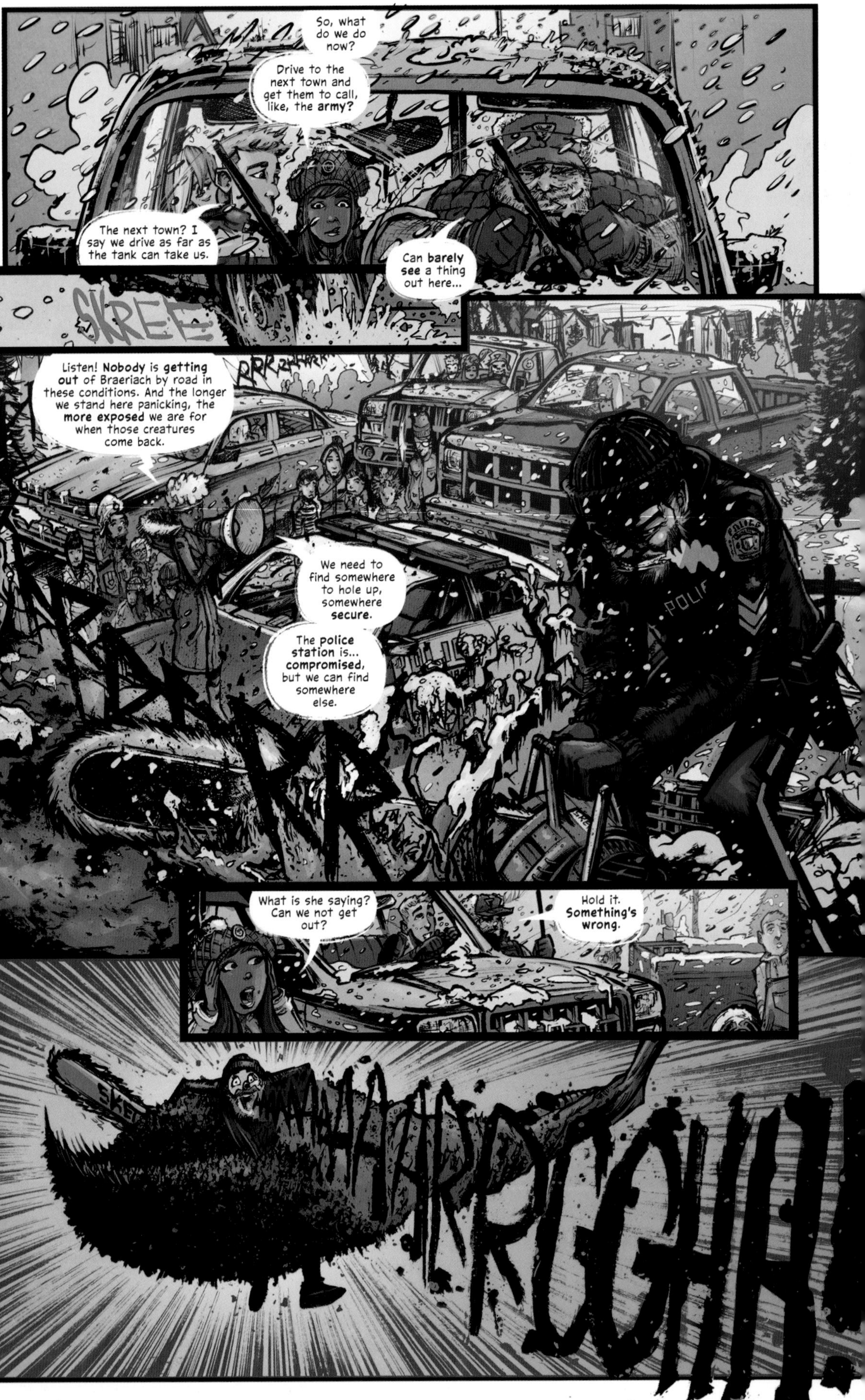

So, what do we do now?
Drive to the next town and get them to call, like, the **army?**
The next town? I say we drive as far as the tank can take us.
Can **barely see** a thing out here...
SKREE
Listen! **Nobody** is **getting out** of Braeriach by road in these conditions. And the longer we stand here panicking, the **more exposed** we are for when those creatures come back.
We need to find somewhere to hole up, somewhere **secure**.
The **police station** is... **compromised,** but we can find somewhere else.
What is she saying? Can we not get out?
Hold it. **Something's wrong.**

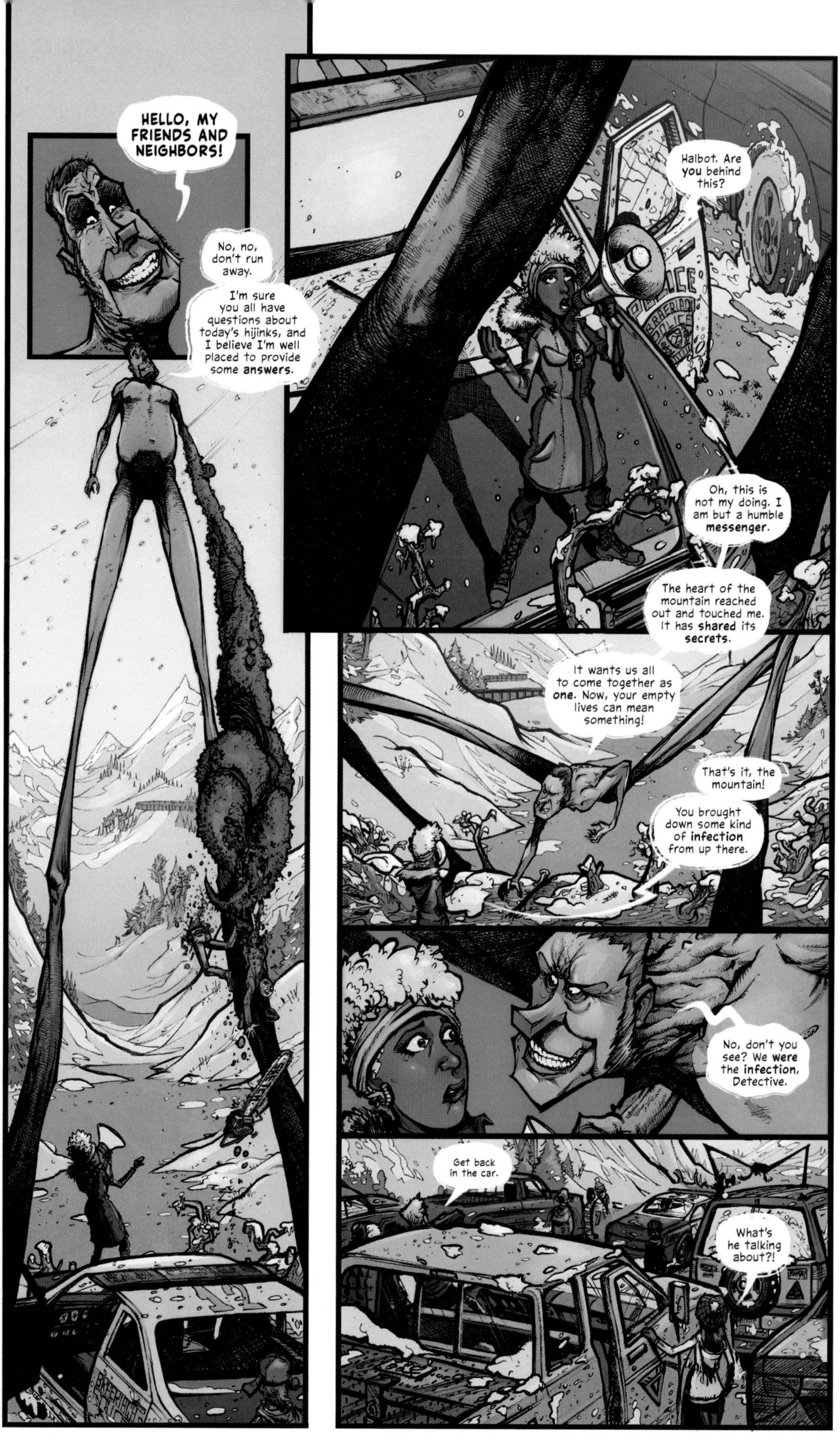
HELLO, MY FRIENDS AND NEIGHBORS!
No, no, don't run away.
I'm sure you all have questions about today's hijinks, and I believe I'm well placed to provide some **answers**.
Halbot. Are **you** behind this?
Oh, this is not my doing. I am but a humble **messenger**.
The heart of the mountain reached out and touched me. It has **shared** its **secrets**.
It wants us all to come together as **one**. Now, your empty lives can mean something!
That's it, the mountain!
You brought down some kind of **infection** from up there.
No, don't you see? We **were** the **infection**, Detective.
Get back in the car.
What's he talking about?!

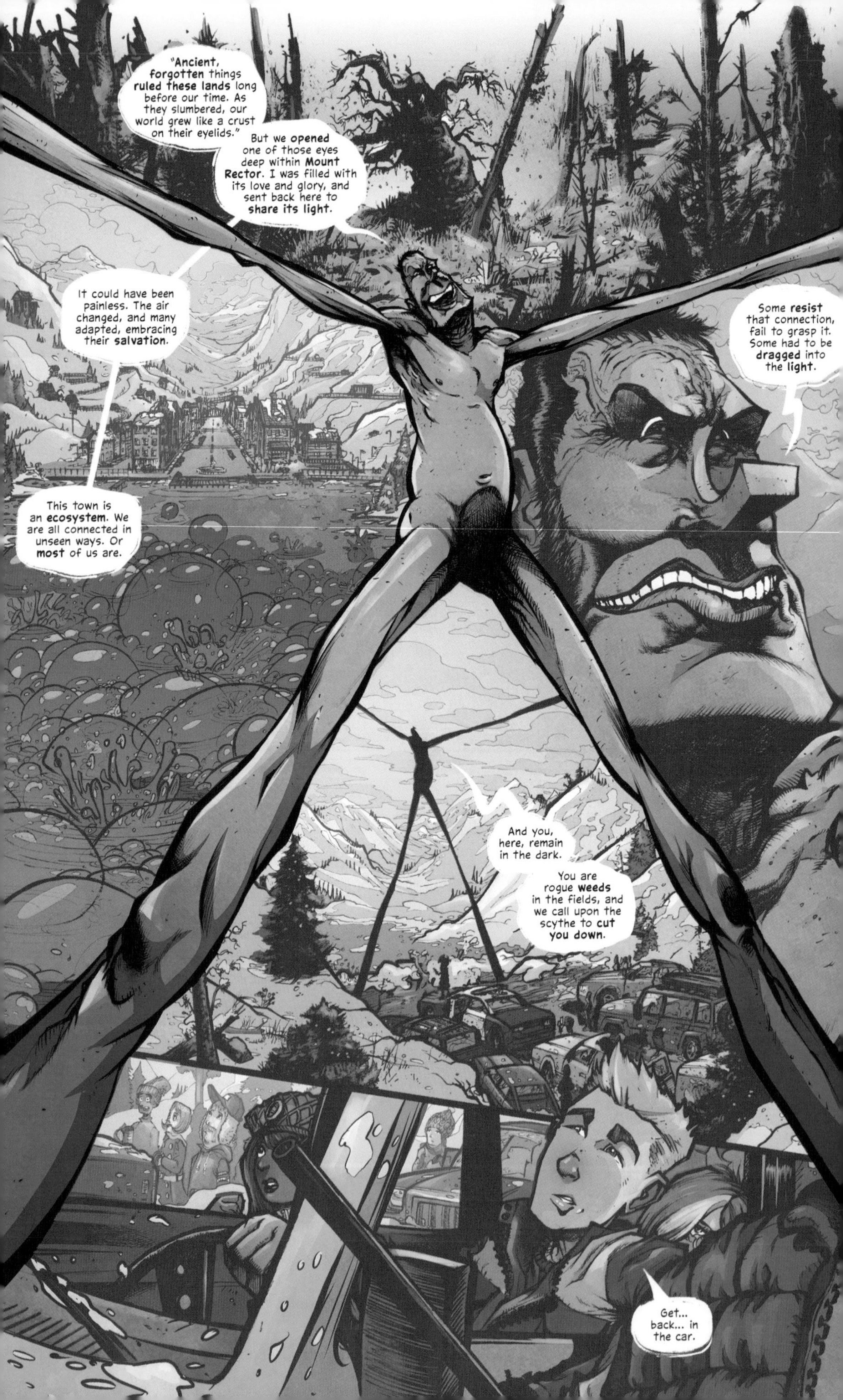
"Ancient, forgotten things ruled these lands long before our time. As they slumbered, our world grew like a crust on their eyelids."
But we opened one of those eyes deep within Mount Rector. I was filled with its love and glory, and sent back here to share its light.
It could have been painless. The air changed, and many adapted, embracing their salvation.
This town is an ecosystem. We are all connected in unseen ways. Or most of us are.
Some resist that connection, fail to grasp it. Some had to be dragged into the light.
And you, here, remain in the dark.
You are rogue weeds in the fields, and we call upon the scythe to cut you down.
Get... back... in the car.

KRR KT

FWSS

KRAK

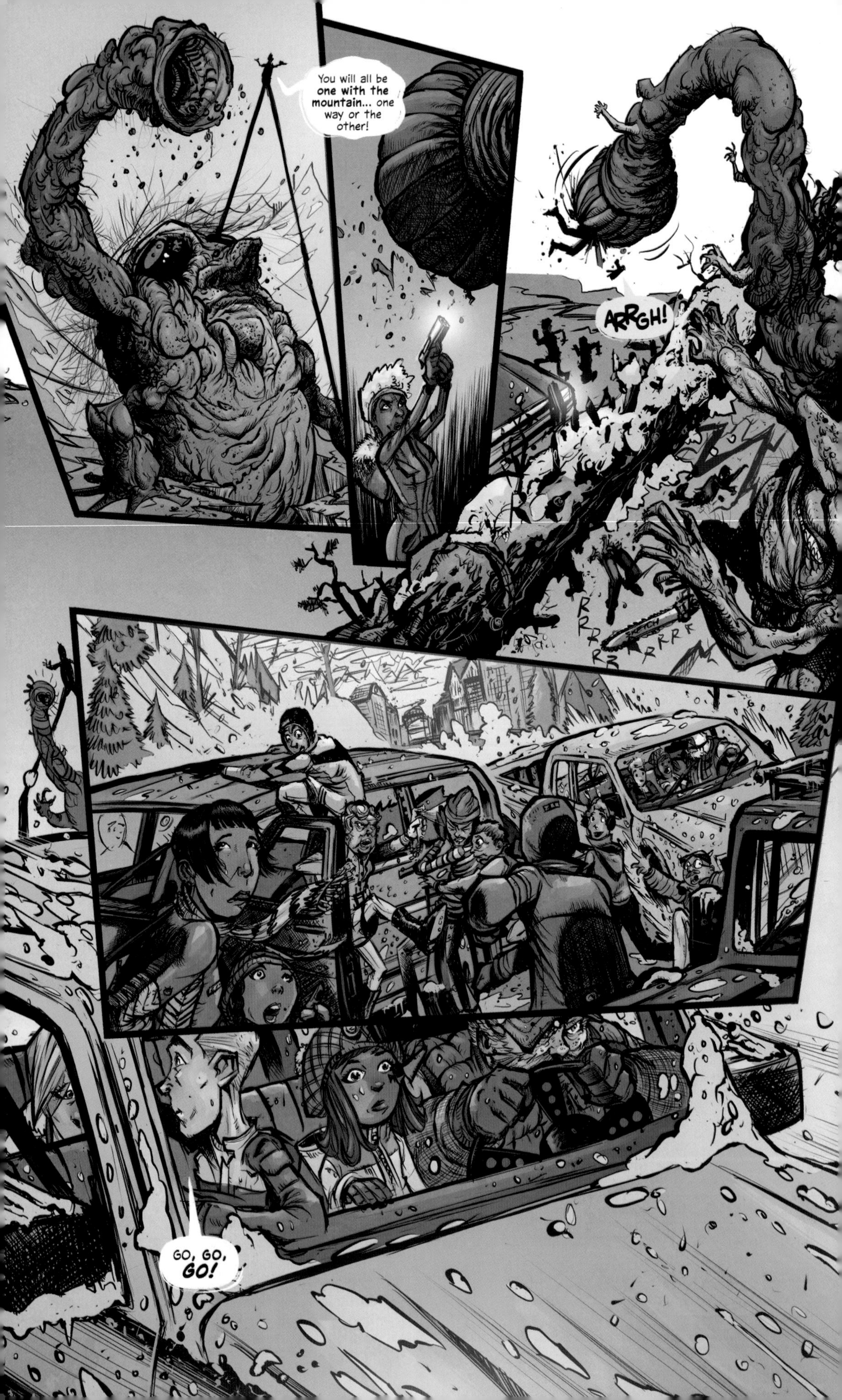
You will all be one with the mountain... one way or the other!
ARRGH!
GO, GO, GO!

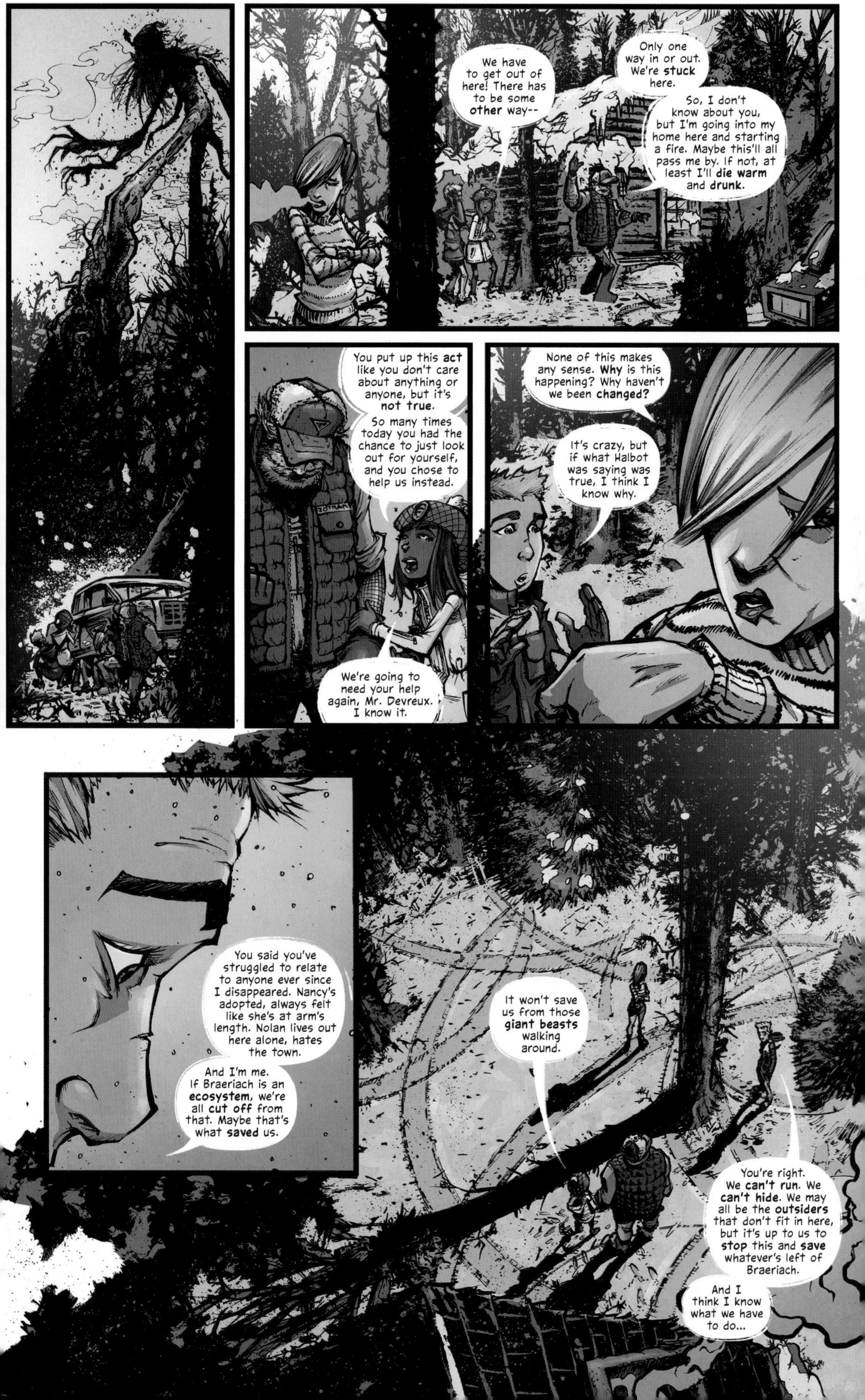
We have to get out of here! There has to be some **other** way--
Only one way in or out. We're **stuck** here.
So, I don't know about you, but I'm going into my home here and starting a fire. Maybe this'll all pass me by. If not, at least I'll **die warm** and **drunk**.
You put up this **act** like you don't care about anything or anyone, but it's **not true**.
So many times today you had the chance to just look out for yourself, and you chose to help us instead.
We're going to need your help again, Mr. Devreux. I know it.
None of this makes any sense. **Why** is this happening? Why haven't we been **changed?**
It's crazy, but if what Halbot was saying was true, I think I know why.
You said you've struggled to relate to anyone ever since I disappeared. Nancy's adopted, always felt like she's at arm's length. Nolan lives out here alone, hates the town.
And I'm me. If Braeriach is an **ecosystem**, we're all **cut off** from that. Maybe that's what **saved** us.
It won't save us from those **giant beasts** walking around.
You're right. We **can't run**. We **can't hide**. We may all be the **outsiders** that don't fit in here, but it's up to us to **stop** this and **save** whatever's left of Braeriach.
And I think I know what we have to do...

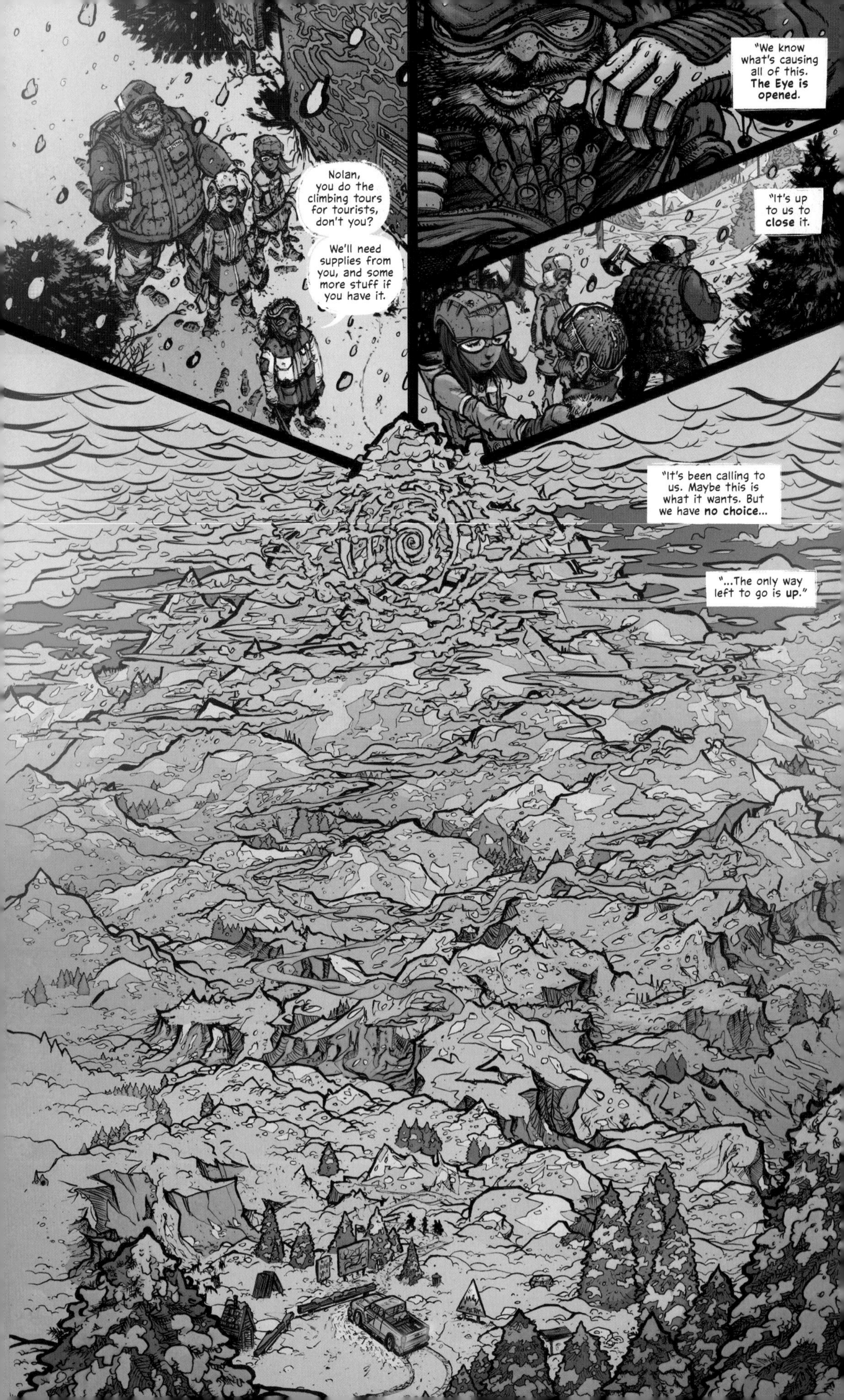
BEARS
Nolan, you do the climbing tours for tourists, don't you?
We'll need supplies from you, and some more stuff if you have it.
"We know what's causing all of this. **The Eye is opened.**
"It's up to us to **close** it.
"It's been calling to us. Maybe this is what it wants. But we have **no choice**...
"...The only way left to go is **up**."

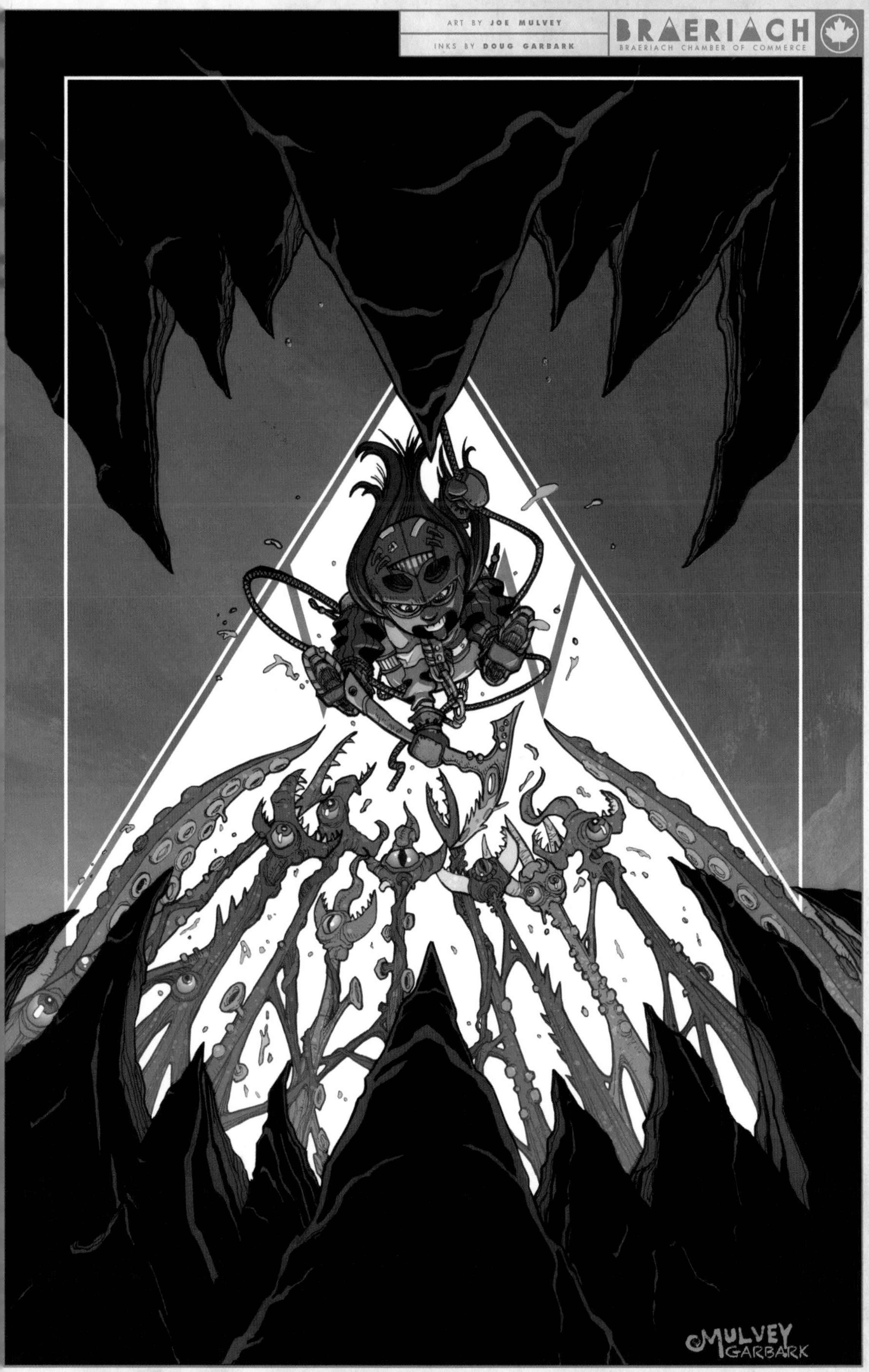

ART BY JOE MULVEY
INKS BY DOUG GARBARK
BRAERIACH
BRAERIACH CHAMBER OF COMMERCE
©MULVEY GARBARK

BRAERIACH
BRAERIACH CHAMBER OF COMMERCE

ART BY RYAN LEE

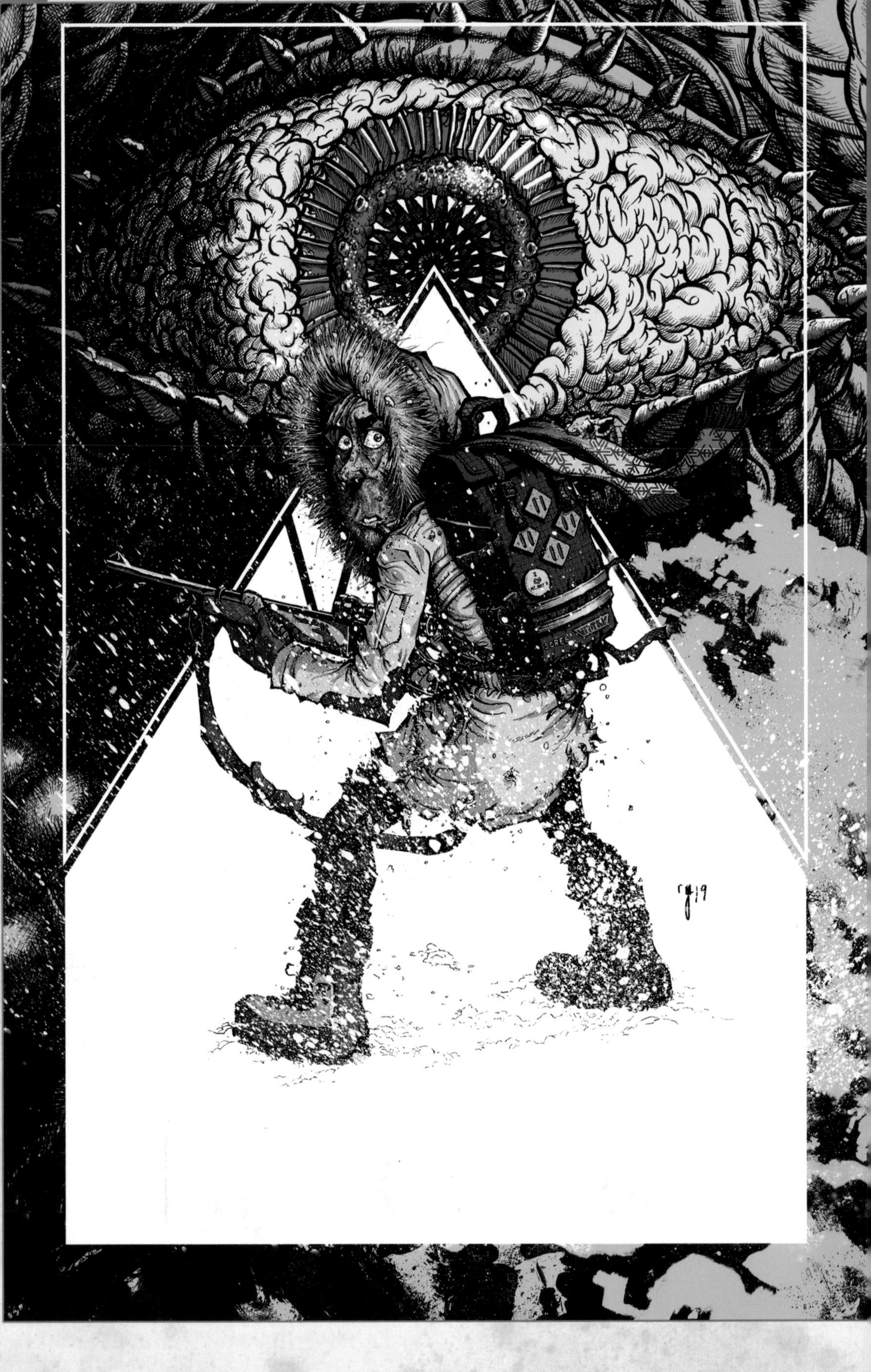

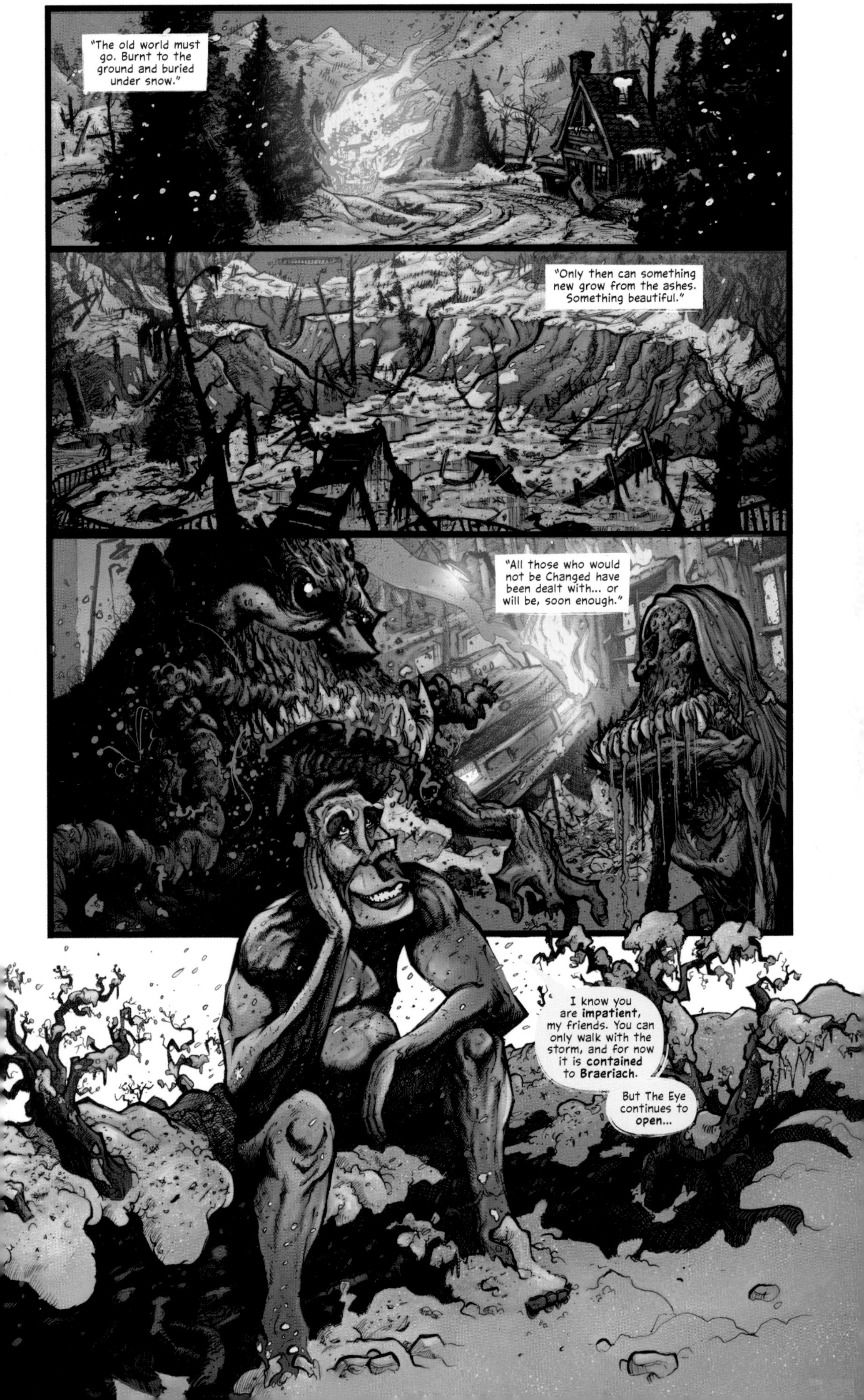
"The old world must go. Burnt to the ground and buried under snow."
"Only then can something new grow from the ashes. Something beautiful."
"All those who would not be Changed have been dealt with... or will be, soon enough."
I know you are **impatient**, my friends. You can only walk with the storm, and for now it is **contained** to **Braeriach**.
But The Eye continues to **open**...

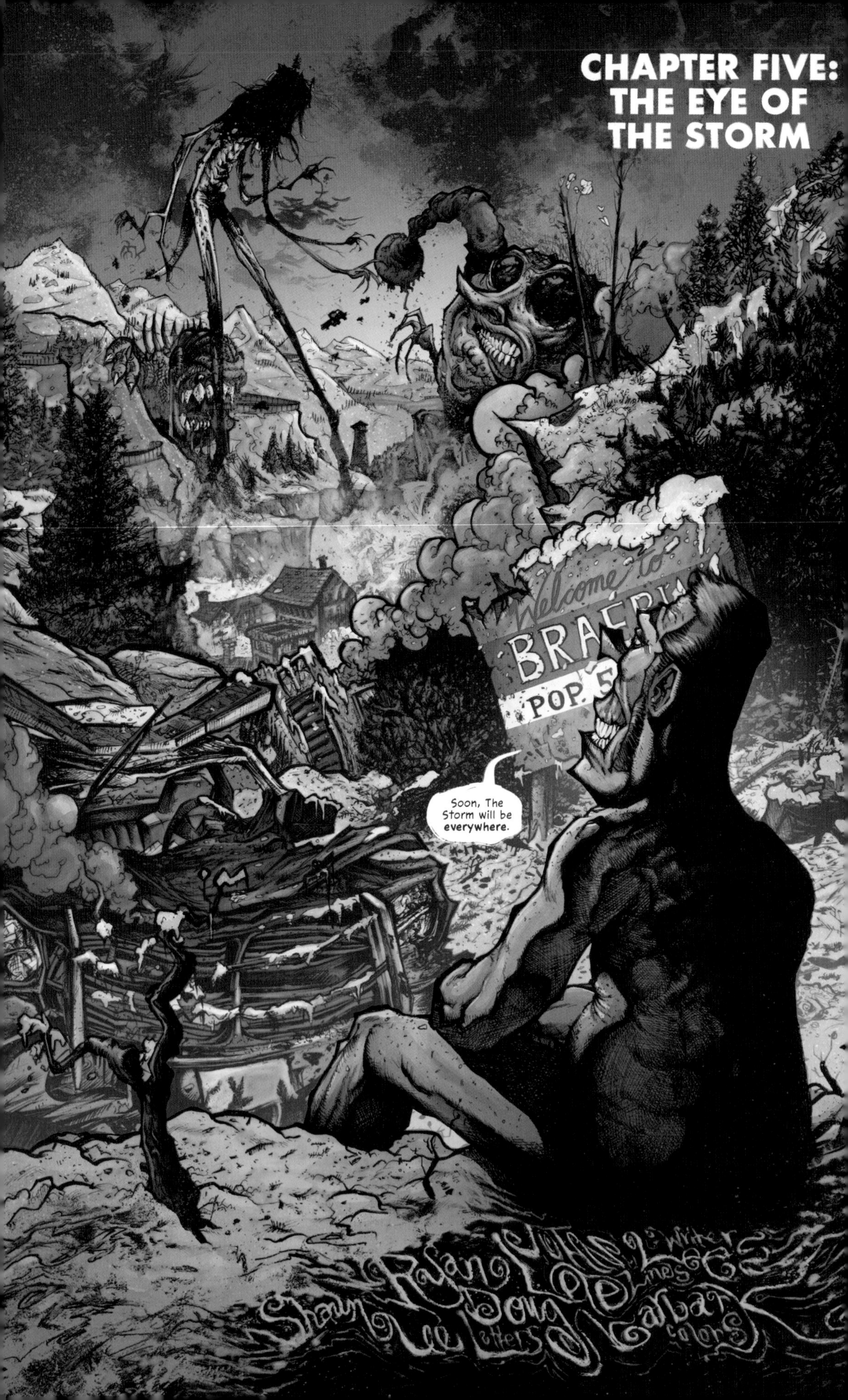
CHAPTER FIVE:
THE EYE OF
THE STORM
Welcome to
Soon, The Storm will be **everywhere**.
writer
lines
Shawn Lee letters
Doug Garbark colors

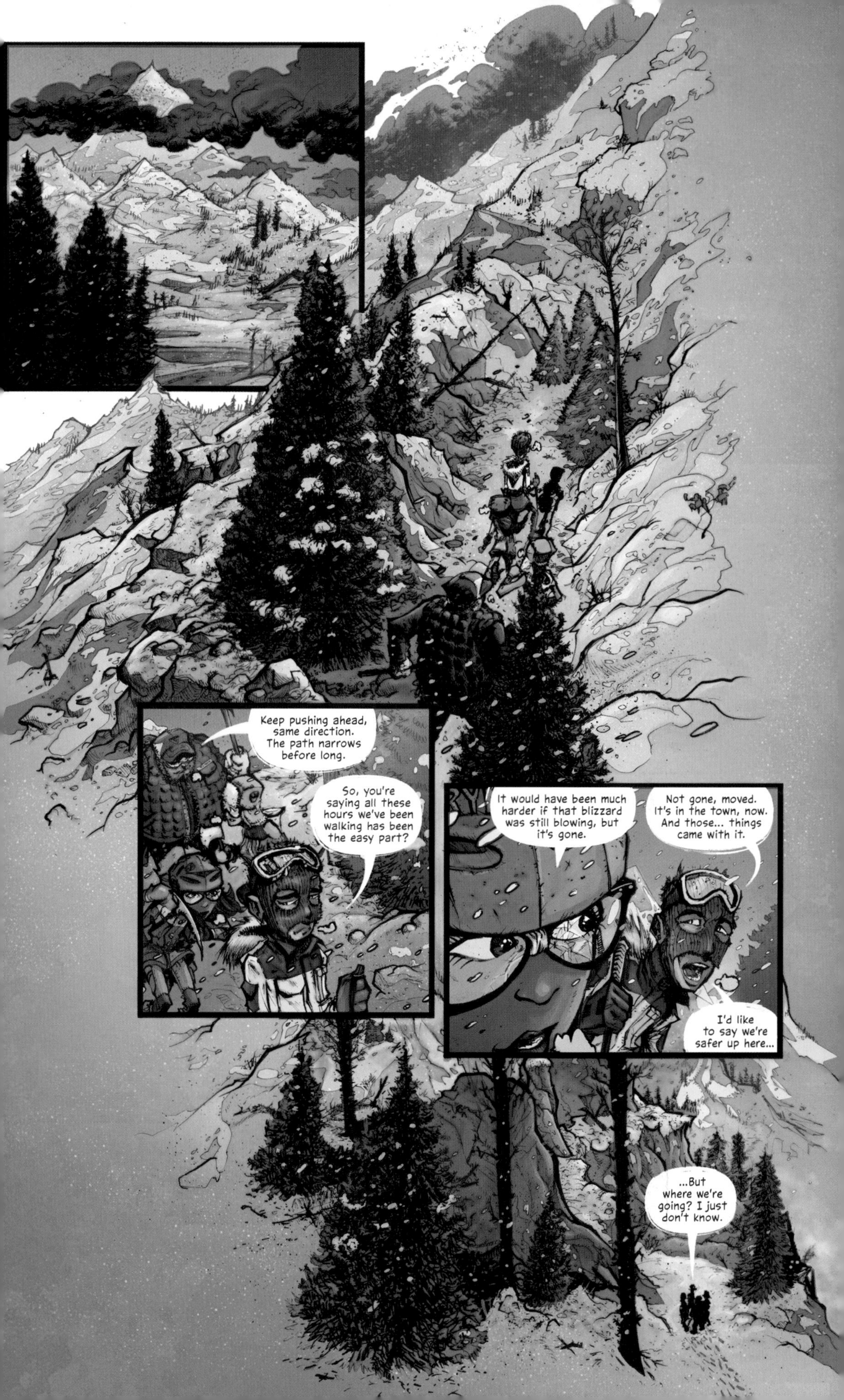
Keep pushing ahead, same direction. The path narrows before long.
So, you're saying all these hours we've been walking has been the easy part?
It would have been much harder if that blizzard was still blowing, but it's gone.
Not gone, moved. It's in the town, now. And those... things came with it.
I'd like to say we're safer up here...
...But where we're going? I just don't know.

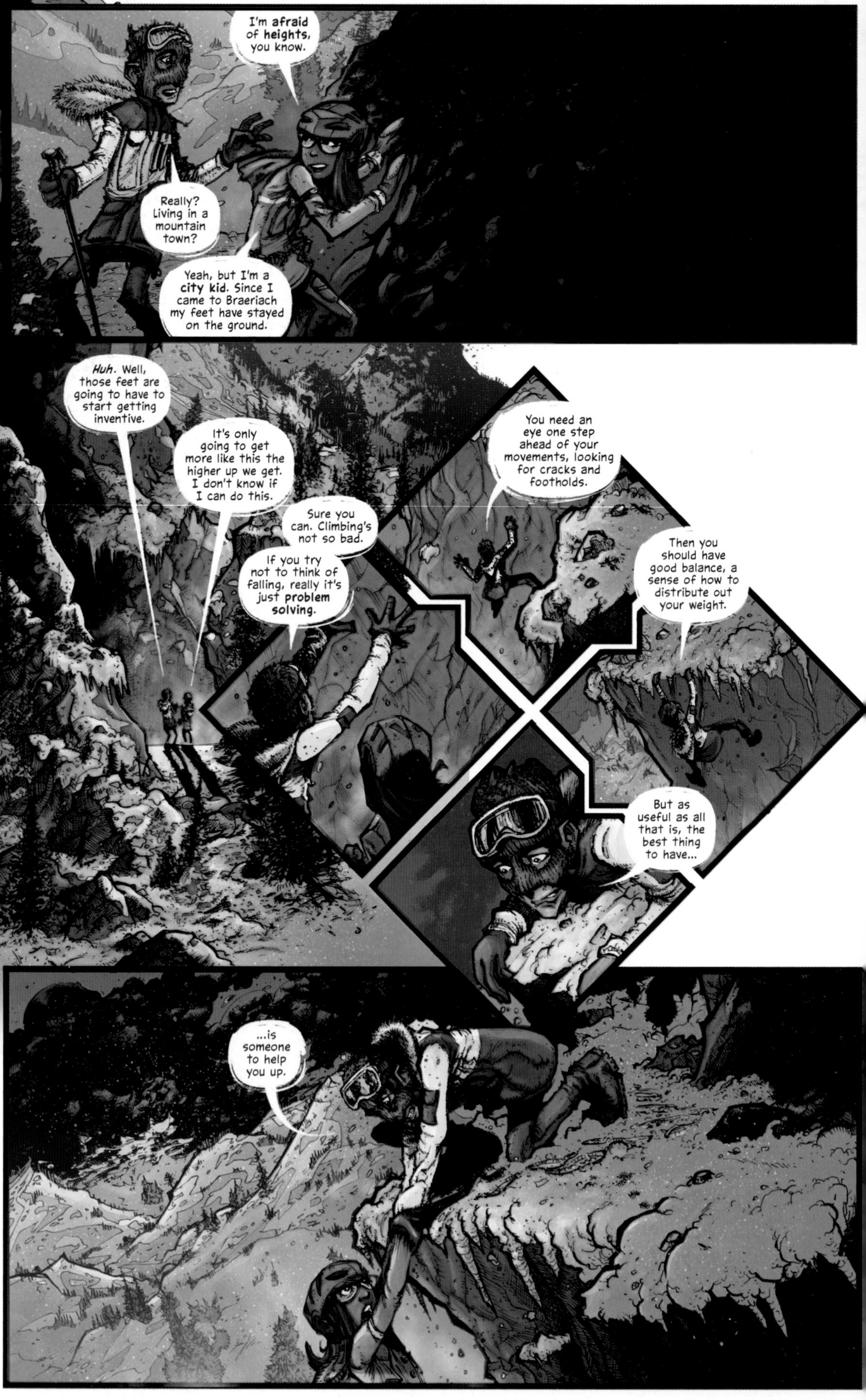
I'm afraid of heights, you know.
Really? Living in a mountain town?
Yeah, but I'm a city kid. Since I came to Braeriach my feet have stayed on the ground.
Huh. Well, those feet are going to have to start getting inventive.
It's only going to get more like this the higher up we get. I don't know if I can do this.
Sure you can. Climbing's not so bad.
If you try not to think of falling, really it's just problem solving.
You need an eye one step ahead of your movements, looking for cracks and footholds.
Then you should have good balance, a sense of how to distribute out your weight.
But as useful as all that is, the best thing to have...
...is someone to help you up.

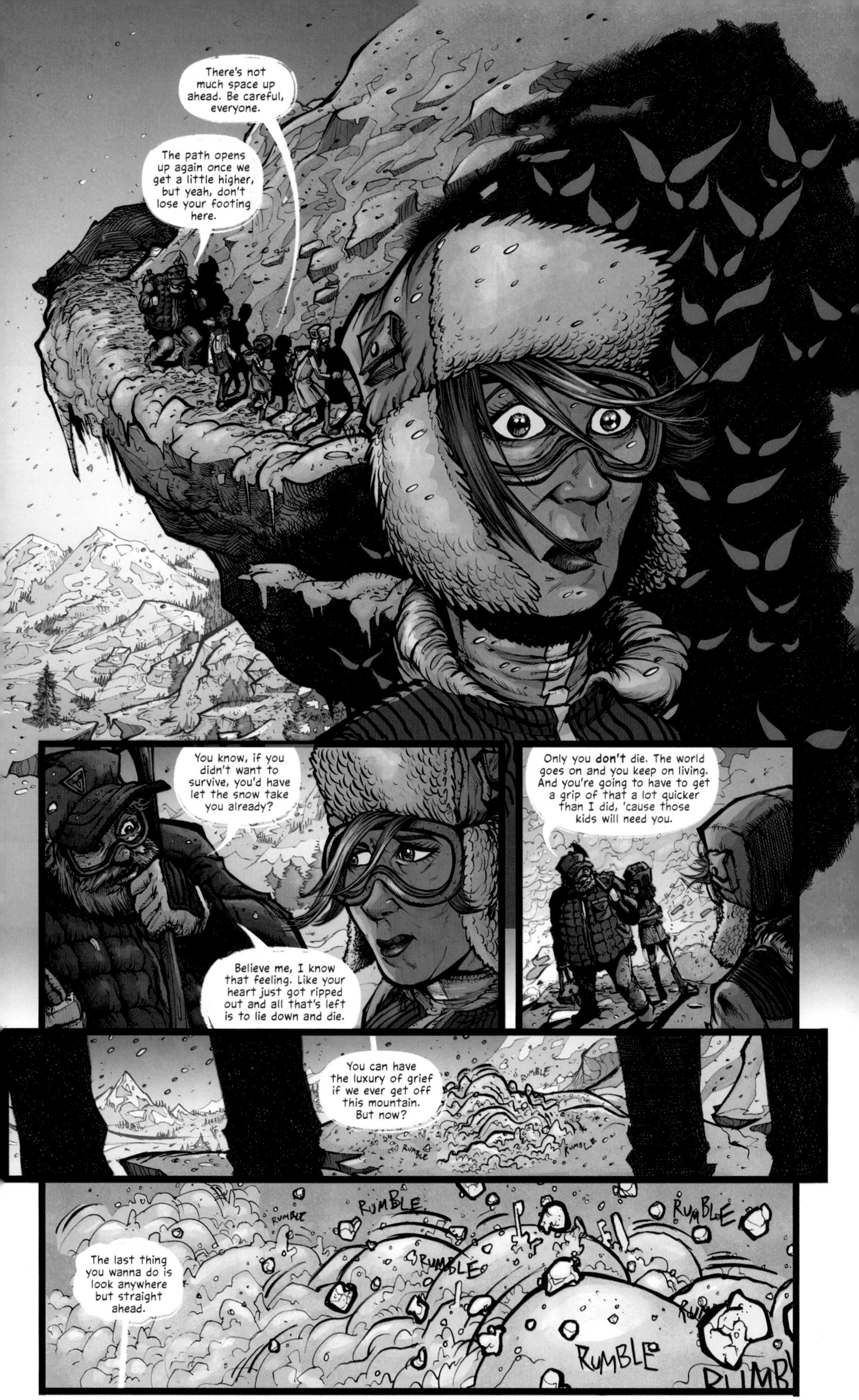
There's not much space up ahead. Be careful, everyone.
The path opens up again once we get a little higher, but yeah, don't lose your footing here.
You know, if you didn't want to survive, you'd have let the snow take you already?
Believe me, I know that feeling. Like your heart just got ripped out and all that's left is to lie down and die.
Only you **don't** die. The world goes on and you keep on living. And you're going to have to get a grip of that a lot quicker than I did, 'cause those kids will need you.
You can have the luxury of grief if we ever get off this mountain. But now?
RUMBLE
RUMBLE
RUMBLE
The last thing you wanna do is look anywhere but straight ahead.
RUMBLE
RUMBLE
RUMBLE
RUMBLE

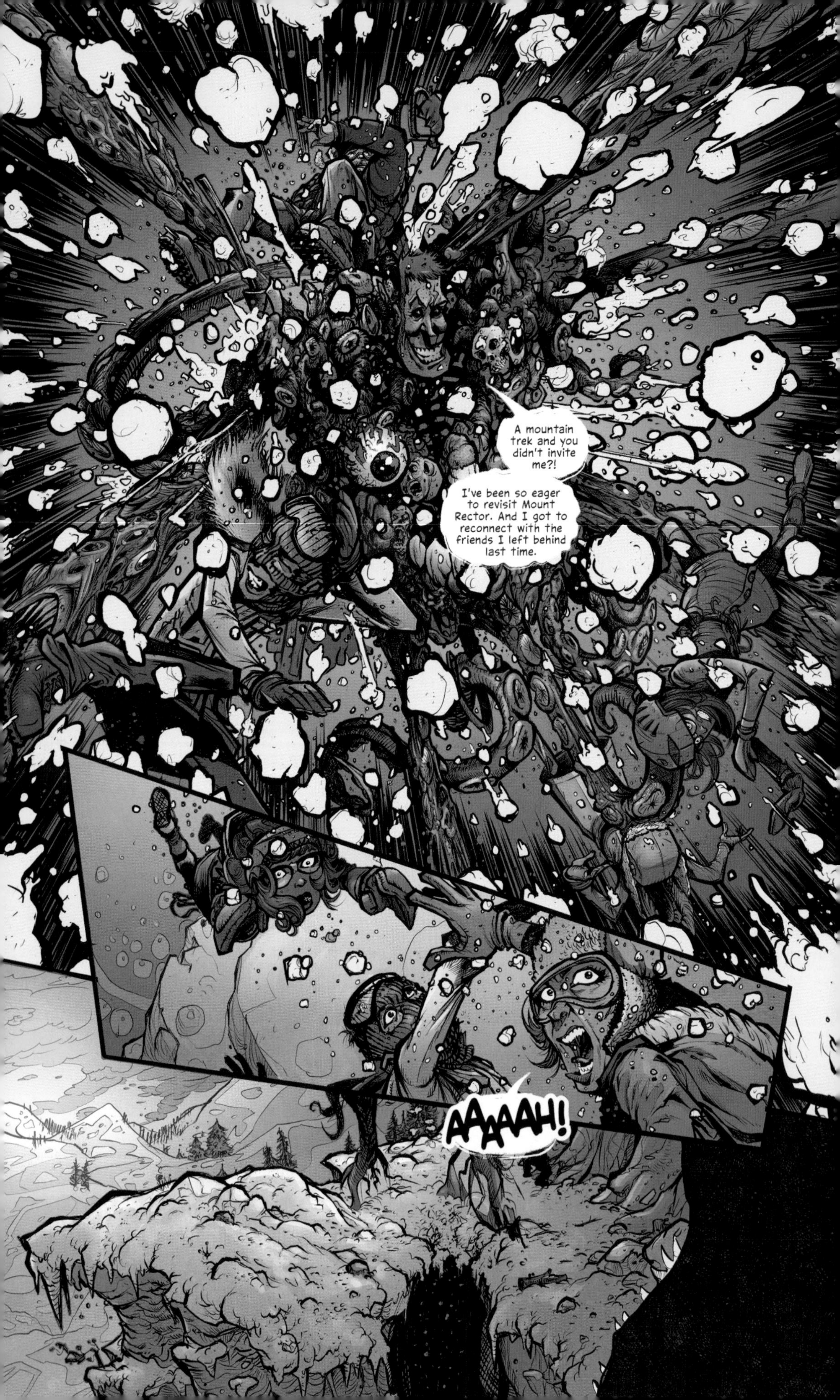
A mountain trek and you didn't invite me?!
I've been so eager to revisit Mount Rector. And I got to reconnect with the friends I left behind last time.
AAAAAH!

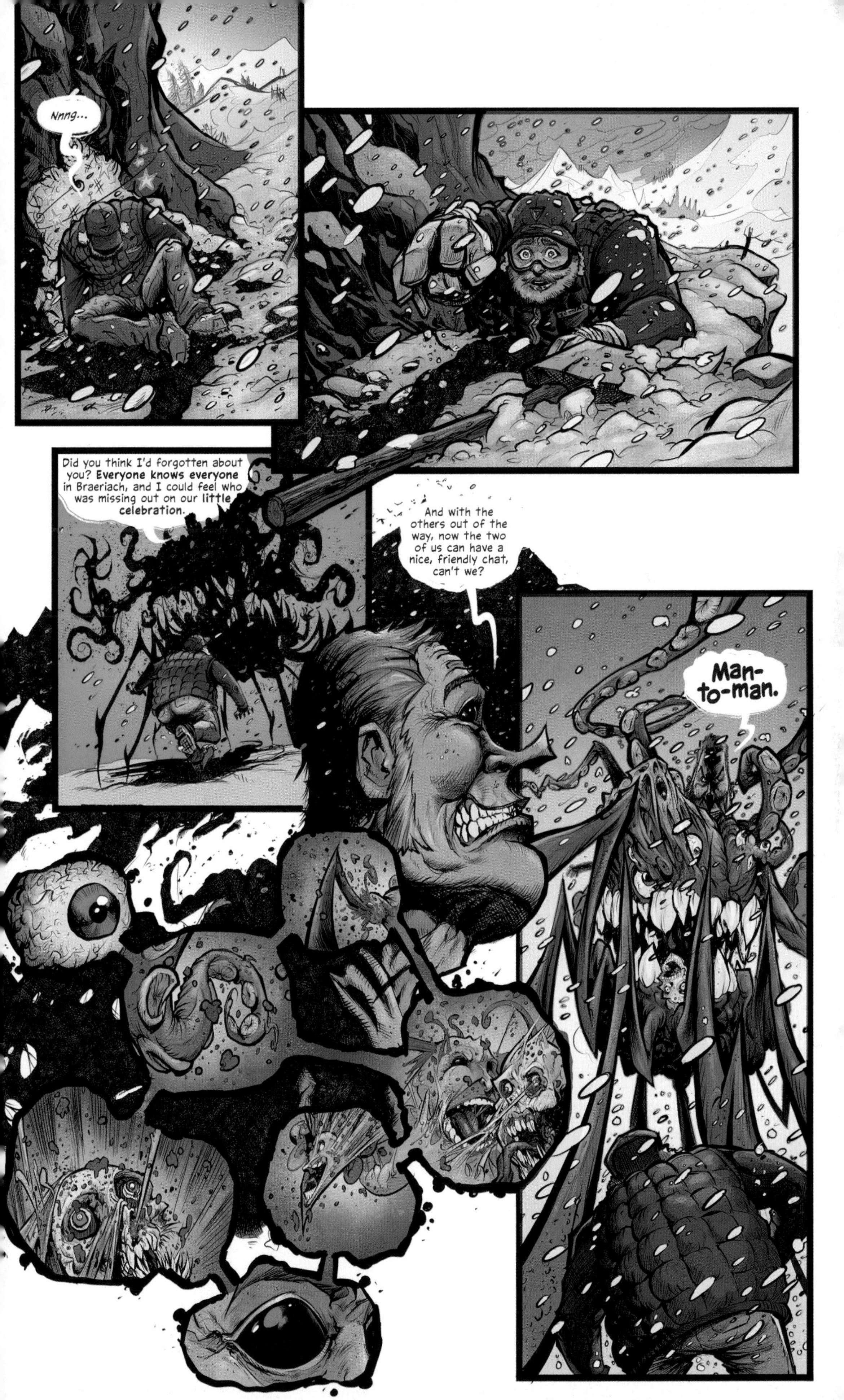
Nnng...
Did you think I'd forgotten about you? **Everyone knows everyone** in Braeriach, and I could feel who was missing out on our **little celebration.**
And with the others out of the way, now the two of us can have a nice, friendly chat, can't we?
Man-to-man.

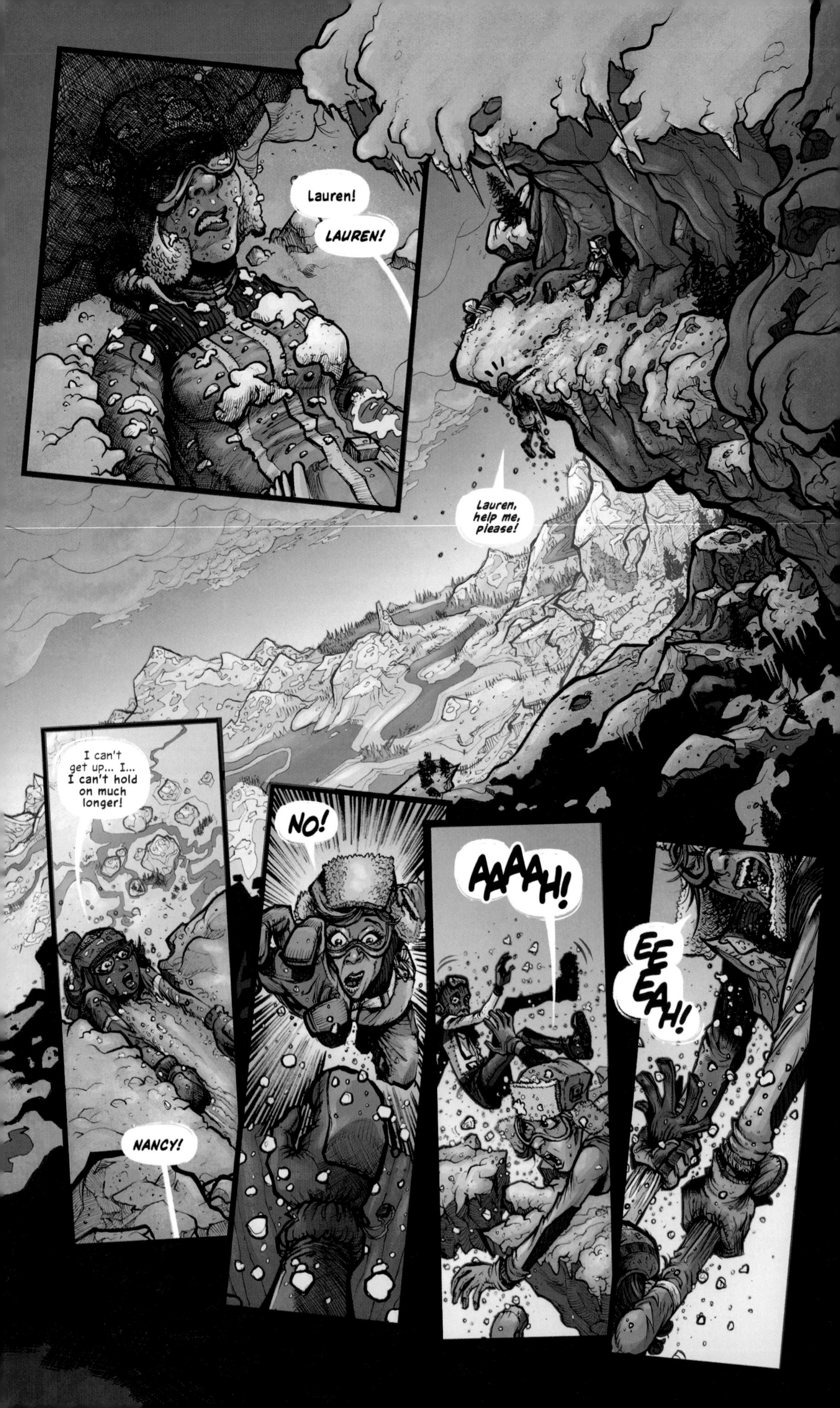
Lauren!
LAUREN!
Lauren, help me, please!
I can't get up... I... I can't hold on much longer!
NANCY!
NO!
AAAAH!
EEEAAH!

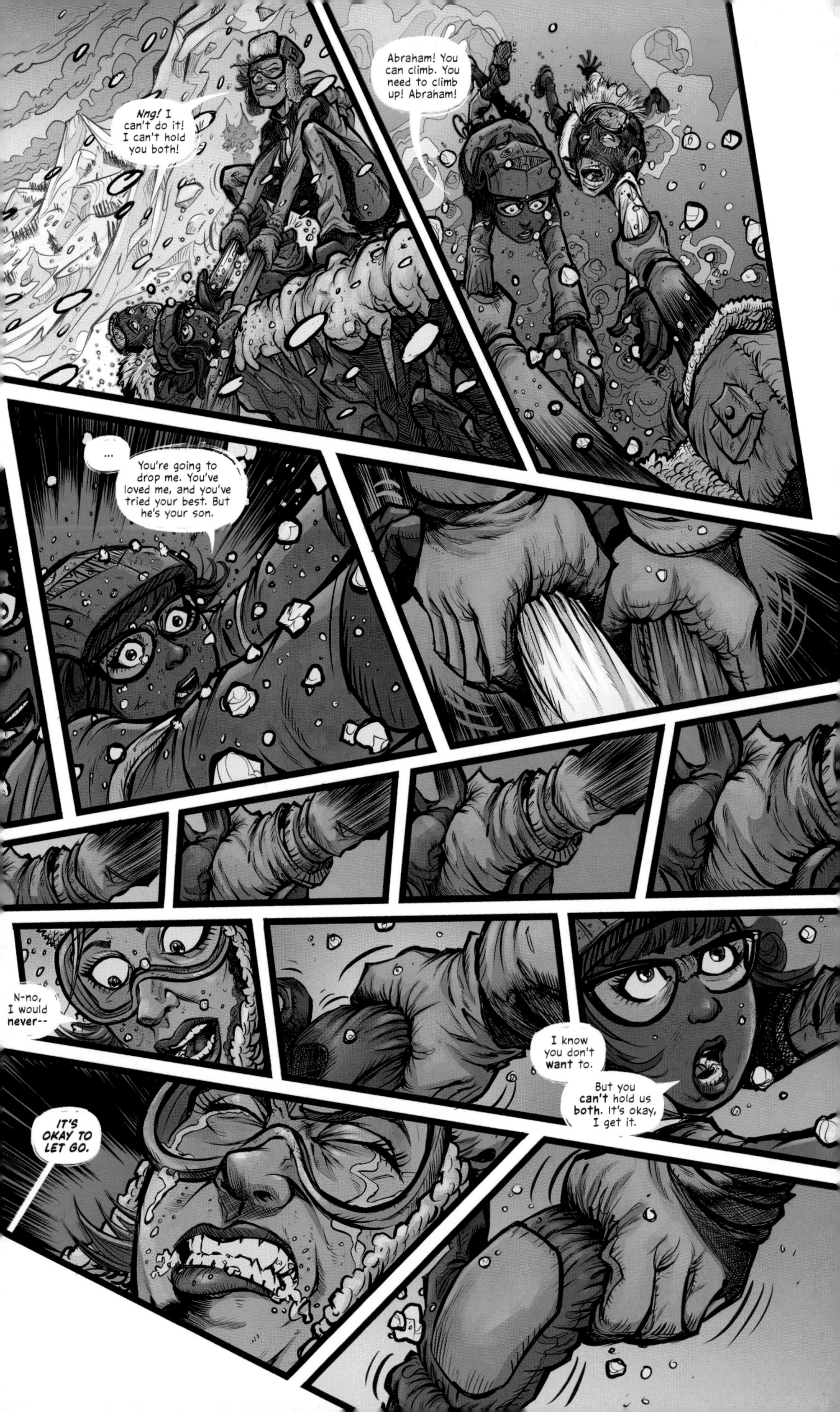

Nng! I can't do it! I can't hold you both!
Abraham! You can climb. You need to climb up! Abraham!
...
You're going to drop me. You've loved me, and you've tried your best. But he's your son.
N-no, I would never--
I know you don't want to.
But you can't hold us both. It's okay, I get it.
IT'S OKAY TO LET GO.

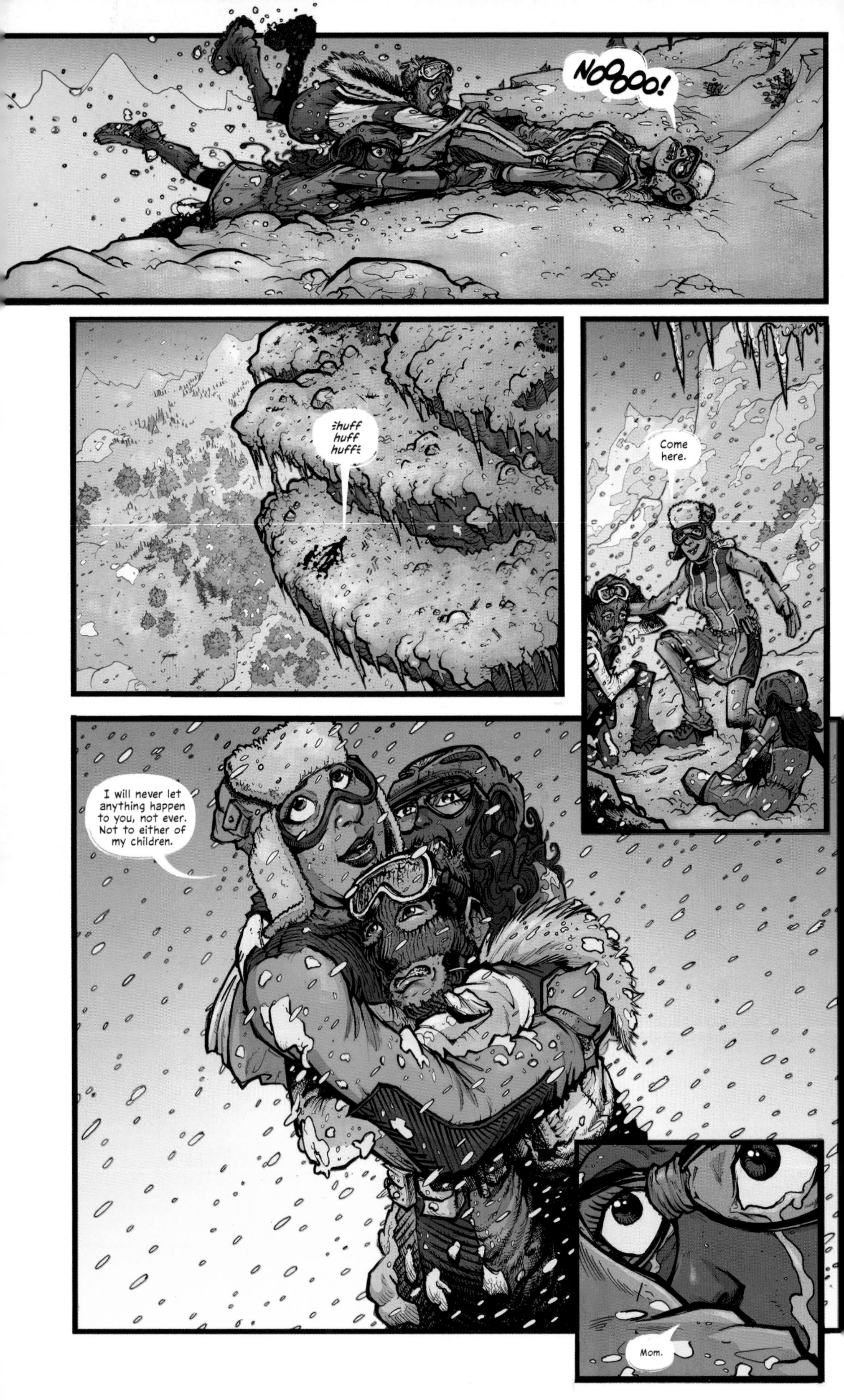
NOOOOO!
huff
huff
huff
Come
here.
I will never let
anything happen
to you, not ever.
Not to either of
my children.
Mom.

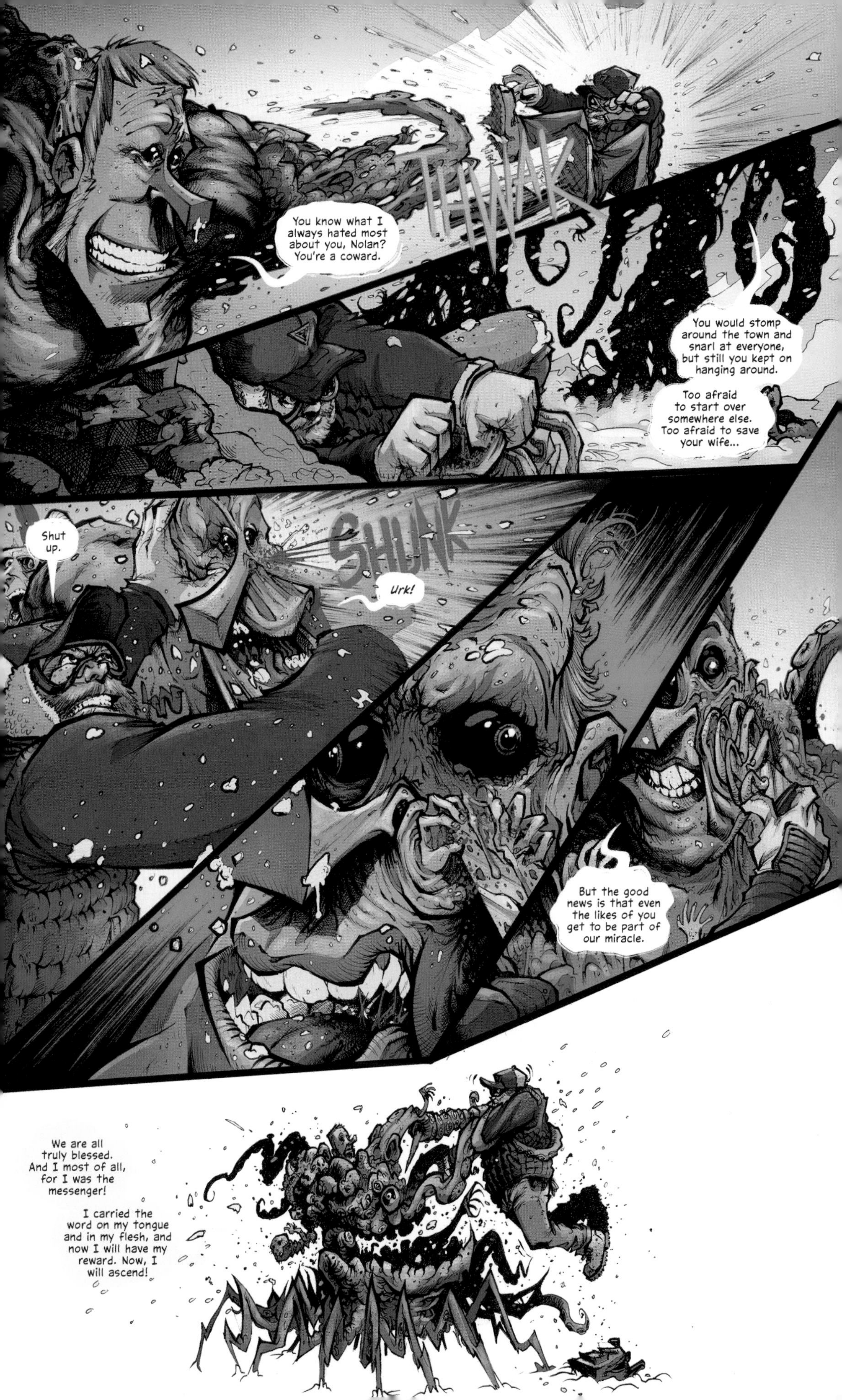
THWAK
You know what I always hated most about you, Nolan? You're a coward.
You would stomp around the town and snarl at everyone, but still you kept on hanging around.
Too afraid to start over somewhere else. Too afraid to save your wife...
SHUNK
Shut up.
Urk!
But the good news is that even the likes of you get to be part of our miracle.
We are all truly blessed. And I most of all, for I was the messenger!
I carried the word on my tongue and in my flesh, and now I will have my reward. Now, I will ascend!

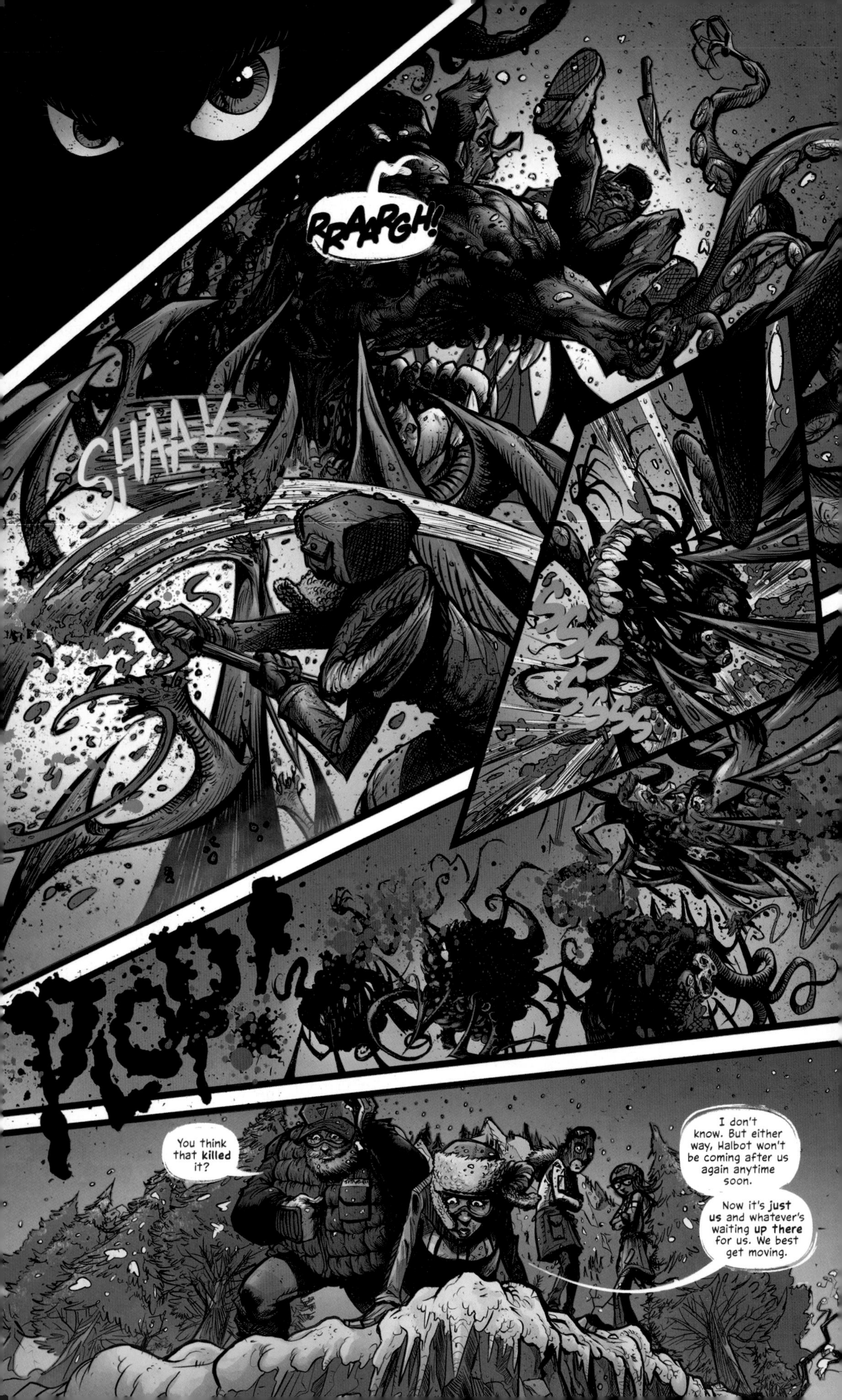
RRAARGH!
SHAAK
SSSS SSSS
PLOP!
You think that **killed** it?
I don't know. But either way, Halbot won't be coming after us again anytime soon.
Now it's **just us** and whatever's waiting **up there** for us. We best get moving.

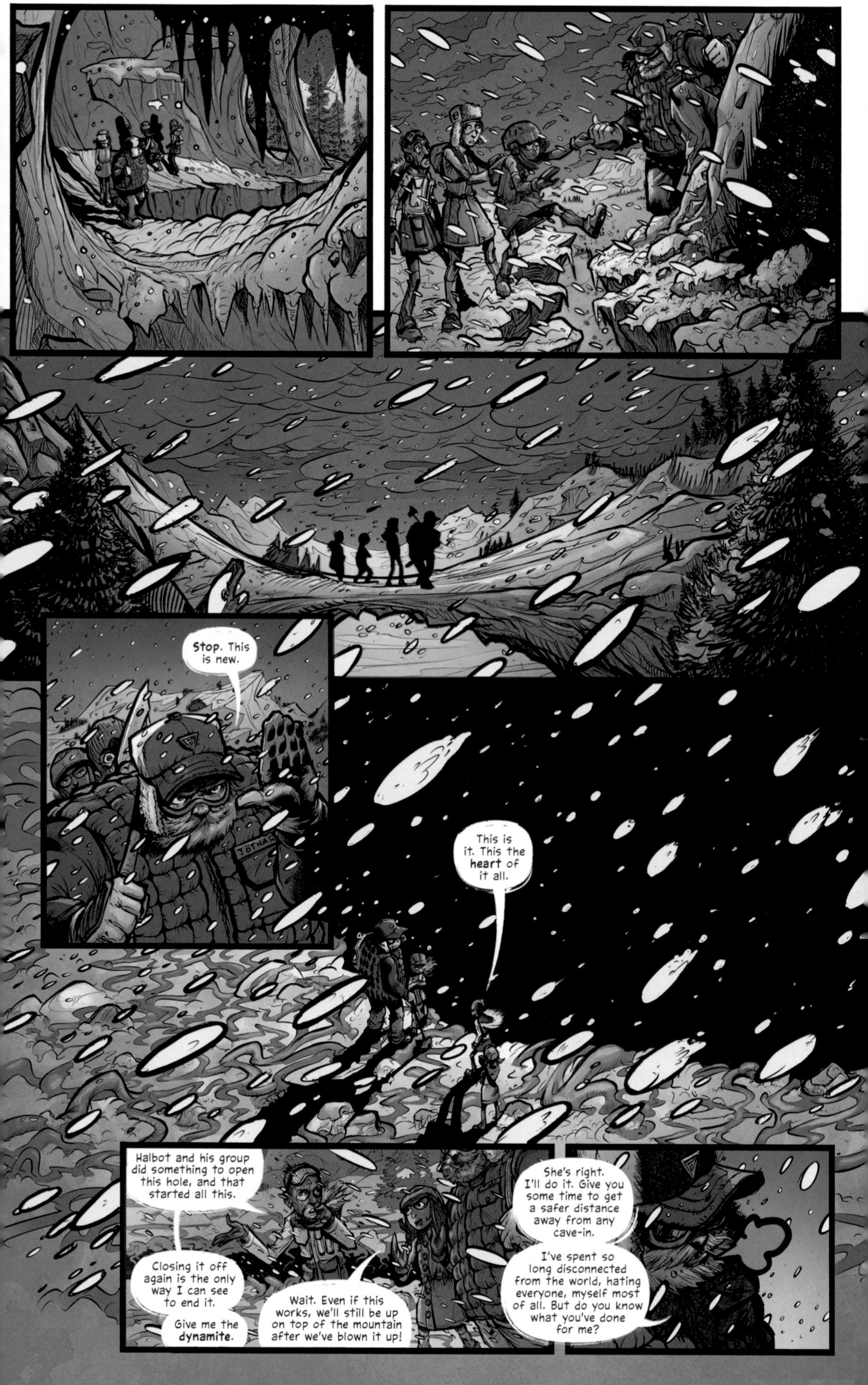

Stop. This is new.
This is it. This the heart of it all.
Halbot and his group did something to open this hole, and that started all this.
Closing it off again is the only way I can see to end it.
Give me the dynamite.
Wait. Even if this works, we'll still be up on top of the mountain after we've blown it up!
She's right. I'll do it. Give you some time to get a safer distance away from any cave-in.
I've spent so long disconnected from the world, hating everyone, myself most of all. But do you know what you've done for me?

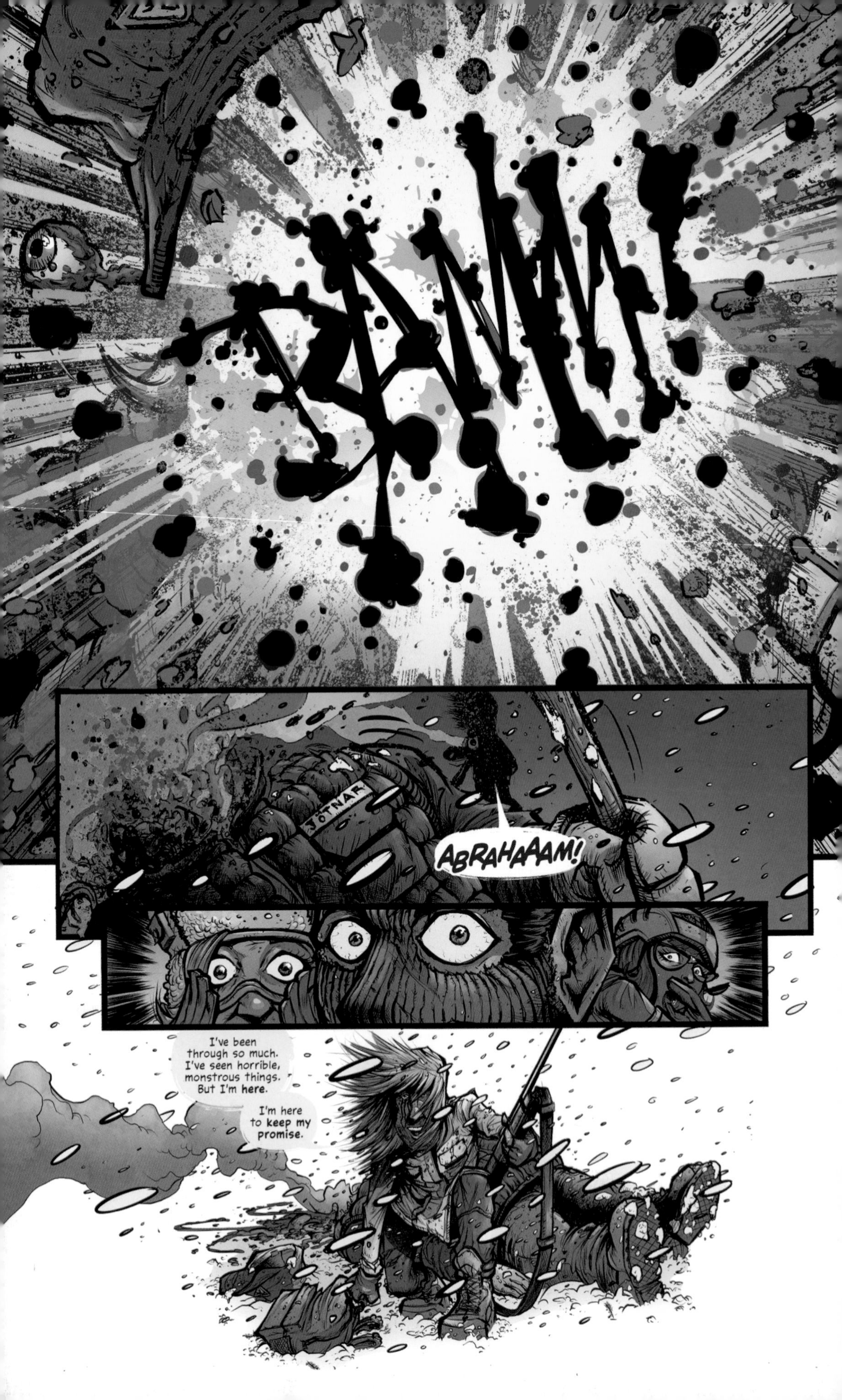
JÖTNAR
ABRAHAAAM!
I've been through so much. I've seen horrible, monstrous things. But I'm here.
I'm here to keep my promise.

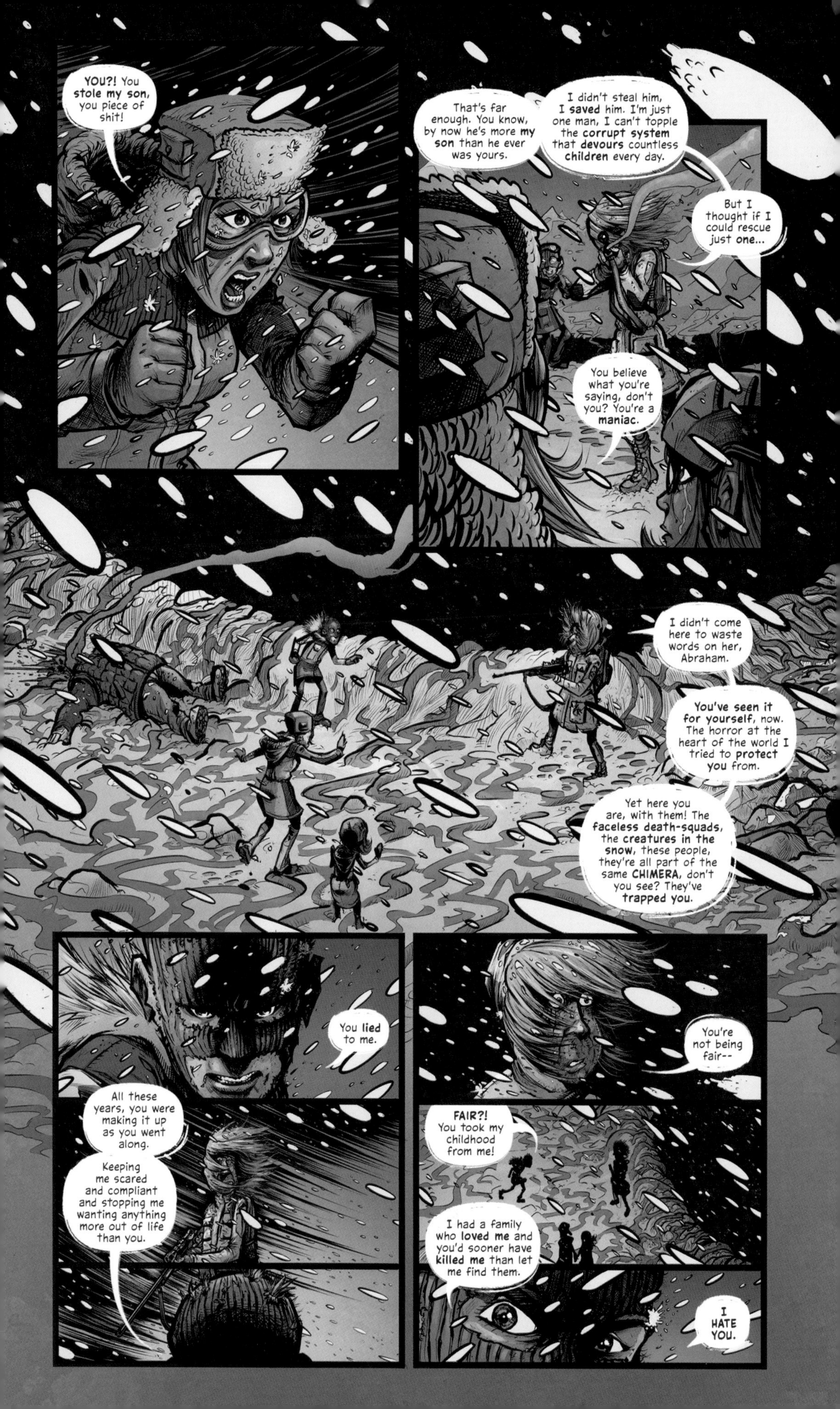

YOU?! You stole my son, you piece of shit!
That's far enough. You know, by now he's more my son than he ever was yours.
I didn't steal him, I saved him. I'm just one man, I can't topple the corrupt system that devours countless children every day.
But I thought if I could rescue just one...
You believe what you're saying, don't you? You're a maniac.
I didn't come here to waste words on her, Abraham.
You've seen it for yourself, now. The horror at the heart of the world I tried to protect you from.
Yet here you are, with them! The faceless death-squads, the creatures in the snow, these people, they're all part of the same CHIMERA, don't you see? They've trapped you.
You lied to me.
All these years, you were making it up as you went along.
Keeping me scared and compliant and stopping me wanting anything more out of life than you.
You're not being fair--
FAIR?! You took my childhood from me!
I had a family who loved me and you'd sooner have killed me than let me find them.
I HATE YOU.

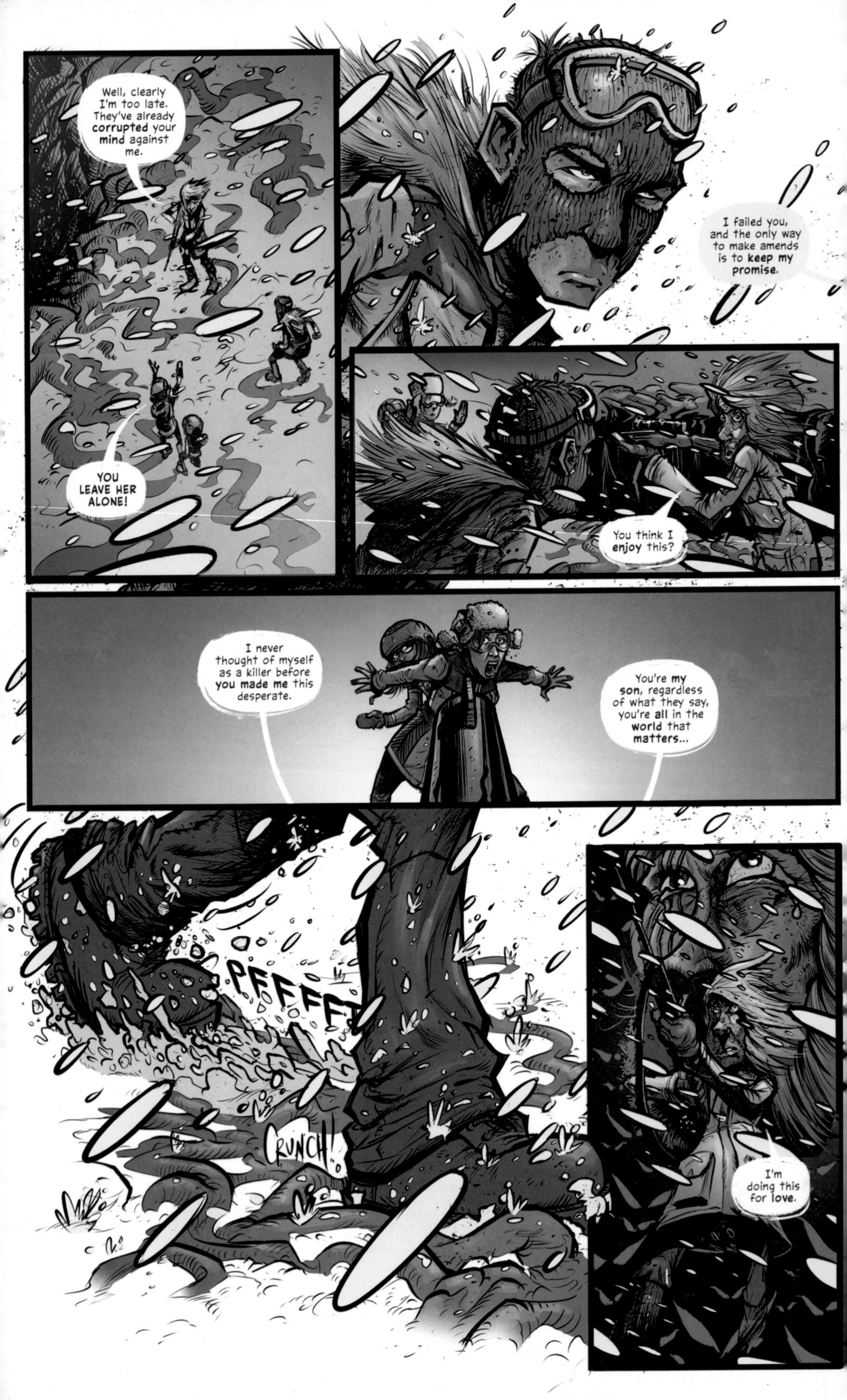
Well, clearly I'm too late. They've already **corrupted** your **mind** against me.
YOU LEAVE HER ALONE!
I failed you, and the only way to make amends is to **keep my promise.**
You think I **enjoy** this?
I never thought of myself as a killer before **you made me** this desperate.
You're **my son,** regardless of what they say, you're **all** in the **world** that **matters...**
PFFFFT
CRUNCH!
I'm doing this for **love.**

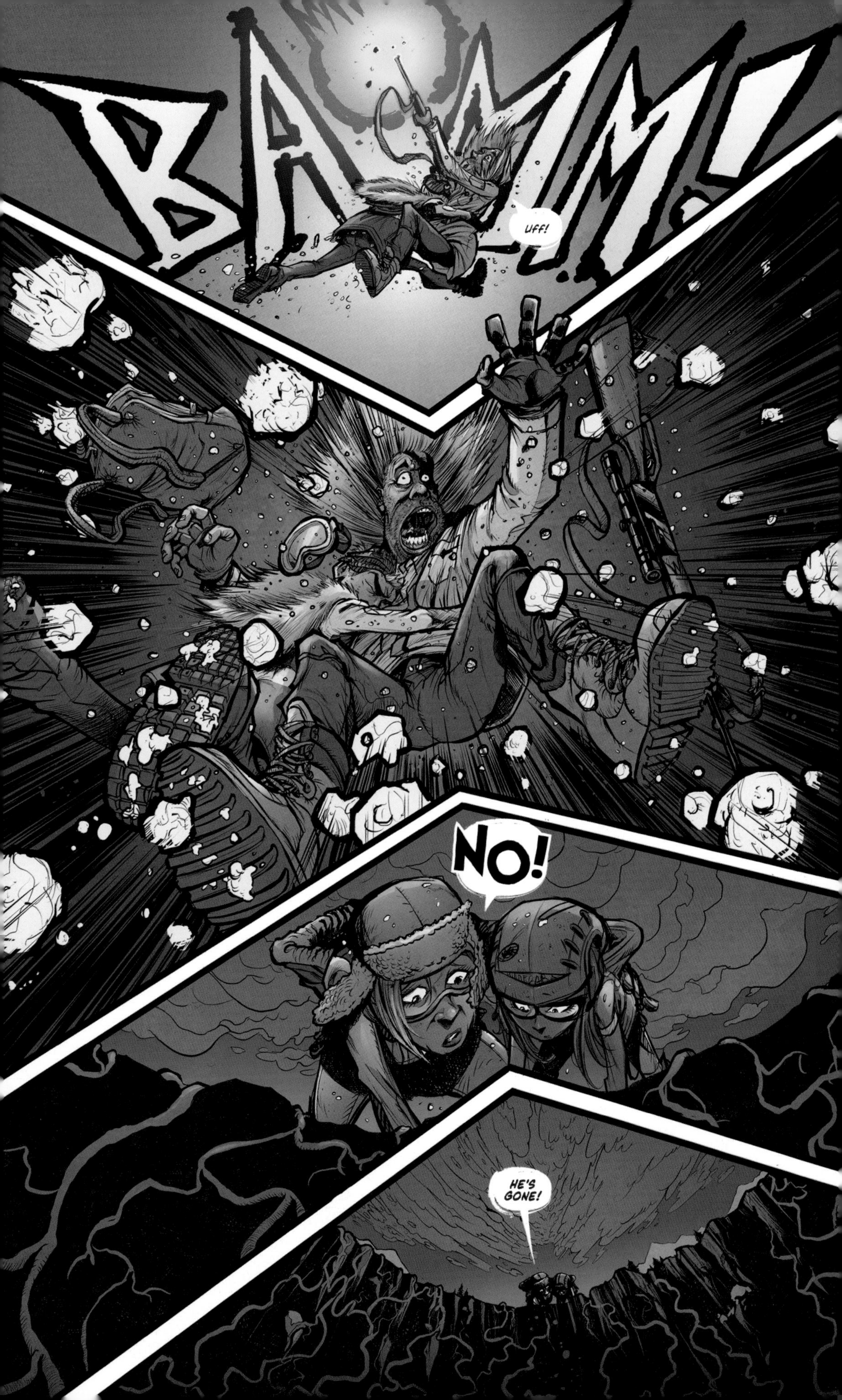
BAMM!
UFF!
NO!
HE'S GONE!

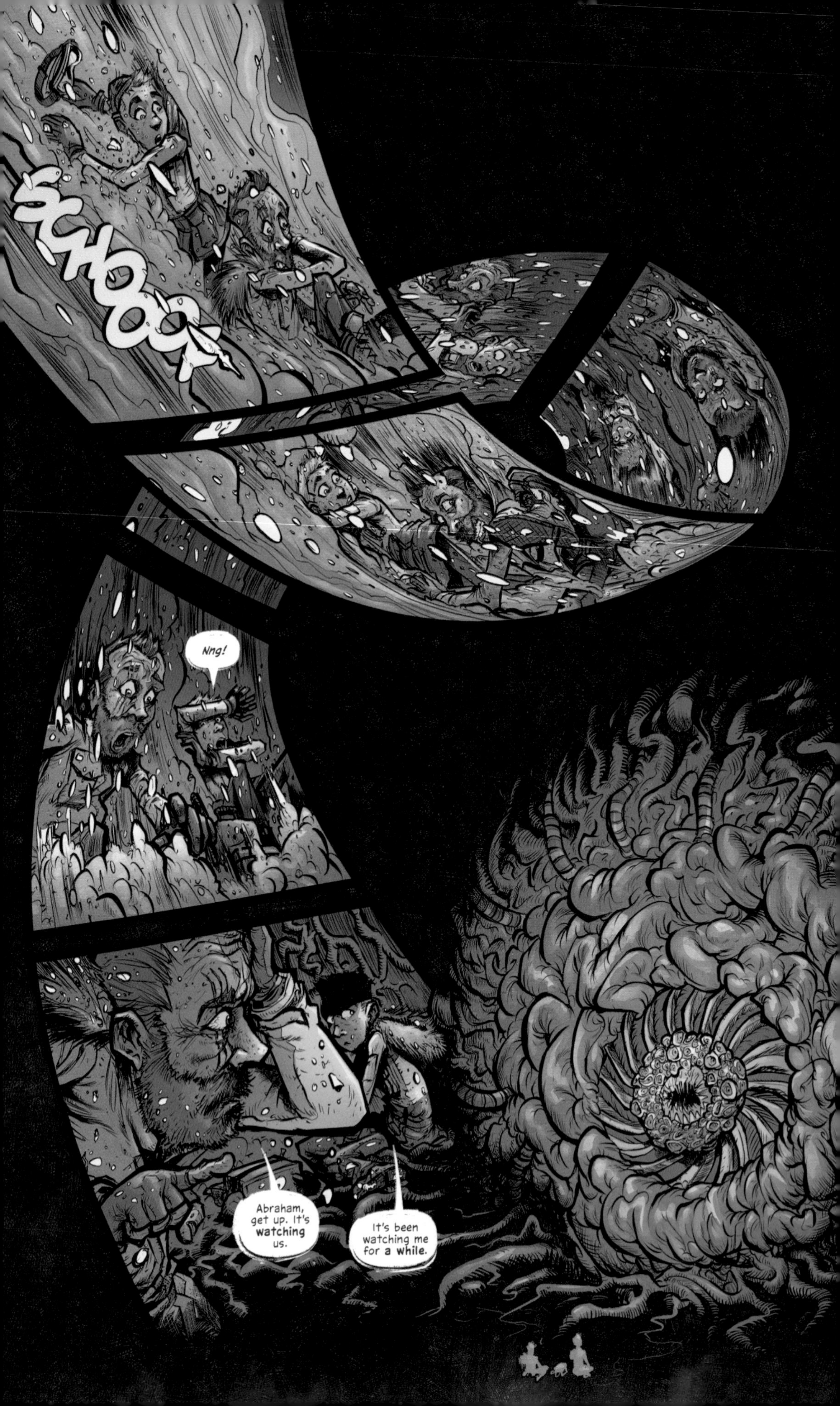
SCHOOOM
Nng!
Abraham, get up. It's watching us.
It's been watching me for a while.

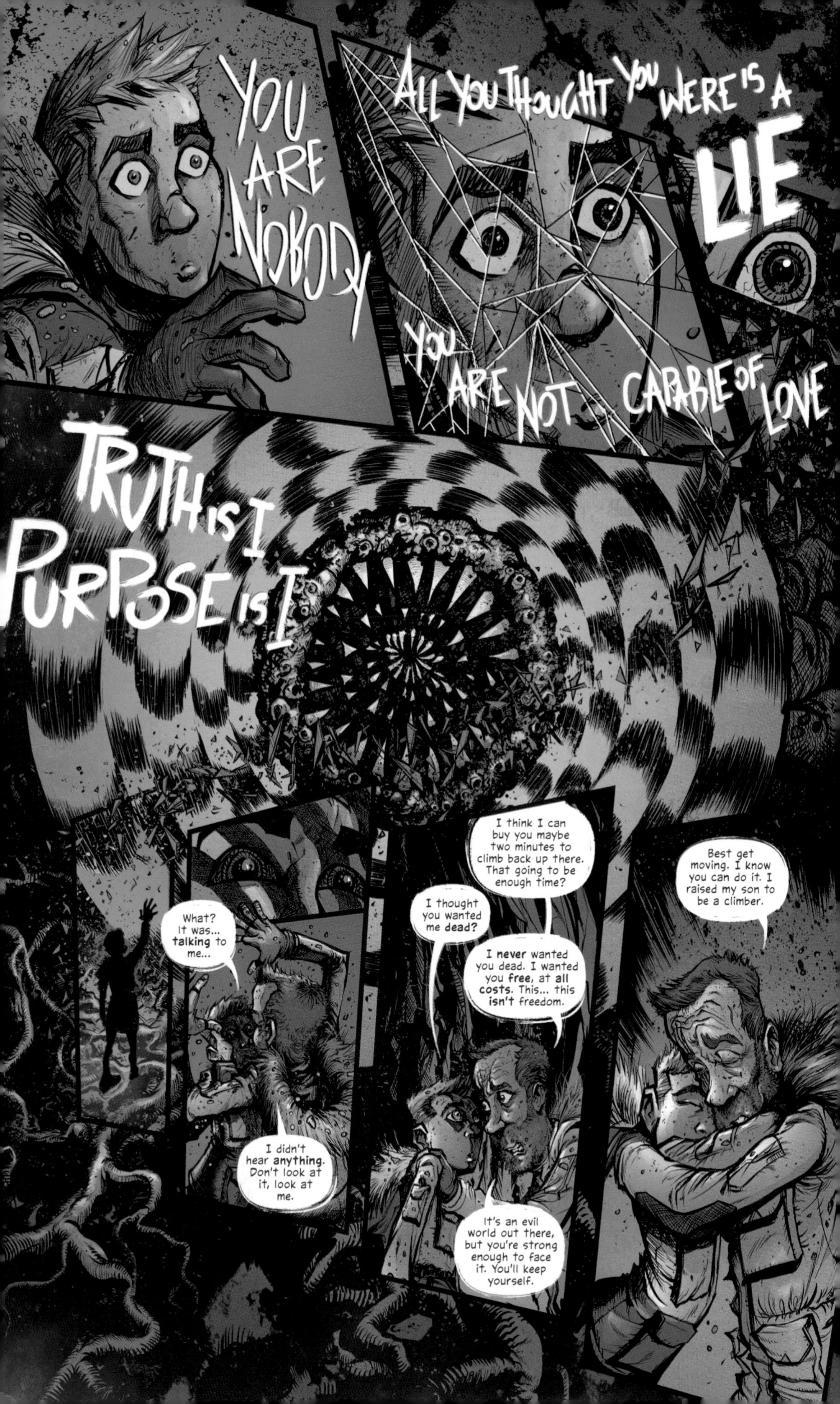
YOU ARE NOBODY
ALL YOU THOUGHT YOU WERE IS A LIE
YOU ARE NOT CAPABLE OF LOVE
TRUTH IS I PURPOSE IS I
What? It was... **talking** to me...
I didn't hear **anything**. Don't look at it, look at me.
I think I can buy you maybe two minutes to climb back up there. That going to be enough time?
I thought you wanted me **dead?**
I never wanted you dead. I wanted you **free**, at **all costs**. This... this **isn't** freedom.
It's an evil world out there, but you're strong enough to face it. You'll keep yourself.
Best get moving. I know you can do it. I raised my son to be a climber.

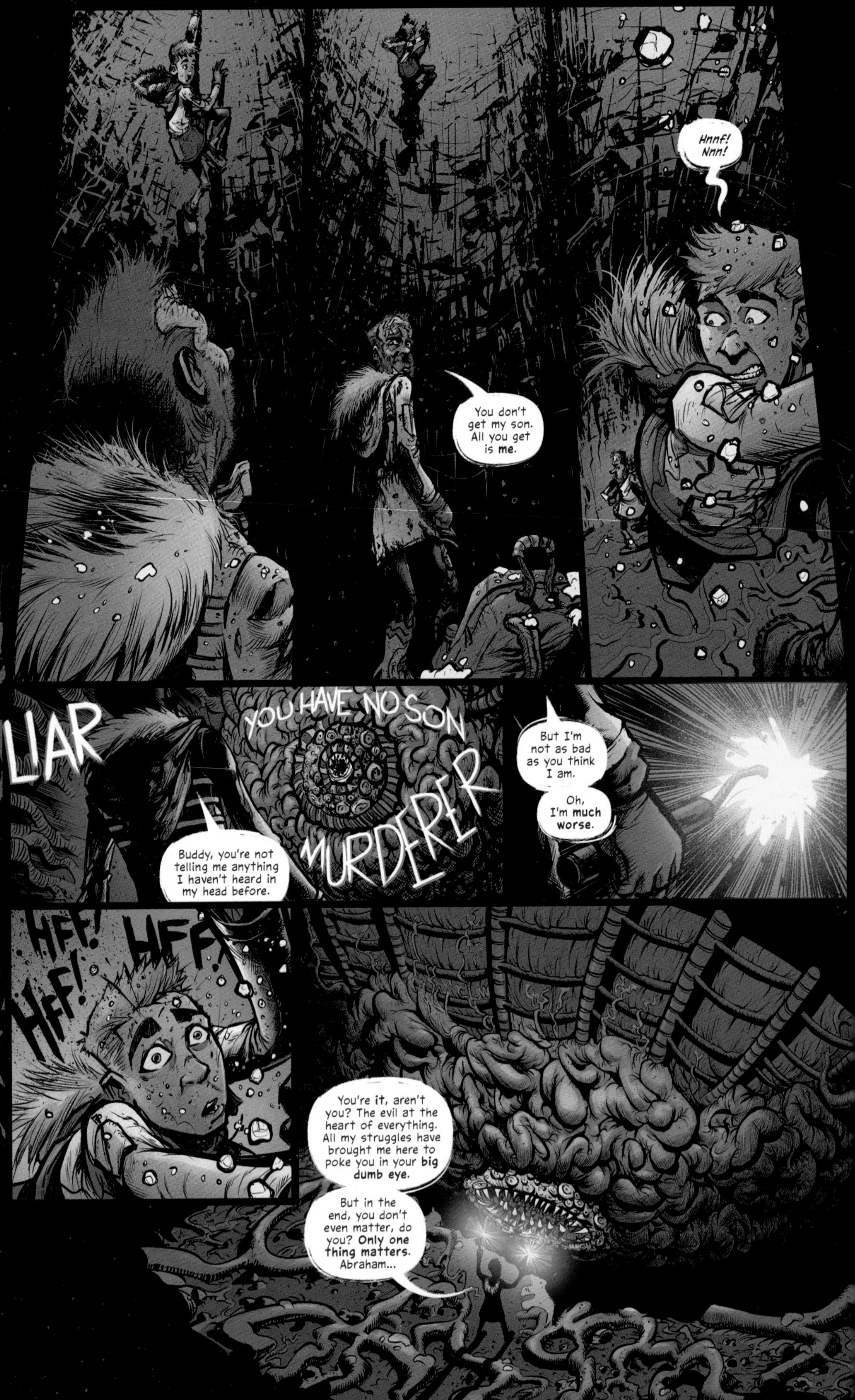
Hnnf! Nnn!
You don't get my son. All you get is me.
LIAR
YOU HAVE NO SON
MURDERER
Buddy, you're not telling me anything I haven't heard in my head before.
But I'm not as bad as you think I am.
Oh, I'm much worse.
HFF! HFF! HFF!
You're it, aren't you? The evil at the heart of everything. All my struggles have brought me here to poke you in your big dumb eye.
But in the end, you don't even matter, do you? Only one thing matters. Abraham...

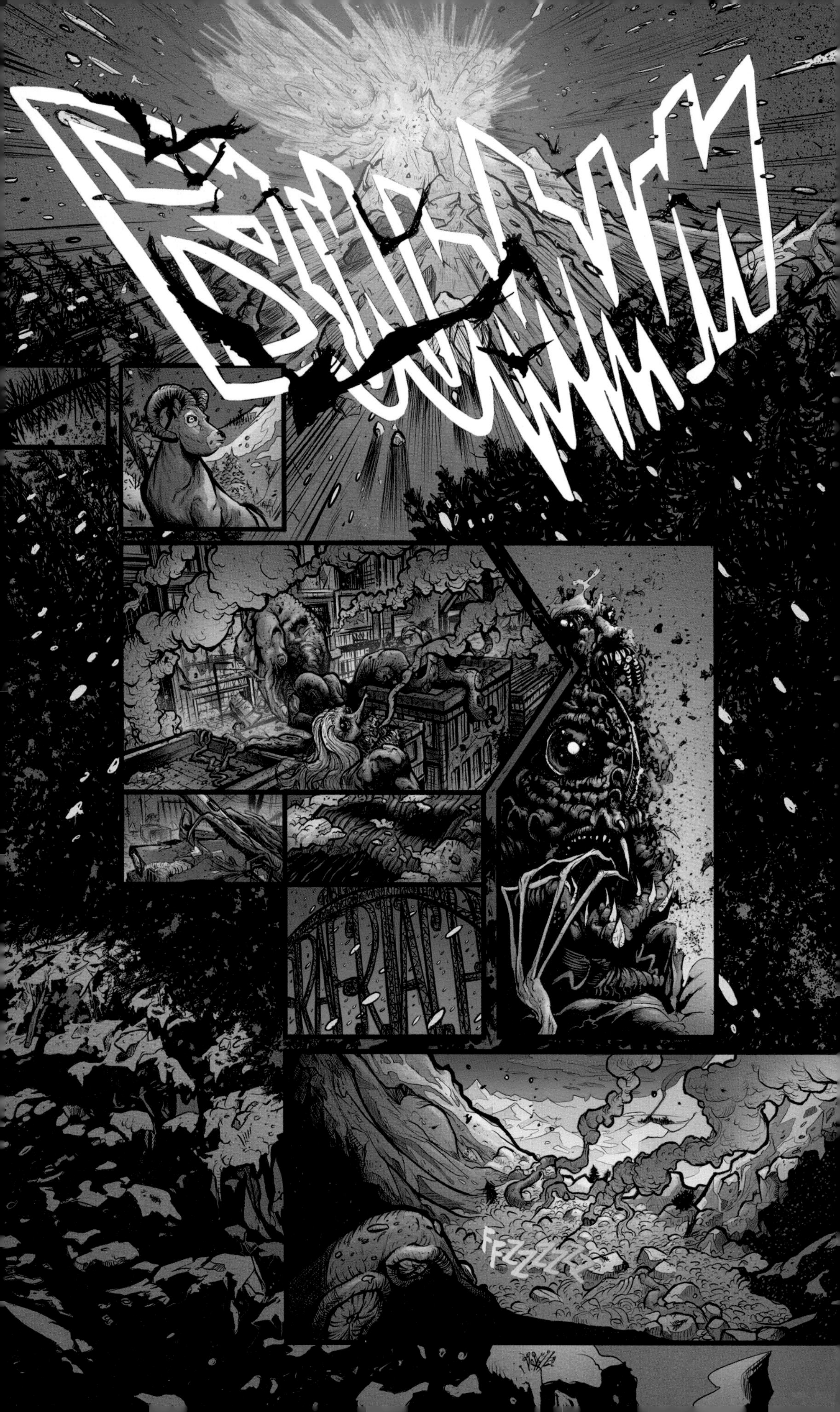
FFZZZZZZ

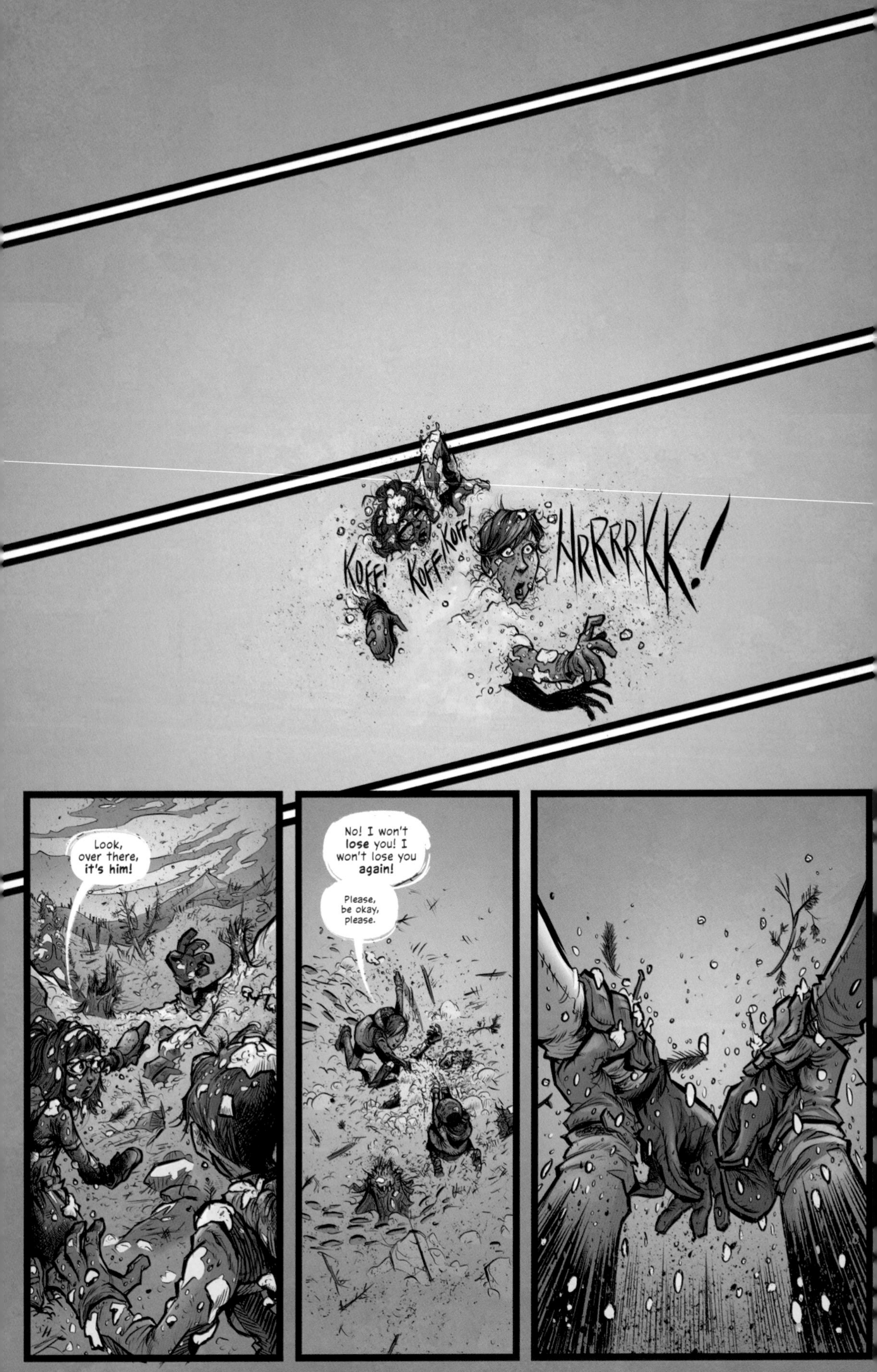
KOFF! KOFF! KOFF!
NRRRRKK!
Look, over there, it's him!
No! I won't lose you! I won't lose you again!
Please, be okay, please.

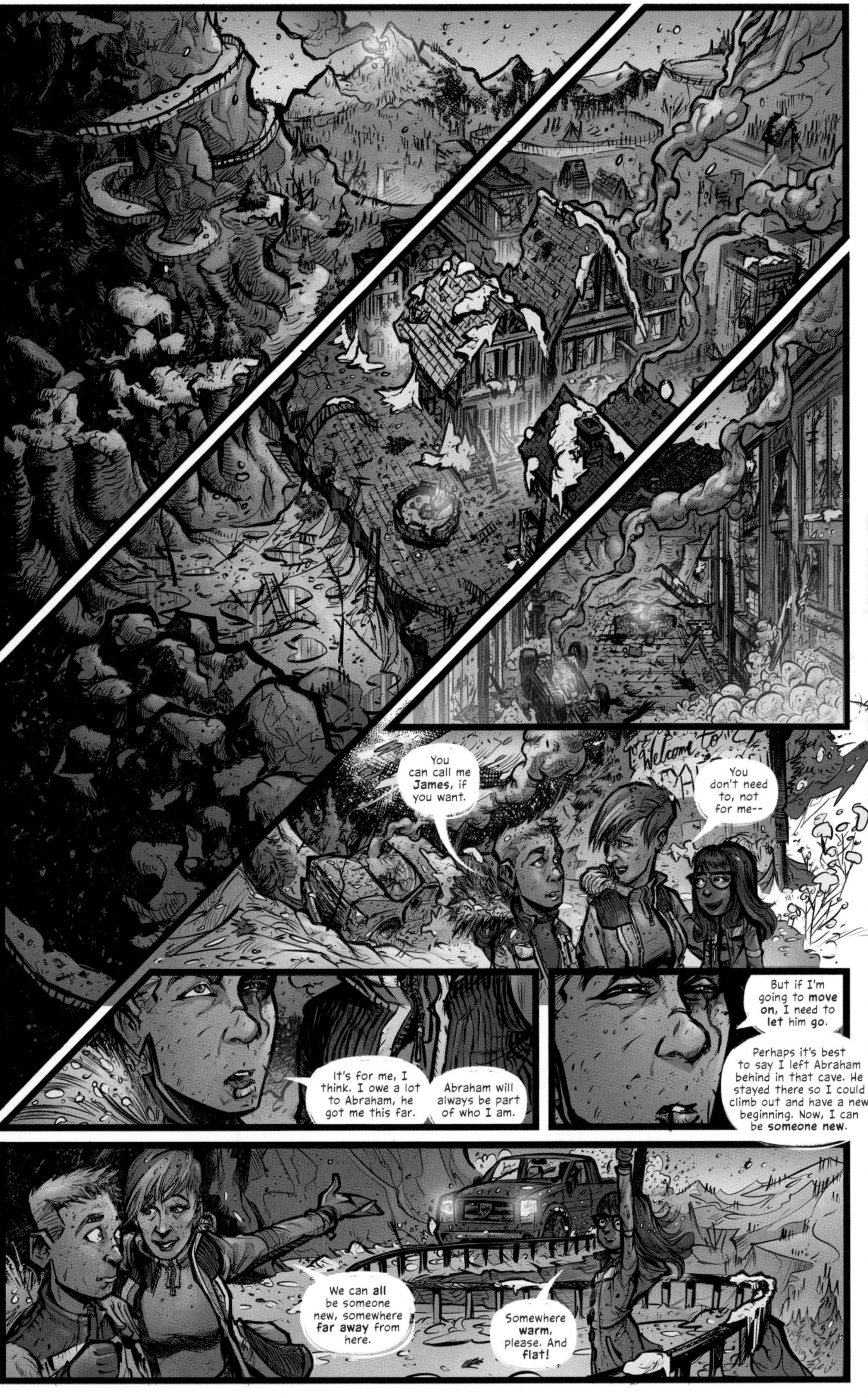

Welcome to
You can call me James, if you want.
You don't need to, not for me--
It's for me, I think. I owe a lot to Abraham, he got me this far.
Abraham will always be part of who I am.
But if I'm going to move on, I need to let him go.
Perhaps it's best to say I left Abraham behind in that cave. He stayed there so I could climb out and have a new beginning. Now, I can be someone new.
We can all be someone new, somewhere far away from here.
Somewhere warm, please. And flat!

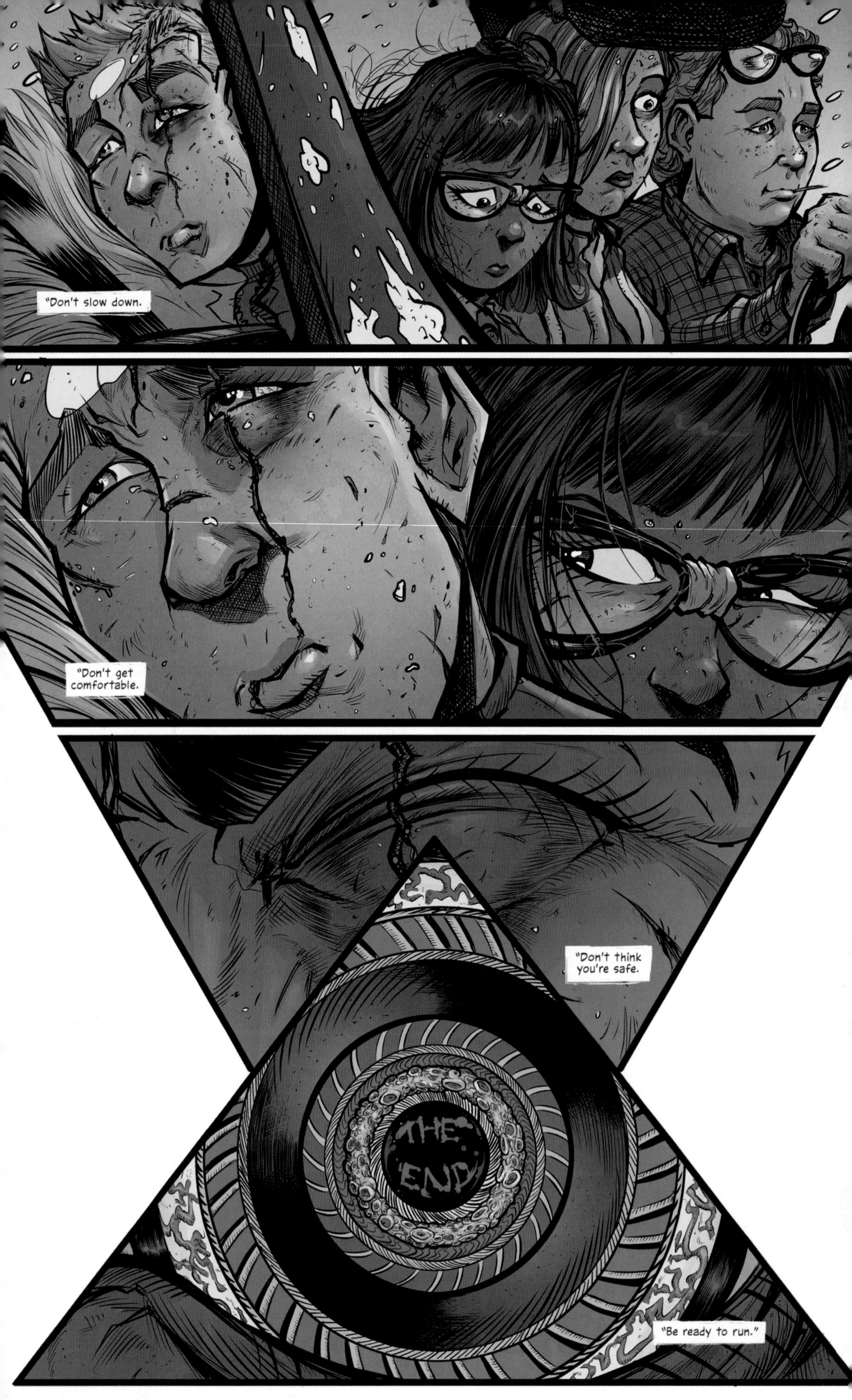
"Don't slow down.
"Don't get comfortable.
"Don't think you're safe.
THE END
"Be ready to run."

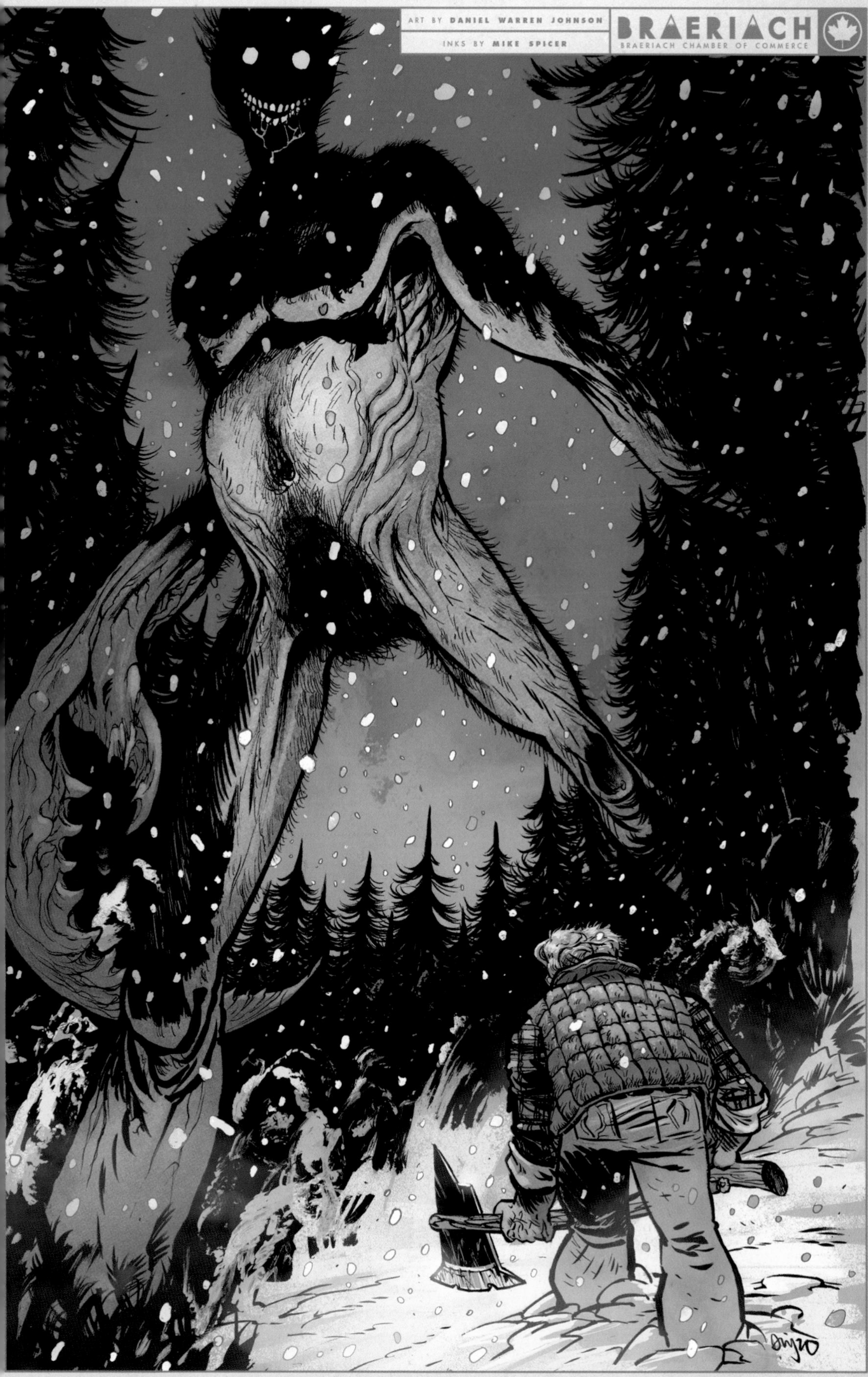
ART BY DANIEL WARREN JOHNSON
INKS BY MIKE SPICER
BRAERIACH
BRAERIACH CHAMBER OF COMMERCE

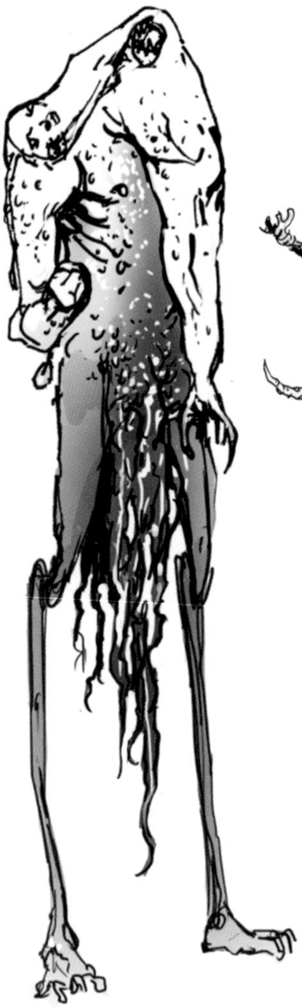
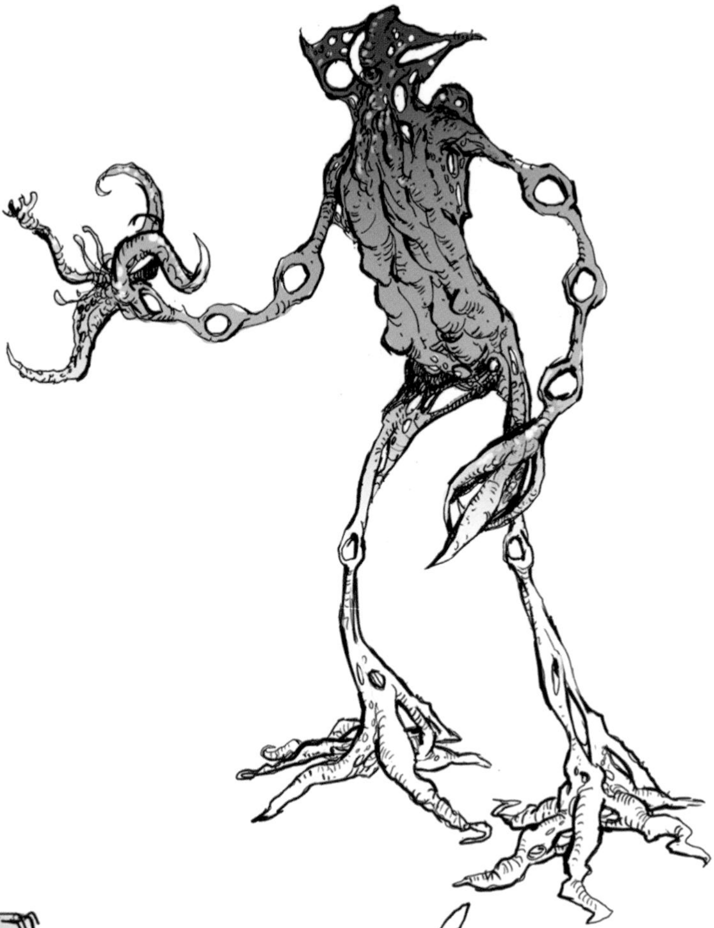
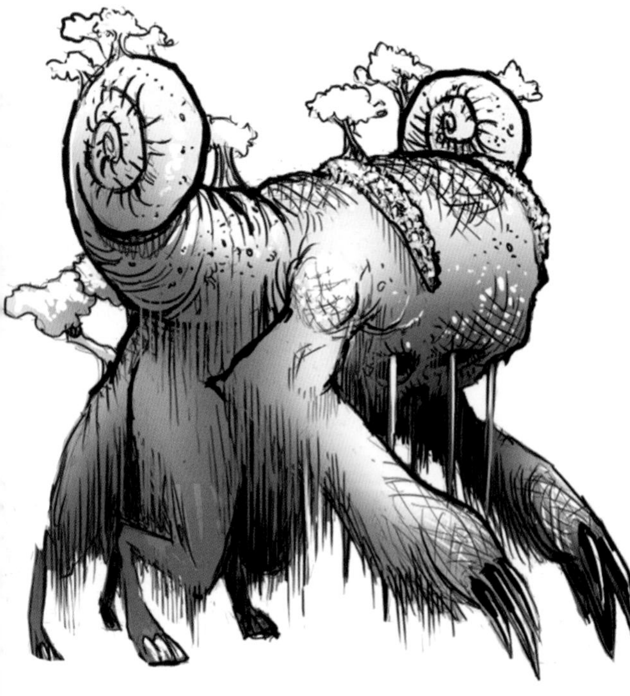
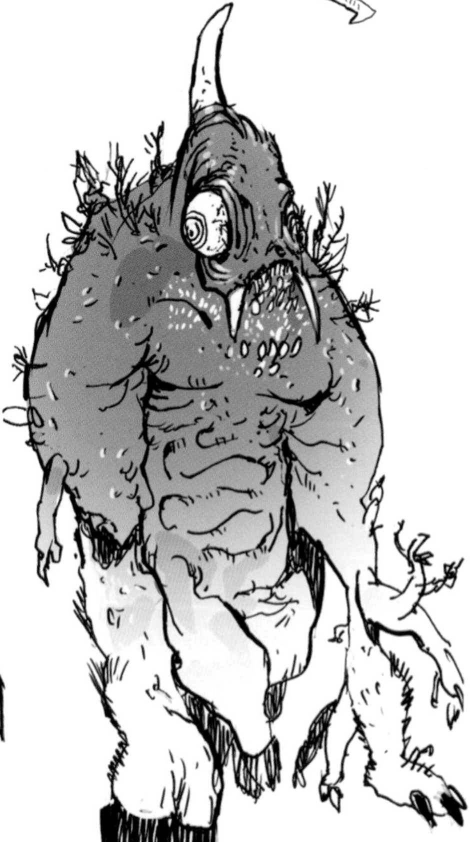

CREATING

BRAERIACH

SOME OF RYAN LEE'S DESIGNS FROM THE ORIGINAL SERIES PITCH

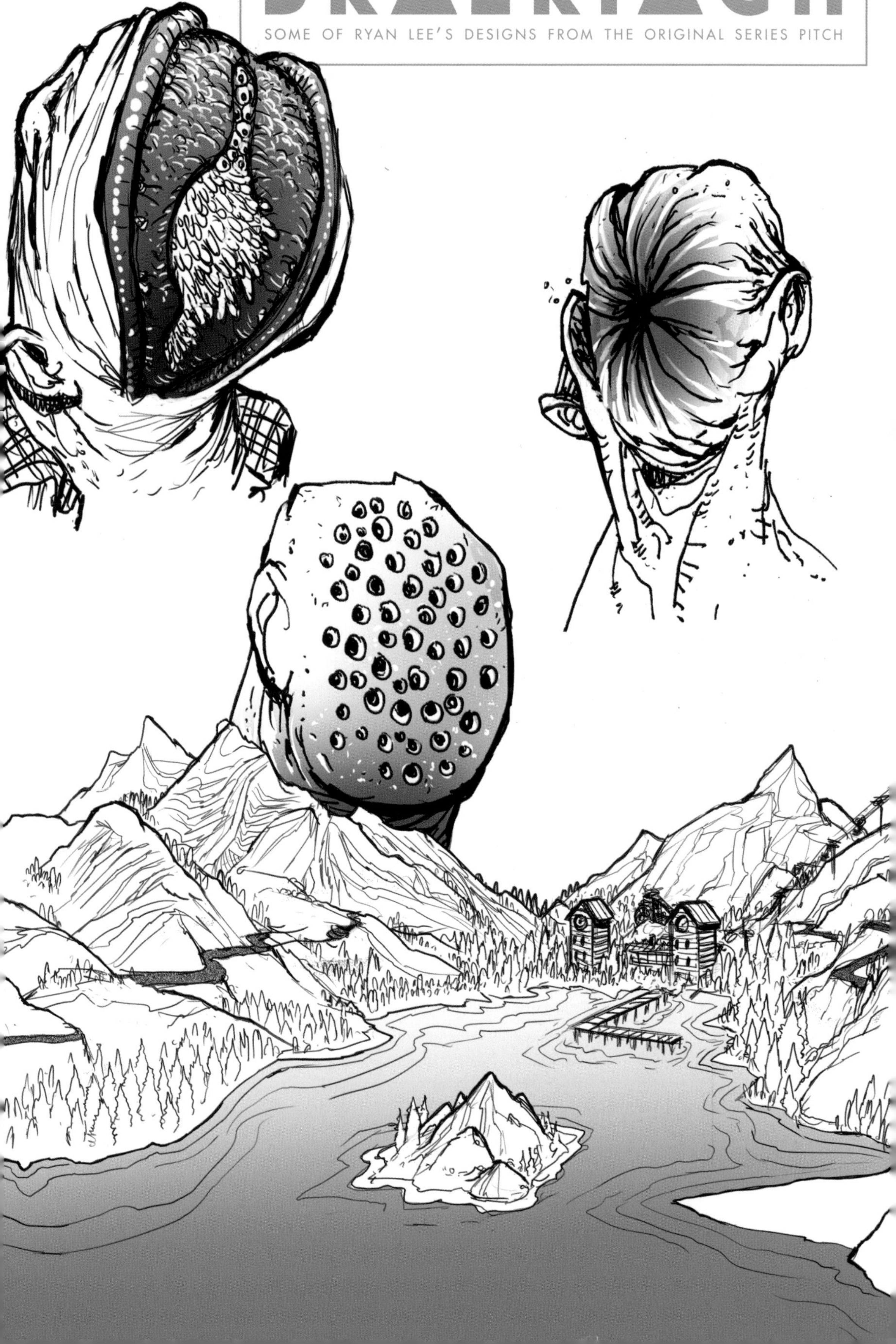

Mt. Rector

MOTOR
LOUNGE

BRAERIACH, B.C.

Don't Stop!